D0257456

MY YEAR OF MEAT

'Smart, funny, irreverent'
Guardian

'A sensitive and compelling portrait of two modern women'
Arthur Golden, author of *Memoirs of a Geisha*

'A meaty first novel about relationships, cultural
boundaries and the beef industry . . . Ruth L. Ozeki masks
a deeper purpose with a light tone . . . *My Year of Meat*
is delightful in many ways'
Jane Smiley

'A wacky combination of love story and exposé,
with observations on growth hormones, sterility, cancer,
early death, television, truth and personal crises. You name
it, *My Year of Meat* has it. It is Ruth Ozeki's achievement to
produce from this a book both marvellously funny and
passionate. *My Year of Meat* had me laughing out loud
and engrossed to the end'
Literary Review

'Original, genuinely funny and mighty strange . . .
provocative, smart and makes you wary of biting into
anything that hasn't actually grown in soil'
Maureen Lipman

'A zany, hilarious romp through the amorality of
television, our preoccupation with meat and what's in it,
and Japanese culture. One of the most original books
of the year – beguiling and entertaining'
Woman's Journal

RUTH L. OZEKI graduated from Smith College, Massachusetts with degrees in English literature and Asian studies, then received a Japanese Ministry of Education Fellowship and emigrated to Japan to do graduate work in classical Japanese literature. She has worked in film and television and has made her own films, two of which have received awards, festival recognition and international distribution.

My Year of Meat is Ruth's first novel. Her second novel, *All Over Creation*, will be published by Picador in 2003. She divides her time between New York City and British Columbia.

Also by Ruth L. Ozeki

ALL OVER CREATION

RUTH L. OZEKI

MY YEAR OF MEAT

PICADOR

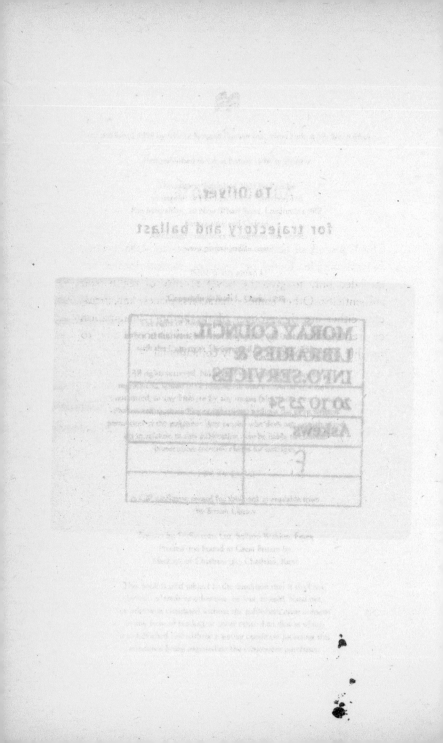

AUTHOR'S NOTE

The Months of the Year

One day Lord Korechika, the Minister of the Centre, brought the Empress a bundle of notebooks. "What shall we do with them?" Her Majesty asked me. . . .

"Let me make them into a pillow," I said.

"Very well," said Her Majesty. "You may have them."

I now had a vast quantity of paper at my disposal, and I set about filling the notebooks with odd facts, stories from the past, and all sorts of other things, often including the most trivial material. On the whole I concentrated on things and people that I found charming and splendid; my notes are also full of poems and observations on trees and plants, birds and insects. I was sure that when people saw my book they would say, "It's even worse than I expected. Now one can really tell what she is like." After all, it is written entirely for my own amusement, and I put things down exactly as they came to me. . . .

As will be gathered from these notes of mine, I am

the sort of person who approves of what others abhor and detests the things they like.

—Sei Shōnagon, *The Pillow Book*, c. 1000 A.D.

The home of the white race in the Old World lies between the lands of the black and the yellow people. . . . In the New World the white race has settled almost everywhere.

It is thought that ages ago there lived somewhere in central Asia a race of white people, now known as *Aryans*. As the race increased in size large bands roamed about in search of new homes, where they could find pastures for their cattle.

—Frye's *Grammar School Geography*, 1895–1902

PROLOGUE

The American Wife sits on the floor in front of a fireplace. The flickering light from an electric yule log, left there all year round, plays across the sweaty sheen of her large, pale face. Legs tucked, toes curling nervously in a brand-new pink shag rug from Wal-Mart, she is leaning forward on one arm, perfectly still. Her lips are pursed. Her husband faces her, his mouth drawn taut, ready, inches from hers. They wait.

"*Takagi!*"

"*Hai!*"

"*Chotto . . . can you please tell the wife not to stare like that! It is creepy. It is not romantic at all.*"

"*Hai . . .* Excuse me, Mrs. Flowers . . . ?"

Without turning her face, the wife glances sideways toward me.

"The director, Mr. Oda, was wondering, do you think you could close your eyes for this scene, just as your husband comes in close to kiss you?"

"Okay," grunts Suzie Flowers. Her jaw remains motionless, but she can't keep her head from nodding ever so slightly.

The cameraman, eye pressed to the finder, groans in exasperation.

"*Takagi, tell her not to move!*" he says.

"I'm sorry, Mrs. Flowers, but I have to ask you once again not to move your head . . . ?"

"*Muri desu yo,*" the cameraman tells Oda. "*It's impossible. We* can't go in any closer than this. Her face is all shiny and blotched. She looks ugly."

"Takagi!"

"Hai!"

"Ask her if she has any makeup she can use to cover up her unattractive skin!"

"Uh . . . Mrs. Flowers? Mr. Oda is asking if you happen to have any foundation? We are having a bit of a problem with the camera, and there's this one little area . . . It's just for the close-up."

"Should I go and get it?" Suzie asks, her jaw still frozen.

"She has makeup. Do you want her to go and get it?"

"Baka . . . Don't be stupid. I don't want her to move. Ask her where it is, and you get it!"

"Uh, Mrs. Flowers? Do you think you could tell me where it is? So I could get it for you?"

Suzie nods. "Do you know in my bedroom?" she says through her teeth. "The dresser? The one next to the mirror on the wall on the left side as you—"

"She's moving!" moans the cameraman, sitting back in disgust.

"Forget it!" Oda barks at me. He turns to the cameraman. "Sorry, Suzuki-san. Listen, just widen the frame out a bit and let's shoot it."

". . . in the top right-hand drawer, underneath—"

"Uh, Mrs. Flowers, that's okay. Actually, we're just going to shoot. . . ."

"Roll camera—and five, four, three . . ." Oda slaps me on the shoulder.

"Action!" I call out.

Suzie squeezes her eyes shut. Like a projectile released from a catapult, Fred Flowers' head lurches forward for the kiss—too fast—and he bangs his teeth hard against his wife's upper lip. Her eyes pop open.

"Ouch!" cries Suzie.

"*Cut!*" cries Oda.

"*Tape change!*" says the video engineer.

Oda shakes his head, disgusted, and walks away.

"I think my lip is bleeding," whimpers Suzie.

"This is stupid," growls Fred.

"Okay," I say soothingly. "Why don't we all relax for a bit, just take a little breather while the cameraman changes tape."

"What is this, anyway?" says Fred, standing and stretching his legs. "Is this the beginning? Is this how the show is going to start?"

"No, honey," explains Suzie. "Don't you remember? This is the last scene. Of the whole program."

"Well, if this is the end, how come you're shooting it first?"

"Well, Fred," I explain patiently. "In TV, sometimes you have to shoot the endings first."

"*Takagi!*"

"*Hai!*" I answer, gently easing Suzie and Fred Flowers back down onto the rug.

"*Get them into position. We're ready to go.*"

THE SPROUTING MONTH

SHŌNAGON

Pleasing Things

Someone has torn up a letter and thrown it away. Picking up the pieces, one finds that many of them can be fitted together.

JANE

"Meat is the Message."

I wrote these words just over a year ago, sitting right here in my tenement apartment in the East Village of New York City in the middle of the worst snowstorm of the season, or maybe it was the century—on TV, everything's got to be the worst of something, and after a while you stop paying attention. Especially that year. It was January 1991, the first month of the first year of the last decade of the millennium. President Bush had just launched Desert Storm, the most massive air bombardment and land offensive since World War II. The boiler in my building had blown, my apartment was freezing, and I couldn't complain to the landlord because my rent was overdue. I had just defaulted to a vegetarian diet of cabbage and rice because I couldn't find a job. Politics and weather aside, the rest was fine. I mean, I was doing the starving artist thing on purpose: I wanted to be a documentary filmmaker, but who could find work in a climate like this?

When the phone rang at two in the morning, I didn't bother to answer. It was unlikely to be a job offer at that hour, and I had just gotten into bed and was lying there, rigid, trying to relax against the icy sheets long enough to fall asleep. I didn't want to lose what little body heat I'd already invested, so I let the answering machine pick up—isn't that what they are for? But then I recognized the voice. It was Kato, my old boss at the TV production company in Tokyo where I had gotten my first job, translating English sound bites into pithy Japanese subtitles. Now, he said, he had a new program and could use my help. I threw back the covers and dived for the receiver. After a brief conversation, we hung up. I wrapped myself in blankets, huddled over my computer keyboard, and, blowing on my fingers to keep them warm, wrote the following:

My American Wife!

Meat is the Message. Each weekly half-hour episode of *My American Wife!* must culminate in the celebration of a featured meat, climaxing in its glorious consumption. It's the meat (not the Mrs.) who's the star of our show! Of course, the "Wife of the Week" is important too. She must be attractive, appetizing, and all-American. She is the Meat Made Manifest: ample, robust, yet never tough or hard to digest. Through her, Japanese housewives will feel the hearty sense of warmth, of comfort, of hearth and home—the traditional family values symbolized by red meat in rural America.

I sat back and read it with some satisfaction. It was a pitch for Kato's new program, a more or less faithful translation of the Japanese text that he had dictated to me over the phone—well, maybe not so faithful; maybe a little excessive, in fact. But I liked it. It would do. I faxed it off to Tokyo and crawled back into bed. As I lay there, shivering, wondering about the new show, I had no way of realizing that what I'd just written would turn out to be some of my most lucrative prose—it would land me a job and keep me both meat-fed and employed for over a year.

My Year of Meat. It changed my life. You know when that

12

happens—when something rocks your world, and nothing is ever the same after?

My name is Jane Takagi-Little. Little was my dad, a Little from Quam, Minnesota. Takagi is my mother's name. She's Japanese. Hyphenation may be a modern response to patriarchal naming practices in some cases, but not in mine. My hyphen is a thrust of pure superstition. At my christening, Ma was stricken with a profound Oriental dread at the thought of her child bearing an insignificant surname like Little through life, so at the very last minute she insisted on attaching hers. Takagi is a big name, literally, comprising the Chinese character for "tall" and the character for "tree." Ma thought the stature and eminence of her lofty ancestors would help equalize Dad's Little. They were always fighting about stuff like this.

"It doesn't *mean* anything," Dad would say. "It's just a *name!*" which would cause Ma to recoil in horror. "How you can say *'just a name'*? Name is very *first* thing. Name is face to all the world."

"Jane" represents their despair at ever reaching an interesting compromise.

In spite of the Little, my dad was a tall man, and I am just under six feet myself. In Japan this makes me a freak. After living there for a while, I simply gave up trying to fit in: I cut my hair short, dyed chunks of it green, and spoke in men's Japanese. It suited me. Polysexual, polyracial, perverse, I towered over the sleek, uniform heads of commuters on the Tokyo subway. Ironically, the *real* culture shock occurred when I left Japan and moved here to New York, to the East Village. Suddenly everyone looked weird, just like me.

Being racially "half"—neither here nor there—I was uniquely suited to the niche I was to occupy in the television industry. I was hired by Kato to be a coordinator for *My*

American Wife!, the TV series that would bring the "heartland of America into the homes of Japan." Although my heart was set on being a documentarian, it seems I was more useful as a go-between, a cultural pimp, selling off the vast illusion of America to a cramped population on that small string of Pacific islands.

As a coordinator, I was part of the production team that shot fifty-two half-hour episodes of *My American Wife!* for the Beef Export and Trade Syndicate, or, simply, BEEF-EX. BEEF-EX was a national lobby organization that represented American meats of all kinds—beef, pork, lamb, goat, horse—as well as livestock producers, packers, purveyors, exporters, grain promoters, pharmaceutical companies, and agribusiness groups. They had their collective eye firmly fixed on Asia. BEEF-EX was the sole sponsor of our program, and its mandate was clear: "to foster among Japanese housewives a proper understanding of the wholesomeness of U.S. meats."

This was how we did it: *My American Wife!* was a day-in-the-life type of documentary, each show featuring a housewife who could cook. My job description, according to Kato, went something like this:

"You must catch up healthy American wives with most delicious meats."

His English was terrible, but I got the picture: Fingers twitching on the pole of a large net, I would prowl the freezer sections of food chains across the country, eyeing the unsuspecting housewives of America as they poked their fingers into plastic-wrapped flank steaks.

Travel, glamour, excitement it wasn't. But during that year I visited every single one of the United States of America and shot in towns so small you could fit their entire dwindling populations in the back of an Isuzu pickup—towns not so different from Quam, Minnesota, where I grew up. I remembered the scene.

It all came back to me during a pancake breakfast in a VFW hall in Bald Knob, Arkansas.

It was our first shoot. I met my Japanese crew at the local airport. A brass band was playing when I arrived, and the ticket counters were decorated with proud banners of spangling stars and stalwart stripes. Yellow ribbons festooned the departure lounge, and Mylar balloons floated like flimsy planets over the cloudlike tresses of blonde girls in pastel who had come to say good-bye.

At the center of all this effusion were the callow recruits, with brand-new crew cuts and bright-red ears, dressed in the still-unfamiliar pale of desert camouflage. Babies were pressed to their clean-shaven cheeks. Mothers' breasts heaved like eager battleships, while the soldiers' fingers lingered over ramparts of stone-washed thigh. Many tears were shed.

My Japanese team was shocked. Stumbling off a twenty-hour flight from Tokyo, jet-lagged and confused, they ran smack into Gulf War Fever. In modern-day Japan, militarism is treated like a sexual deviation—when you see perverts practicing it on the street, you ignore them, look the other way.

Then, at the pancake breakfast where we had been filming, a red-faced veteran from WWII drew a bead on me and my crew, standing in line by the warming trays, our plates stacked high with flapjacks and American bacon.

"Where you from, anyway?" he asked, squinting his bitter blue eyes at me.

"New York," I answered.

He shook his head and glared and wiggled a crooked finger inches from my face. "No, I mean where were you *born?*"

"Quam, Minnesota," I said.

"No, no . . . *What* are you?" He whined with frustration.

And in a voice that was low, but shivering with demented pride, I told him, "*I . . . am . . . a . . . fucking . . .* AMERICAN!"

MEMO

TO: AMERICAN RESEARCH STAFF
FROM: Tokyo Office
DATE: January 5, 1991
RE: *My American Wife!*

We at Tokyo Office wish you all have nice holiday season. Now it is New Year and weather is frigid but we ask your hard work in making exciting *My American Wife!*. Let's persevere with new Program series!

Here is list of IMPORTANT THINGS for *My American Wife!*

DESIRABLE THINGS:
1. Attractiveness, wholesomeness, warm personality
2. Delicious meat recipe (NOTE: Pork and other meats is second class meats, so please remember this easy motto: "Pork is Possible, but Beef is Best!")
3. Attractive, docile husband
4. Attractive, obedient children
5. Attractive, wholesome lifestyle
6. Attractive, clean house
7. Attractive friends & neighbors
8. Exciting hobbies

UNDESIRABLE THINGS:
1. Physical imperfections
2. Obesity
3. Squalor
4. Second class peoples

*** MOST IMPORTANT THING IS VALUES, WHICH MUST BE ALL-AMERICAN.

MEMO

TO: RESEARCH STAFF
FROM: JANE TAKAGI-LITTLE
DATE: JANUARY 6
RE: *MY AMERICAN WIFE!*

Just a quick note to clarify the memo from Tokyo. I spoke with Kato, the chief producer for the series, and told him that some of the points in the memo had offended the American staff. He is very concerned and has asked me to convey the following:

NOTE ON AMERICAN HUSBANDS—Japanese market studies show that Japanese wives often feel neglected by their husbands and are susceptible to the qualities of kindness, generosity, and sweetness that they see as typical of American men. Accordingly, our wives should have clean, healthy-looking husbands who help with the cooking, washing up, housekeeping, and child care. The Agency running the BEEF-EX advertising campaign is looking to create a new truism: *The wife who serves meat has a kinder, gentler mate.*

NOTE ON RACE & CLASS—The reference to "second class peoples" does *not* refer to race or class. Kato does not want you to think that Japanese people are racist. However, market studies do show that the average Japanese wife finds a middle-to-upper-middle-class white American

17

woman with two to three children to be both sufficiently exotic and yet reassuringly familiar. The Agency has asked us to focus on wives within these demographic specifications for the first couple of shows, just to get things rolling.

NOTE ON ALL-AMERICAN VALUES—Our ideal American wife must have enough in common with the average Japanese housewife so as not to appear either threatening or contemptible. *My American Wife!* of the '90s must be a modern role model, just as her mother was a model to Japanese wives after World War II. However, nowadays, a spanking-new refrigerator or automatic can opener is not a "must." In recent years, due to Japan's "economic miracle," the Japanese housewife is more accustomed to these amenities even than her American counterpart. The Agency thinks we must replace this emphasis on old-fashioned consumerism with contemporary wholesome values, represented not by gadgets for the wife's sole convenience but by good, nourishing food for her entire family. And that means meat.

A final note:

The eating of meat in Japan is a relatively new custom. In the Heian Court, which ruled from the eighth to the twelfth centuries, it was certainly considered uncouth; due to the influences of Buddhism, meat was more than likely thought to be unclean. We know quite a bit about Japanese life then—at least the life of the court and the upper classes—thanks to the great female documentarians of that millennium, like Sei Shōnagon. She was the author of *The Pillow Book*, which contains

18

detailed accounts of her life and her lovers, and one hundred sixty-four lists of things, such as:

Splendid Things
Depressing Things
Things That Should Be Large
Things That Gain by Being Painted
Things That Make One's Heart Beat Faster
Things That Cannot Be Compared

Murasaki Shikibu, author of The Tale of Genji, wrote the following about Shōnagon in her diary:

Sei Shōnagon has the most extraordinary air of self-satisfaction. Yet, if we stop to examine those Chinese writings of hers that she so presumptuously scatters about the place, we find that they are full of imperfections. Someone who makes such an effort to be different from others is bound to fall in people's esteem, and I can only think that her future will be a hard one.

Murasaki Shikibu scorned what she called Shōnagon's "Chinese writings," and this is why: Japan had no written language at all until the sixth century, when the characters were borrowed from Chinese. In Shōnagon's day, these bold characters were used only by men—lofty poets and scholars—while the women diarists, who were writing prose, like Murasaki and Shōnagon, were supposed to use a simplified alphabet, which was soft and feminine. But Shōnagon overstepped her bounds. From time to time, she wrote in Chinese characters. She dabbled in the male tongue.

Murasaki may not have liked her much, but I admire Shōnagon, listmaker and leaver of presumptuous scatterings. She inspired me to become a documentarian, to speak men's Japanese, to be different. She is why I chose to make TV. I wanted to think that some girl would watch my shows in

Japan, now or maybe even a thousand years from now, and be inspired and learn something real about America. Like I did.

During my Year of Meat, I made documentaries about an exotic and vanishing America for consumption on the flip side of the planet, and I learned a lot: For example, we didn't even have cows in this country until the Spanish introduced them, along with cowboys. Even tumbleweed, another symbol of the American West, is actually an exotic plant called Russian thistle, that's native not to America but to the wide-open steppes of Central Europe. All over the world, native species are migrating, if not disappearing, and in the next millennium the idea of an indigenous person or plant or culture will just seem quaint.

Being half, I am evidence that race, too, will become relic. Eventually we're all going to be brown, sort of. Some days, when I'm feeling grand, I feel brand-new—like a prototype. Back in the olden days, my dad's ancestors got stuck behind the Alps and my mom's on the east side of the Urals. Now, oddly, I straddle this blessed, ever-shrinking world.

THE CLOTHES-LINING MONTH

SHŌNAGON

When I Make Myself Imagine

When I make myself imagine what it is like to be one of those women who live at home, faithfully serving their husbands—women who have not a single exciting prospect in life yet who believe they are perfectly happy—I am filled with scorn.

AKIKO

2 kilograms	American beef (rump roast)
1 can	Campbell's Cream of Mushroom Soup
1 package	Lipton's Powdered Onion Soup
1.5 liters	Coca-Cola (*not* Pepsi, please!)

"Rumpu rossuto," Akiko repeated to herself. "Notto Pepsi pleezu." She watched the television screen, where a sturdy American wife held an economy-size plastic bottle of Coca-Cola upside down over a roasting pan. The woman smiled broadly at Akiko, who automatically smiled back. The woman shook the bottle, disgorging its contents in rhythmic spurts onto the red "rumpu rossuto." Under her breath, Akiko pronounced the words again. She liked the sounds, the parallel Japanese *r*'s, with their delicate flick of the tongue across the palate, and the plosive *pu* like a kiss or a fart in the middle of a big American dinner.

She liked the size of things American. Convenient. Economical. Big and simple. Like this wife with the "rumpu." Impatient, she shook the bottle up and down, like a fretful infant unable to make its toy work. A close-up showed the plastic Coke bottle so large it made her fingers look childlike as she squeezed its soft sides. The camera traveled down the foamy brown waterfall of cola until it hit the meat, alive with shiny bubbles. The woman laughed. Her name was Suzie

Flowers. What a beautiful name, thought Akiko. Suzie Flowers laughed easily, but Akiko was practicing how to do this too.

Now Suzie was opening a can with her electric can opener. Several children ran through the kitchen and Suzie good-naturedly chased them out with the spatula. Then, never missing a beat, she used the spatula to smear pale mushroom soup over the roast and pat its sides. Pat, pat, pat. She sprinkled the onion soup mix on top and popped it in the oven. Bake at 250° for 3 hours. Easy. Done.

Akiko was so thin her bones hurt. Her watch hung loosely around her wrist and its face never stayed on top. She spun it around and checked the time. The recipe was simple, and if she did her shopping in the morning she would have plenty of time to get to the market and back, marinate the meat, and cook it properly for three hours. She double-checked the ingredients that she had written down on her list and realized she should have a vegetable too. Canned peas, Suzie suggested. Easy. Done. Suzie bent over the oven. Her children pushed between her sturdy, mottled legs and hung off her hem. They must have just poured out, Akiko thought, one after the other, in frothy bursts of fertility. It was a disturbing thought, squalid somehow, and made her feel nauseous.

"It's not spite," Akiko muttered, chewing her lip, "or my contrary nature." She tried a smile again at Suzie, tried to feel happy-go-lucky.

When her periods stopped coming, Akiko's doctor had told her that her ovaries were starved and weren't producing any eggs. Akiko's husband, Joichi, was very upset. He told her that she must put some meat on her bones and he bought her a stack of cookbooks—*Meats Made Easy, Refined Meat for the Japanese Palate, Delicate Meats,* and *The Meat We Eat.* He read each one, cover to cover.

"'A liberal meat supply,'" he said, quoting from this last book, "'has always been associated with a happy and virile people and invariably has been the main food available to settlers of new and undeveloped territory.'"

He held up the book for her to see.

"Professor P. Thomas Ziegler. A wise man. An American."

Joichi believed in meat. The advertising agency he worked for handled a big account that represented American-grown meat in Japan. After a few months of reading cookbooks, Joichi began working late at the office every night. Then he started making business trips to Texas. Akiko didn't mind, but she began to worry when he returned from one of them and told her curtly:

"Joichi is not a modern name. From now on, call me 'John.'"

He was working on a big project, he told her. As his state of suppressed agitation grew, she wondered if he was also having a Texas affair.

Then one day he arrived home and made an announcement.

"*My American Wife!*" he proclaimed, then sat back and waited for her reaction.

Akiko's heart sank. "Who . . . ?" she whispered sadly. "When . . . ?"

"Saturday mornings at eight o'clock. Thirty minutes. Our new TV show. It's a *documentary*."

He swelled with pride—and that's when her meat duties started. Every Saturday morning, she would be required to watch *My American Wife!* and then fill out a questionnaire he had designed, rating the program from one to ten in categories such as General Interest, Educational Value, Authenticity, Wholesomeness, Availability of Ingredients, and Deliciousness of Meat. To complete these last two, she would have to go out and shop for the ingredients and then prepare the recipe introduced on that morning's show. On Saturday evening, when "John" came home from work, they would eat the meat, and he would critique it and then discuss her answers to the questionnaire.

"Kill two birds with one stone," "John" said jovially. They were sitting at the low *kotatsu* table after dinner. "John" was drinking a Rémy Martin, and Akiko was having a cup of tea.

"You will help me with the campaign," he continued, "and learn to cook meat too. Fatten you up a little." Then, all of a sudden, he got very serious. He sat straight up on his knees in front of her, spine stiff, head bowed.

"It was on account of your condition that I was able to have this wonderful idea for the BEEF-EX campaign in the first place," he said in formal Japanese. "I have received great praise from my superiors at the company, and if everything goes well I shall get a significant advancement too." He bowed deeply in front of her, touching his head to the tatami floor. "I am most grateful to you."

Akiko blushed, heart pounding with pleasure, then she realized he was drunk.

It was the Sociological Survey part of the program that Akiko didn't really care for, so she stood up to get ready to leave. She checked the thermometer on the balcony, then stepped outside and looked over the railing at the playground in the courtyard, twelve flights below. It was cold and still quite early on a winter morning to be outside. A toddler, a little girl swaddled in a pink snowsuit, was playing on the swings. Her mother stood near the chain-link fence with an infant strapped to her back, draped in a hooded red plaid cape that made the woman look hunchbacked. She leaned forward under the weight of the child and bounced it gently up and down. Akiko watched the little girl in pink. She could hear the chains quite clearly as the girl swung back and forth. The *kree kraa kree kraa* sound echoed up the sides of the tall buildings of the *danchi* apartment complex, which surrounded the playground like steep canyon walls.

Akiko used to play on a swing set like this one in Hokkaido when she was little. She loved the swing, but it was always crowded with other children. One winter day as she waited her turn, standing off to one side of the set by the upright pipe that supported the crossbar, she pressed her tongue to the cold metal—for no reason, except that she thought it would taste refreshing, like ice. But to her surprise, her tongue stuck fast. She remembered the pain and also the strangeness of being stuck like that, surrounded by people who didn't know. It was lonely. She whimpered a bit to see if anyone would notice, and then stopped when no one did. Finally she held her breath and wrenched her head back, ripping the skin. Separated from the pipe, her torn tongue filled her mouth with blood. She crouched down so no one would see and spit onto the frozen ground. Then she swallowed and stood up. The blood lay on the frozen sand in a little puddle, so she rubbed it out with the tip of her toe and continued to wait her turn.

Akiko shivered. Now, whenever a cold wind brought tears to her eyes and the winter sky turned the color of steel, she could taste the flavor of blood and metal. She went back inside and slid the glass door shut.

Suzie Flowers and her pipe-fitter husband, Fred, were posed in an awkward group portrait with a dozen neighbors and family friends. The Survey was conducted like an informal quiz show; the participants all held two large cards facedown in their laps, and when a question was read off, they answered by flipping up one or the other of the cards to reveal a bold YES or NO. It was the special Valentine's Day Show, so there was a romantic theme to some of the questions, and the cards were decorated with big red hearts.

"Did you marry your high school Valentine?"

"Was he/she a virgin when you got married?"

"Do you think Japan is an economic threat to America?"

The questions mixed current events with a bawdy household humor that made Akiko uncomfortable. She put her coat on, ready to go.

"Have you ever had an extramarital affair?"

Finger on the button to turn off the TV, Akiko watched as pipe-fitter Fred flipped a YES. No one laughed. The camera cut to Suzie Flowers' panic-stricken face and, astonishingly, the sound track reverberated with a loud *boinnggg!* Akiko sank slowly back down to her knees and watched the show until the end. The piece of paper with her shopping list on it was in her pocket, and later, standing in front of the butcher's counter at the market, she pulled it out and realized that she had kneaded it between her fingers until the writing had all rubbed off. The butcher waited impatiently as she stared down at the limp scrap in her palm, trying to decipher the meat. Then she remembered the parallel *r*'s and the plosive *pu*.

"Rumpu rossuto, please," she said to the butcher. "A big one."

SUZIE

Out of habit, Suzie Flowers stifled her crying under a mountain of brand-new floral bedding. From time to time she wiped her nose on the comforter and she noticed that the polyester blend didn't absorb as well as the old cotton one. When Jane, the coordinator, had come for the location scout, she had asked to see all around the house, including the bedroom. The old quilt caught her interest and she had asked all sorts of questions about it. Suzie's mother had made it. It was all stained and torn, and Suzie was so ashamed of it that after the coordinator left that day, she went right out to Wal-Mart and bought new bedding that would look nice on TV. She also bought new guest towels for the bathroom and lots of extra sodas for the Japanese crew. But they never wanted any. They were so well prepared, with their own cooler in the van, filled with mineral water from France. They were polite about it, but Suzie figured that the Japanese people just didn't like American pop.

During the shooting the following week, Jane had hesitated when she saw the new bedding and asked again about the old quilt, which Suzie had already washed and sent off to her sister in Wisconsin, who collected antiques. That was the big joke, that the quilt was so old you could call it an antique. Jane frowned and consulted with Mr. Oda, the director, in Japanese, then she asked if there was any way to get it back quickly. But Suzie had sent the package by parcel post, because airmail was so expensive. There wasn't any real hurry for it to get there, after all, and now it was probably on a mail truck somewhere between here and Sheboygan. Jane had looked stunned. She explained that it was the *old* quilt they liked, because it had old-fashioned, wholesome family values. The new quilt was not interesting, she said, and Mr. Oda seemed very angry and decided not to shoot in the bedroom. Suzie felt terrible.

Fred was furious with her for caring so much, for spending all the money on the new comforter and towels, for agreeing to the shoot to begin with. But when Jane had first called her, all the way from New York City, Suzie thought the TV show might be just the thing to help her and Fred feel positive about their lives again, especially since it was the Valentine's Day

31

Show. And even though the Romantic Evening Kiss scene had been difficult at first, by the end everyone seemed satisfied, and even Fred was in an okay mood by then, but maybe that was just the champagne.

It all went wrong with the Coca-Cola Roast. Jane had seemed so excited when Suzie first described it over the phone to her in New York City. But when it came time to actually cook it, she and Mr. Oda appeared disappointed because there were so few steps. That was the whole point, Suzie tried to explain. It was quick 'n' easy. Yet instead of appreciating this fact, they just seemed annoyed. The meat-cooking section was the most important part of the show, Jane said. It had to be interesting. So to make up for not having *enough* steps, the director decided to take lots of different shots of the *same* steps over and over again. But Suzie had bought only enough ingredients to make *one* rump roast, so they had to go out to the grocery store and buy a dozen economy-size bottles of Pepsi because the store had run out of Coke. Unfortunately they couldn't find another rump roast that looked the same, and in between each take, Suzie had to wash off the raw meat in the sink and pat it dry with paper towels and make it look new again.

It was kind of funny at first. Jane stood off to one side, funneling the Pepsi into the Coke bottle, which Suzie then poured onto the tired rump, over and over again, until the meat turned gray. Finally they told her to put it into the oven a few dozen times, and when that was over she was so relieved—but then, out of the blue, Jane asked for the matching, already cooked roast she was supposed to have prepared in advance, so they could shoot her taking it back out of the oven without wasting time. She was supposed to have prepared the meats in *multiples*, Jane groaned, in *stages*. But Suzie hadn't understood this. There was no help for it, and they all just had to wait for the roast to cook, and it was the longest three hours Suzie had ever spent. The crew went out to the van, where she could hear them laughing.

Later they shot her and Fred and the kids eating the Coca-Cola Roast for dinner, but the kids were cranky because they didn't like the taste of the Pepsi, and Mr. Oda kept screaming at Jane, and Jane kept telling the kids to act like they were enjoying their meat, until finally Fred stood up and walked out the door.

She should have known then. She should have just put her foot down, put a stop to the whole thing. Then Fred would have just come home eventually, like he always did, and the Sociological Survey would never have happened, and she would never have learned about the cocktail waitress, and the neighbors wouldn't have, either. And right now she would be happy—well, not happy, perhaps, but at least asleep. She wiped her nose again and inspected the silvery streak that lay on the nonabsorbent surface of the polyester. It looked like a slug trail. At least, Suzie thought, she would ask her sister to send the old quilt back, since she just couldn't seem to stop crying.

JANE

"Well?"

Kenji, my elegant, sloe-eyed office producer, leaned back in his chair, feet propped delicately against the editing console. He was eating cashew nuts from a small cloth sack. He gazed pensively at Suzie's horrified expression—slack-jawed, incredulous—frozen on the screen.

"The Survey's a bloody bore," he offered. He'd been

33

educated in England, one of the new breed of *issei*, first-generation Japanese immigrants, who wore his British accent like his Armani suit, casually draped, with a sense of perfect global entitlement.

". . . could have cut out quicker and thrown in a couple of reaction shots of someone laughing."

"No one was laughing," I told him.

"Oh."

Our office was located in the East Village. It was an improbable location for a Japanese TV production company, since most tended to cluster around Rockefeller Center, a secure, Japanese-owned neighborhood. Kenji had preferred SoHo, but Kato had nixed the idea because the rents were too expensive, and so we settled here. I thought it was great, five blocks from my apartment, but Kenji, who lived on the West Side, was still annoyed.

When the first edited episodes of *My American Wife!* arrived from Japan after airing, the New York office staff crowded around the VCR in the conference area to watch the fruits of their labors. The disappointment was palpable—*My American Wife!* was dumb. Silly. After the first few shows, the New York staff stopped watching.

The program looked like this: The Wife of the Day appeared in a catchy, upbeat opening . . . she introduced her husband and her children . . . she led us on a tour of her hometown and her house . . . and she ended up in her kitchen, where she cooked the Meat of the Week. Occasionally there would be a special regional or seasonal theme, but at first the programs stuck to this format, embellished with various "corners," with titles like "My Hobby," "Lady Gossip," "Pretty Home," "Romantic Moody," and the "Sociological Survey," which purported to investigate "Timely Topic in American Home and Nation." Okay, it was really dumb.

I was upset. I may have been glib in my pitch and clumsy in my initial dealings with the wives, but I honestly believed I had a mission. Not just for some girl in the next millennium, but for here and now. I had spent so many years, in both Japan and America, floundering in a miasma of misinformation about culture and race, I was determined to use this window into mainstream network television to *educate*. Perhaps it was naive, but I believed, honestly, that I could use wives to sell meat in the service of a Larger Truth.

I mean, this was an amazing opportunity for a documentarian. *My American Wife!* was broadcast on a major national network on Saturday mornings, targeting Japanese housewives with school-age children, who represented the largest meat-eating slice of the population. The show played opposite cartoons, which wasn't easy. But the first episodes we'd shot had scored ratings of up to 7.8 percent and penetrated approximately 9,563,310 households. This was very good. With an average of 3.0 persons per household, an estimated 28,689,930 members of the Japanese population watched our show, and the sponsors were pleased. I mean, that's a lot of sirloin.

Part of the success was due to the marketing angle that the Network chose. *My American Wife!*, they assured the Japanese audiences, was produced "virtually entirely" by a *real* American crew, so the America conveyed was *authentic*, not one distorted by the preconceptions of jaded Japanese TV producers.

But of course it wasn't real at all. Already, by February, I sat through each program out of a sense of responsibility and residual loyalty to an ideal. Kenji watched them all too. He didn't get out of the office much, or out of New York, and maybe that's why he liked the shows. As we stared at Suzie's frozen face, I wondered: Were we even seeing the same thing?

"Fred, the husband, left her right after the Survey. . . ."

Kenji popped another nut into his mouth. "Was it your

fault?" He had taken off his Italian loafers and was trying to operate the edit deck controls with his toe. His socks were made of fine knit silk. "Will we get sued?"

"No. I don't know. I doubt it. He was having an affair with some cocktail waitress, but he got so bent out of shape at us being there, and mad at Suzie for inviting us, that after he flipped his card, he told her. Everything. Right there, in front of us, in front of her family, the whole neighborhood. You see that expression on her face? That's her reaction shot. The director didn't speak a word of English and didn't understand what the guy was saying—he just had Suzuki keep on filming."

"Who was the director?"

"That bonehead Oda. Afterward, when we were watching dailies at the hotel and I explained what had happened, Oda got all excited and suggested using Fred's confession, then cutting to a sex scene with the cocktail waitress."

"He was serious?"

"Totally. He didn't get the concept of 'wholesome.' I had to call Tokyo and get Kato to explain the mandate of BEEF-EX to him."

Kenji shrugged, sat up, and rewound the tape. Suzie's face recomposed briefly, then Kenji hit the Play button again. The Japanese announcer's voice-over asked, "Have you ever had an extramarital affair?" The participants held up their Survey cards, and the camera zoomed in on Fred's big YES. The sound-effect track swelled with canned laughter, and Suzie's face collapsed into its expression of horror, punctuated with a resounding *boinnggg!*

"That's awful," Kenji said, grinning. "But it works. . . ."

"It makes me sick. How can we send this tape to her? The whole thing is a lie. Here, watch the ending."

Suzie and Fred were curled on the pink shag rug in front of the fire, toasting each other with glasses of champagne. They had put the kids to bed early, the narrator murmured, and it was time for that special Valentine's Day moment, time to forgive and forget. They leaned slowly in and kissed, and when their lips met, Oda had laid in a cartoon heart, emanating from the point of contact and throbbing to fill the screen. It was a cheap computer graphics effect, like a TV ad for phone sex.

"It's sweet," Kenji said.

"It's dumb."

"It's television." He rewound it and played the scene again. "Nice graphics. How'd you shoot that kiss, if the husband had left her?"

"Out of sequence. We shot it the first day we got there."

"Smart girl."

"Yeah, I guess."

"Listen, it's great. Makes it look like they had this minor tiff but everything turned out all right in the end."

"But it didn't. It's a lie. Kenji, I should be directing these. I could do a much better job. I could make it real. . . ."

Kenji took out a carefully pressed handkerchief and dusted his fingertips and then the corners of his mouth. He was only in his early thirties, but his tastes—pressed handkerchiefs, fussy wines, antique cameras, and high-end audio equipment—had stiffened into those of a confirmed bachelor. Pachelbel and Delibes composed the sound track to his life, and listening to these melancholy strains, he would gaze eastward, out the window of his TriBeCa loft, past Liberty in New York Harbor, past London, and all the way back to Tokyo. He saw himself as a courtier, banished by his lord to a rude provincial capital.

"Yes, well, bring it up with Kato," he concluded. "But essentially you do direct them now, you know. You choose all the content. The only thing you don't do is cut."

"But that's big, Kenji. Editing is what counts. I mean, look what Oda did. . . ."

"Well, listen," he said, punching Rewind and cutting me

off. "At least you got good meat and the kids are cute and there's enough sidebar activity to keep things lively." He swung his feet to the floor and stood to leave. At the door, he turned back.

"What do you want me to do about sending her the tape?"

"Can we cut out the *boinnggg?*"

"No. Anyway, that's dishonest too."

"Well, then we can't send it. If she calls, tell her the show got canceled."

The rewinding image on the monitor caught his eye and he smiled. I turned just as the large Coca-Cola bottle sucked the last of its contents upward, off the bubbling meat.

"Mmm," said Kenji. "Great product shot."

I shook my head. "It's Pepsi, Kenji. Not the real thing at all. . . ."

THE EVER-GROWING MONTH

SHŌNAGON

Shameful Things

A thief has crept into a house and is now hiding in some well-chosen nook where he can secretly observe what is going on. Someone else comes into the dark room and, taking an object that lies there, slips it into his sleeve. It must be amusing for the thief to see a person who shares his own nature.

JANE

I imagine Shōnagon, the master thief, hiding in her nook of history, watching me slip in and out of darkened rooms and steal from people's lives. I hope she is laughing from behind her long silk sleeves.

One requisite of a good documentarian: you must shamelessly take what is available.

It was March, the "Ever-Growing Month,"[1] and we'd been shooting since the beginning of the year. Suzuki was the cameraman, one of the best videographers in the business. He had an enormous face, like a big round moon, that sweat like a Gouda when he got drunk. His hair was long, and while he worked he wore it tied back tightly in a ponytail like a Heian courtier, but after work, at the bar, he would untie it and let it flow like molten obsidian down his back. His eyes were Heian too, mere slits, as though someone had taken a razor blade and drawn bloodless incisions into the swollen skin. You could never tell if they were open or shut, or if he was watching you. "He has a great eye," I liked to say to Americans and watch them glance dubiously at him and wonder, Where?

Suzuki had a passion for Jack Daniel's, Wal-Mart, and American hard-core pornography. "*Waru-Maato wa doko?*" It was the first thing he'd ask when we pulled into a new town or had some time off. Not that I blame him. There wasn't anyplace else to go in those towns. I mean, if you took a Sociological Survey of the people who lived there, they all spent their days off at Wal-Mart too.

The soundman, Oh, was a quiet man who spoke in monosyllables out of the corner of his mouth. He was always turning away. He was walleyed and mean, except to animals. He loved animals. Sometimes you'd see him holding his boom pole, taking sound, and his coat would be alive, stuffed with a writhing litter of barnyard kittens poking out from his collar and cuffs. But if he loved animals, he worshiped Suzuki. The two of them would get drunk on Jack Daniel's and tape pictures of blondes from *Hustler* all over the Sheetrock walls of motels across America, then use the girls for target practice, shooting out their tits and crotches with air guns they'd bought at Wal-Mart.

The PA was American, an ex–flight attendant. He was a short but handsome young man who wore cowboy boots with heels for added elevation and blue jeans with carefully pressed creases. He sent his laundry out to valet services at every hotel we stayed in and racked up huge bills on toll calls to phone-sex chat lines. I'd hired him because I thought his chiseled blond looks would come in handy wrangling the wives. He loved to talk about Making It on Airplanes and the Mile High Club. This made him popular with Suzuki and Oh.

The directors were sent from Japan on a rotation basis, showing up every couple of months to shoot a show or two. The ones I remember were like Oda—dumb, or disaster prone.

We left our mark in truck stops and motels across the country. So much was new to them. In Taos, New Mexico, Suzuki and Oh stayed in a pink adobe suite with a fireplace. They got drunk and made a small, cozy fire in the hearth, and when they ran out of firewood they burned the telephone book and the Bible, then a chair and a bed-post, and finally the bedroom itself. After the fire department had left, Oh explained, somewhat sheepishly, "In Japan fireplaces are not so common."

In Austin, Texas, after Suzuki passed out while running a bath and flooded thirteen floors of the Radisson Hotel, I asked him if baths, too, were not so common in Japan, but he just shrugged. "Of course we have baths," he said. "We are famous for our baths. It's just that our tubs are so much deeper."

But what really impressed them was the sheer amplitude of America. I'll never forget the look of astonishment that lit up Suzuki's moonlike face the first time he walked into a Wal-Mart. To a Japanese person, Wal-Mart is awesome, the capitalist equivalent of the wide-open spaces and endless horizons of the American geographical frontier. All this for the taking! Your breast expands with greed and need and wonder. I followed Suzuki around the store as he pored over a dozen brands of car caddies, fingered garden hoses, and lingered on the edge of Lingerie, watching farmwives choose brassieres. He loved the fact that you could buy real firearms, not just air guns, over the counter at Wal-Mart, but that was where I drew the line.

I was learning. *This* was the heart and soul of *My American Wife!*: re-creating for Japanese housewives this spectacle of raw American abundance. So we put Suzuki in a shopping cart, Betacam on his shoulder, and wheeled him up and down the endless aisles of superstores, filming *goods* to induce in our Japanese wives a state of *want* (as in both senses, "lack" and "desire"), because *want* is *good*. We panned the shelves, stacked floor to ceiling, tracked women as they filled their carts with Styrofoam trays of freezer steaks, each of which, from a Japanese housewife's perspective, would feed her entire family for several days. "Stocking up" is what our robust Americans called it, laughing nervously, because profligate abundance automatically evokes its opposite, the unspoken specter of dearth.

Locating our subjects felt like a confidence game, really. I'd inveigle a nice woman with her civic duty to promote American meat abroad and thereby help rectify the trade imbalance with Japan. Overwhelmed with a sense of the importance of the task, she'd open up her life to us. We'd spend two or three days with her, picking through the quotidian minutiae of her existence, then we'd roll out of town and on to the next one. We tried to be considerate, but you have to remember that *My American Wife!* was a *series*. You are doing a wife or two a week. While you are shooting them, they are your entire world and you live in the warm, beating heart of their domestic narratives, but as soon as you drive away from the house, away from the family all fond and waving, then it is over. Their lives are sealed in your box of tapes, locked away in the van, and you send these off with the director to edit back in Tokyo, and that's it. Easy. Done.

That was the idea, anyway. Sometimes, though, it doesn't happen exactly that way.

"Mrs. Flowers?" I knocked loudly on the door. "Uh, Suzie?"

Finally she answered, opening the door a crack and peering around the edge. She was dressed in an old bathrobe. Her face was mottled and her eyes were swollen shut from tears. "Yes," she whispered.

"I am so sorry to disturb you. . . ." I was struggling. "Uh, I just wanted to tell you we're leaving and that I'm so sorry about what happened."

She sobbed once, then gulped. "It's okay, Jane. It's not your fault, really." She opened the door a little further, even tried to smile.

"Well, we just wanted to say good-bye, and . . ." I gestured toward the street, where the van was waiting. The PA had the engine running, and Oda, Suzuki, and Oh were inside. Oda flapped his hand at us from the front seat. He hadn't even wanted to come to the door with me. Suzie waved back.

"... and, uh, Suzie? One last thing ... Mr. Oda wanted me to ask you for the photographs. You know, the ones you said you'd lend us? I mean, if it's still all right ..."

They were her wedding photos, in her wedding album, and Oda wanted to shoot some of them to use in the show. I had tried to talk him out of it—it just seemed too cruel—but he was adamant. Suzie stared at me, then nodded. "Sure. I'll go and get it."

When she came back, she was hugging the big puffy album to her breast.

"You won't forget to send it back?" she asked anxiously.

"No, I won't forget," I promised.

"And a videotape of the show too? You said I could have that. . . ."

Reluctantly she handed me the album.

"You see," she said, as her tears welled and her voice dissolved, "it's all I've got left. . . ."

Mind you, I had Kenji send the album back promptly, although without the tape. But even so, I felt bad about Suzie Flowers—like I'd stolen something from her that could never be replaced.

AKIKO

Sometimes Akiko felt like a thief, sneaking through the desolate corners of her own life, stealing back moments and pieces of herself.

It hadn't always been like this. She and "John" had been married for three years. Before that, Akiko had a job at a *manga* publishing house, writing copy for comic books. She had studied the classics in college, but there wasn't much of a market for that these days. Not that she ever really thought she'd have a career or even continue her education.

She liked the job at the comics because it gave her a chance to write things. Her specialty was action-adventure and her coworkers teased her, said she had a knack for gore. When she got married, she gave up the job in order to learn to cook and otherwise prepare for motherhood. Since then she'd written articles for maternity magazines from time to time, but she could tell that the young mothers from the *danchi* thought it presumptuous of her to write on subjects she knew nothing about. "John" was a great believer in positive thinking, though. He had taken an American course in it. He believed that if she concentrated on positive thoughts of maternity, she would get pregnant, so he had forbidden her to write about anything else. His meat campaign to fatten her up and restore her periods was part of the same training. Positive Thinking leads to Positive Action which leads to Success.

But it wasn't working. Akiko had a hard time with positive thoughts. After dinner, when the washing up was done, she would go to the bathroom, stand in front of the mirror, and stare at her reflection. Then, after only a moment, she'd start to feel the meat. It began in her stomach, like an animal alive, and would climb its way back up her gullet, until it burst from the back of her throat. She could not contain it. She could not keep any life down inside her. But she knew always to flush while she was vomiting, so "John" wouldn't hear. She also knew that she felt a small flutter in her stomach, which she identified as success, every night when it was over.

Things That Give a Clean Feeling
An earthen cup. A new metal bowl.
A rush mat.

48

The play of the light on water as one pours it into a vessel.
A new wooden chest.

Things That Give an Unclean Feeling
A rat's nest.
Someone who is late in washing his hands in the morning.
White snivel, and children who sniffle as they walk.
The containers used for oil.
Little sparrows.
A person who does not bathe for a long time even though the weather is hot.
All faded clothes give me an unclean feeling, especially those that have glossy colors.

The effete somnambulance of Heian court aesthetics was reassuring to Akiko, late at night in a dim pool of light, lying next to "John," who was snoring with his back to her. She turned the pages of *The Pillow Book* with exquisite care so as not to wake him. Shōnagon was so sure of herself and her prescriptions, and Akiko found that it comforted her to read them.

Oxen should have very small foreheads.
Small children and babies ought to be plump.
On the fifth of the Fifth Month, I prefer a cloudy sky.
A preacher ought to be good-looking.
To meet one's lover, summer is indeed the right season.

Akiko could not imagine what such certainty would feel like. She never felt at all sure of anything, even of her likes and dislikes. She had bought a pillow book of her own, a small locked diary that she kept under the futon, and from time to time she tried to make some lists like Shōnagon's: "Splendid Things" and "Things That Arouse a Fond Memory of the Past."

49

"Snow," she wrote, trying to recall Hokkaido in her mind. "Cows. Countryside. Farmhouse." But then her mind would stray and she would see instead the dour face of the aunt who'd raised her, and the leer of her uncle, drunk and lurking by the outhouse. A car accident had killed her parents and her younger brother. She had been in the car too, thrown safe, but she had seen the rivers of blood, seen their bodies. . . .

These were not fond memories at all and Akiko wondered if perhaps they ought not to be listed under "Regrettable Things" instead. In the end, she found that she couldn't really get past Shōnagon's headings. She did a bit better with more concrete topics, like "Clouds." Maybe her choice of categories was wrong, she thought. Too lackluster. She picked up a pencil and flipped through Shōnagon's lists, looking for a topic with more gusto.

Squalid Things
The back of a piece of embroidery.
The inside of a cat's ear.
A swarm of mice, who still have no fur, when they come wriggling out of their nest.
The seams of a fur robe that has not yet been lined.

The problem with Shōnagon, Akiko thought, is that she was hard to improve on. Even if the things that she described, like unlined fur robes, weren't so common in everyday life nowadays, you could, if you thought about it, still imagine perfectly how squalid they would seem. Of course, other items on her lists were timeless.

Darkness in a place that does not give the impression of being very clean.

A rather unattractive woman who looks after a large brood of children.

That was a perfect description of Flowers, the Coca-Cola lady, and she was a housewife from Iowa in the United States of America. Not that Flowers was unattractive to start with. At first she seemed quite charming, but by the end of the show Akiko felt that something was wrong. After all those squirming children and the sweet, greasy roast and the cheap champagne that her cheating husband brought home, her life seemed squalid indeed. Akiko had given the show a 3 for Authenticity, and "John" was still angry with her.

"I thought . . . ," Akiko tried to explain. "I don't know why . . . maybe it was the computer graphics."

"But it's just like cartoons," he complained, as though she'd betrayed him. "I thought you liked *manga*. . . ."

"Yes, but this is supposed to be real, isn't it? It just . . . it felt like they were hiding something."

"John" sighed with irritation. "It still deserves better than a three."

Akiko knew better than to argue. Ever since the production of *My American Wife!* had gotten under way, "John" was irritable all the time. "It's out of my hands now," he declared. "It's a good, solid program concept, and the Americans are ruining it." He came home regularly every night and had turned his restless attention back to her menstrual difficulties, annoyed that the increase in their meat consumption still hadn't fleshed her out. She was as pale and anemic as ever.

A woman who falls ill and remains unwell for a long time.
In the mind of her lover, who is not particularly devoted
to her, she must appear rather squalid.

And there it was, thought Akiko, her own sad self. What could she possibly add to a list like that? She put down her pencil. It was depressing. Some things hadn't changed in the last one thousand years. As she closed her pillow book and tucked it under her mattress, she realized there was one thing she felt sure of. However squalid, the meat was critical. She glanced over at "John," then turned off the small lamp. She must continue to make a big deal of the meat.

JANE

"His name is Joichi Ueno," I explained to my ex–flight attendant PA. "That's pronounced 'Wayno.' He likes to be called John."

The flight attendant groaned. I shrugged. Actually, I was the one who had given him the nickname, during the initial planning meetings for the show. Kato told me he was so proud of it that he insisted on using it all the time, even to his colleagues in Japan.

"Listen," I continued sternly. "Don't give him attitude. This is the big man, the Chief Beef. I'm giving you a major responsibility here. I want you to pick him up at the airport and fall in love with him, and more importantly, I want him to fall in love with you. Got it? Your job is to take care of him, keep him out of the way. You are uniquely suited to this assignment. The two of you have similar tastes."

As the representative of the ad agency in charge of marketing the meats, Ueno was my de facto boss. He was a real hands-on kind of guy and he always showed up for the commercial shoots. Each episode of *My American Wife!* carried four attractive commercial spots for BEEF-EX. The strategy was "to develop a powerful synergy between the commercials and the documentary vehicles, in order to stimulate consumer

52

purchase motivation." In other words, the commercials were to bleed into the documentaries, and documentaries were to function as commercials.

We had bigger crews for the commercials. I didn't coordinate them, since I am a documentarian, but I was asked to help out, in order to reinforce the synergy.

It's good to unbalance these agency guys right from the get-go, and renaming them is an effective way to start. Ueno was a large, soft-bodied man, with smooth, damp skin and a stunningly profound halitosis, indicative of serious digestive problems, that rose, vaporlike, from the twists of his bowels. He had gone to a Christian college and been a member of the English Speaking Society, where he studied the language assiduously in order to explain to Americans why the Japanese were unique. He had one weakness, which I happened to know all about, having done my part on previous shoots to both cultivate and exploit it: he loved big-breasted American women. Strapping Texas strippers were a very effective tool in the unbalancing of John Wayno.

So I assigned my flight attendant to him with specific instructions to "get Wayno wasted." The two of them toured all the strip joints in Austin that night, and accordingly, on the first day of the shoot, John was still drunk and docile. We were shooting a square dance scene; the girls were wearing short, frilly dresses that looked like inverted chrysanthemums, and John sat quietly on a sandbag in a corner of the set where he could look up their skirts as they sashayed by. We finished Day One on schedule.

That night, though, he resisted our combined efforts at temptation and got a good night's sleep. Day Two was a nightmare. It was the most important day, ten hours of tabletop, and we were shooting the Presentation of the Meat. To stay on schedule, we needed to get two shots: the Sizzle Cut, a big fat slab of raw steak hitting the griddle; and the

Presentation, the same steak on a platter, perfectly seared and carved to reveal a moist and tender pink interior.

John hated everything. The choice of plates was inadequate. The vegetable accessories were unappetizing. The meat was dull and lifeless. He complained about the marbling and fussed with the hues, peering over the shoulder of the food stylist as she labored with her little camel-hair brushes to achieve just the right blush of pink. Eighteen hours later he was still unsatisfied with the Sizzle, then the meat wranglers ran out of glycerin to make the beef glisten and the American crew walked. I found him all by himself on the empty set, leaning over a platter of steak, breathing on the lettuce and morosely tweaking a pea. John Wayno had a dark and lonely side to his personality.

Of course, when he saw the dailies, everything was gorgeous, and he was as pleased as if he'd shot every plump and juicy frame himself.

That night we all went club hopping. Between the whiskey and the lap dancing and the warm sense of a job well done, old John Wayno was in heaven. The young Texas beauties were breaking his heart. He wept freely as one—her name was Dawn—straddled his tenderloin and offered up her round rump for his inspection. When she pivoted to face him, the tears in his eyes rolled down his mottled cheeks and splashed the pert pink tips of her nipples.

"Japanese girl not like this," he cried out mournfully. "Scrawny, you know? Not happy-go-lucky."

Dawn winced at the warmth of his carrion breath. She lifted her ample tit to her mouth and licked off his tear, then scampered away with a hundred dollars of our production budget tucked inside her G-string.

John sighed mightily and wiped his eyes with his neatly pressed handkerchief. You could tell that his wife back in

Tokyo had packed his bags. He looked around the room with great longing. His eyes came to rest on me.

"You, Takagi, are good example of hybrid vigor, you know?"

"No." I was sitting in the corner, minding my own business, making mental notes for a fax I was going to write later on that night. I didn't think I needed to be drawn into this conversation.

"Yes."

John Wayno surveyed me critically. He reached across the table and took my jaw in his hand, turning my head from side to side. I held my breath. I fully expected him to pry open my mouth to inspect my gums and teeth. Then he let go of my face and shook his head sadly.

"We Japanese get weak genes through many centuries' process of straight breeding. Like old-fashioned cows. Make weak stock. But you are good and strong and modern girl from crossbreeding. You have hybrid vigor. My wife, never mind her. We try for having baby many, many years, but she is no good. Me, I need mate like Texas Dawn to make a vigor baby."

He leaned back in his chair, took a long drink, then waved at another dancer, who came trotting obediently over. As I exhaled and watched him, I started counting categories:

Hateful
Unsuitable
Depressing
Annoying
Presumptuous
Things That Give a Hot Feeling
Things That Give a Pathetic Impression
Things Without Merit
Things That Are Unpleasant to See

When I'd put enough distance between us, it occurred to me that I was probably the only person in the history of the world who has ever recalled Shōnagon in a strip joint in Texas. I liked that.

People Who Look Pleased with Themselves

I was at the top of that list.

AKIKO

Three years earlier, when they moved into the *danchi* complex after their honeymoon, "John" had instructed Akiko that it was her duty to purchase condoms until such time as it was appropriate to cease practicing birth control and start a family. Kneeling on the futon next to her, he broached the subject as he plucked a condom from the box.

"That's the last one," he said, "from the honeymoon supply." He ripped open the foil packet. "You have to take care of buying them from now on. As a married man, it's not appropriate for me to do it. Make sure you always have plenty on hand—this brand."

He dropped the torn wrapper onto her bare stomach. She smoothed the ripped foil carefully and studied the label, "Mandom SuperPlus," then pressed it carefully between the pages of the cooking magazine she'd been studying.

"You don't suppose you could possibly learn to do this too?" There was an edge to his voice. He straddled her head, his penis inches from her nose. She watched, cross-eyed, as he slowly unrolled the thin rubber sheath down the shaft. She reached up and held it between the tips of her finger and her thumb and tugged obligingly.

How does one buy condoms? During their sex that night, she had been wholly preoccupied with the problem.

Next to the market there was a neighborhood pharmacy, but when Akiko went the following day, she saw that the condoms were behind the counter, out of reach. She deliberated for a long time over American painkillers and then bought a spare bottle of shampoo and an unnecessary box of mineral bath salts from a famous local hot spring. It was hopeless, she realized as she paid. *A box of Mandom SuperPlus, please.* She could hear the words in her head, but she would never be able to say them out loud to the salesgirl.

The only other option was the vending machine on the corner by the liquor store just down the block from the train station. Akiko waited until dusk.

There were actually three machines on the corner. One sold the condoms. The one next to it sold pornographic magazines. The magazines were displayed in two vertical rows, with strips of mirrored foil discreetly shielding from view the nude parts of the girls on their covers. But in the dim yellow glow of the streetlamp you could still see the top halves, and you could still get the gist, whether it was high school girls in sailor uniforms, or tortured women bound in fetal positions with ropes that crisscrossed their breasts, or nude nuns, even.

The third machine sold batteries.

Akiko was in a hurry, afraid that one of her neighbors, returning home from work to the *danchi*, would pass by and see her. She put her coins in, pressed the button, and quickly pocketed the pack that came out. As she turned away, she caught a glimpse of her eyes reflected in the foil that shielded the girls in the magazine machine. The girls peered back from their covers, but her own eyes, fractured in the wrinkled foil, were the ones that looked lifeless.

On the way home, seeing that the street was still empty, she sneaked a quick peek at the package in her pocket. They were the wrong brand, not Mandom SuperPlus. "John" would be angry. He would stare at her with contempt.

"Just don't think about it," she counseled herself, taking a detour so she could walk a little longer along the embankment by the train tracks. She liked it there. Plum trees lined the tracks; since it was March, they were just starting to bloom, and the blossoms, lit by the streetlamps, were bright against the cold, dark sky. "Think about something else instead." So she thought about the vending machines, but couldn't understand why the three types of machines were grouped together, next to each other like that, occupying the same street corner. If you bought the pornography, why would you need condoms? And how did the batteries fit in?

The extra shampoo would never go to waste. She decided that she would pack the bath salts in "John"'s suitcase, as a surprise, the next time he went to America. It would be a considerate, wifely gesture, if indeed he noticed, and would perhaps make him feel nostalgic for home.

As it turned out, he did notice. He returned the gesture by bringing her a package of prickly neon-colored rubber rings, "Texas Ticklers," that he'd bought in a vending machine in the men's bathroom of a truck stop in America. She looked curiously at the quivering apparatus sitting in the palm of her hand. It looked like a small pelagic squid, like something she remembered from her cousin's fishing tackle box. "John" lay on his back, waiting, and she attached it to him with a dexterity that she was practicing to hide her distaste.

Sex with the squids on was more abrasive than usual, and after a couple of tries, she asked "John" if it would be all right not to use them anymore.

"Fine, whatever." He shrugged, obviously offended. "I bought them for your pleasure."

"John" felt it was unseemly for couples to announce a pregnancy too early in a marriage, but after a year, he announced it was time to try. By then, though, Akiko had lost weight and her menstruations were beginning to dry up. She hadn't told "John" because it hadn't mattered. But suddenly her periods became his business, and as soon as they did, she stopped having them entirely. After the second year, he began to grumble; his mother was expecting a grandson, he said, people at work were beginning to talk. But still, nothing. Now, in the third year of their marriage, he was stony with rage.

THE DEUTZIA[2] MONTH

SHŌNAGON

Hateful Things

A good lover will behave as elegantly at dawn as at any other time. He drags himself out of bed with a look of dismay on his face. The lady urges him on: "Come, my friend, it's getting light. You don't want anyone to find you here." He gives a deep sigh, as if to say that the night has not been nearly long enough and that it is agony to leave. Once up, he does not instantly pull on his trousers. Instead he comes close to the lady and whispers whatever was left unsaid during the night. Even when he is dressed, he still lingers, vaguely pretending to be fastening his sash.

Presently he raises the lattice, and the two lovers stand together by the side door while he tells her how he dreads the coming day, which will keep them apart; then he slips away. The lady watches him go, and this moment of parting will remain among her most charming memories.

Indeed, one's attachment to a man depends largely on the elegance of his leave-taking. When he jumps out of bed, scurries about the room, tightly fastens his trouser-sash, rolls up the sleeves of his Court cloak, over-robe, or hunting costume, stuffs his belongings into the breast of his robe and then briskly secures the outer sash—one really begins to hate him.

JANE

I had a lover in the Year of Meat. His name was Sloan and he was a musician from Chicago. A mutual friend had sort of set us up, but I was never in New York much and he was always on the road, so it was months before we actually met in person. Instead we got into this phone sex thing. I'd call him up late at night from some trucker's motel in Gnawbone, Indiana, or wherever we happened to be shooting, and we'd have these libidinous conversations that went on into the night. Production paid the bills, so it didn't matter how long we talked. When we weren't on the phone we'd fax, and I could usually count on a transmission waiting for me at the front desk when I'd check into a new motel. It made things interesting, helped mark the time. I always wondered if the desk clerks read our faxes or listened in to our calls.

"Exotic? Well, botanically speaking, yes, but not what you'd expect. I'm more of a hybrid or a mutant. . . . I'm tall. Very tall, pole thin . . . .

"Green eyes, shaped like my Japanese mother's with her epicanthic fold. My dad's eyes were blue. The green's not traceable, but Ma thinks it's the *oni* and I'm the devil's spawn. . . .

"Brown hair. Usually. Sometimes I dye it when I'm not working. Short, but respectable. No, like *really* short. Like boy short. Yeah, with a couple of AWOL parts that stick out in front. . . .

"Breasts? Upstanding, small. Never discouraged, never lethargic . . . Yes, quite sensitive . . . Hmm, yes, some pain is good. . . .

"Now? At a truck stop. Lying on the bed looking up at the drop ceiling . . . An old army-green sleeveless undershirt and brand-new boxer shorts from Wal-Mart . . . Haven't been near a laundromat in weeks. Yes, men's shorts . . . More room to move around in . . .

"The room? Lurid. Weeping walls and peeling ceilings, and it reeks of Tiparillos. The wallpaper's flocked, harvest gold with a floral pattern. The walls are riddled with pockmarks, looks like from an air gun, and the mirror has a large crack in it. Mattress like a sponge. The carpet is golden, too, and sticky, so I'm wearing my combat boots . . . unlaced, no socks. . . . No. You know what it's like? A 1960s porn set: exotic Eurasian of ambiguous gender, dressed in men's under-wear and combat boots, lying on her back having phone sex on the damp polyester bedspread—sort of post-Vietnam nostalgia-porn thing. A quick little R and R fantasy in Tokyo or Seoul. I should call the boys in to film it. There must be a market for this. . . ."

We finally met in Nebraska. I got back to the motel after a day of shooting a Mrs. Beedles and her Busy-B-Brisket, to find Sloan sipping a martini at the motel bar. He had no trouble recognizing us, of course, being as we were the only Japanese television crew in the 77,355 square miles of high plains that is Nebraska. He strolled over to us and extended his hand.

"Jane Takagi-Little? Sloan Rankin, Nebraska Film Com-missioner. It's my distinct pleasure to welcome you and your distinguished crew to the Cornhusker State."

I tripped over the tripod I was carrying. Suzuki and Oh and the director were right behind me, so I introduced them all, and that's when I noticed something peculiar about the Japanese crew—they would not look an American in the face. The director, a shy, sweet man this time, approached the ersatz Commissioner with desperation and gusto. In a valiant simulation of a hearty American greeting, he pumped Sloan's hand, but he was unable to raise his eyes from the floor. When Oh's turn came, his body just seemed to rotate like a magnet driven away by an opposing charge. Suzuki was the most successful; he fixed his gaze in the region of Sloan's solar plexus and haltingly greeted the string tie Sloan had purchased as part of his Commissioner disguise. Along with the cowboy hat. Or so he told me later.

"Will you be visiting our national forest during your stay?" Sloan drawled with unctuous aplomb. "It truly is one of Nebraska's more notable attractions, being as it's the only man-made forest in the United States of America."

The crew stood quietly, heads bowed, and withstood this onslaught of English like schoolboys being singled out for unfair punishment, so I excused them and they escaped to their rooms with the equipment. Later I gave them petty cash and asked them to fend for themselves; I had to eat with the Commissioner. He'd been such a valuable asset during preproduction, I explained, and had introduced us to Mrs. Beedles and her Brisket and all the nice folks of Nebraska ... but Suzuki and Oh and the director were already deep into communion with Jack Daniel's, cackling convulsively about something esoteric pertaining to their choice of video entertainment for the evening.

I left them in the motel room, cabling up the Betacam to the motel TV. In our equipment case was a small but well-curated collection of prerecorded tape stock with titles like

"Texas T-Bone Does the Hoosier Hooters." These were little-known regional delights that the crew had acquired during our travels, and needless to say, the climax was always about meat.

It was a cinematic night. A seedy motel room. A tall, dark stranger in cowboy boots, who followed me through the door, shut it firmly behind, then locked it. The unfamiliar hand, resting heavily on my shoulder, letting me know that I wouldn't get away. In the cool night, beyond the venetian blinds, the nervous light of the neon flickered red and hot. Sloan was unapologetic as he pushed me down onto the flimsy bed and lowered himself on top. As the Commissioner, he was relentless.

"Nebraska," he breathed into my ear. "Population: one million, five hundred eighty-four thousand, six hundred seventeen. Birth rate: seventeen per thousand. Death rate: nine point two per thousand. Population density: twenty point seven persons per square mile. Thirty-seventh state in the Union."

He kissed me for a long time, then turned me over onto my stomach. "Major agricultural products," he continued, "—corn, soybeans, hay, wheat, sorghum, dry edible beans"—he gnawed on the back of my neck—"sugar beets"—he doubled me over—"cattle, pigs, sheep . . ."

He ran his hands around me, up under my T-shirt and down into my boxer shorts. With a quick yank, he pulled them down, then pressed against me. "Nebraska state motto: Equality Before the Law."

There was to be no discussion.

Sloan played the sax. He had a remarkable embouchure and a memory for facts. All the things I'd told him on the phone over the previous months he remembered and now put to use, in an ebb and flow that lasted until morning. It was odd. Since I knew him so intimately from the phone, I felt emboldened to do or say anything—but at the same time, since I'd never met the physical man before, I was rocked by the heart-pounding terror of fucking a total stranger. He felt the strangeness too. During a rest, I opened my eyes and caught him staring.

"Is it what you'd imagined?" I couldn't help myself. I had to ask.

"More or less. You're younger looking. Like a prepubescent boy after a growth spurt."

"Do you feel like a pedophile?"

"A bit. But I like it. What about you?"

"I knew you. Your descriptions were good. Gaunt, cadaverous."

"Do you feel like a necrophile?"

"No."

"Good. I don't mind looking like a corpse, but you shouldn't think I fuck like one. I'd be upset."

He rolled onto his back and closed his eyes. His face was rough and his eyes were deep-set, curtained by a forelock of dark-brown hair, which diffused their intensity. He was tall. Taller than me, and lanky, but still somehow elegant. He had the most remarkable fingers, long and dexterous, and a habit of pressing his fingertips against his lips, as though to seal them shut. He could do wonderful things with his fingers.

In the morning, when it was still dark, I dragged myself out of bed, showered, and dressed. I left Sloan asleep, sprawled across the bed; he was an exquisite corpse. The crew was in the parking lot, silently loading the equipment into the van. We drove through the deep-blue, shadowy dawn to shoot the sun rising over the Nebraska dunes. Throughout the long day I thought about Sloan incessantly. He had insinuated himself under my skin. Whenever I could, I would disengage from the scene at hand, and my mind would retract like an oyster to its shell, to worry this newfound nacreous pebble. When we got back to the motel later that day, he was gone. He had chartered a flight from the municipal airport and disappeared as abruptly as he'd come. The room had been cleaned, sheets changed, bed made. I thought perhaps he might have left a note on the night table, or perhaps in my suitcase, or on the bathroom mirror. Perhaps a message at the front desk. But he hadn't. I went to bed. Lay there and waited. By the time he called, I was dead asleep.

"You're not here," I told him groggily.

"No. That's right. I'm here." His voice was low, a rough whisper. Suddenly I was wide awake.

"Oh. Weren't you just here?" A deep, sleep-induced indifference was the effect I was after, but my heart was in my throat and pounding.

"Yes. I was there last night."

"Oh." I yawned. "I don't believe you."

"No?" I could hear him smile.

"No. Because I don't think you exist. Good night."

"That's too bad. It's sad that I leave such a transient impression. I will try to fix that. Let's see, Bloom on Saturday, isn't it? Just south of Dodge City?"

"How'd you know that?"

"Called your office. Told them I was the Kansas Film Commissioner, calling to complain that you hadn't submitted your location permits. They faxed me your itinerary for the rest of the month."

I liked him. He produced records in New York, scored films in L.A., and his band, based in Chicago, played a dark, demented brand of postmodern jazz that was popular in Tokyo and Berlin. He was always flying across the country, so it was relatively easy for him to touch down for a night or two.

I worried about the crew at first. The ex–flight attendant knew right from the start, but I bought him off by approving his phone sex. He smirked a lot, but he kept quiet. The directors from Japan changed from week to week, so they would never catch on. Suzuki and Oh were the problem, but somehow they never seemed to notice that the film commissioners from Kansas and Utah looked the same as the one from Nebraska, and Sloan changed his shirt and the shape of his tie on a state-by-state basis. I kept waiting for the boys to raise their eyes, to recognize his face, but they never did. Maybe they were just too drunk, or Sloan was too tall, or maybe it was that all Americans looked the same, so why bother? More likely, they just didn't care.

Sloan regarded these trips as opportunities for sex and sociological surveys. So did I, but that was my job. The sociology part, I mean. It's not easy to find My American Wife and you have to initiate a broad base of inquiry. First we'd look for an area with distinctive geographical features and scenic appeal and then we'd undertake a survey: chambers of commerce, churches, PTAs, agricultural extension offices. The researchers would sit in the New York office, phoning these bastions of small-town culture; what I learned is that there's precious little culture left, and what's managed to survive is mostly of the "Ye Olde" variety.

Main Street is dead, which is no news to the families whose families ran family businesses on Main Street. When I returned from Japan and visited Quam, I found that all the local businesses from my childhood had been extirpated by Wal-Mart. If there is one single symbol for the demise of regional American culture, it is this superstore prototype, a huge capitalist[3] boot that stomped the moms and pops, like soft, damp worms, to death. Don't get me wrong. I love Wal-Mart. There is nothing I like more than to consign a mindless afternoon to those aisles, suspending thought, judgment. It's like television. But to a documentarian of American culture, Wal-Mart is a nightmare. When it comes to towns, Hope, Alabama, becomes the same as Hope, Wyoming, or, for that matter, Hope, Alaska, and in the end, all that remains of our pioneering aspirations are the confused and self-conscious

71

simulacra of relic culture: Ye Olde Curiosities 'n' Copie Shoppe, Deadeye Dick's Saloon and Karaoke Bar—ingenious hybrids and strange global grafts that are the local business-person's only chance of survival in economies of scale.

Anyway, once we'd found a town, we'd start homing in on its married women. Using Tokyo's list of Desirable Things, we'd extract the names of plausible candidates from our initial contacts—local clergymen and newspaper reporters made the richest sources—then we'd start phoning the wives. It was easy to get information from them about their families, hobbies, and favorite cuts of meats. Even wholesomeness could be ascertained over the phone. The challenge was to find out what they looked like. But there were ways. You could phone up the local Nu U Unisex Salon or Chez-Moi Hair Styling and Life Insurance and appeal to the owner as a colleague:

"'So, Cindy, you've known Mrs. Crumph for five years, you said? Great. Now, just between you and me . . . you're a beauty professional, and what I really want to ask you for is your *professional* assessment of her appearance. . . . I mean, this is television, and we need someone who looks attractive—not necessarily glamorous, but you know, not horribly overweight, or with a walleye or goiter or anything.'"

"You really ask them that?" asked Sloan, bemused.

"Of course. We need to know these things."

"You can't shoot a wife with a goiter?"

"No. The BEEF-EX people are very strict. They don't want their meat to have a synergistic association with deformities. Like race. Or poverty. Or clubfeet. But at the same time, the Network is always complaining that the shows aren't 'authentic' enough. Well, I've been saying if only they'd let me direct, I'd show them some real Americans. So this is it, Sloan. This is my big chance. . . ."

Sloan was entertained. I lay on the bed at the Outlaw Inn as he applied Wet 'N Wild nail polish to the reddened clusters of chiggers that were breeding all over my legs and thighs. They burrow under your skin and the only way to get rid of them is to cut off their oxygen supply.

I got the chiggers in Texas, in a field outside Lubbock, but it was worth it. We'd been standing there for a good part of an afternoon, shooting a very small child playing with his piglet. In the background was a white farmhouse. The boy, whose name was Bobby, lived there with his parents, Alberto and Catalina Martinez. Alberto, or Bert, as he now preferred to be called, was a farmworker. He'd lost his left hand to a hay baler in Abilene seven years earlier, a few months after he and Catalina (Cathy) had emigrated from Mexico, just in time for Bobby to be born an American citizen. That had been Cathy's dream, to have an American son, and Bert had paid for her dream with his hand. Since then he had worked hard in the fields to support the family, and Cathy had worked too, in factory jobs, and finally their efforts had paid off. They had scraped up the money to buy the little white farmhouse and a few acres of surrounding land, and the way I figured it, Alberto, Catalina, and little Bobby were on their way to becoming a real American success story. The problem was getting the chance to tell it. After four months, the BEEF-EX injunction on the demographics of our wives was still in effect, and we continued to shoot primarily middle-class white American women with two or three children. The Martinez family would obviously break this mold.

To make matters worse, the director for the shoot was the bonehead Oda, back for his second round.

"Takagi, don't be stupid," he told me. "The program is not called *My Mexican Wife!*, you know. . . ." I had given up trying to sell him on the idea.

But then the oddest thing happened. We had been filming in Oklahoma, the "Sooner State," just across the border in a town at the tip of the Panhandle. Oda had this great idea that the entire meal should be cooked in frying pans with handles, and our wife, a Mrs. Klinck, agreed. She made German Fried Potatoes and Succotash and Griddle Biscuits, and her meat was a delicate Sooner Schnitzel, made with thin cutlets of veal, dredged in crushed Kellogg's Krispies and paprika, then pan-fried in drippings with sautéed onions and sour cream. Mrs. Klinck insisted we try a cutlet or two, and to my surprise, Oda dug in with gusto. He had a fondness for German food, it seemed, but after the first few bites, he dropped his fork and clutched his neck as though he were choking.

"Oda-san! Dame da yo! Stop it immediately!" I hissed at him, furious that he should make such cruel fun of Mrs. Klinck's cooking. I mean, she was sitting at the table, facing us and watching to see how we liked her Schnitzel.

But he didn't stop. Instead, the strangling noises he was making intensified, and as Mrs. Klinck watched him, her eyes grew wide and round. She stood up, knocking her chair over, and ran from the room.

"Call nine-one-one!" I heard her cry, and that's when I realized something else was happening.

Oda's entire body had suddenly grown rigid and was starting to swell. Within minutes his windpipe had closed, and by the time the local paramedics arrived he could barely breathe. They gave him a shot of adrenaline and we airlifted him in a crop duster to the nearest hospital.

"Anaphylactic shock," the emergency room doctor said. "What was he eating when it started?"

I described the menu in detail.

The doctor shrugged. "Sounds a bit heavy," he said, "but basically okay."

After the seizure had passed and I was helping Oda fill out the medical history forms, he answered yes to the question about antibiotic allergies. When the doctor saw this, he nodded.

"That's it," he said grimly. He was a young man just out of medical school and had come to Oklahoma from San Francisco. He was cute and really tall, so we'd been flirting a little.

"What's it?" I asked.

"Antibiotics," he said. He looked at me. "You're a city girl. You've probably never been to a feedlot, have you."

"What, you mean for cows?"

He rolled his eyes. "No, cattle. Meat."

"No, but it's funny you should bring it up. What do feedlots have to do with anaphylactic shock?"

"Well, if you'd been to one, you'd know what I was talking about. They're filthy and overcrowded—breeding grounds for all sorts of disease—so cattle are given antibiotics as a preventive measure, which builds up and collects in the meat."

"But this was veal. . . ."

He looked at me. "Are you kidding? *Especially* in veal. Whew! Those calves live in boxes and never learn to walk, even—and the farmers keep them alive with these massive doses of drugs just long enough to kill them. What sent your director into shock was the residue of the antibiotics in the Sooner Schnitzel."

"You're kidding."

"Nope. What's his name . . . Oda? He must be the sensitive type."

"Oh, please . . ." If he only knew.

The young doctor's smile faded. "You know, it scares me. I mean, allergies are one thing. But all these surplus antibiotics are raising people's tolerances, and it won't be long before the stuff just doesn't work anymore. There's all sorts of virulent bacteria that are already resistant. . . . It's like back to the future—we're headed backward in time, toward a pre-antibiotic age."

I remembered this conversation much later on, but at the moment all I could think was damage control. I phoned Kato in Tokyo to let him know what had happened, and to my immense surprise, he turned the shoot over to me. To direct.

This was it. Without bothering to ask for anyone's permission, I rerouted us south into Texas and straight into the Martinezes' kitchen.

Bert wore a mean-looking hook in place of his missing hand, and during lunch he had taught me how to two-step, resting its point in the middle of my spine, while Cathy took a turn around the kitchen table with Suzuki. They were excellent dancers. Bert used to play the guitar beautifully, Cathy told me, when they were still in Mexico, before the accident.

"So now"—she shrugged—"in America we have not so much music. But we can still dance."

We filmed them stepping out on Saturday night, and on Sunday afternoon after church, Cathy prepared Texas-style Beefy Burritos, made with lean, tender slices of Texas-bred sirloin tips. The burritos were the symbol of their hard-earned American lifestyle, something to remind them of their roots but also of their new fortune. Afterward, Bobby wanted to show us his 4-H project piglet. So there we were, in the chigger-filled field, filming little Bobby in a sea of golden grass that rippled in the wind. Bert and Cathy stood arm in arm, watching. The piglet, whose name was Supper, was so big and heavy that Bobby could barely hold it up in front of him. Bobby was wearing his Sunday suit, a hand-me-down from a neighbor, which was still a bit big for him and the trousers flapped against his bony shins. His head was dwarfed by an old felt hat of his father's. He had given the piglet a bath and the animal was still wet, sending glistening droplets into the sunlight as it squirmed in his arms. Bobby smiled at the camera, a little Mexican boy shyly offering his American Supper to the nation of Japan. Everything was in slow motion. It was a surreal and exquisite moment.

AKIKO

The alarm clock rang at seven-fifteen on Saturday morning. Akiko woke in panic, which subsided into gentle dread when she realized she was alone. She lay in her futon, staring up at the acoustic ceiling tiles and fluorescent light fixture. Out on the balcony, she could hear the dull rhythmic thump of someone's wife beating the bedding hung over the balcony rail. Children were awake too. Their voices drifted up from the playground. When Akiko went to market, she always took great care to avoid the playground and the young mothers who congregated around its periphery, just inside the gate. Akiko found it difficult to walk by them along the path outside.

Akiko found it difficult to do many things: to go to bed at a reasonable hour, for example, when "John" stayed overnight in the city or was out of town on business. The air in the small apartment smelled damp and sweet. Sweet poofy exhalations all the night through. She turned over on her side and spotted the squat little whiskey bottle that she'd emptied last night in her exaltation. It had felt so good to be alone. Unmolested. She felt the hard lump of Shōnagon under her pillow. Then she spotted her pillow book diary, its pages scrawled with her own pickled lists.

Things That Make One's Heart Beat Faster
Rain clouds massing before thunder. To stand on one's balcony looking toward the city. To see the dull green-

ocher ring forming around the point of impact, that bruised sky, *my Tokyo heart*.

To contemplate his key in the latch, the scraping of his shoe, his sock-clad heel hitting the hollow floor. To feel the sweet, humid steam from the meat bathe one's face as one carries it in on the platter. To retreat, to purge—not a soul sees, yet *these* produce inner pleasure.

It is night and one is feigning sleep. One becomes aware of his critical mind grazing one's sparrow ribs, considering the cavity of one's pelvis, fingering the knob of one's spine, disdaining one's breasts. Suddenly one is startled by the sound of his deep snoring.

Soused, she'd had this dumb idea that lists could become poetry. She ripped out the pages from the diary and crumpled them in her fist, then made up another.

Things That Give a Hot Feeling
The shame of drinking.
Disobedience.
Drunken poetry, full of imperfections.

She got up slowly, head pounding, and carefully folded the top quilt and the sheets. Then she folded the bottom futon and the thin foam mattress into accordion sections of three. She piled the covers on top of the mattress, laid the buckwheat pillows on top, picked up the entire heap of bedding, and staggered to the closet. She shoved it all inside, onto the shelf, and slid the door shut quickly to keep it from tumbling out. Then she boiled water for tea. By eight o'clock she was dressed and sitting at the low *kotatsu* table in front of the television. Toes tucked neatly beneath her, she watched the screen, where a young Mexican child stood in the middle of a waving field of wheat, smiling shyly up at her and offering her an enormous pig. It was squirming in his arms, so heavy he could barely hold it. He teetered back and forth on the tips of his toes.

Then, in slow motion, the wind caught his big felt hat and blew it up into the air, the pig gave a wriggle and flew from his arms, and the little boy broke into peals of laughter as he chased them both in circles. Akiko felt the tears well up in her eyes as, pen in hand, she smoothed out the sheet of paper, ready to take down the day's recipe, for Texas-style Beefy Burritos, on the back side of her crumpled poem. The haunting a cappella strains of "Amazing Grace" drowned out the noise of the Tokyo suburb.

JANE

FAX

TO: S. Kato
FROM: Jane Takagi-Little
DATE: April 12, 1991

Dear Kato-san,

Thank you for your fax. I was very happy to hear about the high ratings for the Martinez show, and I want to thank you for your vote of confidence in allowing me to direct another episode of *My American Wife!* I will do my best to increase the Authenticity and General Interest of the program while maintaining the high standards of Helpfulness, Knowledge Enhancement, Wholesomeness, and of course Deliciousness of Meat.

Please assure Mr. Ueno that I understand his concern that an American director might not be able to satisfy the unique sensibilities of the Japanese audience. I will do my best, and I will be sure to send you proposals in advance for your approval.

Up until now we have chosen our American Wives based on characteristics that market studies indicate will be attractive to Japanese married women. I think the reason the Martinez family show received such high ratings is because it was different. It widened the audience's understanding of what it is to be American. I would like to continue to introduce the quirky, rich diversity and the strong sense of individualism that make the people of this country unique.

Here is my proposal for the next show.

BEAUDROUX FAMILY
Askew, Louisiana

OPENING: Imagine *Gone With the Wind*. The frame is locked and neatly circumscribes a classical Southern perspective. The long drive cuts straight down the center toward the house, lined on either side by ancient oaks whose branches are laden with beards of Spanish moss. The brick plantation house defines the end of the drive and plugs up its vanishing point. We hear a slow Zydeco "Valse Bébé" or a sliding Cajun blues riff like "Ma Petite Fille Est Gone" by Rockin' Dopsie.

An attractive middle-aged woman with faded blonde hair and a glimmer of quiet humor in her eye enters from the left of the frame. She turns to face the camera. "Hi, y'all," she says, with a slow smile. "I'm Grace Beaudroux. I'm your American Wife today. Now, let's meet the family."

Her words motivate a slow camera dolly forward to reveal a lanky, balding man, deeply tanned.

"I'm Vern," he drawls. "Gracie's loving husband."

Again the camera pushes forward, this time to discover a fair-haired daughter, whose pregnancy burgeons at the bottom of the frame.

"I'm Alison," she says. "I'm the oldest." The camera continues to move.

"I'm Vernon," says a tall, sandy-haired young man. "Junior. I'm the second." The camera booms down to a considerably lower angle, and suddenly an Asian teenager with raven-black hair and bangs cut low across her forehead confronts the camera.

"I'm Joy," she says aggressively. "I'm the third." She has a pierced eyebrow.

"I'm Newton," says the Asian boy who follows. "The fourth."

"I'm Cici," says the next girl. "I'm fifth." And then one after another, Asian children in varying shades, descending in size and age, take their turns.

"I'm Elvis. I'm sixth."

"I'm Page. I'm seventh."

"I'm Jake. I'm the eighth."

"I'm Emily May. I'm ninth."

"I'm Duncan. I'm tenfth." The little ones have accents still.

"I'm Joey. I'm elevenst."

"I'm Chelsea," says the tiniest girl, dark and suddenly quite different. Her black eyes glisten with confusion. She looks around for help. Various whispers can be heard off-camera, which seem to hearten her. Bravely she faces the camera. "I'm the last one."

CUT TO:

Wide Shot of Family, lined up in front of the plantation house. Gracie is in the center, flanked by her husband and the smiling ranks of her family.

Just think of the meat this gang can eat at a single sitting!

CUT TO REGIONAL CORNER:
With a burst of raucous Southern Funk—Bobby Joe Creely singing his cover rendition of "Poke Salad Annie"—the small town of Askew, Louisiana, comes to life with the annual Pig Festival. In the center of town, whole pigs are splayed and roasted over open pits, and people are spitting watermelon seeds, calling hogs, and chasing greased piglets for prizes. The festival concludes with the crowning of the Pig Queen.

CUT TO MEAT:
Vern is a professional chef and on his day off from his restaurant, as a special treat, he gives Grace a late-afternoon nap; while she dozes, he cooks dinner. In keeping with the Pig Festival theme, he makes his specialty: Cajun-style Baby Back Ribs. His recipe is quite original and well suited to Japanese tastes. The kids all pitch in and help him, and the Cooking Corner becomes quite a rough 'n' tumble affair.

CUT TO CHERRY STREET:
Cruisin' Cherry on a Saturday night. Cherry Street flows like a slow molten river of metal and chrome as the teenage population of Askew gathers in a ritual that hasn't changed since Grace and Vern were young—only now the vehicles are Nissans and Mazdas, and the music is House of Pain. The cars cruise slowly up Cherry to the Civil War memorial at the edge of town, swing around the monument, then drive back down to the parking lot of the Dairy Queen, where they pull a U-turn and do it again. At seven o'clock,

the unofficial start, the occupants of the vehicles are rigidly segregated by gender. As the cars pass each other, subtle agreements are struck, and then, as if by chance, two vehicles will pull to a stop side by side and swap some of their occupants.

"That's the point," said Grace. "Right, Joy?"

We were in the car and Vern was driving and they were giving me a tour of Askew. Joy rolled her eyes at me and scowled at the back of her mother's head. "How should I know?" she said. "I didn't make it up. You guys did."

Grace turned and looked at me over the seat back.

"It's one of our primitive Southern customs," she explained. "Joy just does it to humor us."

CHERRY STREET (cont.)

Grace Peabody and Vernon Beaudroux met cruisin' Cherry. Gracie was new in town. So was Vern. Neither had a car, but as both were attractive teens, they got lucky and were invited to join the crowd, Grace in the back seat of a gun-blue Barracuda, and Vern in a cherry-red Chevy Impala. But by the end of the evening, when they'd both been required to vacate the back seats for more expansive couples, they found themselves perched on the memorial at the end of Cherry, discussing their dreams for the future. Vern straddled the rump of the great bronze horse, sharing the saddle, back to back, with a proud Rebel cavalryman. Gracie sat demurely at the horse's feet, leaning up against the hip of the Rebel's Negro manservant.

"That's it right there," Grace said, pointing out the statue to me as Vern drove us slowly around it. "It's shameful. I don't know if y'all oughta film it."

"Elvis and some of the kids at school are trying to get it taken down," Joy told me.

"It was 1968!" Vern exclaimed. "We were sixteen-year-old white kids, but we just didn't . . ."

"We just didn't *think*," Grace concluded, pursing her lips sternly.

CHERRY STREET (cont.)

In the next thirty minutes Vern and Gracie knew everything about each other that mattered: that they'd both been to the city but preferred country living; that they both liked Zydeco, funk, and especially Bobby Joe Creely, but they also liked singing in the church choir; that they both loved kids and wanted a big family, but neither felt it was right to have more than two children of one's own.

"The way I figure it," said Vern, "two's enough. And then if we wanted a big family we could just adopt some. . . ." He looked at Grace, wondering if she'd noticed that he'd practically proposed to her.

"That's perfect!" exclaimed Gracie, clapping her hands as though what he'd suggested was nothing more than a neat decorating theme for the school prom. "Like all the little Oriental babies from Korea and Vietnam who don't have anyone to care for them or buy them toys or educations . . ."

Then suddenly she got real serious. "I've always thought folks should just replace themselves in the world, you know, one kid for each parent, so you're not really adding anything. If everyone does that, we won't have the population explosion. . . ."

"She always had a talent for numbers," Vern said, smiling at Grace.

Grace frowned. "It used to bother me like crazy!" she exclaimed. "Thinkin' about all the billions of people on the earth multiplying, having more and more babies—I swear it used to keep me awake at night. It still does. It's the single most underdiscussed issue in the world."

"What, having babies?" I asked.

Joy groaned. "Don't get her started," she warned in a loud whisper.

Grace ignored her. "I mean, we talk about the environment, the economy, human rights, but no one ever talks about population."

"She gets totally insane about this," Joy said ominously.

"Well, it's the heart of all the other problems," Grace protested, turning around to face us. "Or it will be. You just wait and see, Joy. You'll still be alive when the you-know-what hits the fan. Havin' babies is going to be the big topic of the millennium—who gets to do it, who's still even capable of doing it. . . . I mean, it can't go on like this. The math just doesn't work out." She sank back down into her seat. "It's all these religious nuts," she muttered darkly. "We can't even have a sane conversation about abortion."

CUT TO FAMILY HISTORY CORNER:
Grace and Vern got married, and during the next three years their project began to materialize. Alison was born,

then Vernon Junior followed two years later. Vern Senior had a talent for food, and Gracie had her talent for numbers. Together they bought a run-down mill outside of town and turned it into one of the most famous Cajun restaurants in Louisiana. When Alison was seven and Vernon Junior just turned five, they bought the old plantation house, opened the gates, and started to fill it with children.

Joy was first. She was five, just a few months younger than Vernon Junior. They found her in a Christian adoption magazine. She was the Amerasian daughter of a GI and a Korean prostitute. She'd been abandoned at the age of three and a half on the steps of a Catholic church with a note attached to her wrist that read, "This girl's mother is a whore and her father is an American. God, please raise her for me. Thank you very much." The adoption magazine had this description of her:

Min Jung is an alert and intelligent five-year-old who can be a true delight. She is generally quiet and obedient and shows a sensitivity to sound and music. Because of early institutional neglect and lack of stimulation, she has been slow to develop verbal skills and is prone to occasional outbursts of obstinacy.

"*Some* things never change," said Grace. We were sitting in the living room, waiting for the family to congregate.

"Shut up, Mom," replied Joy. She pointed to the old adoption magazine, holding it up so I could see. "'True delight. Quiet and obedient.' She always leaves out those parts."

"Well?" Vern Senior had opened the floor for discussion. Their family meeting was a weekly event, when everyone got together and reviewed the events of the week and made all the decisions that would affect them.

"She's so cute," said Alison. "She looks like a little doll."

"I want a brother," said Vernon Junior.

"Outbursts of obstinacy?" inquired Vern Senior.

"Sensitivity to music," concluded Gracie, who was by now the assistant leader of the church choir.

They voted to name her Joy. When she first came to live at the large brick house at the end of the drive, she spoke no English and certain things seemed to terrify her: Vern Senior kissing Alison good night, for example, or birthday parties with noisemakers, or blinking Christmas lights. Other things—the sight of the full Louisiana moon or a black child smaller than she was—would set her off in a different way. It was like something inside her heart just snapped. She would turn to face the nearest vertical surface, press her forehead against it, squeeze her eyes shut, and emit a high-pitched keening that split ears. She would stand like this for hours, humming like a tuning rod to the pitch of her grief.

"Musical?" Vern Senior asked mildly.

Gracie pursed her lips and waited. In the dead of the night under the moon, or in the toy aisle at Wal-Mart, she would pry her strange new daughter away from the supporting wall, crouch, and wrap her arms around her. But the child remained unbending, unable to explain. The wellspring of her rigor was too deep to reach, and normally serene Grace fretted endlessly.

It took the better part of the year, but the episodes

diminished. As Joy learned English, the means of expression seemed to assuage her terrors. Her voice was harsh and nasal at first, but as her language developed and she gained confidence and velocity, it softened. Grace realized then that the girl was a soprano and the keening was the first expression of her talent. She brought Joy to choir practices, and before too long she was singing solo.

Grace regained her composure and called another family meeting. Good-natured Newton came next.

> Dong Chul has a cleft palate, but he laughs easily and babbles well. His good nature, cooing, and laughing endears everyone to him.

And then bold Cici:

> Ha Young is a baby who shows good response to light and sound, holds her head up well.

And big Elvis:

> Young Bum is a loving, healthy, happy baby with a good strong cry.

And calm Page:

> Nam Hee watches TV well.

And then came restless Jake:

> Now isn't that a winning smile? This energetic baby explores his surroundings by creeping all over the room.

And curious Emily May:

> Mee Ree is sensitive and entertains herself by playing with her fingers and toes.

And wise Duncan:

Ho Young makes good eye contact with his caretakers.

And sweet Joey:

> This little winner had polio, but now he is walking well
> and doing his best, if not to run, to move very quickly.

And finally dark, conflicted Chelsea:

> This bright-eyed orphan from São Paulo is missing
> fingers from both hands. She may have been mutilated
> during a round-up of homeless children by the police,
> but she is responding well to tender loving care.

"You guys keep all your descriptions?" I asked the kids.
They screamed with laughter.

"Yeah, man. It's cool. 'Good strong cry . . . ,'" said Elvis.

"We had to go through a lot," said Newton quietly. "I
guess we're proud."

"I bring mine to show-and-tell at school," Joey said. "I am
a winner. I move fast!"

Chelsea burrowed her head into Elvis's side. He put his
arm around her. "I didn't mean it," he said to her. "It's not so
cool, really. It's just some stupid thing someone said about
you. They didn't even know . . ."

Joy leaned over. "She doesn't know what 'mutilated' means
yet," she whispered, "but she doesn't like the word 'homeless.'"

FAMILY HISTORY CORNER (cont.)

As the reputation of the Beaudroux restaurant grew,
adoption became a yearly event. Once a year, at Christmas,
Gracie and Vern called a special family meeting to decide
whether to expand the family and, if so, to choose a new

sibling. They started by adopting children from one country, with the hope that eventually, in a town with a population of just over a thousand, the adopted kids would form a majority of their own. Several of the children were biologically related. Elvis was Joy's younger brother, who was six months old when Joy was abandoned. Joy was beside herself when, after an arduous and expensive search in Korea, seven-year-old Young Bum was discovered cleaning rooms at the brothel where their mother had worked before she died. His father was African-American, and his skin was darker and his hair curlier than the rest of the Korean siblings. Joy would beat up anyone who teased him about either his color or his name. Later Elvis was the one who picked Chelsea out of the catalog and lobbied to adopt her, despite her different racial background. Chelsea, for her part, stuck to Elvis like a burr, locking the thumb and forefinger of one hand around his belt loop and sucking the remaining fingers of the other. At number twelve, Chelsea made an even dozen. The family came to a consensus that she would be the final sibling.

"But now there's Alison," said Grace with a sigh. "She's due any day now. Her boyfriend ran off on her and it doesn't look like he's coming back. I shouldn't be so conservative, but I'm havin' trouble supporting her decision to have this baby by herself. It's damn hard to raise kids, and it's just not the time for ambivalent breeding, you know? In this day and age . . ."

We were walking around the rear of the main plantation house, down by Vern's large kitchen garden, looking at the former slave cabins, which Vern and the boys were renovating, one by one. My boys were packing up the equipment in the van, getting ready to go.

"Do you have any kids?" Grace asked.

I shook my head. "I tried. I was married once, but it just didn't work out. . . ."

"Well, you're still young. You got plenty of time. Are you seeing anyone now?"

"Sort of. But it's pretty casual."

"I guess you don't have a lot of time, huh?" Grace smiled. "Is it rude for me to ask all these questions?"

"Not at all. It's only fair. I know all about you, after all."

Most of the little cabins were dilapidated and sagging and overrun with kudzu, but two were renovated, and they were charming. Alison would live in one of them with her baby.

"Joy has dibs on the second cabin," Grace said. "It's a privacy thing. She's at that age. . . ." She smiled at me. "You really made a big impression on her."

"It's the tattoo." I'd shown her the delicate tiger, my Chinese birth sign, that I'd had tattooed on my shoulder blade in Kyoto. Joy was born in the Year of the Tiger too.

"Well, I guess that's part of it. But it's also that y'all are cool, you know? Good role models. They really took to all of you. Suzuki and Oh too."

"Well, that goes both ways," I said.

I'd never seen Suzuki and Oh so engaged with a family before. It all started with the kudzu. We'd shot Grace and Vern working in the kitchen garden and then had moved on to the cabin renovation. Vern and his sons were pulling up the kudzu vine, ripping it from the roof and walls so they could get at the wood underneath. When we'd finished shooting the scene, Suzuki put down the camera, dumbfounded. He hadn't realized that in the South, kudzu was a weed—the whole time he was shooting it, he'd thought it was Vern's prized crop.

Suzuki stashed the camera in the van and returned with a tire iron, which he used to dig up an armload of the tubers. Back at the house, he showed Vern how to turn them into starch, then how to use the starch to thicken sauces and batters. He made a salad with the shoots and the flowers, and even a hangover medicine that resembled milk of magnesia. Vern was astounded. He'd never thought of the plant as anything but an invasive weed.

It was an interesting story, I thought, especially for a Japanese audience.

CUT TO DOCUMENTARY INTERLUDE:

Kudzu, honored by Japanese farmers for generations, is the most infamous exotic to shoot its root through the thin mantle of American soil. This humble member of the pea family is native to many parts of Asia. It was introduced at the Centennial Exposition in Philadelphia in 1876, when the alien twiner was touted as "The Miracle Plant" and praised for its versatility, hardiness, and speed of growth. It could shade a bower in a matter of days and feed a herd of cows and pigs to boot. But this was just the beginning.

By the early part of the century, decades of careless cotton and tobacco farming had depleted Southern soil, and bankrupt farmers were fleeing their barren fields. In 1933, desperate to keep the South from washing away, Congress established the Soil Erosion Service, and kudzu, with its deep, binding roots and its ability to reintroduce nitrogen into the soil, was seen as Dixie's savior. It could survive drought. It would grow anywhere, even where other plants couldn't. It could rehabilitate the land. The government paid farmers up to $8.00 an acre to plant the vine.

But kudzu was predaceous, opportunistic, grew rampant, and was soon out of control. By the end of World War II, the invasive Asian weed had overrun an estimated 500,000 acres of the southeastern United States. It engulfed the indigenous vegetation, smothered shrubs and trees, and turned telephone poles and houses into hulking, emerald-green ghosts.

Under ideal conditions it will grow a foot a day. You can measure its growth in miles per hour, say embittered farmers. Drop it and run. Mothers threaten to toss their naughty children into the kudzu patch, where they'll strangle and drown. Its economic and practical uses have been forgotten. Mostly, nowadays, its only use is metaphoric, to describe the inroads of Japanese industry into the nonunionized South.

"We're real glad y'all came," said Vern. "And not just because of the kudzu, either." He shook Suzuki's hand.

Grace put her arm around me and walked me to the van. "Y'all come back now anytime, you hear?"

AKIKO

Bobby Joe Creely was singing "Poke Salad Annie." Akiko sat by the window on the express train to the city and scrutinized the lyric sheet that came with the CD. She liked the song. It felt like Bobby Joe was telling her a story and if only she could understand the words she would be able to identify with it perfectly. Unfortunately, there was no Japanese translation on the lyric sheet. It was a song about a girl who liked salads, she was sure of that. Akiko liked salads too, far more than meats. But there was also something in the song about alligators and chain gangs. She didn't know what a chain gang was. It was a phrase she had never looked up in her dictionary.

She'd heard the song on the *My American Wife!* program about the Korean children in Louisiana. It was a good show, and she had given it a 9 in Authenticity. She'd especially liked the music. She'd written down the names of Bobby Joe and also Rockin' Dopsie at the bottom of the paper where she copied the week's recipe. The next day she took the bullet train to town and found the CDs at Tower Records in Shibuya. It took her most of the day, but it was worth the trip. When she got home to her apartment she put on the Rockin' Dopsie CD and cooked the Cajun-style Baby Back Ribs. They had turned out exceptionally well and she gave them a 9 in Deliciousness, but even this hadn't made "John" happy, although he ate them with gusto.

"How stupid can she be?" he muttered darkly as he tore the sticky meat from the bone with his teeth.

"Who?" Akiko asked, trying hard to be conversational.

"That stupid American coordinator. She goes and shoots the husband cooking! Husbands aren't supposed to cook. The show is called *My American* Wife!"

"Well, it is nice for a change . . . ," Akiko started, then thought better of it. "But of course you're right, it makes no sense."

"And she has been instructed to make programs about beef, but no." He sucked the bone, then added it to the growing pile on his plate and grabbed another. "She goes and chooses pork, clearly a second-class meat. I mean, really! A pig-roasting festival! Not to mention all those Korean children . . ."

He shook his head. "John" had a way of changing the mood of any room he entered.

But before he had come home, while Akiko was still cooking, the small apartment was filled with the sweet, fragrant steam of the stewing meat and the happy, humid music of the bayou. "Hot Tamale Baby." All that was missing was the children. Lots of them, clambering over each other like puppies. They looked just like Japanese children, but in their forthright manner and their solemn sense of responsibility they were so unlike the kids in the *danchi*, who tended to be withdrawn and self-conscious. It would be nice to raise a child in a rough 'n' tumble family. Maybe she and "John" could adopt, if this problem of hers didn't work itself out.

Akiko removed the earphones. The pressurized silence on the train, eerie at such a high speed, filled her ears like wads of Kleenex. Replacing the phones, she jacked up the volume on her portable CD player. She liked Bobby Joe's voice, the way he grunted between verses. She thought she would be a little scared if she met him in person, but his songs made her feel reckless and even a little dangerous. Basically, she thought he was just a down-to-earth man. The notes from his guitar shimmered like heat rising off a hard-packed country road. She'd never seen heat rising before, or met a woman like the one in the song, who carried a straight razor. Akiko didn't know what a straight razor was, but suddenly she wished she could have one too. She wondered if this music was what the Deep South felt like. "Lord have mercy . . ."

She looked out the thick window at the terraced paddies, flooded now and scored with neat green rows of young rice. The songs had a driving beat that went well with the rhythm of the speeding train, but the scenery was all wrong. Rice grew wild in Louisiana swamps, she thought, but this was different. The Japanese rice fields had no funk.

In under an hour, the train pulled into Tokyo Station. Akiko eased herself into the flow of people that eddied toward the subway lines. She took the Marunouchi Line to the Ginza, and when she had climbed to street level, she consulted the piece of paper where "John" had written the address of the specialist for her. The office was on the eleventh floor of a building near the Mitsukoshi Department Store.

There were three women ahead of her in the waiting room. One, visibly pregnant, gave Akiko a smile and a nod when she entered. The other two, reed thin and hollow as Akiko herself, ducked their heads and looked away as though they'd done something terribly wrong. One by one they were called in to the examination room. The pregnant one rose slowly when summoned, arching her back with an apologetic smile. The thin ones kept their eyes to the ground and scurried, crablike, out of sight.

When Akiko's turn came, the nurse told her to undress and handed her a paper gown to put on. She sat on the edge of the table in the examination room and waited. Finally the specialist arrived and told her to lie down on the examining table and put her feet into the metal stirrups. He tossed a sheet across her knees, snapped on a pair of latex gloves, and stood at the foot of the table. He was wearing a white coat and the bottom half of his face was covered with a white gauze mask, held on by elastic that looped over his ears. The thick black rectangular frames of his glasses appeared to perch along the top edge of the mask, giving his face a boxlike symmetry. His hair was oiled into place, and as he examined her, dipping up and down over the limp horizon of sheet, Akiko noticed that the crown of his head was dusty and speckled with large, embedded particles of dandruff.

The examination hurt, and when he had finished, he peeled the gloves from his hands and gravely told her to get dressed and come into his office. She obeyed. She knocked timidly on his door and found him seated behind a large desk. He waited until she sat down across from him. Without the surgical mask, his face looked childlike, with plump, bow-shaped lips that formed a little pout of disapproval.

"Mrs. Ueno, quite frankly, I think I am the wrong doctor for you to be consulting. I told your husband this, but he insisted. Physically, there is nothing wrong with you that a few extra pounds wouldn't take care of. You are severely malnourished and that is why your menstruation has ceased, but apparently you already know this? Of course, the odd thing is that your husband tells me you get plenty to eat. In fact, you have quite a robust appetite, he says."

Akiko nodded mutely, keeping her eyes fixed on her hands, which were folded in her lap. The doctor watched her carefully from behind his glasses, then he leaned forward.

"I'm not a psychiatrist. I'm used to looking for real illnesses, with real symptoms and causes, but if I were to hazard a guess, I'd say that you were doing something. Am I right? That you are doing something to yourself on purpose, to keep your menstruations from coming back?"

Akiko watched her knuckles whiten.

"Very well." He sat back and shook his head. Akiko tried to relax her shoulders.

"I must say I have no patience with stubborn wives like you. There are so many young women who are desperate to have a baby, who would cut off an arm or a leg in order to conceive and are honestly incapable of doing so. But you, you are not honest. You lack fortitude. Simply put, you have a bad attitude. This is my diagnosis, which I will give to your husband. I hope, for both your sakes, that he will be able to help you correct your problem."

In the public rest room of the Mitsukoshi Department Store, Akiko felt the meat start to rise inside her, although she had eaten nothing all day. She flushed the toilet, leaned over and heaved, but nothing came out. When the spasms settled, she reached up and flushed again. The smell of the rushing water refreshed her. She stood and leaned against the side of the stall, rubbing her empty stomach with her hands, and she thought about cutting off her arm to trade for a baby. Stupid. At the sink, she dampened her handkerchief and patted her face with it, then straightened out her blouse and plugged the earphones back into her ears. The gravelly voice of Bobby Joe made her heart jump. She moved to the syncopated beat, out the washroom door, across the department store, through scarves, perfumes, and cosmetics, and into the accessory department. Her arm brushed against a display shelf. She glanced quickly up and down the aisle. No one was watching. As Bobby Joe groaned, "Oh, Lord," she reached toward a pearl-studded barrette, fingered it, then slipped it into her pocket. Bobby Joe's voice shook with his muted pain, then broke free and soared.

It was all Akiko could do to keep from singing along with him.

GRACE

Grace yawned and stretched her toes, squeezing the last bits of physical pleasure from her afternoon nap. It was warm, but there was a breeze blowing, and the room was filled with a soft dappled light that filtered through the leaf-covered window. Something in the moment, some fleeting conjunction of the senses, of light and air, of warm and cool, of smell and sound and memory, made her shiver with the irrepressible *life* of it all. It was like a sexual feeling, only self-contained, immaculate.

She could hear Vern in the kitchen with some of the kids. That was nice too. Elvis was there for sure, she could hear his booming voice, and since he was there, so was Chelsea. If they were cooking, Page would be helping also, with Duncan, and if there were scraps to eat, then Joey would be begging for them. Emily May would be reading on the porch. Vernon Junior was away at college. Newton was at football practice. Cici was at cheerleading. Jake was at band. Was that everyone? No, Joy. Joy would not be in the kitchen. Joy would be in Alison's cottage, lurking by the baby.

A few days after the baby was born, Alison had found Joy next to the crib in the middle of the night. It frightened her, and she had complained to Grace the next day—she didn't want her child to imprint on this image of Joy's pierced face looming over his horizon like a cloudy harvest moon. Grace told her to relax. The kids had all been older when they were adopted, so newborns were a bit of a novelty, and Joy was at that age when it was natural to find infants fascinating. But privately Grace worried. Maybe it was Alison's choice of words, comparing Joy to the moon like that, but it reminded Grace of all the trouble they'd had.

This was the problem with trying to prolong naps, she thought. You let in one single thought, even a pleasant one, and the rest all tumbled in afterward, and soon they started crashing into each other and worrying you and it was hard to recover your napping composure. Sometimes, though, you could get it back if you thought about something pleasant, something completely different. . . .

The TV shoot had been fun and unexpectedly constructive. It suddenly occurred to Grace that the kids had probably never spent time with an Asian adult since coming to Askew. Certainly there weren't any Asians among her or Vern's friends. They knew lots of African-Americans, but of course that wasn't the same. She had never thought about race when she was growing up, and now she saw that she'd been blind to it. The colors had been all around her, endlessly complex, with shades as variegated as the genetic spectrum could permit. Joy told her that Elvis was hanging out with the black kids at school, lobbying to have the Civil War memorial on Cherry taken down. That was good. Change was good, and Elvis had a peer group, and his stability was rubbing off on Chelsea. Alison was settling in nicely, and despite Grace's reservations, she had to admit it was nice to have an infant around. No, it was Joy she was worried about. It always came back to Joy.

The fragrant smell of fried chicken wafted up the stairs from the kitchen. Vern was experimenting again. Grace smiled. Ever since the shoot, Vern had been obsessed, researching the various uses for kudzu and perfecting recipes for food and herbal remedies. He had taken to loading all the kids into the minivan on the weekends and setting them loose in the countryside to harvest kudzu roots. They would come back at the end of the day, dirty and exhausted, with their backpacks full, and process the roots into starch. The kids were happy because Vern was paying them an hourly wage. He had high hopes of winning at the state fair with his kudzu-based crispy chicken batter.

"They'll never believe it, Gracie," he crowed. "When I win and then tell them my secret ingredient, they'll just never believe it!"

With a little ingenuity and a few pointers from the Orient, Vern was certain he could find a way to turn this old weed into a solid cash crop. It just goes to show, Gracie thought, sitting up in bed. Sometimes you had to look at things from another angle.

THE RICE-SPROUTING MONTH

SHŌNAGON

Times When One Should Be on One's Guard

The sea is a frightening thing at the best of times. How much more terrifying must it be for those poor women divers who have to plunge into its depths for their livelihood! One wonders what would happen to them if the cord round their waist were to break. I can imagine men doing this sort of work, but for a woman it must take remarkable courage. After the woman has been lowered into the water, the men sit comfortably in their boats, heartily singing songs as they keep an eye on the mulberry-bark cord that floats on the surface. It is an amazing sight, for they do not show the slightest concern about the risks the woman is taking. When finally she wants to come up, she gives a tug on her cord and the men haul her out of the water with a speed that I can well understand. Soon she is clinging to the side of the boat, her breath coming in painful gasps. The sight is enough to make even an outsider feel the brine dripping. I can hardly imagine this is a job that anyone would covet.

JANE

SUPERMARKETS TO INTRODUCE
VENDING MACHINES FOR MEAT

The modern Japanese housewife finds the human interaction necessary to purchase meat distasteful.

This is the conclusion of a market survey conducted by the Super Marushin Grocery chain, which claims that Japanese housewives between the ages of 20 and 65 find it embarrassing to say the names of meat cuts out loud. The wives also complain that too much conversation is needed to conclude a purchase, and that the human contact at the butcher shop is too personal.

The majority of housewives say they would prefer to buy meat from vending machines, where they would not be called upon to make conversation about the weather or answer questions like "How are you today?"

"The modern Japanese housewife, living a hermetic existence, increasingly cut off from contact with the world, is literally losing her voice. Is it any wonder she prefers to interact with a machine?" asks Dr. Yoko Horii, of Tokyo University. Dr. Horii studies eating disorders, depression, substance abuse, suicide, and other dysfunctional behaviors among Japanese housewives.

These new findings may be a cause of concern to

sociologists like Dr. Horii, but the challenge for meat marketers is clearly how to "de-humanize" meat.

—*Asabi Gazetteer*
(English translation)

I read this article in a Tokyo newspaper and found the market trend toward dehumanized meat quite interesting. After my year, I have my own thoughts on the matter.

A sixteen-year-old high school exchange student from Japan named Yoshihiro Hattori was shot to death in Louisiana. Rodney Dwayne Peairs, the man who shot him, worked at a Winn Dixie supermarket as a meat packer. Hattori had rung Peairs's bell to ask for directions, and Peairs shot the boy in the chest with his .44 magnum. He had yelled "Freeze" before he fired. The case went to court, and Peairs was acquitted by the jury of manslaughter, on the grounds that he had acted in a reasonable way to defend his home.

Japan was shocked at the verdict. It was murder, or at the very least it was an act of wanton and reckless manslaughter, and the Japanese media went into overdrive, trying to explain what was so clearly a miscarriage of justice. On TV talk shows, professors from Tokyo University who were experts on U.S. culture discussed the profound feelings Americans have for their guns. Japanese news crews brought cameras into gas stations and 7-Elevens to show viewers the vast array of magazines on guns, ammo, and hunting for sale. They filmed bars with firearms displayed in glass cases like works of art, next to the stuffed heads of the animals they had killed. One crew even visited Wal-Mart to show how easy it is to buy a gun over the counter. A newspaper article attempted to analyze the profound feeling Americans have for guns by comparing it to the Japanese attachment to rice, and a TV show offered lessons in idiomatic English, explaining that *freeze* was not just something that was done to meat.

"Do all Americans carry guns?" was a question my Japanese friends used to ask me. "What kind do you have? Where do you carry it?" I became a documentarian partly in order to correct cultural misunderstandings like this one, and it made me crazy to see them so effectively reinforced.

Hattori was killed because Peairs had a gun, and because Hattori looked different. Peairs had a gun because here in America we fancy that ours is still a frontier culture, where our homes must be defended by deadly force from people who look different. And while I'm not saying that Peairs pulled the trigger because he was a butcher, his occupation didn't surprise me. Guns, race, meat, and Manifest Destiny all collided in a single explosion of violent, dehumanized activity. In the subsequent civil trial, evidence that had been suppressed during the criminal trial was introduced, including Peairs's affiliation with the Ku Klux Klan. The civil court found him guilty.

I started collecting local stories and would test them on the boys as we drove around in the van. If they liked a story or found it surprising, I would use it in the show. I was a full-fledged director now, and I'd promised Ueno I would do my best to satisfy the "unique sensibilities" of the Japanese television audience; since I wasn't Japanese, I used the boys as my barometer. Traveling across America, they were astonished at how deeply violence is embedded in our culture, how it has *become* the culture, what's left of local color. We are a grisly nation.

In Green River, Wyoming, a bartender told us a story about a rancher who was traveling into town, when he spotted a campfire. As it was growing late, he rode closer, glad of the company and the promise of a good meal. Sitting there were two scruffy-looking men, stirring a large pot full of delicious-smelling stew. The rancher asked if he could have some, and reluctantly they agreed. He sat down and ate a bowl, then, finding it quite tasty, he asked what it was. "Pigeon stew," they answered somewhat curtly. They were not very sociable, so rather than linger, he rode on into Green River, where he stopped at the bar for a drink. The bar was crowded. Seated to one side, he overheard some townspeople discussing a doctor back East who was looking to purchase clean human skulls. On the other side, a couple of cowhands were talking about the mysterious disappearance of a local rancher named Lloyd Pigeon.

"*Sooo da ne . . .*," said Suzuki, considering. "Cannibalism is interesting to Americans."

"We Japanese eat mostly fish," explained Oh.

Sloan used to love this stuff. He was an entirely modern, urban musician and had never been exposed to the macabre under-belly of small-town America. The crew and I would come back from a day on the sagebrush steppes, clambering about the buttes, scrabbling down riverbeds, jumping barbed wire, hop-ping tracks, searching for the perfect shot of the lowering skies, and I'd find Sloan lounging in a local bar like the one in Green River, buying drinks for laid-off trona miners and railroad men. It was great, like having a researcher in the field. He'd cull stories, then feed them to me later in bed.

Bed with Sloan. He was a masterful storyteller, but that was only a small part of it. First I have to explain. I had hit my adult height by the time I was fourteen and spent most of my adolescence freakishly taller than my classmates. My first sexual experiences felt like geographical surveys; I was a continent, a landmass beset by small, brave pioneers. Like Gulliver. It was amusing, in a distant sort of way. Later I learned about pleasure, but procuring it always felt masturbat-ory, like my partner was a tool, something I could hold in my hands and manipulate.

Few men could make me feel diminutive. Sex became sleek

and narcissistic, but I never experienced that queasy, uneasy paradox of boldness and fear. I never felt submissive and certainly I never lost control.

Until Sloan. He overwhelmed me. Is it regressive of me to talk this way? The word "masterful" comes to mind, but he could be that. In the motel room in Nebraska, with the neon spitting red and blue and turning the air electric, Sloan took charge. In life, I am the most competent person I know. It can get in the way. But Sloan was such a master of sex that my competence in life was irrelevant. He relieved me of choice. And self-consciousness.

That was the charm of it. I was a director now, in control of my crews and my shoots. Yet in hotels and motor lodges across the country, in seedy rooms or from time to time in penthouse suites, the moment the door closed behind us, the parameters of my reality would shift—violently, like the list of a ship, or, on a plane, the way your stomach pitches during a problematic descent through turbulence—that is how he would tip me.

In the quiet corridor on the way to the room, he walked behind me and his focus made me cower. The hairs on my neck would prickle and rise, and there was this moment of fear. . . . I'd seen nature documentaries about the sexual behavior of large felines in the wild. I've *made* nature documentaries about the sexual behavior of large felines in the wild. I'd just never felt like one before.

I just assumed that, like any dominant male, he had a harem. Okay. There was this one thing Sloan did that was antithetical to nature, at least the documented animal kind: He always wore not one but two condoms, the heavy-duty kind that seemed to be made out of synthesized latex and Kevlar, which he would secure in place before anything resembling a penetration took place. Not a nudge, not a bump or a brushing up, was allowed to happen unprotected. I assumed that his precautions reflected the peculiar exigencies of his profession: Musicians of course would have multiple partners. Still, while I was a firm believer in safe sex, and while I was grateful to him for initiating such durable care, there was something disturbingly neurotic about that second condom.

Lying in bed in New Jersey, I asked him about it. He was stunned at my assumptions regarding his promiscuity. On the contrary, he protested, he was protecting himself from me. Standard precaution. And thus we arrived at a juncture of sorts.

"Takagi, where I grew up, people are careless. All the guys I went to high school with got their girlfriends pregnant and are stuck working shitty factory jobs in Akron, trying to pay child support. . . ."

"I'm not your girlfriend, Sloan. And I don't get pregnant."

"And then with AIDS and all . . . I'm a musician, a lot of my friends have died. And you're in the *film* business, for Christ's sake. For all I know, you've got a Commissioner in every port."

"Sloan, that's the most insane . . . How could I? Getting you in and out of these backwater towns is hard enough."

"Yes, but once you figure out the logistics for one Commissioner, it's simple to bring in a second or third. . . ."

"I don't have the time—"

"Or you could just hire locally. . . ."

"Never mind the energy—"

"Or you could get a travel model, something compact and portable, like your flight attendant? I always thought that he . . ."

"That's disgusting. Anyway, it was never my intention to be monogamous with you, believe me. I never even intended to *like* you, but that's just the way it's turned out."

From the parking lot outside the motel window, the air brakes of an enormous semi squealed and decompressed. The motel was in a strip mall by the interstate.

"Is that comment significant?" Sloan asked.

The truckdriver checked into the unit next to ours. He slammed the door and went straight into the bathroom. I listened to him urinate.

"I don't know, Sloan . . . Do you want it to be? And if it is, can we go to the next level of intimacy—you know, use just one condom?"

"We could get tested."

"I have. Repeatedly. Well, twice since you . . . *I'm* fine."

The truckdriver flushed. I listened to him reenter the bedroom and turn on the television, flipping through the channels. Looking for porn.

Sloan rolled over onto his side and propped himself up on his elbow. "Me too."

The driver turned off the television and turned on the radio. Surprisingly, the sounds of Mahler filtered through the hollow Sheetrock. I looked over at Sloan.

"It's Mahler's Sixth," he said, "his most completely *personal* symphony, according to his wife. Listen, it's his old orchestra too—the Boston Philharmonic—but it's Tilson Thomas conducting." He was watching me. "So, that means we're safe," he concluded tentatively. "At least from the disease standpoint, right? I haven't slept with anyone else since you, either."

"So . . . ?" I didn't know what he was getting at. He had this wicked grin on his face as he rolled on top of me.

"Takagi, do you mind if I . . . I mean, could we . . . Here, just for a moment . . . I won't come inside you, I promise."

"Sloan, what are you . . . ?"

He had lowered himself, half laughing, and was whispering relentlessly in my ear. "It's perfect, Jane, please. . . . Come on, it's such a *personal* moment. . . ."

"Sloan, you're crazy."

"Jane, I trust you completely."

"Yeah, well, I trust you too. . . ."

Which was a lie. I mean, I trusted him about testing negative because I knew him to be scrupulous in areas of empirical truths and health care. But emotionally he was an enigma. I didn't understand him, so how could I trust him?

And maybe that's why I went along with it. I was curious. Suddenly I needed to know things: Why did he want this? What did it mean? I needed to know if, unprotected, he would be different, if he would lose his control, if he would suddenly fall in love with me, and if he did, would I fall in love with him? And just as suddenly, the need for answers turned physical, and I found myself craving the heightened contact of total nakedness and the thrill of the truth or dare. Suddenly it seemed so personal.

We fucked without a condom, which sounds banal, but fueled by the urgency of all those ifs, it was as if the sex opened up and swallowed us. And I let him come inside me because I knew I was safe, and when it was over and the shuddering had slowed but the trembling was still raw and sporadic, Sloan raised his damp head from my sweaty breast and thanked me politely. In the desultory conversation that followed, I discovered that in the two decades he'd spent developing his sexual connoisseurship, he had never once fucked without a condom. He'd been curious—and so, of course, had I. But afterward, curiosity sated, I was only terribly aware of the sounds that filled the room: the distant whine of cars on the interstate; the soft exhalations of Sloan sleeping; the muted movements of the truckdriver next door, padding back and forth across the stained carpet, popping the flip top of a can of Budweiser, opening and closing drawers, all the while listening to Mahler's most completely personal symphony on NPR, which was a reminder to me that maybe I didn't know so much about musicians or truckdrivers after all.

AKIKO

A light, reassuring tone was what the editor wanted, but Akiko found this difficult to achieve. It was, after all, an article on complications.

> *Toxemia of Pregnancy*: This is a serious condition, but happily these days, because of our modern and superior prenatal care in Japan, the condition can be detected early and treated. So it is very important to be on the lookout for these symptoms: swelling or bloating of your fingers, face, and legs, caused by water retention; raised blood pressure; excessive weight gain; blurry vision; severe head-aches; fits, followed by unconsciousness or coma. If you experience any of these symptoms, don't be ashamed, but tell your husband and your doctor immediately.

Writing this article was not an exercise in the type of positive thinking that John was so adamant about. It was not putting her in a good frame of mind for pregnancy at all.

It was no good, Akiko thought. She just didn't enjoy writing magazine pieces like this. It wasn't that she didn't like writing. She used to enjoy her old job at the *manga* publishing house, filling in gory details in the serial stories for the illustrators to put pictures to. She had hoped to have a strip of her own one day. But that was before her marriage.

Akiko's marriage to John was proposed by John's boss at the advertising agency to Akiko's boss at the *manga* house. They were business associates and drinking companions, and one night, at a small, intimate members' club in Shinjuku, John's boss had confided to his friend that he had a promising young employee who needed a wife, and he asked for help.

Akiko's boss had thought for a minute, accepted another watery scotch from the hostess, and shook his head. He couldn't think of anyone appropriate at his company, he said regretfully. The hostess nudged him with her blunt elbow and chided him. How untruthful and ungenerous you are, she said. A handsome man like you must have many pretty young ladies working under you, but you are so selfish you want to keep them all to yourself. The two elderly men chuckled, and Akiko's boss laid a hand on her leg. He slipped his fingers under the edge of her miniskirt. You've gained some weight, he said, squeezing her plump thigh, and that's when he remembered Akiko. The hostess slapped his hand and he withdrew it, then offered his friend a bride.

Akiko wasn't exactly fat. On the heavy side was how people described her. She was very aware of this, especially on her first date with John. It wasn't a date, exactly. More like a meeting she'd been required by her boss to attend. He had walked by her desk one day and stopped, as though remembering something, then turned back and stood beside her. He had never done this before, and she was terrified. Her heart was thumping and she didn't dare to look up.

"Tanaka . . . Akiko, isn't it?"

"*Hai*," Akiko whispered.

"Mmm. What are you working on?" he asked.

She mumbled the name of the strip.

"Good, good. How old are you, anyway?"

"Twenty-nine."

"About time to marry, don't you think? Any prospects?"

Akiko's face turned crimson. "No," she gasped.

"Good. Good. I have someone in mind for you. A good, solid salaryman, works for my friend's company. We'll have tea with them tomorrow. We'll leave here at three."

The meeting took place at an elegant tea parlor in the

Ginza, decorated all in aqua blue, with huge fish tanks built into the partitions separating the deep cushioned booths and a shimmery ceiling above. John and his boss sat on one side, Akiko and her boss faced them.

Akiko had worn a navy-blue suit because dark colors were slimming. She ordered Earl Grey tea because she'd read it was worldly, but her hands were trembling so hard she couldn't lift her cup. She sat with her hands clenched in her lap, picking at the edges of her lace handkerchief. She dared look up only once at the heavyset young man with slicked-down hair who was being proposed as her future husband. Bright-tailed fish swam back and forth behind his head and she felt herself mesmerized by their flitting and darting, so she looked back down again quickly. She could feel the men's eyes fixed upon her. The two bosses tried to keep a conversation going, asking each of them questions. John answered his tersely; she could only nod or shake her head. She knew she was making a bad impression, but her throat had constricted and she could barely swallow. Words were impossible. Have some pastries, John's boss urged. Have some more tea. But it was no good. She was bloated, she had a terrible headache, and the blood pounded in her brain with such force she felt like she was deeply submerged, far underwater, diving past the fishes for pearl oysters at the bottom of the sea. She was afraid she would lose consciousness before she reached the surface again. She also felt like she needed to pee.

> A sudden gush of water generally means that the amniotic bubble where your baby is growing has burst and the fluid is leaking down your leg. If this occurs between the 28th and 36th week, you will have to go immediately to the hospital, where you will be given modern, superior sedatives and drugs to halt premature labor. If it happens after the 36th week, then your doctor will most likely decide

to allow the labor to continue, and before you know it, you will be a mother!

In the taxi on the way home from the meeting, Akiko's boss had reproached her for her silence.

"Why are you so shy?" he asked. "You must make more of an effort or you will never be successful in finding a good husband."

"I'm sorry," she whispered.

"You do want to get married, don't you?"

She nodded silently.

He sighed. "Oh, well. You never know."

It was true. You never knew. How could you know if you wanted to get married or not? At the time, when the prospect of a good marriage was offered to her, she'd never even considered the possibility of an alternative desire. She had been simply grateful. But now, after more than three years of marriage, she realized she might have had plenty of desires, but she gave them all up before she even knew what they were.

The following day her boss stopped by her desk again and chuckled.

"Well, we got lucky this time. Ueno liked you after all. He wants to see more of you. He's going to call you for a date."

Akiko again felt her throat constrict.

"Now listen. It's fine for a girl to be shy, it's attractive, even, but a man likes a wife he can talk to. Eventually you are going to have to learn to be more outgoing, understand?"

Akiko nodded. But on that date, and on subsequent ones, it turned out not to matter, because John was able to fill up any conversational spaces with his own words and opinions, and Akiko was grateful to him for that. They would go out to dinner together, but she could never eat much. After that first meeting and long into the marriage, her throat frequently clenched and went into spasms, making it difficult for her to swallow. That's when she started to lose weight. She managed to train herself to relax enough to get the food down, but in order to do that she had to eat very quickly and think about something else. The problem was that most of the time, the food wouldn't stay down for long, but the way she figured it, at least it looked like she was eating. She knew she was deceiving John, but she didn't want him to worry.

> Severe abdominal pain accompanied by bleeding can indicate *abrupto placenta*, or separation of the placenta prematurely from the uterus, but you needn't worry. In most cases of *abrupto placenta* the child survives. Only 25% result in termination.

When Akiko stood up from her desk, the severe abdominal pain continued. She limped into the bathroom to get a drink of water. She stared at her face in the mirror above the sink. The scab above her eye had come off, leaving a thin white indentation.

The day she visited the specialist in the Ginza, she had come home expecting the worst. The doctor had threatened to call John at work with his diagnosis. John had been acting strange and the last thing he needed was the news that his wife was sabotaging her own fertility. Akiko attributed his edginess to stress at work and problems with the meat campaign. She had been doing her best to be supportive, to watch the programs and give her opinions for what they were worth, and to cook the meat as best she could. But it wasn't easy. Most of the recipes were crude, inaccurate, and not at all delicious. She found herself cheating more and more, cribbing from other cookbooks and adding ingredients that the original American wives had never heard of.

So that night, when she got back from the Ginza, she had

made the special Texas-style Beefy Burritos that she'd learned from the Mexican family. It was one of the best recipes on the show and she had secretly improved it with the addition of some spicy Korean bean paste and ground ginger root in the marinade. John seemed to like the dish. He hadn't liked the show very much, but he thought the Beefy Burritos were good. He was a big fan of anything from Texas.

He was late. When he finally walked through the door and kicked off his shoes, he was holding himself very stiff. He walked through the living room into the kitchen and stopped, inches from her nose.

"So. Let's get this straight. You don't want to have children, is that right?"

He had heard from the doctor and he was drunk. He spoke slowly, deliberately, trying not to slur his words.

"Is that right? That is what the doctor told me on the telephone today. He was very annoyed with you. And with me too. He said that as a fertility specialist he was accustomed to seeing patients who wanted to conceive, not ones who damaged themselves in order to prevent it. What do you say to that, Akiko?" He swayed a little, peered down, and squinted in her face.

Akiko was silent, blinking her eyes, trying not to wince. His breath reeked of beer and greasy *gyoza* dumplings.

"Perhaps you lied to me," he continued. "Perhaps you married me under false pretenses. Is that right?"

Akiko shook her head.

"No? So. You do want children, then?"

Akiko nodded.

"If that is indeed true, why do you stop your menstruation by throwing up? There. You see, I know everything. I know your secret. Hah!" The force of the single, malodorous blast of laughter propelled him backward toward the wall. He caught

118

himself before he fell, and leaned casually against the china cabinet for support.

Akiko shook her head again. "I . . . I can't help it," she said weakly.

"Well, well. That is not what the doctor said at all. He said you were perfectly capable of controlling it if you wanted to. So now, how can you explain that? You obviously don't want to get pregnant, but you say you want a family. That makes you either a liar or a fool. Which is it? Which is it I'm married to?"

"We . . . we could . . ."

"Speak up. I can't hear you."

"We could adopt . . ." She got her voice back and almost shouted. "We could adopt *ten* children! Ten Korean children, like the Beaudroux family of Askew, Louisiana!"

John reeled as though she'd hit him. He strode over to her, grabbed her by the shoulders, and shook her so hard that her head flipped back and forth on her thin neck.

"I want *my own children*. Mine. Do you hear? *Mine!* Not some bastard of a Korean whore and an idiot American soldier. I want *my* genes in *my* child. That's the point! *Mine!*"

And with that, he gave Akiko one last violent shake, with such force that she slipped from his hands, spun once, fell over the back of a kitchen chair, which caught her squarely in the abdomen, then collapsed against the china cabinet. The cabinet was one of the first pieces of furniture that she and John had bought together and they'd chosen it for its blunt and rounded edges—a baby couldn't hurt himself if he fell against it while learning to toddle. But they hadn't reckoned on the sharp-edged handle that now gouged Akiko right above the eye. Blinded by the sudden blood, she groped her way into the bathroom. When she reemerged, John was gone.

*

Now, examining her face in the mirror, she saw that the scar would actually be quite small. The skin around the eye itself was healing too—

> an ever-brightening aureole
> of yellow, green, and blue.

Soon she would be able to go outside again. John had forbidden her to leave the house until the injuries stopped showing. But he had been coming home early to help her ever since the accident. In fact, when he came home the next day he was sober and contrite. He apologized to her, formally, by getting down on his knees and bowing until his head touched the floor. He had even been doing the grocery shopping. Akiko faxed a shopping list to his office, and he would pick up the items on the way home from the station. He had told his boss that Akiko was ill, and the boss, who took a special interest in their marriage, having helped arrange it, excused him from overtime. Akiko was finding it difficult to breathe very deeply, partly because of the severe pain in her abdomen from falling over the chair, and partly because John was now spending so much time at home. But he was being very kind and polite to her, and it was a relief, a treat, even, not to have to face the market and the shopping every day. Still, she was looking forward to his next business trip, so she could relax.

JANE

> We are lost, we are lost, we are lost, we are lost . . .
> Without your help, sweet Jesus, we are lost.
> We are lost, we are lost, we are lost, we are lost . . .
> O Lord . . .

The tinny Yamaha organ laid down a bridge of notes, like stepping-stones, for the Preacher to walk along as the voices of the Harmony Five subsided and the congregation released them with a last "Hallelujah" and a lingering "Praise the Lord." The Preacher didn't miss a beat.

"And now I ask those of us here who are newcomers, I ask our new brother and sister, to stand *up* now and *tell* us your names and how you came here today, so we can *truly* welcome you among us. . . ."

The Preacher had fixed his gaze upon us, and as far as I could see, there were no other newcomers jumping to their feet. I elbowed Ueno, who was sitting rigidly beside me on the wooden pew. I thought it was only polite to let him go first, on his own. He was so damn cocky about his English ability, and besides that, I was furious at him.

"Self-introduction," I hissed in Japanese. "Stand up and tell them who you are."

He looked around, stricken. The church was small, but the entire population of Harmony, Mississippi, had turned out to look at us. He got shakily to his feet.

"I . . ." His throat was dry and his voice cracked. He swallowed hard.

The congregation watched politely. The church hadn't been this hushed since the service started. The members were all dressed in their Sunday best and were being remarkably patient and tolerant, to my mind, given that as far as Miss Helen could recall, no white person had ever crossed the threshold of the Harmony Baptist Church. Miss Helen had been very hesitant when I first contacted her. She didn't really understand what I wanted.

"We want to bring a camera to the church. To film there . . . ," I explained.

"Uh huh." Miss Helen's voice was barely a whisper and it was hard to hear her over the phone.

"Do you understand what I mean?" I felt like I was screaming. The noise outside the East Village office was deafening, police sirens, ambulances, jackhammers in the street, drowning out our conversation.

"You want to bring a camera to our church," she whispered.

"Yes, to film the church for Japanese TV. And then to film you and your family too."

"I don't think we ever had no white person inside of our church before. . . ."

"Well, we're not technically white, Miss Helen. We're Japanese, so really we're mostly yellow. . . ."

"Uh huh."

I was excited about doing a program with Miss Helen Dawes. She lived in the tiny Mississippi town of Harmony, which hugged the Tennessee border. Miss Helen and her husband, Purcell, had nine children: one son, followed by eight daughters, the youngest of whom was in grade school. Mr. Purcell and the boy, Lewis, were both members of the Harmony Five and were quite well known in the Southern gospel circuit. Miss Helen was known in Harmony for two things, her chitterlings and her fast sinking curve ball, and all her girls took after her, excelling in either cooking or sports. In the field in back of their house, Mr. Purcell had built a real baseball diamond, with bleachers, a scoreboard with numbers that hung on hooks, and a chain-link fence for a backstop behind home base. Every summer Sunday after church, the family and neighbors would gather for fast-pitch softball games. Miss Helen would make chitterlings. Sometimes a neighbor would bring fried chicken, or beans, or biscuits and gravy. The girls would make lemonade and cake and hit home runs all afternoon. Miss Helen was proud of the way her family and friends stuck together when times were hard, "which is just about most of the time, I guess," she had whispered to me over the phone.

I had been working hard for weeks to explain the program to her and to overcome her reluctance. She just couldn't seem to understand why we found her interesting. Finally she had agreed to let us come, at least for the location scout, and now Ueno was about to blow it.

"I . . ." Ueno had recovered his voice. It was unbelievably hot and he was sweating profusely and looking more red than yellow at the moment. The black faces surrounding us were gleaming with sweat too, and there was an oddly unsettling quality to the scene, caused by the rapid flicker of hundreds of identical white paper fans, all printed with the name of the church. Ueno took a deep breath. I could tell he was ready now, and I braced myself.

"I am Joichi Ueno," he announced, "but you may call me by my nickname. That is 'John.' You get it? 'John Wayno'!" He paused expectantly. "It's joke!" he said. But no one laughed. There was no reaction at all, just the politely suspended anticipation, the sound of the fans, beating the air like bird wings, and a single sour note from the organ, which trailed its reverb behind it like a wake as Ueno deflated. "Thank you," he mumbled, and sat back down.

I stood and the organ changed key. I looked around and smiled.

"I'm Jane Takagi-Little." At moments like this I hated the arcane complexity of my name, but I persevered, speaking slowly and, I hoped, sincerely.

"Thank you for letting us come to your church today. We are so happy to be here. We have come all the way from Japan to make a television program to teach the Japanese people about America. Miss Helen Dawes and her family have generously agreed to help us, and she asked us here today to meet you, because you are part of her family. We believe that people all over the world should try to learn about each other and understand each other, and that is what our television program is about, so I am here to ask you to share your faith with the people of Japan and give us your permission to film you all here, inside the church, during a Sunday service later this month. Thank you for listening. God bless you."

As the organ swelled, the congregation broke into smiles and applause. I sat down and an ancient lady with mahogany wrinkles and snow-white hair grasped my forearm with one wizened claw and patted me with the other. Perched on her head was a tiny hat made of straw and tulle and decorated with tiny cloth flowers on stems that wobbled like antennae as she nodded her vigorous approval. A nodder and a patter, just like a Japanese auntie.

My neighbor to the other side was Ueno. He was damp all over and was staring at me with an abject look of defeat and resentment. It wasn't really fair. I knew we'd be called upon to introduce ourselves and I'd prepared my speech in advance, but I hadn't warned Ueno. Like I said, I was mad at him.

I had spoken to the Preacher on the phone several weeks earlier and he said that he could give us permission to film, but if I wanted to gain the acceptance of the congregation, I should come to church and petition them myself, in person. So I arranged the scout for that Sunday and had flown into Memphis two days earlier. Unfortunately, so had Ueno.

When I checked into the Holiday Inn on Friday, the desk clerk handed me a fax. At first I thought it was from Sloan and my heart leapt. I hadn't seen him since Fly and had left a message on his answering machine, inviting him to Memphis. I wanted to see him so badly. But the fax was from Tokyo.

FAX NOTICE

Takagi:

I hope you are feeling fine in Memphis, but there is change of plans a little. Mr. Ueno from Agency will be arriving there on Friday evening flight. He will accompany with you to hunting the two Wives, so you must meet him at the airport, please.

I think you will be inconvenience but it cannot be helped. His job area is only Meat, but because of Synergy he ask that NY office must be more careful to choose American Wives with best meats, so he will help you this time. (Maybe he didn't like last story about pork and adoption so much, I think?) Also he is hands-on guy.

This is not regular procedure so I am sorry for inconvenience to you, but our company need good relation with Agency for future. Also by the way, I agree with your thinking about putting minority peoples on our show. So please persevere as much as you can.

S.Kato

I appreciated Kato's support, but frankly Ueno's participation was not good, was quite detrimental, in fact, both to my personal needs—I wouldn't be able to see Sloan—and to my agenda for the show.

It was customary for the New York office to propose two wives for each shoot. The first, and as far as I was concerned the only, candidate was Mrs. Helen Dawes. The alternate wife was Becky Thayer. She was the owner of a bed-and-breakfast in Magnolia Springs, a small but well-known town along the plantation tour circuit. She and her husband, Tom, were eager for us to come because so many of their guests these days were Japanese tourists, part of the *Gone With the Wind* boom that had mysteriously swept that country, and they thought an appearance on *My American Wife!* was just the thing to increase their exposure. Mrs. Becky Thayer was a gourmet cook and an antiques collector, and the bed-and-breakfast was her hobby.

"I had no choice!" she exclaimed to me on the phone. "I had to start the B-and-B just to have somewhere to exhibit all my junk! But I never expected it would turn into *this!*"

By "this!" she meant a thriving business that was ranked at the top of every B-and-B guide in America for authenticity of decor, gracious accommodation, and mouthwatering cuisine. She had started offering dinner on the weekends too and she faxed us sample menus to choose from, with entrées ranging from a regional Southern-style Filet Mignon served with black-eyed peas and a purée of collard greens, to an exotic Chicken-fried Steak Orientale, marinated in seasoned soy sauce, then dipped in a delicate tempura-style batter made with free-range eggs, cornmeal, and Szechwan peppercorns. She always served a salad garnished with nasturtiums and daylilies from the kitchen garden, which, she assured me, looked real charming on-camera.

Mr. Thayer was a real estate agent and the head of the Magnolia Springs Chamber of Commerce. They had two young children, both of whom were in day care. Oh, did I mention the Thayers were white?

The New York office had sent profiles of both families to Tokyo, but I was so dead set on the Daweses, I hadn't intended to visit the Thayers at all. Now that Ueno was coming with me, clearly I was going to have to change my plans. So I phoned Becky and made an appointment for noon the following day, left another message for Sloan, rescinding my invitation, and then booked two rooms at the Peabody, the best hotel in Memphis.

In my experience, Japanese men on business trips are generally more tractable if you put them in one of the better hotels in town, and I knew Ueno was particularly susceptible to this treatment. On the way back from the airport, he was gruff and taciturn, but the ornate lobby with its palm-and-gilt decor sweetened his mood. He'd eaten dinner on the plane, so we had a perfunctory meeting in the bar and I filled him in on the location-scout schedule. We were sitting adjacent to each other in large overstuffed armchairs, with a low coffee table in between. He leaned back into the velvety forest-green upholstery and raised his glass of Rémy.

"To *My American Wife!*" he said, and took a long drink. He sighed with contentment. He was feeling rich. He looked around the room, and his eyes came to settle on me. "So, now you became a director. . . ."

"Yes." I smiled, trying to look benign and neutral.

He frowned. "I tell to Kato is not good idea. You are still incompetent and cannot make correct choices for proper program topics. So I must come here to teach you." He waited, watching me to see how I would react.

"Thank you. I appreciate your guidance." I smiled again, I hoped demurely.

"No problem," he grunted. He took another long sip, set the glass on the coffee table, then reached over and squeezed my knee. "It is my pleasure," he said, leaving his hand there. I stood up and excused myself. I rode the elevator up to my room, muttering darkly, vowing to teach him a lesson. As it turned out, I didn't have to.

In the lobby of the Peabody Hotel there's a pond with real ducks that swim around during the day. The ducks spend the night on the roof and every morning at eleven they are herded into one of the elevators and brought downstairs. This is an event full of pomp and circumstance: a red carpet leading from the elevator to the duck pond is ceremoniously unrolled, the pianist starts to play, the elevator doors open, and out waddle the ducks, all in a row, down the red carpet and across the lobby to the pond, where they plop into the water, one by one. Lots of people come to watch. It's the tourist thing to do when you're in Memphis.

I don't know how he got into that elevator, but on Saturday morning, when the music started and the elevator doors opened, out waddled Ueno. Gripping his briefcase, he headed straight down the middle of the red carpet. A snicker or a stare from an American tourist must have clued him that something was wrong. He glanced around nervously, then tripped over his feet when he saw the neat row of ducks following hard on his heels. Catching himself before he fell, he kept walking, trying very hard to pretend that nothing out of the ordinary was happening, that he wasn't being followed by ducks or jeered at by a gauntlet of American tourists lining the carpet on either side of him. When he reached the edge of the duck pond, he stopped and looked around in panic, then, realizing this was precisely where the ducks were heading, he veered quickly out of the way. The crowd was disappointed and started to boo. The ducks continued in a straight line to the edge of the pond, where one by one they raised their rumps in a sporty salute and slid into the water.

I'd been standing behind a potted palm by the side door and didn't want to add to his embarrassment, so I slipped outside, walked around the block, and reentered the building from the front. I found Ueno sitting in an inconspicuous corner.

"Good morning! Did you sleep well?" I asked him cheerfully.

"I've been waiting for you for a long time," he said, surly as hell.

"Oh, great! You must have seen the ducks, then. They usually walk right by here. . . ."

It was a beautiful day, and we drove to Magnolia Springs through the emerald-green kudzu-drenched countryside. The Thayers were entirely predictable and by afternoon Ueno was considerably mellowed by Becky's gracious Southern hospitality. But I was beginning to worry. At dinner back at the hotel that evening, he started making a shot list of all the areas in their exquisitely appointed home that he wanted to see in the program. I reminded him that we had a second family to scout, but he flapped his hand dismissively and continued to design the opening camera dolly through the foyer. This was not his job. This was my job. I ordered him a double shot of Wild Turkey, wondering if I could make him black out retroactively. I was hopeful. I was determined not to do the Thayers.

I took him to a blues club on Beale Street—I didn't care where we went, as long as it was too loud to carry on a conversation. Ueno was really happy, because the atmosphere was a hundred percent authentic. I could tell by the casual way he slouched, one loafer balanced on the edge of the chair in front of him, trouser leg hiked up to reveal the white sock, and also by the way he flagged down the waitress, arm in the air, with his head ducked and his eyes half closed—but the real clue to his mood was the upturned collar on his golf shirt. I don't know exactly when he flipped it. One minute it was lying down, the next minute it was standing up. He continued to pop back shots of Wild Turkey and by the time we left he was loaded.

Of course, I'd seen him this way on the commercial shoots, so I knew what to expect, but I'd never had to deal with him single-handedly before. He was heavy. His big blocklike head lolled and swayed to the echoes of the blues in the night. Random notes bounced around its hollow interior. He could barely waddle. He draped his arms around my neck for support, knocking his head against mine and occasionally turning to face me, square on, and confide the innermost feelings from his heart. The feelings were noxious enough, but they were borne along on gaseous clouds rising from his innermost bowel and they made me gag.

We made it up the elevator to his floor and all the way to his door before he collapsed. I thought about just leaving him there, but then I took pity on him. However distasteful, I had to find his key, so I stuck my fingers gingerly into his pants pockets and fished around, trying not to touch anything. I found the key in his wallet, opened the door, and tried to drag him inside, but he was too heavy, so I got a wet towel from the bathroom and slapped his face with it for a while. Finally I managed to bring him around enough to get him up on his feet. Once standing, he swayed like a top, then he fell against me, pushing me through the doorway and onto the floor.

Suddenly something kindled in the man. He was a sneaky bastard, and quick too. He kicked the door shut with his heel, and before I knew what was happening, he had landed on top of me. I couldn't fight him off. He was enormously heavy and put all his weight into his shoulder to pin me to the floor. He ripped my shirt open in front and grabbed my breast and started squeezing it and moaning, while he got his knee wedged between my legs and my skirt up around my hips.

"*Yarashite, Jane-chan, yarashite*—let me do it, please. I want to do it so bad. . . ."

He pulled down the front of my underpants and jammed his fingers into my crotch and I felt them, blunt and cold, fumble at the opening of my vagina. I struggled but couldn't shift his weight, and this just seemed to excite him further. He moaned again.

"*Jane-chan, wa kawaii*—you are so cute. Listen to me. . . . My wife, she is fruitless woman, but . . . Jane, *akachan ga tsukuritai*—I want to make baby with you. . . ."

130

That was his mistake. The idea of being impregnated by this foul-breathing man gave me the jolt of strength I needed to jam my knee into his groin and my knuckles into his windpipe and roll him over. I stood up. He lay on the ground, writhing and groaning.

"*Tsumetai*, Jane. How can you be so cold?" He gripped his crotch in both hands.

It was revolting. I suppressed an upsurge of nausea and an overwhelming urge to kick him as hard as I could.

"*Oi, Ueno*. Call time's at seven." I paused. "Did you hear me?"

He groaned and I turned to go, then stopped at the door.

"Take the right-hand elevator, you dickhead. The left one's for the ducks."

I took about ten showers that night. By the following morning I was still feeling queasy, but most of that was psychological. I had managed to circumvent the worst of a physical hangover by taking a tonic of kudzu that Suzuki had made for me in New York. However, when Ueno stumbled out of the left-hand elevator at seven-fifteen, I felt like throwing up all over again. Still, I could tell he felt worse. It was like seeing his face on a TV monitor when the color bars haven't been set correctly and there's too much green in the skin tones. He was sweating. When he saw me in the lobby he mumbled an apology for being late and waddled meekly after me to the front, where the valet had my car waiting. I was still too angry to talk to him, and during the drive to Mississippi I had to pull the car over three times so that he could vomit on the side of the road.

When we finally arrived in Harmony, I stopped the car on the outskirts of town.

"Ueno, listen to me. I have worked very hard to gain this family's trust. They are not used to people like us, and unlike the Thayers, they do not know a lot about the way the TV business works. I don't care how rotten you feel or how rotten you are, but we are going to church now and you are going to behave like a decent, civilized man, do you understand? Not a sleazy agency rep. Not a television producer. A human being. That is all you are for the next few hours, until we leave this town. If you have to throw up again, do it now. This is your last chance. Do you understand?"

He nodded meekly, opened the car door and retched.

We reached the church. The small dirt parking lot was full of cars, but there was no one outside and the doors were closed. I parked and led Ueno up the steps, straightened him, stood to one side, and knocked quietly. I was still somewhat hungover, and feeling ill, so when the doors opened and a nurse stepped out to greet us, it made perfect intuitive sense to me. But not to Ueno. He saw her, a monumental black woman dressed in a starched nurse's uniform so tight it accentuated every pinnacle of breast and palisade of thigh, and he gasped and reeled and almost fainted.

"Shhh!" she hissed as she caught him by the cuff with her white-gloved fist and dragged him through the door.

We stood with a group of latecomers, guarded by the big nurse, in the foyer between the church's outer and inner doors. They all had their heads bowed as though in penance, so I kicked Ueno and bowed mine too. The Harmony Five were singing the opening hymn, and when they finished, the doors opened and we were all let through. Two more nurses—I realized now they were ushers—met us and took us by the arm. I'd been hoping to find seats near the back, where Ueno could slip out should the need arise, but instead the nurses led us to the very front pew, the seats of honor, which apparently had been reserved for us. We sat down. I looked around, hoping to recognize Miss Helen or Purcell, but I'd never met them, and everyone in the church was staring at us with equally curious attention.

The Preacher was talking, and it took me a while to identify him as the same man I'd spoken with on the telephone. He'd had an accent then, but nothing compared with this thick blanket of honeyed sound, from which I could extract neither words nor meaning. It would be offensive for me to try to re-create it here and I also have to confess that I wasn't paying much attention. At the time, I was concentrating less on the intricacies of the Preacher's theology and more on whether Ueno was going to throw up. I was worried. We were sandwiched on either side and it would not be easy to escape. It was a bad situation.

But at that moment, the Preacher segued into the next hymn, which was "Without Your Help, Sweet Jesus, We Are Lost," and the Harmony Five burst into song and the congregation followed:

We are lost, we are lost, we are lost, we are lost . . .
O Lord . . .

And as the music gathered momentum and people got to their feet, singing and clapping, I discovered that my worries were dissipating. There was no room for them. The music filled every crevice of heart and soul and washed away my sickness, and it was clear that although we were lost, we would be found.

And when the song subsided and the Preacher called for our introductions, I understood perfectly the words he was saying, and I spoke, and it was all right. And the old ladies around us commenced their nodding and their patting, and I think they reminded even Ueno of his aunties in Japan, so I felt him relax a bit too.

And then the Preacher launched into the body of his sermon, which was about how the world seems so big and strange, but really it's just made up of countries, which are made up of states, which are made up of towns, which are made up of communities, which are made up of neighbors, which are made up of families, and so on. And when there is sickness in the family you must turn to your neighbors and to your community to help cure that sickness, because the community is there to help each member and the community is only as healthy as each member. And then a young man from the congregation stood up and turned his palms to the sky to give testimonial. He told of how he had grown up in Harmony, gone to school here all the way through high school, but had turned his back on his family and community for a job in the big city.

As he spoke, he moved from the back of the church to the front, until he joined the Preacher near the pulpit, next to the Harmony Five, who were giving him a little background vocal support. He testified that he *knew* he was blessed to be given the chance of a job in the big city, but he had become *seduced* by the big-city ways and had *abdicated* his responsibilities to his family and his community and had committed many sins, including drinking liquor and sins of the flesh, and he was *sickened.* . . .

And now, whenever he was *emphatic*, when he came *down* on a word, his knee would jerk *up* and his elbows would *contract* into his sides. . . . And he told them how, one day, he realized how the job and the big city were working a *change* on him, and it was *up* to him, it was his *duty*, to come home to his *neighbors*, to his *community*, and stay *true* to his church, that *here is where his true health is, here is where he can be delivered from sickness, from temptation.* . . .

And now, suddenly, he was overcome with spastic convulsions, and his limbs shot out, first an arm, then a leg, and the Yamaha punctuated each syncopated spasm with a chord, and the Harmony Five roused the congregation to a frenzy. They were waving their palms over their heads, shouting out "Praise the Lord!" and "Amen, brother!" and "That's right, tell it like it is!" The young man threw his head back and fell to the ground, kicking his feet until his shoe loosened, flew through the air, and landed in Ueno's lap. Ueno responded as though it were a live thing, brushing it off in terror, and then the Preacher started in again. The ladies on either side responded, grabbing Ueno and me and wrapping us in their arms, then passing us off to another neighbor, to be similarly embraced. Catharsis was close at hand. I dimly understood it, felt it gathering all around me. And the miracle was, so did Ueno.

The combination of terror and hangover had pushed him over the edge. All around him, people were dancing and writhing and singing and shaking and speaking in tongues, and others were caring for them, laying on their hands, supporting their frenzy. Sweat was pouring down Ueno's face, pure distilled alcohol by the smell of it, and he was sobbing. A tall, sturdy woman, wearing a navy dress with little raised Swiss polka dots, cradled his head like a baby on her bosom and patted his heaving back. He raised his head and it wobbled a bit, as though his neck were not yet strong enough to support the weight. His puffy, tear-stained face retained the impressions of her little polka dots. He smiled at me, blissful, then he laid his head back down again and sniffled. The polka dot woman just kept patting and patting, and she looked at me over his shoulder and smiled.

"Hi," she said softly. I recognized her voice. It was Miss Helen Dawes.

Just then the Preacher's words started to rise. His voice focused the congregation, gathering up all the disparate frenzy into a single concerted expression of faith and healing, cresting now, teetering on the razor edge between earthbound speech and song, and when it broke, it soared up to the vaulted ceiling of heaven. This man could *sing!* The Harmony Five led the congregation in the background refrain, and when the song was over, the Preacher bade us all to take the hand of our neighbor in prayer. The skinny old lady grasped my right hand and Miss Helen held Ueno's. He and I stood there and just looked at each other. Then we turned and faced the pulpit. I could feel the link of brotherhood, broken and dangling limply between us, but as the Preacher commenced praying, Ueno surprised me. He reached over and took my hand in his damp, sticky paw and held it, quietly, firmly. All through the prayer I let him hold it, clenching my teeth as nausea alternated with forgiveness.

It wasn't so unreasonable. I mean, after seeing him stripped so bare, sobbing and raw on Miss Helen's shoulder like that, how could I hold a grudge? I was astounded that this tightly wound Japanese businessman was able to let himself go. Maybe I'd underestimated him. Maybe he was simply starved for affection, and the warm and generous contact here in Harmony had broken the bonds of his repression and liberated his wellspring of love. It was possible. Anything was possible. At the end of the prayer the Preacher bade us embrace our neighbor in the spirit of brotherly love, and I allowed Ueno to take me in his sweaty arms and even managed to suppress a violent shudder. I was never going to like this man, I realized as I gritted my teeth and hugged him back. On the other hand, I could be generous—I was going to get to do my Helen Dawes show after all.

After the service, Miss Helen and Mr. Purcell claimed us and proudly introduced us to the members of the congregation, all of whom, even down to the littlest child, wanted to shake our hands. We were very exotic, but more than that, I think Miss Helen had been honestly moved by Ueno's religious feeling. We drove to the Dawes house, which was just down the dirt road from the church, and went inside. We were going to have lunch with them and then see a bit of the softball game, but first I wanted to do a quick interview with Miss Helen and Mr. Purcell, to get more information about them for my script and to lock down a few details of the shoot.

Filming food preparation is always difficult with amateur cooks. Since the Flowers show, I'd learned that you have to work with the wives to break down their recipe into stages and then explain how each stage must be prepared in advance so that during the actual shoot we would not have to wait for the food to cook. In addition, each stage must look like the one that came before, so the audience won't know that there's been a cheat. Miss Helen was going to make chitterlings for us and I wanted to prep her and to figure out what the rest of the menu would be.

We sat in the small living room. The faded pastel-green walls were decorated with department store portraits of all nine children. A collection of gilt trophies for softball, baseball, and basketball, and singing awards for the Harmony Five, covered the side table, spilled over onto the bookshelf, and reached all the way to the top of the television. A dusty bouquet of blue plastic roses sat there too. When the children ran in and out of the kitchen, thudding down the corridor into their rooms, the walls shuddered and set the roses quivering. But the running children seemed very far away all of a sudden. As the world outside receded and the living room closed in around us, I realized that we had entered one of those funny warps in which the social paradigm shifts out from under you. After all the commotion and the naked outpouring of emotion at church, we were suddenly all alone together. And silent. Stricken with self-consciousness.

Miss Helen sat on an upright wooden chair from the kitchen with her hands folded in the lap of her polka dot Sunday dress, still wearing her hat. She was a large woman, but lean and strong, and you could see the muscles running down her calves, underneath the thick nylon stockings. She knew how to hold perfectly still, head bowed, barely there. Next to her, Mr.

Purcell sat on the couch, wearing a shiny green suit with big wide lapels. The springs of the couch had collapsed and the seat cushions sank so low that his knees stuck up, and this in turn hiked up the cuffs of his pants to expose his skinny callused ankles. His shoes were worn but meticulously polished. He was nervous and smiled at us broadly, flashing a mouthful of huge, crooked gold-capped teeth.

Ueno and I were seated side by side on the two chairs that were obviously meant for guests. It was up to me.

"Miss Helen, I wanted to ask you a bit about your family's diet—the kind of things you like to eat?"

Miss Helen sat very still and stared at her lap. Mr. Purcell just smiled and smiled.

"I was wondering if you could tell John here a little bit about your chitterlings?"

"Yes, ma'am," whispered Miss Helen.

The "ma'am" caught me by surprise and threw me off. It was so formal. We waited for her to continue.

"You know, the chitterlings that you're famous for?" I prompted.

"Yes, ma'am."

Again, she was silent.

"What do you eat with the chitterlings?" I didn't know what to do. The "ma'am" had turned me into a teacher or a social worker giving her a test, its questions so inane as to be incomprehensible. It was safer for her just to say nothing. "Do you eat something with the chitterlings?"

"Yes, ma'am."

"What do you . . . Do you eat vegetables of some kind?"

"Yes."

"Like . . . collard greens?"

"Yes, ma'am."

"And anything else? Like . . . corn bread?"

"Yes, ma'am."

It was a guessing game, but my preconceived notions of Southern cooking were limited by what was available on the menus of country-style, home-cooking restaurants in SoHo, and I was running out of suggestions.

"Uh, anything else? Do you eat anything else?"

"Hog maws," offered Mr. Purcell.

Ueno snorted. He was sitting back in his chair, arms crossed, retracted back into his impassive Japanese businessman persona. He was making me very nervous.

"How about other meats?" he asked. "You like another kind meats too?"

"Chicken," Mr. Purcell said. "We sure do like chicken, but even chicken ain't cheap now. Used to be they had these *parts* that was real good. And cheap down at the packin' house . . ."

Miss Helen let out a hiccup that turned into a burst of laughter.

"Yeah, we *thought* they was real good . . . until Mr. Purcell's barrytone came out soundin' serpraner!"

Ueno looked at me questioningly, but I didn't get it, either.

Purcell explained. "It was some medicines they was usin' in the chickens that got into the necks that we was eatin'. . . . An' that medicine, well, if it didn't start to make me sound just like a woman!"

"And look just like one too, with them teeny little titties and everything!" Miss Helen chimed in.

I still didn't get it, but Ueno cut them off with another snort. He leaned forward.

"What about beef? You like beef?"

Miss Helen looked up in surprise. "Oh, no, sir."

"No? But why you don't like it? Steak is most delicious."

Purcell shrugged. "You got kids?" he asked. Ueno stiffened slightly and shook his head. "Red meat's too costly with so many mouths to feed," explained Purcell apologetically.

"We get hamburger sometimes," offered Miss Helen.

"That's right, we do. Miss Helen'll fry up some for the kids ever so often. But to my mind red meat ain't half so tasty as white. . . ." Mr. Purcell's voice trailed off into silence.

Ueno sat back and I wrapped up the interview as quickly as I could. I waited for Ueno to say something, but he kept quiet. We had dinner with the family while the neighbors gathered, and then the softball game got under way. Ueno didn't eat much, or say much. After the meal, he played a few innings and even scored a hit off of Miss Helen, although I suspected she let him. But the whole time, I was worried. I didn't trust him one bit.

"We'll be back," I said loudly, for Ueno's benefit, as we got ready to leave. "We'll see you again, soon." Miss Helen walked us to the car and hugged first Ueno, then me.

"I gotta confess I was nervous at first," she said softly, holding on to my hands. "We never met no Japanese people before and we didn't know what kind of folks you'd turn out to be. But we're all real glad you came. We're lookin' forward to when you come back with the camera."

Mr. Purcell shook Ueno's hand, pumping it up and down like he was priming a well.

We got in the car and backed down the driveway. As we drove away from Harmony, Ueno pulled out his handkerchief and wiped his hands. The tension in the car started to build. Ueno dropped the ax at the Tennessee border.

"I have decided you must make program about the Thayer family."

Of course. I had been expecting this.

"Why?!" I exploded. "That is absolutely insane. The Dawes are wonderful. They're perfect. It took them a while to warm up, but you'll never get a more interesting show than that. The Thayers have *nothing*, there's no comparison. Think about the church! How can you even *consider* not filming there, after what you went through today?"

"It's not about me. It's a question of meats."

"What about the meats?"

"Mrs. Becky Thayer has better meats. She has beautiful beef."

"But I thought 'Pork is Possible!'"

"Yes, but 'Beef is Best!' And as you know, chitterling is not pork, Takagi. It is the intestine of pig. *My American Wife!* is for Japanese people, not for Koreans or black peoples."

"You racist bastard."

He turned and stared at me, narrowing his eyes. "I didn't make up rules. This is U.S.-sponsor show and U.S.-sponsor instruction." He looked away again, at the brilliant green curtains of kudzu draping the trees and spilling down the berm by the side of the road. He folded his arms across his chest.

"Meat is the message, Takagi," he said, surveying the landscape with a grim air of accomplishment. "If you cannot learn this, you cannot be director for my program. That is all I will say."

THE WATER MONTH

SHŌNAGON

The Way in Which Carpenters Eat

The way in which carpenters eat is really odd. When they had finished the main building and were working on the eastern wing, some carpenters squatted in a row to have their meal; I sat on the verandah and watched them. The moment the food was brought, they fell on the soup bowls and gulped down the contents. Then they pushed the bowls aside and finished off all the vegetables. I wondered whether they were going to leave their rice; a moment later there wasn't a grain left in the bowls.[4] They all behaved in exactly the same way, so I suppose this must be the custom of carpenters. I should not call it a very charming one.

JANE

Anyone who travels around the sprawling heartland of this country must at some point wonder why Americans are so uniformly obese. Are we *all* so ignorant about diet and health? Or so greedy, or so terrified of famine that we continuously, and almost unconsciously, stockpile body fat? Or is there something else? These are the questions that Suzuki and Oh would ask me, confronted with yet another bleeding steak the size of a manhole cover, spilling over the sides of the plate. And the potato, stuffed with butter and sour cream? Why both? they would cry in dismay.

I am not fat, but my tallness amounts to the same sort of gross affront to nature, at least to my Japanese mother, who comes up to my rib cage. She sees my height as a personal insult and something that could have been avoided. It's all tied up in her mind with her efforts to counteract the Little in my name—she thinks I grew just to mock her. On her saner days, she gazes skyward at my face and blames the red meat she fed me as a child. But it was Minnesota, Ma. There were lots of cows and not a lot of sushi.

When Miss Helen blurted out that remark about chicken necks causing Mr. Purcell's voice to change and his breasts to grow, I was shocked. I knew about antibiotics from the cute doctor in Oklahoma, and I guess I knew that hormones were

147

used too. I'd just never given it much thought before. But now I couldn't get the image of Mr. Purcell out of my head. "Meat is the Message," or so I'd written, and suddenly I wanted to know more. Once I started researching, it didn't take me long to stumble across DES. It was a discovery that ultimately changed my relationship with meats and television. It also changed the course of my life. Bear with me; this is an important Documentary Interlude.

DES, or diethylstilbestrol, is a man-made estrogen that was first synthesized in 1938. Soon afterward, a professor of poultry husbandry at the University of California discovered that if you inject DES into male chickens, it chemically castrates them. Instant capons. The males develop female characteristics—plump breasts and succulent meats—desirable assets for one's dinner. After that, subcutaneous DES implants became pretty much de rigueur in the poultry industry, at least until 1959, when the FDA banned them. Apparently, someone discovered that dogs and males from low-income families in the South were developing signs of feminization after eating cheap chicken parts and wastes from processing plants, which is exactly what happened to Mr. Purcell. The U.S. Department of Agriculture was forced to buy about ten million dollars' worth of contaminated chicken to get it off the market.

But by then DES was also being widely used in beef production, and oddly enough, the FDA did nothing to stop that. Here is a brief recap:

In 1954, a ruminant nutritionist at Iowa State College had discovered that if you feed DES to beef cattle they get fat quicker. In fact, the DES-"enhanced" cattle could be "finished" (brought to slaughter weight) more than a month sooner than unenhanced animals, on about five hundred pounds less feed. Obviously this was a good thing for meat producers. DES was trumpeted as a "miracle" and "a revolution in the cattle industry," and without further ado, that very same year, the FDA approved DES for livestock. A year later DES received a patent as the first artificial animal growth stimulant. By the early 1960s, *after* the ban on implants for chickens, DES was used by more than 95 percent of U.S. cattle feeders to speed up production. Sure, there were accounts of farmers who accidentally breathed or ingested DES powder and started showing symptoms such as impotence, infertility, gynecomastia (enlarged and tender breasts), and changes in their voice register. But in the face of all that promised profit . . . And after all, farming has always been a dangerous business. Everyone knows that.

DES changed the face of meat in America. Using DES and other drugs, like antibiotics, farmers could process animals on an assembly line, like cars or computer chips. Open-field grazing for cattle became unnecessary and inefficient and soon gave way to confinement feedlot operations, or factory farms, where thousands upon thousands of penned cattle could be fattened at troughs. This was an economy of scale. It was happening everywhere, the wave of the future, the marriage of science and big business. If I sound bitter, it's because my grandparents, the Littles, lost the family dairy farm to hormonally enhanced cows, and it broke their hearts and eventually killed them. But I'd never understood this before.

Meanwhile, all this time, since it was first synthesized, DES was being used for another purpose entirely. Researchers and doctors were prescribing it for pregnant women in the belief that DES would prevent miscarriages and premature births. The pharmaceutical companies ran ads in professional medical publications, like the *Journal of Obstetrics and Gynecology*, recommending the drug for all women to produce "bigger and stronger babies." Many doctors prescribed it as casually as a vitamin, to an estimated five million women around the world. *Five million!* This was despite evidence, right from the start, that hormone manipulation during pregnancy was dangerous. In the 1930s, researchers at Northwestern University Medical School gave doses of estrogen to pregnant rats and discovered that the babies were born with various deformities of their sexual organs. But those were rats.

Then, in 1971, a team of Boston doctors discovered that DES caused a rare form of cancer, called clear cell adenocarcinoma, in the vaginas of young women whose mothers had taken the drug during pregnancy. And as if that wasn't bad enough, DES was finally exposed as a complete sham. That was the real tragedy. It was all hype. As early as 1952, researchers had found that DES did absolutely nothing to prevent miscarriages. On the contrary, a University of Chicago study showed a significant increase not only in miscarriages but also in premature births and infant deaths due to DES. Ironically, it was even used as a morning-after pill to terminate pregnancy. But again, this evidence was ignored.

Once the link between DES and human cancer was established, other effects were discovered as well. In addition to the cancer, DES-exposed daughters were suffering from irregular menstrual cycles, difficult pregnancies, and structural mutations of the vagina, uterus, and cervix. DES sons developed congenital malformations including undescended and atrophied testicles, abnormally undersize penises, defective sperm production, and low sperm count, all of which increased the risk of testicular cancer and infertility.

Of course, there was an immediate outcry to ban DES in cattle feed. But cheap meat is an inalienable right in the U.S.A., an integral component of the American dream, and the beef producers looked to cheap DES to provide it. So it took almost a decade of bitter political struggle to ban the drug, overcoming tremendous opposition launched by the drug companies and the meat industry, who argued that the doses of DES given to cattle were minuscule and harmless to humans and that the residues in the meat were far below the levels of danger. Finally, in 1979, the government banned DES for use in livestock production.

In 1980, however, half a million cattle from one hundred fifty-six feedlots in eighteen states were found with illegal DES implants. Three hundred eighteen cattlemen had decided that since they didn't agree with the ban, they would simply ignore it. Frontier justice. You take the law into your own hands. They were given a reprimand. None were prosecuted.

Today, although DES is illegal, 95 percent of feedlot cattle in the U.S. still receive some form of growth-promoting hormone or pharmaceutical in feed supplements. The residues are present in the finished cuts of beef sold in the local supermarket or hanging off your plate.

In 1989, Europe banned the import of U.S. meat because of the use of hormones in production. BEEF-EX started looking for a new market.

In 1990, as a result of pressure by the U.S. government, the New Beef Agreement was signed with Japan, relaxing import quotas and increasing the American share of Japan's red-meat market.

In 1991, we started production on *My American Wife!*

This was my first glimpse of the larger picture. Of course, I didn't put these pieces together all at once. I started reading about the meat industry, and little by little, over the course of the next few months, the chronology sort of dawned on me. Please keep this in mind.

HELEN

Miss Helen stood in front of the church, shaking her head and saying the same thing over and over to her friends and the members of the congregation.

"Yes, today was supposed to be the day, but now she says she ain't comin' after all. . . ."

Mr. Purcell added, "And after Miss Helen went and got the fixings all bought and set."

And the friends and members of the congregation were saying, "It's too bad, it surely is" and "It's a pity for the children to get so excited" and "She didn't give you no reason?"

And Miss Helen just kept shaking her head from side to side, saying, "I guess we just weren't the right sort" and "What would all them people in Japan be interested in us for, anyway?"

Then Mr. Purcell tried to make things better with laughter by saying, "Well now, Miss Helen, maybe you shoulda just slowed down that pitch of yours a little and let that producer man get a few more hits, now."

And the Preacher agreed and said, "Sure enough that pitch of yours could scare off anyone!"

And everyone laughed except Miss Helen, who just stood there saying, "It's a pity, it surely is a pity," and shaking her head, like she'd expected it to go wrong from the very beginning.

AKIKO

"Authenticity—two! You only gave it a two for Authenticity?"
John put down Akiko's questionnaire for the Becky Thayer
Show and stared at her. "What were you thinking? What did
you think was wrong with it?"

Akiko shook her head. "There wasn't anything *wrong*...."

"Then why did you only give it a two?"

"I ... I don't know. I gave it an eight for Wholesomeness,
though. See? And a nine for Deliciousness of Meat ..."

"Now, what's the point of Wholesomeness if it's not
Authentic? A two for Authenticity undermines a high mark for
Wholesomeness. Why did you only give it a two? You must
have had a reason."

"Because ... I didn't believe it."

John slammed his hand down on the *kotatsu* and Akiko
flinched.

"How could you not believe it?" he shouted. "It's the truth.
It's a documentary program, isn't it? What is there not to
believe?"

"I don't know," Akiko whispered. She made a grab for the
paper. "You're right. I don't know what I was thinking. I'll
change it."

John snatched it back. "Don't be ridiculous. This is a
questionnaire. You can't just change your answers because
something I say makes you change your mind. These are
supposed to be your honest impressions of the show."

He scowled at the paper again. "Okay. Now what, precisely, did you find hard to believe? Please, *try* to be specific if
you can."

Akiko hated these sessions. No matter what answers she

put down, John always got angry and told her they were wrong. And then she had to defend them.

"I . . . I don't know. It seemed like they were making things up. Like it was artificial, just something they were doing for the program."

"Who?"

"The Thayer family. They were so . . . perfect, you know? I guess maybe they just didn't feel like a real family to me. . . ."

"Hmmph. What would you know about a real family?"

"No, of course. You're right. I don't know much about families at all. . . ."

"You're missing the whole point." John sighed, exasperated. "You just don't get it. The whole *point* is to show perfect families. We don't *want* families with flaws. And anyway, you should have seen the other family. . . ."

Akiko nodded her head. It always seemed to make sense when he explained it to her, so she couldn't understand why she always got the answers wrong. But still, she supposed it was nice of him to try to teach her about the way television worked and talk to her about his job, so she did her best to listen. Many husbands wouldn't share their work concerns with their wives at all.

"Of all the stupid ideas, she actually thought this black woman could be an American Wife!"

"Who?"

"Takagi, that American woman director I told you about. The one I had to go all the way to Memphis to help with the program."

"What was wrong with the black woman?"

John rolled his eyes and snorted. "You should have seen her family. First of all, they were extremely poor. Their accents were so uneducated that even with my level of English I could barely make out what they were saying. And that was just the beginning. The husband had terrible dentistry, gold teeth everywhere, and the wife just looked, well, badly dressed. Their house was not beautiful at all, and the food she cooked! Pig intestines! Entirely inappropriate."

"It sounds . . . different."

"It certainly was. We even went to their church service. Remember I told you? The day I was so sick with the flu I kept having to throw up? That was an experience. They all went into trances and fell down on the floor."

"Did they sing authentic gospel music? I like authentic gospel music very much. . . ."

"I guess that's what you call it." He scowled at her enthusiasm. "But the *point* is, the family was wrong. How could a Japanese housewife relate to a poor black family with nine children? That Takagi keeps choosing the wrong kind of families. Sometimes I think she is doing it on purpose."

"Yes, I see exactly what you mean, I think. . . . Do you mean like the Beaudroux family? Was that her choice too? They weren't at all perfect, because most of the kids were adopted and were Korean, and the real daughter was having an illegitimate baby, and the other girl had a pierced eyebrow. . . ."

John nodded approvingly. "The Beaudroux family was a terrible choice," he concurred.

"I gave them a very low mark in Wholesomeness. . . ."

"Yes, but you gave them a nine in Authenticity."

Akiko hung her head.

"Why did you do that?"

"I don't . . . I mean, as a family . . ."

"Tell me!" He leaned across the table and gripped her wrist.

"I liked them," she whispered.

He released her, sat back, and crossed his arms. "Finally. The truth. And the Thayers? What did you think about them?"

"I didn't like them at all." Akiko's voice was now barely audible. "I thought they were phony."

"So what you are saying is that your evaluation has nothing to do with true Authenticity. It's just an arbitrary number based on your own questionable and subjective tastes. Is that right?"

"Yes. But I thought . . ."

"Good." John crumpled up the questionnaire and shot it across the room toward the wastebasket. "I'm glad you told me. I guess we won't have to waste time with these anymore, then. If that's all it is, if I can't trust you to give me accurate and reliable impressions, then it's simply a waste of time."

Akiko let out her breath slowly.

"Does that mean . . . ?"

"Yes, I no longer trust you to fill out the questionnaire. Just try to make the recipes as accurately as you can, please. That's the least you can do."

"Yes. Of course." Akiko picked up her tray. Carefully she placed the coffee cups and saucers on it and brought them to the kitchen. She put them in the soapy water left over from the dinner dishes, then stepped down the hall, into the bathroom. She leaned against the sink and closed her eyes, resting her forehead against the mirror of the medicine cabinet. No more weekly questionnaires. She rolled her head from side to side, enjoying the cool feeling of the glass against her hot forehead. Suddenly she heard a footstep just outside. The door slammed open with a crash. Akiko gasped and jumped away.

"I told you *never* to close this door," John screamed. "Do you understand? You are *never* to be in the bathroom after meals with the door *closed!*"

"I'm sorry," Akiko whimpered. "I wasn't going to . . . I forgot."

JANE

FAX NOTICE

Dear Kato-san,

I received your fax. I am sorry to hear that the Network did not like the Thayer show, but as I told Ueno, the Thayers are phony. It's a pity that we didn't do the Dawes family, but now it is too late. Miss Helen does not trust us anymore.

The next program I would like to do is about the Bukowskys. They are perfect candidates for *My American Wife!*, as I think even Ueno will agree. They are middle class, of Polish descent (white), they live in Indiana, and the daughter's physical handicap is the result of an automobile accident, not poor diet or health. The way that the family and the entire community have rallied during their time of need is truly an American story. The daughter is very beautiful, and we just won't film her legs.

Sincerely yours,

Takagi

Here is what happened: The girl, Christina Bukowsky, was riding her bicycle down the frontage road that bordered the interstate and was run over by a delivery truck making a right-hand turn into the Wal-Mart parking lot. Her legs and spine were crushed by the monstrous wheels, leaving her paralyzed from the waist down. The doctors said she would never walk or even sit up unassisted again. But worse even than that, when she was knocked off her bicycle she hit her head on a stretch of concrete curbing, and the force of the blow fractured the back of her skull. The trauma to the left temporal lobe rendered her more or less a vegetable, uncomprehending, incapable of speech.

Mrs. Eleanor Bukowsky and her husband, Dale, refused to believe this diagnosis. When Christina's condition had stabilized somewhat, they took their daughter out of the hospital and brought her home. By this time, Christina was conscious and she could open one eye, but she still was not moving her limbs, nor was she responding to external stimuli.

Eleanor Bukowsky asked for time off work so she could rehabilitate her daughter. She was an associate at Wal-Mart, a job that she needed because Dale had been laid off at the mine. He had been doing some part-time contracting, but work was increasingly hard to find. There wasn't a lot of building going on in the town of Quarry, Indiana.

When Mrs. Bukowsky asked for time off, however, her boss turned her down. He was a nice guy, a local guy, but he was being pressured by management, who felt that since the Bukowskys were suing Wal-Mart, granting her request would be admitting liability for the accident. Discouraged, Mrs. Bukowsky asked her boss to fire her so at least she could collect unemployment, but again he refused, since it would be bad publicity for Wal-Mart first to crush the daughter, then to fire the mom. So she quit without severance, and she and Dale set up a twenty-four-hour-a-day watch over the girl.

They installed their still-life daughter in the living room, outfitting it with a hospital bed. They read books, they consulted with specialists, and they developed a method of treatment that involved the entire underemployed population of the town. Eleanor posted sign-up sheets with visiting times on the bulletin boards at the schools, at the beauty salon, and even at Wal-Mart, and soon they had a steady stream of visitors coming over to their living room to sit with Christina.

"Thank you for coming, Albert," Eleanor would say, ushering in a sitter. "Right this way. Here she is, in the living room. You know. The Room for Living."

"That's very nice, Mrs. Bukowsky. That's absolutely right."

The way she figured it, each sitter would bring the girl something different. If there was any small spark of consciousness left inside her vegetable mind, and if enough people came, then someone would be able to rekindle it. It might be the most unlikely person, Eleanor figured, but the more people came, the greater the odds. In addition, each sitter was asked to bring a small contribution of food. It was close to begging, but the fact was, the Bukowsky family was broke. Wal-Mart was contesting its responsibility, and since Mr. Bukowsky had lost his job, the family of course had no health insurance.

For seven months after the accident, Christina Bukowsky lay in the converted living room, silent, immobile, dribbling a silvery thread of saliva from the corner of her mouth. It was one of the few precious signs of her life, and Eleanor wiped the drool with love and respect. At first Christina's one blue eye would open and close, for no apparent reason, not triggered by any particular noise or change in her environment. One minute it would be closed, and the next, open. The only other movements came intermittently from her bowels and regularly, if reluctantly, from the heave-ho, heave-ho of her emaciated rib cage.

For seven months, a thin stream of townspeople (there were only 973 people in the town of Quarry, Indiana, after all) trickled through the door of the Bukowsky household, which was always kept open. And each person brought something that he or she loved. That was the other part of it. Along with the contribution of food, you had to bring the Thing in Life That You Love Best, to share with Christina. A Hope was okay too. And if, like Alfred Cotter with his brand-new John Deere tractor, or old Lettie Crumb with her new cemetery plot under the weeping willow, which she'd exchanged for the one by the dying oak—if you couldn't actually carry the Thing You Love Best into the living room, it was okay to just bring a photograph. It was all about compassion, Mrs. Bukowsky figured. Compassion: "com" (with, together, in conjunction with) plus "passion."

Whatever it was, it worked. Slowly Christina's good eye started to respond to stimuli. It would open when she had visitors and close when the visitors left, and track their movements around the Living Room in between. Then her little fingers started to move too, an aimless, slow-motion wriggle like anemones in the deep sea. Hope grew among the townspeople, and when the second eye opened and looked around, the Bukowskys were cautiously ecstatic.

Then, after seven long months, the miracle they'd been waiting for finally happened. It was the same day that young Daryll Spilkoff finally saved enough money to buy the new Crash Test Dummies CD. He arrived early for his sitting, ollied up the front porch steps, and dropped his skateboard in the middle of the Living Room floor. He attached the earphones of his portable CD to Christina's immobile head and played her the cut "At My Funeral." At the end of the song, Christina opened both her eyes, licked the spit off her cracked lips, and spoke:

"amchob," she said.

"What?" said Daryll.

"aamchop," said Christina.

Daryll got up and walked to the back porch and called out to Mrs. Bukowsky, who was watering her tomato plants.

"Uh . . . Mrs. B.?" he said. "Uh . . . I think, like . . . Christina wants a lamb chop."

It had been her favorite food before the accident.

That was the beginning. By this time, the townspeople of Quarry were invested in Christina's rehabilitation. They had grown to look forward to, and in fact even to count on, their visits to the Living Room and the opportunity it gave them to talk freely about the things they loved best—topics of conversation that would send their own loved ones at home into eye-rolling, mind-numbing catatonia. And miraculously, these same topics appeared to have a therapeutic effect, provided the listener was already, literally, catatonic.

Whatever the reason, the outcome was quick and linear. The media got hold of the story and pumped it for all it was worth from every angle, including the exploitation of small-town America by the corporate retail giants. Wal-Mart did the right thing, paid a handsome settlement, and the family used the money to transform the Living Room into a Deluxe Physical Training Center. Mr. Bukowsky outfitted their house with a gothic web of ramps and lifts and pulleys and elevators for his daughter's wheelchair. It was the work of a zealot. Mrs. B. hired a physical therapist from Chicago, enlisted the townspeople, who continued to come by at their appointed times, and had the therapist train them in the most modern of rehabilitation techniques, which they took turns practicing on Christina. The girl had no choice but to get better.

And then, as though right on cue—just when the house was ready and the townspeople were trained and Christina could get around by herself in her wheelchair and didn't need so much individual attention anymore—then came the supplicants, the prayerful and those full of hope. They were parents with damaged offspring, like Mr. and Mrs. Bukowsky, and soon, before anyone really understood what was happening, additional beds had been installed to accommodate the variously crippled children, and the townspeople were doing double and triple shifts. The town of Quarry had discovered a new natural resource—compassion—and they were mining it and marketing it to America. At the March town meeting of 1989, the town voted to change the name officially on its charter. Quarry became Hope, and Mr. Bukowsky was elected mayor. Within a year the Hope Renewal Center, run by Mrs. Bukowsky, had moved into a brand-new two-hundred-bed long-term-care facility. The townspeople found jobs with the Center or started their own businesses as affiliated service providers. Motels and restaurants were necessary to house and feed the relatives of the Center's clients. A CD store and a butcher's shop were among the businesses that sprang up along the newly thriving Main Street. The Mayor and Mrs. Bukowsky starred in a promotional videotape, *Welcome to Our Living Room: The Bukowsky Method of Compassion and Renewal*, and published a best-selling book by the same name.

There was only one unanswered prayer. "We had hoped . . . ," Mrs. B. confided to me wistfully. The Mayor reached over and took her hand. He looked worried, but she smiled at him reassuringly.

"It's okay. I don't mind her knowing. And it helps me to talk about it." She turned back to me. "You know, Christina is going to be sixteen in a few days, and, well, we'd hoped that in spite of her legs that perhaps she'd be all right, you know, inside."

I didn't know. "Is there something wrong with her internally?"

"It's just that her periods . . . we'd hoped that . . . she's an only child, you see . . . but it looks like she won't be able to . . ."

"She's such a beautiful girl," the Mayor explained. "We had

hoped one day that she might be able to have a husband and a family of her own, you know, in spite of her legs. . . ."

But Christina's body and her mind were not cooperating. She'd never shown the slightest interest in boys, even Daryll Spilkoff, and aside from the wounds from the accident, she had never shed a drop of blood from between her crushed and lifeless legs. It was as though her lower regions had just had enough of bloodletting.

This was the Bukowsky story, and as far as I was concerned, it was almost perfect. My only problem was the lamb chop.

Pork was Possible. Beef was Best. I knew that now. But Ueno had never said anything about the relative status of lamb. BEEF-EX represented domestic lamb and mutton interests in Japan, and although I had a hunch that these were second-class meats, technically my chops shouldn't be a problem. Of course, it was also true that most of the lamb products imported by Japan came from Australia, not the U.S., and that Australia was America's main foreign competitor for the Japanese meat market. Featuring lamb could be seen as tantamount to treason. But frankly, my loyalty to BEEF-EX was pretty stressed. And I couldn't make a program without a Meat of the Week.

We were scheduled to shoot for three days, the third of which was to be Christina's Sweet Sixteen party, and Mrs. Bukowsky was going to serve Hallelujah Lamb Chops. I didn't tell Ueno. I figured he'd learn soon enough, and I'd never get another meat like this, so beautifully integrated into the core of the family narrative. Documentarians are suckers for good narrative, since we have to wait patiently for them to happen and can't just make them up from our imaginations. It was a rare storytelling opportunity, not to be passed up for a small discrepancy in the species of meat.

You see, Christina Bukowsky was beautiful. Not beautiful in any ordinary, earthbound, Midwestern sense of the word, but transgressively so. During the seven months of her withdrawal from our world, her skin had grown so clear that you could see life moving below the surface of her cheeks. Her hair shone like a mutable golden corona, whose shiftings and waftings sent fractured particles of light into the leaden air of Hope. Her eyes were blue, but not the hue she'd been born with, not the steel blue of Eastern Europe, dulled by gazing daily at the blighted postcapitalist landscape that was formerly Quarry, Indiana, at the end of the twentieth century. No, she'd once had eyes like that, but she had closed them tight in terror as the monstrous Goodyears crushed her. Those blue eyes were gone forever, and when she opened them again, her new blue was pellucid, the eyes of an angel that had rested for a while on Another's countenance.

And the best was that you could see it on-camera. Back at the Compassion Inn, I watched dailies with the crew. We'd done an interview with Christina and her parents that day, and the results were startling. Christina was simply and heartbreakingly radiant. Sitting in her wheelchair on the porch, as a mild breeze toyed with her golden locks, she talked about her accident and her parents and her community of Hope, but she could have been counting chickens and still have made you weep. Suzuki was superb. In the most exquisite approach I've ever witnessed, he dollied almost imperceptibly around her radiant face, and then, slowly zooming in to the source of her luminescence, he penetrated the blue of her eyes at the exact moment they spilled crystalline tears of beatitude and joy.

It was the oddest moment. Sitting on the edge of a pastel polyester coverlet on a king-size bed in the Compassion Inn, I felt an overwhelming sensation, a tremendous shudder that I imagine must have been akin to grace. Suzuki and Oh felt it too.

"Too bad about those legs, huh?" said the flight attendant. "She's great from the waist up, though. I wonder, do you think she still can, you know . . ." He pantomimed a bit of the old in-and-out with his fist and forearm, and looked to the boys for confirmation.

Oh turned silently away, which was perfectly in character, but Suzuki surprised me. He stood up and crossed the room. His face glowed like a red paper lantern, and when he was nose-to-nose with the flight attendant, he let loose a torrent of Japanese expletives that I'd never before heard or even imagined. It was like being transported back in time, into the thick of a samurai drama, and this effect was only heightened when, having finished cursing him, Suzuki stepped back and slapped the flight attendant's face. Twice. Once in each direction. Like a lord disciplining a retainer. Of course, this being America, the subtleties of this feudal interaction were lost.

The flight attendant quit on the spot and later tried to sue us, but by then the New York office had closed and no one was left to care.

It seemed that Suzuki had fallen deeply in love, and so had Oh. The following day we borrowed a wheelchair to use as a dolly, and with the Betacam braced on his shoulder, Suzuki chased Christina up and down the ramps and lifts and elevators and all through the house. Oh pushed. I knew the footage would be splendid. When a cameraman gets under the skin of his subject like that, the resulting images are zen in their oneness. I left them alone. The Bukowsky parents and I stood at the bottom of the stairs as they thundered above us, Christina's laughter ricocheting through the house and making the floorboards shiver with pleasure.

"She's never laughed like that before," said Mrs. Bukowsky softly. "No one's ever *played* with her like that before."

"After the accident, it's like she's on another plane," said the Mayor. "Above us somehow, but not really here. I mean, she's physically here, and happy, but at the same time she's not fully participating. But I guess maybe it's our fault, the way we've been treating her—"

At this moment the two wheelchairs came hurtling down the ramp next to the staircase and spun to an abrupt halt. Christina's cheeks were pink from the infusion of blood to the surface of her skin. She looked up at her parents and paused just long enough to flash a wide-eyed smile, then she glanced quickly back at her pursuers, who were momentarily tangled up in camera cables. Then she spun away. Suzuki heaved the camera onto his shoulder, and Oh, brandishing the boom pole like a lance or a banner, gave a mighty thrust to the wheelchair and they took off in pursuit.

"It's like I always said, dear," said Mrs. B. to the Mayor. "You never know who it's going to be, or what they'll bring, but whatever it is, it's always exactly what is needed."

Suzuki? Oh? It was a disturbing thought. I spent a sleepless night worrying if I should leave them behind, to woo Christina into a successful puberty, but the next day, after the Sweet Sixteen party, we all left as planned. Christina was sad, yet she was still too young to have her heart seriously broken, at least by the likes of my camera crew. But at the party she had this new way of turning her wheelchair off-center from the person she was talking to and shooting a veiled glance and a heavenly smile back over her shoulder. It was positively coquettish. There was no mistaking it.

Suzuki was quiet in the van and on the plane and for several weeks afterward. I noticed that he and Oh stopped shooting out the crotches of blonde girls in their motel room. Our visit to Hope had changed them.

*

Each sojourn into the heartland had its own viscosity—a total submersion into a strange new element—and for the duration, the parameters of my own world would collapse, sucked like a vacuum pack around the shapes of the families and the configurations of their lives. But as we settled on the plane, and took off, and flew out of Indiana, I felt a slow return to my forgotten skin as the world reinflated, and I began to dip into all the corners and crevices of my own dormant concerns.

I had only two weeks to do the edit.

Ueno would learn about the lamb.

I was feeling kind of queasy. Just nerves. Or my period. It was way overdue. Maybe I'd stopped out of sympathy with Christina.

I still hadn't seen Sloan. Hadn't seen him since Fly.

Ueno was going to be furious about the lamb.

He would try to have me fired.

But how could he? Screw the Beef. Lamb was Lovable, and I had just shot the most mouth-watering show of the season.

And with that thought, I unbuckled my seat belt and walked to the lavatory at the back of the plane, closed the flimsy folding door behind me, and vomited into the metal toilet.

AKIKO

The girl in the wheelchair struggled down a rutted dirt road toward the camera. A plaid lap robe shielded her damaged legs and covered something on her lap, large and lumpish, which she took great care to keep from tipping over. The wind was strong and it was blowing her hair about her face. Akiko wanted to help her. Why didn't anyone help her? The wheel of her chair got caught in a rut, and the girl rocked back and forth, careful not to upset her bundle, until she freed herself, then continued valiantly forward. Then, when she reached some invisible mark, she stopped, looked up, and smiled triumphantly. She lifted the lap robe and revealed a domed platter underneath. She uncovered the platter and offered it up to the camera. It was the prettiest ring of Hallelujah Lamb Chops, each upturned rib decorated with a little white angel skirt made of frilly paper that looked like wings. In the center of the ring was a heart made of mashed potatoes, with cranberry lettering that read "Sweet 16." The girl looked steadily at the camera, her blue gaze melting the lens, penetrating its glassy barrier and capturing the hearts of housewives throughout Japan. Then laboriously she maneuvered her wheelchair around, but before she went, she shot one more heavenly smile back over her shoulder.

At the market, the butcher had only six chops left. They were Australian, but Akiko figured that John wouldn't know the difference.

With a pair of scissors she cut the fringe on the frilly angel skirts for the lamb, carefully following the steps demonstrated on television. Why the girl wanted a lamb chop after waking up from her coma was a mystery. Well, it hadn't been a coma, exactly, but almost. The girl couldn't move or speak or eat. Akiko wondered what it would be like to be incapacitated like that. After she fell into the china cabinet, her stomach had hurt so badly she couldn't get out of bed, and all she wanted was to slip into a coma and not move, not speak, not eat. There were no townspeople. Nobody came. Their cluster of *danchi* high-rise buildings had a population five times that of the town of Hope, but no one knew about her illness. If her neighbors had known, maybe some of them would have come, if only out of curiosity, to stare, but they wouldn't have thought to bring her the Thing in Life That They Loved Best. Akiko tried to think about the things that she loved, but she couldn't come up with a single idea, except maybe her secret purging. But it wasn't a secret anymore. And it wasn't about life. It was about dying. Maybe she was in a coma after all and just didn't know it.

Akiko had read somewhere that pointed toes were a symptom of comas. Ever since she had fallen into the china cabinet, she'd been having a dream that was causing her to flail her arms at night and point her toes so hard she got cramps in her calves. She couldn't understand the dream. It was about Moses. In a Western art history class she'd taken in university, she had seen a sculpture of Moses by Michelangelo from the Church of San Pietro in Vincoli, in Rome. Moses had bull horns on his head and this was how she recognized him in her dream. He was standing by the Red Sea, only it wasn't a sea but more like a fast-flowing river, and he walked out into the middle of it and the waters parted for him, just as one might expect. There he stopped and waited for her to come, but whenever she tried, the red waters closed again, over her foot. Moses stood safe and dry, tossing his horned head like a bull, impatiently, holding his hand out to her to lead her to safety. There was no choice. She had to follow. Arms flailing in circles so as not to lose her balance, Akiko ran on stiffened tiptoes in a headlong tilt toward Moses as the waters of the Red Sea closed behind her.

She'd wakened John with all her flailing and finally she told him about her dream. He'd gone to a Christian university, so he was very offended that she should dream she was an escaping Israelite, since that would make him an Egyptian oppressor. Akiko tried to convince him that this couldn't be the case: she hadn't remembered why Moses was crossing the Red Sea in the first place. But John insisted she must have known. It was common knowledge, even if you hadn't attended a Christian university.

The lamb was in the oven when John got home and the timing was almost perfect. He was a little late, which was fine because it had taken a bit longer to cut the tiny skirts than Akiko had anticipated. When she took his jacket at the door, she could smell beer on his breath. It made her nervous. She hesitated in the kitchen, in front of the refrigerator, but he called out for a beer, so she had no choice but to bring him one on a tray. Something was wrong. He was sitting at the *kotatsu*, holding the remote, flicking through the news programs on the television. Akiko retreated, glad dinner was almost ready and that it was such a special one. She reentered the living room proudly, holding up the pretty crown of lamb chops like an offering. She knelt down in front of him. He took one look at the meat and recoiled violently.

"How dare you serve Australian lamb in my house!" he hissed, then he lunged forward and knocked the platter from her hands. She raised her arms to ward off a blow. He obliged, boxing her ear with his fist and knocking her into the television.

"Australia is a land of criminals and traitors," he declared as he got to his feet and headed toward the door. "That is where you belong. How could you do this? I can't stand the sight of you! I wish you would go away to Australia!"

After he left, Akiko lay against the television for a while. The nine o'clock news was on, but she couldn't hear it over the roaring in her ears. Eventually she picked up the meat from the floor and put it back on the platter. She pulled off a little piece and tasted it. It was delicious. She went to the whiskey cabinet and poured a glass. The next few hours she spent sipping whiskey and nibbling at the delicately charred fat of the lamb. It was the best meat she'd ever eaten. She gnawed all six chops, then sucked the bones dry. Afterward, she went to the bathroom and waited, but the animal inside her was quiet. Instead she felt a vague cramping in her pelvis. She pulled down her underpants and sat on the toilet, thinking it might be the onset of diarrhea caused by the strange meat. She waited, but nothing happened. She stood again to pull up her underpants, and that was when she noticed the faint, pinkish-brown stain.

THE POEM-COMPOSING MONTH

SHŌNAGON

Surprising and Distressing Things

While one is cleaning a decorative comb, something catches in the teeth and the comb breaks.

A carriage overturns. One would have imagined that such a solid, bulky object would remain forever on its wheels. It all seems like a dream—astonishing and senseless.

A child or grown-up blurts out something that is bound to make people uncomfortable.

All night long one has been waiting for a man who one thought was sure to arrive. At dawn, just when one has forgotten about him for a moment and dozed off, a crow caws loudly. One wakes up with a start and sees that it is daytime—most astonishing.

One of the bowmen in an archery contest stands trembling for a long time before shooting; when finally he does release his arrow, it goes in the wrong direction.

JANE

After the edit of the Bukowsky Show, I was still feeling sick and oddly exhausted. I sent the show in, got on a plane, and flew to Minnesota, to visit my mother in Quam. I didn't even wait around for the approval from Tokyo. Kenji knew how to contact me if there was a problem.

Quam, Minnesota. It is always odd to go back. When I was growing up there, I don't remember seeing a single Asian other than Ma, and maybe that's why it never crossed my mind that I was different. I was a Little, after all. I look at the Little family photos now, taken at my grandparents' dairy farm, and I can't understand how I could have been so blind. I mean, here is this solid embankment of weather-beaten Anglo-Saxon farmers, Grampa in his overalls, Grammy in her faded flowered dress—I swear she's holding a pitchfork—and then the pale-eyed, pale-haired sons and daughters flanking them, all equally eroded by the sun . . . and then there is me. An American Gothic gone wrong. The earliest picture shows Grampa holding me in the palm of his hand, like a pet rabbit, or something he might skin for dinner. I am staring straight at the camera, eyes shaped like little almonds, with kernels inside that are as black and hard as coal. Grampa is watching the top of my head with his rheumy blue eyes, and my pitch-black hair is standing on end, long, perfectly straight, astonished. Like young wheat. Grampa told me that Grammy and Ma used to take turns spitting on it to make it lie down and that this was the thing they could do together, without language, which made them feel closer and more like a family; but it never stayed down for long.

I should have known I looked different, because when I played cowboys and Indians with the neighborhood children, I was always the Indian princess. I was tall for my age even as a kid and generally won most of the battles, and I used to get into terrible arguments with this boy named Farley, who said I was cheating by winning because the Indians were supposed to lose. I didn't get it. I knew I wasn't cheating, but I definitely wasn't going to lose, either, certainly not to assuage Farley's sense of historical propriety.

And now I remember, there was this game that my best friend, Polly, and I played during the first snowfall of every year. When the snow had just dusted the ground, we would take long sticks and draw faces on the asphalt road in front of my house. I would make Japanese faces, with big circles for heads, and then eyes, a nose, and a mouth. Polly would make American faces the same way. Only the eyes were different. Mine were just two slanty lines, slashed quickly in the snow, but Polly had to draw entire little circles. It took her a lot longer to do this, and since it was a race to see who could draw more faces, she always lost. The faces represented our two countries' soldiers and we called the game World War II. We'd play and play, breathlessly rallying our troops until the entire street was filled with faces and it was dark and my Japs had won. I guess I did know something about difference after all. But it didn't feel racial yet. More like different color teams in gym class. Later I learned in school that the Japanese had lost that war, so once again I'd been practicing revisionist history. I didn't mean it. I just couldn't seem to avoid it—and maybe that's why I ended up in television.

I finally got it one day at a Peewee League softball game. It was an away game, and this black girl from another team called me a "chink." She was the third baseman, and I had just hit a triple and had run as fast as I could and was standing on her base, panting. The girl sort of reached over and tapped me on the butt with her glove. "Nice hit, chink," she said, smiling. I didn't know what it meant, but she was so friendly when she said it and it sounded like this special thing, sort of like "slugger." I remember standing there catching my breath and smiling at her and feeling so proud, and when the next batter up bunted to first I took off, but not before I heard her softly call out, "Go, chink! Run!" I made it safely home and scored, and afterward I went around for a couple of weeks calling all my friends "chink" and slapping them on the butt. Finally my teacher asked me if I knew what it meant. When I admitted I didn't, she called my father.

In my early teens, when Polly and the other girls were assembling ideal boyfriends from the body parts of teen movie idols and lead guitarists, I was conjuring a mate along very different lines. The way I figured it, I had the chance to make a baby who could one day be King of the World. An embodied United Nations. I went to the Quam Public Library and looked up "The Races of Men" in an old Frye's geography book.

If we were to travel through all the countries, we should see many different classes of people. We may divide them into five great groups called races. . . .

This sounded promising. I liked lists and categories even back then.

All of Africa south of the Sahara is the home of the *black* or *Negro race*. . . .
These people have crude weapons, such as darts, bows

and arrows, wooden clubs, and blowguns made of hollow reeds.

Such natives are very ignorant. They know nothing of books; in fact, they know little, except how to catch and cook their food, build their rude huts, travel on foot through the forests, or in canoes or on rafts on the rivers, and make scanty clothing out of the skins of animals or fibers of grasses or bark. A few of them know how to raise grains in a crude way. Such people are savages.

I'm a documentarian. I'm not making this up. The book is the Frye's *Grammar School Geography* published in 1902 by Ginn & Company, Boston. I know because I went back to the library to look for it, and it was still there, so I checked it out again. The Quam Public Library is not computerized yet, so you have to fill out the slip at the back of the book. You write your name under that of the last borrower and hand the slip to the librarian. When I took the card out of the manila pocket pasted inside the back cover, I recognized, about halfway up and written in pencil, my twelve-year-old script. Five kids had checked it out since then. I wrote my name again and gave it to the librarian. I was going to put a stop to this.

In the hot belt of the New World, in South America, are also found millions of savages, but they belong to the *red* or *Indian race*. . . .

In their home life these "red men" resemble the black savages of middle Africa. They wear but little clothing and use about the same kinds of weapons. They hunt and fish, and lead a lazy, shiftless life. . . .

The people of the *brown* or *Malay race* also live almost wholly in the torrid zone. . . .

The people of the *yellow race* have slanting eyes, coarse black hair, flat faces and short skulls. . . .

And more specifically . . .

The people of the yellow race living on the islands of Japan have made more progress than any other branch of the race. They are eager to learn how the white men do all kinds of work, and they have been wise enough to adopt many of the customs of the white race. . . .

Even as a kid, I knew there was something very wrong with this picture of the world—after all, I had gone to the library as a twelve-year-old searching for amalgamation, not divisiveness. Still, I learned what I needed: a mate who was black, brown, or red, to go with my white and yellow. At the very least, I was aiming for three out of five. I returned the book to the library, then forgot about my breeding project for the next decade or so. But when I arrived in Japan at the age of twenty-one to study Shōnagon, I was suddenly overcome with the swampy urgency of maternal lust.

Emil triggered it. A graduate student like myself, he was at Kyoto University on exchange from Zaire via Paris, and I fell in love with him. I saw him for the first time on the banks of the Kamogawa, just downriver from the university. I was jogging, and when I spotted him he was being held hostage by a gaggle of country schoolgirls on their annual class trip to historic Kyoto. His smile, benign and wry, drew them like flies, or maybe it was the color of his skin. The girls were dressed in identical uniforms—middy blouses and long pleated skirts—and they surrounded him, practicing their English and pushing up next to him to have their pictures taken. *"Dis is a pen, dis is a pen,"* the girls cried, convulsing into giggles. *"Hallo, hallo!"* He towered over them—tall, coal black, utterly different. Our eyes met over the tops of the schoolgirls' heads and he froze like a panther, hungry after a long nap, at the sight of an antelope jogging by. Dazzled, I couldn't help but glance back over my shoulder, and I saw him as he shook off the girls, broke free, and sprinted. I turned my head, but not before our eyes met again and he fixed his sights on me. I picked up the pace. He was dressed in a suit and a tie and leather dress shoes, and I was running flat-out now, but it still took him less than a minute to catch up.

"Don't run away!" he said softly, right behind me, and his voice was like chocolate. He overtook me, then, without breaking stride, he turned in his tracks to face me and ran backward, still matching my pace. I gave up and slowed.

"Do you always chase after women like this?" I asked, querulous, out of breath.

"Nah," he said smoothly. "Women, they chase after me. I mean, look at yourself! Who is chasing whom now, I ask you?"

His eyes widened in mock innocence, and when I scowled at him he threw his head back and laughed. It stopped me dead.

"Are you a professional athlete or something?" I asked. Kyoto is a sweltering bowl of a city in the summer, and that year the heat had lingered, still and muggy, into the fall. The sweat ran down my forehead, stinging my eyes, but his dark face was perfectly dry.

"Nah," he said. "I'm an engineer."

Which perhaps explains why, when I eventually told him about it, months later, he approved of my experiment in biotech.

"So that is the reason you chased me along the banks of the Kamogawa, then?" he said, rolling over onto his back. We were lying in bed, under the futon that was always too short and left our feet exposed down at the end, and it was winter now, and cold. "You spotted a handsome black man and recognized my genetic potential."

"Emil, I didn't—"

"Some people might call that racism, you know?"

"Listen, *you* chased *me*."

"Well, I consent. I will gladly be the genetic engineer of our love, but perhaps we ought to marry first?"

In racially homogeneous Japan, we were a radical couple. We waited until the following year, until Emil finished his master's degree, and we got married in the spring. Immediately we set about the creation of our family, first with abandon, then with precision, and finally with despair, but to no avail. I couldn't get pregnant. It wasn't Emil, we were fairly sure of that. He'd impregnated a girlfriend in Paris, so it had to be me. I have thought of myself as mulatto (half horse, half donkey—i.e., a "young mule"), but my mulishness went further than just stubbornness or racial metaphor. Like many hybrids, it seemed, I was destined to be nonreproductive.

I underwent a battery of fertility testing and discovered that I had a precancerous condition called neoplasia, an *in situ* carcinoma consisting of malignant cancer cells growing in the tissue of my cervix. *In situ* means that the cancer wasn't going anywhere, and my Japanese doctor wasn't worried. He also insisted that this wasn't the reason for my infertility. But as soon as I could, I had an operation called a conization to remove the malignancy, and afterward the surgeon told me that he'd discovered something else. He showed me an X-ray.

I've always pictured the triangular uterine cavity as the head of a bull, with the fallopian tubes spreading and curling like noble horns, and that's what I was expecting to see. But when he showed me the filmy negative against the light, what I saw instead was less symmetrical. The left side of the bull's broad forehead was caved in, less triangular, as though my uterus had been coldcocked.

Still, we hoped. The doctor said I should be able to conceive, despite my diminished capacity, but he was wrong. We tried again and again. . . . No, that's not quite true. I tried. And I made Emil comply. Every month I would monitor my temperature, time my cycles, and test my secretions until that magic interval of life's potential opened its portals. Emil was a sport. He never made me ask, he never rolled his eyes or sighed deeply or made excuses or stayed late at school. He would come home and politely become aroused, and again we would try. And fail. As far as I know, we never even managed to fertilize an egg.

Barrenness took its toll, infected my studies, and so when Emil received an offer of a job in Tokyo, I was more than happy to give up Shōnagon and her lists. Tokyo was a welcome change. I made friends with Kato, who gave me a job at his production company, translating English-speaking interviews for the Japanese subtitlers and dialogue editors. I cut off my hair and discovered androgyny as a tool for sexual politics in the workplace. Emil and I continued to try, but slowly, inevitably . . .

After almost five grim years, we woke to the realization that we just didn't love each other enough. It wasn't the frustration of our biological imperative; I think we could have survived that and accepted childlessness with grace. But neither of us could recover from the overwhelming sense of failure. It poisoned every single thing we tried to do as a couple. By the end we couldn't even go out to dinner and think of the evening as a success. So we split up. He stayed on in Japan and later married a Japanese woman and had several kids. I moved back to America and into my tenement apartment on the Lower East Side of New York City, reconciled to my stubborn solitude and mulish sterility.

In Fly, when I told Sloan I don't get pregnant, this is what I meant.

Call it censorship, but on that trip home to visit Ma after the Bukowsky show, I stole the Frye's *Grammar School Geography* from the public library. It was the least I could do for the children of Quam. But to be perfectly honest, I wanted the book, and it's not the kind of thing you can easily pick up at a Barnes & Noble superstore. It felt like antique pornography to me, with its musty old text, quaint etchings, and poisonous thoughts. From time to time I still pore over its stained, chamois-soft pages, satisfying my documentarian's prurient interest in the primary sources of the past. Today, with a frisson of delight, I discovered the Preface, complete with typographical flourishes:

> In this book, **man** is the central thought. Every line of type, every picture, every map, has been prepared with a single purpose, namely, to present the *earth as the home of man*,—to describe and locate the natural features, climates and products that largely determine his industries and commerce, as well as his civic and other relations,—thus bringing REASON to bear on the work.

It isn't Mr. Frye's use of the generic "man" for "human" that I'm interested in. Other women might object to his choice of words, but as far as I'm concerned, that's an intraspecific quibble. The conflict that interests me isn't *man* versus *woman*, it's *man* versus *life*. Man's REASON, his industries and commerce, versus the entire natural world. This, to me, is the dirty secret hidden between the fraying covers.

Ma is waiting for me when I come back from the county medical center. It's been three days since I've been home, and there is no hiding it from her. She's seen me run to the toilet in the morning, she's hovered by the bathroom door, listened as I retch. I've gone for a test, and it's positive—I am one and a half months pregnant. When I walk through the door, Ma is standing hesitantly in the kitchen, supporting herself on the back of a stuffed vinyl kitchen chair. She is tiny, a miniature Ma, bent and gray and accusing.

"Is the baby," she declares. She has never learned to speak English well and is particularly awkward with her articles and prepositions.

"Yeah," I tell her. "It's a baby."

She moves around the chair and sits down on the edge. "Why you get pregnant now? You not even married anymore."

"I should think you'd be relieved, Ma." She had never met Emil. She refused to meet him. Before we were married I sent her a picture of him and me, in front of the Great Buddha at Kamakura. It was a great picture of the three of us: pitch black, pale yellow, and a looming greenish-blue. She wrote back that she would not come to the wedding.

"Who is father? Is it another one of black Africaman?" That's what she used to call him: never Emil, just "Africaman."

"No, this one's green." She drives me crazy. I mean, as the only Asian in a place like Quam, how could she still be so prejudiced?

"Good. Is better you have green baby. Is matching stupid color of your hair."

She smiles grimly. She is impossible.

"At least you tall girl. Big bones. Not so bad for you to have . . ." She spreads her legs and makes a shooing gesture with her hands between them, pantomiming childbirth but looking more like she is chasing away flies. "Me, I have very bad time. Very bad. You are much too big baby for me." She looks at me accusingly.

But I don't really notice. Something is stirring at the back of my mind.

"Mom, when you were pregnant, did your doctor tell you to take any medicine? Any pills?"

She shrugs. "Maybe. I don't know. Don't remember."

"Come on, Ma, you must remember. Please. Think back. Little pills maybe you had to take every day, to help you, so you wouldn't lose me . . . ?"

She shakes her head. "I don't know. Everything crazy then, and I don't speak good English at all. Maybe sure I take some pill, some vitamin, I don't remember. It was bad time. Doctor say I am *so* delicate."

She looks so delicate, sitting on the edge of the chair, her callused feet, in their old rubber thonged slippers, swinging clear of the linoleum floor. Her hands are crossed in front of her on the kitchen table, fingers interlaced, like those of an obedient schoolchild at her desk, as she watches me expectantly. Suddenly it seems perfectly clear. I know what happened. The bludgeoning my uterus received occurred when I was still only a little shrimp, floating in the warm embryonic fluid of Ma. I can imagine the whole thing. Ma, frightened, pregnant, not speaking a word of English, sitting in the doctor's office, maybe with Dad, maybe with Grammy Little. I sat in a doctor's office today. I know how scary it is. Of course old Doc Ingvortsen, the family doctor in Quam, decided she was delicate. And from there, it would have been only a reasonable precaution. After all, he was used to treating large-bodied Swedes and sturdy Danes, with ample, childbearing hips—the farthest east he'd probably ever imagined was Poland or possibly the Ukraine. But Ma was Japanese. My birth certificate, signed by this doctor, lists her race as "yellow." And she was narrow. Doc must have subscribed to the *Journal of Obstetrics and Gynecology*, seen the ads. So he gave her a prescription, probably about 125 milligrams of diethylstilbestrol, otherwise known as DES, to take once a day during the first trimester of me. To keep me in place, floating between her delicate hips.

"Ma, where is Doc Ingvortsen now?"

"Oh, he long time dead."

"Who took over his practice? Is there a new doctor there?"

"No." She flapped her hand at me in disgust. "Old Main Street office long time burn down. No Quam doctor no more.

Only brand-new, sooperdooper Medical Center. Too far away. But all doctor stay there together. I say, why need so many doctor in same sooperdooper place? Better to spread out, little doctor here, little doctor there. Better the old-fashioned way."

The next few days seemed like a dream—astonishing and senseless. I tried to track down Dr. Ingvortsen's records, but they had been lost or destroyed in the fire. It was thirty years ago, after all. I searched Ma's files and medicine cabinets but didn't expect to find anything. I didn't tell her about the DES. Maybe I should have, but I figured what good would it do? She would only feel guilty. She couldn't really offer me solace. We just didn't have that type of relationship. Later in the week we talked again.

"Ma, I have to tell you. I don't know if I can keep the baby. . . ."

She shook her head. "You keep, you throw away. Always you do only what you want. Not thinking about other people. What his father say?"

"I don't know."

"You don't know father?" She turned away from me. "You are wicked girl."

"No, Ma. I know who the father is. I just haven't told him."

"He nice man?" She turned back hopefully.

"I don't . . . I mean, yes, I guess he's a nice man."

"You tell him, then he marry you? Maybe?"

"No, Ma. I don't think so."

"Then he not nice man and is better you throw away his baby." She narrowed her narrow eyes at me. "But you not sure, right?" she persisted.

"That's right, Ma. I'm not sure. I'm not sure at all."

*

It is my job to be sure about things. Every day, I must reassure my crew, my wives, the local sheriff who's about to arrest us for trespassing, or treason, or public intoxication . . . that really, sir, ma'am, everything is just fine, under control, the check is on the way, in the bank, whatever. I have an honest, earnest face. It's the Asian-American Woman thing—we're reliable, loyal, smart but nonthreatening. This is why we get to do so much newscasting in America. It's a convenient precedent. The average American is trained to believe what I tell him.

It can also be an occupational hazard. I am so good at convincing people that I know exactly what I am doing, I end up fooling myself.

But here is a truth, regarding Sloan.

At first he was a lark, primarily funny. I was twenty-seven when Emil and I got divorced. For two years afterward I didn't date at all. My relationship with my body had been irrevocably altered by my failure to conceive. With a shriveled uterus and a predisposition to cancer, I was not in the mood for love. I was deformed, barren, and scared. I suspected I might die young, and I didn't think I'd ever be able to view sex as recreational again. Sex was about precision and despair, the antitheses of pleasure. It was a production, and I was the director and had run it ruthlessly. Maybe that was the problem. Maybe my little egg, in the middle of her placid descent, simply recoiled in horror when she saw these beleaguered genetic envoys, joyless and exhausted, bushwhacking their way up my tortuous reproductive tract. So when they finally arrived and came knocking, she slammed her door, and there they died, defeated in the murky, lukewarm threshold of becoming.

Anyway, two years after the divorce, a girlfriend told me about Sloan. He was a good friend of hers. They used to discuss their sexual proclivities, as did she and I, and in a magnanimous curatorial gesture of friendship, she suggested to both of us that we might like to fuck. She thought we'd have a lot to talk about.

She was right. We had that long prelude by telephone, and by the time we finally met, in Nebraska, we had talked so much and my defenses were so far down that the sudden embodiment of sex shook me.

What hooked me was the suspicion that he was not equivalently shaken. This is not easy to admit. But I sensed it. Perhaps his sexual mastery and my abandonment indicated nothing more than the discrepancy in our desire. I should say, the goals of that desire: I am pretty sure that our enjoyment was on a par—at least he told me as much, and I had no reason to disbelieve him, but I soon suspected that we just didn't want the same things to come of it.

I started to realize that the world Sloan roamed was much larger and richer than mine. Although we normally met on my turf, small backwaters you could reach only by pickup truck or Greyhound bus, on a couple of occasions when I was in transit we met in L.A., which was one of his towns. He knew that I loved food. He took me to exquisite restaurants, where we ate rich urchin roe that melted like butter, and paper-thin *fugu* with chili *ponzu* sauce, and a thimbleful of black-market caviar, wrapped in a translucent skin and tied with a chive, then covered with trembling pieces of gold leaf; it was called a Beggar's Purse and each one cost fifty dollars. After weeks of Denny's, I loved it.

He knew people. Everywhere we went. People whose names and faces I recognized but whom I had never seen in person before. Musicians. Film people. I got the sense he was showing me off, and I began to wonder if perhaps I wasn't primarily a rustic curiosity, a story he recounted to his friends or his therapist. It was a point of pride with me to show up in his world covered in mud and chiggers, with torn jeans and a filthy T-shirt, traipsing cow dung across the cropped carpets of the Chateau Marmont. He liked this. I never had the right clothes, and he would take me shopping and buy me things so we could go out to dinner, and then he would take them off me later on. He had a few stores that he knew well—I mean, *really* knew: the collections, the designers, the girls. I got it. I am not stupid. Just underdressed.

This type of relationship was normally not my style, but then again, nothing was normal in the Year of Meat.

The episode in Fly undid me. The almost accidental conversation about trust released all these unexpected hopes. I'd thought they were all dead. That's the thing about involuntary infertility—it kills your sense of a future, so you hide out in the here and now. Of course, lots of people choose a child-free life. But when you don't get to choose, when it is thrust upon you, you equate the loss of posterity with the loss of hope.

So there in Fly, I was overcome with this soft and screwy sense of hopefulness, followed by this titanic sex that laid me out, and when I came to, all these ifs were flying around, blackening the air like an infestation. When they cleared, they left me looking squarely at a brand-new desire. After resolutely keeping him at a distance, suddenly I knew that Sloan was important. He meant something to me. I'm not sure why, but I wanted him at the center of my life, not just orbiting its periphery like a spare moon.

That dank, moldy room by the interstate was a threshold of sorts. After the sex was over, we lay in the middle of the spongy mattress, and my heart pounded and swelled with all this massing, nebulous expectation. His head was on my chest, and he lifted it and shifted slightly, as though he'd felt the pulse of it too.

"Takagi?"

"Yes . . ."

"Thanks."

"Uh . . . sure."

He rolled over onto his side and propped his head on his hand and looked at me.

"Jane, when you said you didn't get pregnant, that you were safe . . . ?"

"Yes?"

"Are you sure? I mean, what exactly did you mean?"

I didn't want to tell him at first. I don't know what I thought. Maybe that he wouldn't take me seriously if he knew. And I wanted him to take me seriously. As seriously as I was taking him. And that's when I realized I had to tell him.

"Sloan, I can't have kids."

"Really?"

"Yeah. I was married, remember? We tried, I got tested, nothing. Zip. That's what broke us up, finally."

"I'm sorry."

"Yeah, well . . ."

"Thanks. For telling me."

"Well, I guess you should know."

He rolled over onto his back. "You know, I've never had sex without a condom before. I've always wondered what it feels like, but what with AIDS and paternity suits and all . . . I've never had a lover who was perfectly safe. . . ."

And that was that. What it all boiled down to. A discrepancy in desire. He wanted a simple answer to a nagging question, like scratching an itch. I wanted something else. With Sloan, for the first time in so long, I wanted more. But no. Not to be safe. Not *perfectly safe.* That was not at all what I wanted.

It was the strangest thing. As I stared up at the stained acoustic ceiling tile, the tears started to leak from the corners of my eyes. This had happened to me once before, when I was in the hospital after the operation and the doctor showed me the X-ray of the imploded forehead of my uterus and its decrepit curling horns. The tears for my thwarted posterity just ran down the sides of my face, into my ears, and onto the pillow. I wasn't crying, really. Rather, life and all my stupid hopes for the future were simply draining out of me. And in Fly it happened again. I couldn't make the tears stop. After a while, Sloan got up to go to the bathroom and noticed.

"Are you all right?"

"I'm fine, Sloan, really," I reassured him, in a perfectly normal, reliable voice. "Everything is just fine."

"Really, Ma, I'm fine." She stands on the porch watching me as I carry my suitcase to the rental car parked in the driveway. She is worried, I can tell. But what can I say to her? I told her about the neoplasia, just to get her used to the idea that I might not be as durable as she imagines. But from what I'd read about DES, and what I'd seen of my imploded uterus, I can't promise to have the baby at all, even if I wanted it, which I'm not at all sure I do. And I certainly can't promise to marry Sloan. But at least I will tell him, I promise her. Before I abort I will tell the nice green man, just to see what he says. "Ma," I say to her as I lean way down to kiss her good-bye on the top of her gray head. "Don't worry. Everything will be just fine."

Returning from the Midwest to New York is like driving full speed into a wall. The city slams you. Middle America is all about drift and suspension. It's the pervasiveness of the mall-culture mentality; all of life becomes an aimless wafting on currents of synthesized sound, through the well-conditioned air. In New York, you walk down the streets like that, you're dead meat.

I slipped back into the city and spent a week at home pretending I was still out of town. I made appointments with an obstetrician for an ultrasound and an oncologist to check my uterus for more malignant forms of life, and then I unplugged the phone, got down on my knees, and cleaned every corner of my tiny apartment. It's a ritual I perform every year. I go through all my possessions, touching each, one by one. I reconsider everything I own and either choose it again or throw it away. It's a deterrent to shopping, and stuff stays special that way.

My apartment is small but fits me perfectly: a long, slim railroad with tall ceilings, exposed brick walls, and broad oak-plank floors. The walls are decorated with *hanga* wood-block prints and some old hand-tinted photos of my Japanese relatives that I'd gotten from my aunt in Tokyo. Some of my furniture had belonged to them too: a lacquered chest of drawers inlaid with mother-of-pearl, a low table made from a slab of twisted ironwood, polished to a rich, knotty glow. Mixed with these were the things from Grampa Little's side. A scarred wood-and-enamel kitchen sideboard from the farm. Grammy's pink double-globe lamps with their hand-painted flowers and the lace table runners that her mother crocheted. An old love seat and a couple of milking stools from the farm that Grampa couldn't bear to throw away, even though he hadn't used them for milking in several decades.

At the end of my week of reevaluation, I emerged and walked over to the office to announce my return. Souvenir exchange is a ritual glue in Japanese offices, and I'd bought shot glasses for the American researchers and refrigerator magnets for the Japanese staff. We were aiming for complete sets in both categories from all fifty states. The shot glasses said "Indiana—The Hoosier State," and the magnets had the slogan "Crossroads of America" emblazoned across the top and a cartoon of a baffled-looking Japanese tourist reading a crossroads sign with some of the more colorful Indiana town names—Brazil, Holland, Mexico, Peru, Alexandria, Delphi, Carthage, Gnaw Bone, Pinhook, Popcorn, and Santa Claus—written on rickety wooden arrows that pointed in all directions.

My desk was covered with mail, faxes, and Post-it phone messages. There were brochures from PR firms representing small-town tourist interests, faxes from film commissions, and a couple of messages from Suzie Flowers, which I tossed in the trash. She had been calling me regularly ever since the shoot. Kenji told her the program had been canceled, but she persisted, saying she wanted some of the footage even if the show hadn't aired. I felt bad, but it was Kenji's job to deal with her.

The two faxes that I was interested in were pinned to my bulletin board. One was from my mole at the Japanese Network and the other was from John Ueno. I read the mole's fax first.

----

7 July
Dear miss Takagi,
      Congratulations on your program of Indiana's
Bukowsky family that earned highest ratings for the time
slot in this season, penetrating more than 10,000,000
households, perhaps! Our Network producer is quite satisfy
and say please to continue good work on authentic
American family that only you can choose. But I warn you
please to beware of agency rep Mr. J. Ueno who is
exceedingly anger or so I have heard.
      Sincerely,
      Tashiro
P.S. if you like to know why is J. Ueno exceedingly anger it
is because of your show causing all of the lams to sell out
of butcher stores in Tokyo on Saturday afternoon, which

became so famous story as to be highlight on national evening news! Maybe this is very funny for you but not good for American sponsor and especially Mr. J. Ueno!

The second fax read:

----

10 July
Dear Ms. Jane Takagi,

This is to inform you of your grave flaw in last program of *My American Wife!*, which is the Mrs. Bukowsky program, and that is the LAMB. You must never put LAMB into the program of *My American Wife!* ever because LAMB come mostly from Australia, which is not good for program sponsor of BEEF-EX since it is unAmerican. Do you understand? I must say very severely to you even though this is a needless to say thing. TV program depend on sponsor. It is business. Please do not do again. I hope you will understand my meaning.

Sincerely,

Joichi Ueno

"It's your gig, primarily. You can handle it as you like. But I'd watch it if I were you. . . ."

Kenji had a habit of sneaking up behind you on his soft Italian soles. I knew he had read the faxes and posted them on the board. He watched my reaction, then added:

"Kato called."

Kato was a man of vision who could see beyond the

196

narrow promotional concerns of sponsors and could imagine programming that was truly unique yet served the needs of the market.

"What did he say?"

"'Congratulations. Don't do it again.' He told me to keep an eye on you."

Kenji's position was complex, I knew, as the despised and lowly courtier, exiled from the capital of Tokyo to the island of Manhattan, U.S.A. On one hand I think he genuinely liked me and wanted to support me. On the other, he wanted me to fall on my face so he could take over directing and get to go to exotic parts of America, where he could take photographs with his antique Leica and eventually get himself noticed and recalled to the capital. And maybe find a wife. I understood his ambivalence and was accordingly a bit wary.

"Great, so now you spy for the enemy."

"*Baka na koto*—don't be an idiot. Here. This call just came in." He handed me a pink telephone message slip.

It was from the Indiana State Film Office. The number on it was Sloan's.

I turned my back on Kenji and dialed.

"BEEF-EX is paying your rent," Kenji continued. "And mine too. So don't get all *auteur* on me, Takagi. It's just too boring."

"Screw you, Kenji," I said as he walked out the door. I mean, I was happy about the ratings. It wasn't an Emmy, and eight o'clock on Saturday morning wasn't the greatest slot in the world, but still I wanted to celebrate a little or at least have someone to commiserate with. I was annoyed that everyone was getting so bent about some dumb lamb chops, when obviously it was the *story* that counted. Then Sloan answered the phone, and as soon as I heard his voice my heart was in my throat, and suddenly I remembered that nothing was simple anymore. But he sounded really glad to hear from me, and the blood was pounding in my face, and by then it was too late to change my mind, so I invited him to New York and told him I'd pick him up at La Guardia.

Sloan sauntered off the plane carrying a brown paper bag with two bottles of champagne that he'd asked the stewardess to chill in the first-class kitchen, and he looked great, a long-limbed, languid musician. I had intended to bring him home, but at the last minute I changed my mind. There was nothing wrong with my apartment. I was actually quite proud of it, newly cleaned and gleaming. But at the last moment I had a total crisis of the imagination—I just couldn't picture him superimposed on all my ancestors' photos and pieces of my family history as I told him I was pregnant with his child. It was far too cozy, too personal. I was scared.

Then it occurred to me all of a sudden that maybe I loved him precisely because he was *not* part of my life, and what turned me on about our relationship was its anonymity. Until Fly, anyway, it had been as neutral, sanitized, and comforting as a plastic ice bucket and a well-stocked minibar. And if I couldn't have more, I certainly didn't want less. I flagged a gypsy limousine at La Guardia and we drove across the George Washington Bridge to the Palisades Motor Lodge, just over the New Jersey border. I imagine Sloan was relieved. He liked these semipublic spaces, rooms just recently vacated and still redolent of someone else's miseries, spurts of joy, and jaw-cracking ennui. We spent the weekend tangled in the polyester sheets, celebrating the mouthwatering diversity of meats, and then he took a cab back to the airport. I didn't tell him about the pregnancy. I figured it could wait until I'd seen the doctors, had the ultrasound, had more information.

When I got back to my apartment, I reread Ueno's fax. Of course he had never mentioned the ratings. That was fine with me. But the reprimand pissed me off, as did his attempt to curtail my freedom as a documentarian. I understood that he had to answer to his superiors at the agency, and ultimately to his American clients, and that my programming was undermining his credibility with BEEF-EX. But I chose to ignore this understanding, as I would ignore the new censorship he imposed. I couldn't help it. "Beef is Best." Hah. He was base. His wanton capitalist mandate had nothing to do with my vocation.

Thinking back now, I wonder that my rage was so misdirected. The real targets were closer to home: Ma, for her credulous nature, for taking a drug that deformed me; Sloan, for impregnating me so casually and wanting so little from me; and me, for wanting so much more and yet not even able to tell him I was pregnant. Ueno was a distraction. I plunged furiously back into work again, hounding the researchers for a new American Wife. I wanted to make a real statement with my next program, really teach Ueno a lesson. I didn't want to think about Sloan. I didn't want to think about the baby, a small bean by now, clinging by a slender root hair to such insubstantial soil. If I had paid more attention, things might have turned out differently. But I was like Shōnagon's archer, standing there with my trembling bow, unable to launch the arrow, yet aware somehow that when I did, it would go off in the wrong direction entirely.

THE LEAF MONTH

SHŌNAGON

Things That Give a Pathetic Impression

The voice of someone who blows his nose while he is speaking.

The expression of a woman plucking her eyebrows.

AKIKO

Prick. Prick.
My blood
lips lick
dew drop
dew drop
pretty ruby red.

The air in the bathroom was thick and humid. Akiko could smell her fertility whenever she peed or even spread her legs. She'd stopped wearing skirts because of this, afraid John would notice. For a while after the incident with the lamb chops, when Akiko fell into the television, John stayed away at night, sleeping in town at a capsule hotel. When he returned he seemed to have forgotten all about the incident. Now he was sleeping in the futon next to hers, but he still hadn't touched her.

"Still nothing?" he asked.

"No."

"Tell me when," he said, rolling away from her. "Just tell me when it starts. Otherwise there's no point."

She was lying to him, of course. She'd menstruated twice since the lamb chops, and she took great care to wrap up her soiled pads, tuck them into the waistline of her trousers under her shirt, then smuggle them out of the bathroom and into the deep pockets of her winter coat, which hung in the closet. She collected them there, and first thing in the morning, after John left for work, she wrapped them in a plastic bag and took them downstairs to the large cement trash can near the playground. She had never learned to use flushable, internal methods of sanitary protection. Never felt comfortable sticking things up there.

> Slash, slash,
> my pretty
> gash.
> Run,
> river run,
> so ruby
> ruby red.

One day, chopping green onions to garnish the miso soup, she cut herself on the fleshy part of her forefinger. The cut was deep, and she stood there for a long time, bouncing her hip against the kitchen counter, watching the blood infuse the pale walls of flesh, collect in the crevice, then swell up over the edge as she squeezed the wound open and shut. She had stopped writing articles on "Complications Need Not Be Complex," "Breast Pumps: It's the Fit That Counts," and "Yes, You're a Mother, But Don't Forget You're a Wife." Now she was writing only lists and poetry. Not good poetry, perhaps, but exciting poetry, words she'd never dared write down before. And ever since the lamb chops, she had stopped purging. The animal stayed down. She felt it, rutting and brooding in her darkness, exuding its fecundity from time to time and fueling her imagination. This excitement coexisted with the dread that John would discover her new secret. The two emotions followed each other with such regularity that they seemed to have blended into a continuum, the two halves of her thumping heart.

TWO SCENES

1.

Lara and Dyann stood side by side on the small lawn in front of their split-level ranch house in Northampton, Massachusetts. They were nervous, laughing and bumping softly into each other for support. From time to time the backs of their hands brushed and their fingers entwined for a brief squeeze before releasing, quickly, well-trained in circumspection. Oh stood in front of them, holding up a sheet of white paper, while Suzuki set the white balance on the Betacam. When they were ready, I stood next to Suzuki, asked him to roll, focused the women's attention on the camera, then counted down their cue for action.

"Hi, I'm Lara," said Lara, with a straight face and a rigid smile, ". . . and this is my wife, Dyann."

"I'm Dyann," said Dyann, starting to snicker, ". . . and this is my wife, Lara."

"Today we'd like to give new meaning to *My American Wife!*" They burst out laughing, and we cut. The line was dumb, but the translation into Japanese would be just fine. Suzuki was beaming. He liked the lesbians a lot.

Maybe America had radicalized him, but it was Suzuki who convinced me that it would be fine to put lesbians on the show. There was nothing unwholesome about their lifestyle, he argued. The women were pillars of their community: one was a district attorney, the other a well-published author; their tiny children were unusually smart and cute; and they were exemplary mothers, both of them. If I was serious about wanting to use *My American Wife!* as a platform to further international understanding, he urged, then why not do a show about alternative lifestyles, something that was not often tolerated in Japan. He was right, but I was nervous. It had seemed like a good idea at the time, with the added benefit of twisting Ueno's knickers, but one small hitch had come up— the women were vegetarians. Lara and Dyann suggested Pasta Primavera for the Recipe of the Day, yet even with a scene of the sweet babies in the garden picking plump and luscious vegetables, I didn't think I would get away with this. I mean, lamb was one thing, and lesbians were another, but vegetarian lesbians were something else entirely.

2.

The two women sat on the couch. On the coffee table sat a gilded turkey baster, mounted like an obelisk on a small square marble base. Suzuki had just finished shooting a family por-trait—Lara and Dyann on either side, sandwiching the two little girls, who held the baster proudly in front of them like a pet or a trophy they'd won. Now the girls were playing with Oh. They had made animal eyes and ears and stuck them on the fuzzy wind sock that covered his boom mike, and Oh was using it to nuzzle their faces. Suzuki nodded that he was ready to start, and the girls settled down on my lap to watch.

Dyann: We shopped for the sperm together, you know, tried to find donors who matched each other.
Lara: Dyann wanted to give birth first, and it was easy to find a match for me ... more or less generic white, Eastern European peasant stock, you know.
Dyann: A gorgeous blonde, with blue eyes ...
Lara: Without my cataracts, however ...
Dyann: Interested in computer programming. . . .

Lara: That part was easy. Most of the donors were computer programmers.

Dyann: Now, *that* truly frightened us. . . .

Lara: But for Dyann it was difficult because she's black, and what we didn't know is that there just isn't a big market for black sperm.

Dyann: Yeah, apparently black men don't have a lot of problems with potency . . .

Lara: Or maybe it's that only whites are obsessed with their progeny . . .

Dyann: Or have the cash to buy it if they ain't got it.

Lara: So it took us quite a while to find a bank that had more than one black donor, but finally we found one in California that had a match for Dyann.

Dyann: He ain't no computer programmer, old Mr. 0579. He's a writer, just like me, jerking off, you know, only he gets the option of doing it with his dick into a bottle for money. I do it with a pen on paper and get paid shit. . . . Now, who's the smarter father? I ask you.

Lara: Dyann, don't be silly. . . .

Dyann rolled her eyes at us and pursed her lips in a prim imitation of Lara, who caught her at it, reached over, and punched her tenderly in the arm. The two little girls, seeing the potential for a tumble, squirmed in my lap, and I set them on their feet and pushed them forward. They didn't need any encouragement. They careened across the room and hurled themselves into the thick of it. Suzuki snatched the camera off the tripod head and followed them. Oh brandished the fuzzy boom-pole animal and made the little girls squeal.

Again, I felt the warm smugness that comes over me when I know that there is another heart-wrenching documentary moment at hand, being exquisitely recorded.

EDITING ROOM

Truth lies in layers, each of them thin and barely opaque, like skin, resisting the tug to be told. As a documentarian, I think about this a lot. In the edit, timing is everything. There is a time to peel back.

I was not always so cavalier with my wives as I sometimes sound. To some extent that pretense was necessary in order to keep up with our production schedule and get the programs out. But the fact is, I did care, and at the same time I couldn't afford to care, and these two contrary states lived side by side like twins, wrapped in a numbing cocoon that enabled me to get the work done. Psychiatrists call this "doubling."

Here's another example: I wanted to make programs with documentary integrity, and at first I believed in a truth that existed—singular, empirical, absolute. But slowly, as my skills improved and I learned about editing and camera angles and the effect that music can have on meaning, I realized that truth was like race and could be measured only in ever-diminishing approximations. Still, as a documentarian, you must strive for the truth and believe in it wholeheartedly.

Halved as I am, I was born doubled. By the time I wrote the pitch for *My American Wife!* my talent for speaking out of both sides of my mouth was already honed. On one hand I really did believe that you could use wives to sell meat in the service of a greater Truth. On the other hand, I was broke after my divorce and desperate for a job.

Suzie Flowers. Miss Helen Dawes. Certain women stuck to me, flickering around the edges of thought. In the dim, inchoate hours of the morning, when I woke up to pee, they'd insinuate themselves like tapered ghosts into my sleep-addled

210

brain. Once there, they worked like ammonia, delivering a jolt of clearheaded dread. My skin prickled, my pores leached sweat. In Japan, ghosts have no legs. Often they are wronged women who are not even dead yet, whose extremity of suffering forces the spirit from the body to torment their oppressors. Living ghosts. Neither here nor there. They are well documented in the works of Heian women, but they had exorcists to deal with them.

I can defend myself; that's not the problem. Miss Helen was not my fault. As things go, she barely counts as a casualty at all. But the fact is that I forced my way into her life, overcame her reservations, and I will never forget her wistful acquiescence when I called to cancel the shoot. And it wasn't my fault, either, that Suzie Flowers' pipe-fitting husband was bonking the cocktail waitress. It was her life and I had no part in its making. Still, the worn fabric of her life tore like tissue under the harsh exposure of my camera; I watched it happen, took aim, exposed her, then shot her in the heart.

A crack in consciousness is a dangerous thing. The slightest tremor can turn it into a gaping abyss. There was something else lurking in the darkened corners, some fact trying to come to light, and when it did, I was in the editing room, finishing the Lesbian Show, cleaning up Dyann's sound. The program was uplifting, a powerful affirmation of difference, of race and gender and the many faces of motherhood, and I was filled with a moral certitude that would sustain me through the fight I knew would ensue when Ueno found out that I'd gone and shot a biracial vegetarian lesbian couple. Then suddenly it occurred to me—I never got around to telling Lara and Dyann about the program sponsor. I never told them about BEEF-EX.

Lara and Dyann were vegetarians for political reasons. I didn't know this at first, but I'd suspected as much, then I'd learned it for sure during the cooking scene.

"Are there a lot of vegetarians in Japan?" Lara had asked, as she washed the parsley.

Suzuki was filming Dyann chopping garlic on the other side of the kitchen, so I answered in a whisper. "No, not so many, really. The traditional Japanese diet has more fish than meat." But Dyann heard and joined in.

"Yeah, well, that's a good thing," she said. "You know, we're vegetarians by default. I mean, we like meat, like the taste of it, but we would just never eat it the way it's produced here in America. It's unhealthy. Not to mention corrupt, inhumane, and out of control, you know?"

"Uh, Dyann, Suzuki's filming you and we need you just to chop, you know, and not talk, just for now. . . ."

"Oh, sorry."

But Lara continued. "When we were trying to get pregnant, it was amazing what we found out. Do you know that sperm counts have dropped by about fifty percent in the past fifty years? That's just one report, but a lot of scientists think there's something to it. They think it's related to the increase of hormones used in industry, especially in meat production. So we just figure, with the babies, you know, why risk it? I mean, you are what you eat, right?"

Dyann couldn't resist. She looked straight into the camera and, using a nearby parsnip as a mike, smiled like a TV announcer. "Recent studies show that today the average man produces fewer morphologically normal sperm than your average hamster."

"Uh, Suzuki, could you cut, please. . . ."

It was an insignificant exchange, suppressed in the chaos of the moment and easily edited out. But recalling it in the editing room, I knew for certain that they would never consent to their image being used to advertise meat.

There was nothing I could do. No possible way to shoot another program in time to meet the broadcast deadline. I'd pushed the schedule to the very limits because I didn't want Ueno to have a choice about airing this one. I wanted to force his hand.

If I told them, they would probably refuse to let it air, and I wouldn't have a show to deliver to the network and would lose my job. I would probably lose my job in any case, for broadcasting vegetarian lesbians. I couldn't imagine Ueno letting this go unpunished.

Why hadn't I realized? If I'd just dealt with it earlier, I could have talked them into agreeing, as a subversive political statement or something. But it was too late now.

Too late . . .

My heart sank.

My ghosts.

My baby.

Sloan still didn't know.

I hadn't dealt with this at all.

But then again, why bother? Why make a big deal about it when the problem would surely go away by itself? Although the ultrasound had been fine, and so were the tissue tests, my uterus and my life were obviously too unstable to support a child. The fetus would realize that its mooring was defective and just quietly slip away. A little nut, like a cashew, with translucent, threadlike limbs. Smaller than my thumb. No color yet, really. I'd never thought it would last this long. Nine weeks? Ten? Sloan didn't need to know. It was just a matter of time.

Dyann and Lara had signed the releases. I could send them a "white mother" copy of the show, before the titles or commercials were inserted, and they would never need to know anything about BEEF-EX.

The program was a good one, really solid, moving, the best I'd made. It could even effect social change.

And so I continued, taking out the stutters and catches from the women's voices, creating a seamless flow in a reality that was no longer theirs and not quite so real anymore.

FAXES

Dear Miss Takagi,

I regret to inform you that your program of vegetarian lesbians is unacceptable to Mr. J. Ueno who insist that you must resign from director of *My American Wife!* ever again. Your program will not be aired and our company must suffer grave humiliation of admitting failure to provide fresh program to Network and must air old rerun program in the slot.

Sincerely yours,
Mariko Nakano
(for Mr. J. Ueno)
cc. Mr. S. Kato

Takagi,

How stupid to think of putting lesbians on Saturday morning family television! This is not late night TV, you know! You have acted like selfish American, not thinking of your company, which will be disgrace if this show cannot air. Mr. Ueno is trying to stop show but I have sent it to network and hope that they will say O.K. to airing.

If show will not be allowed, you must be fired, I am afraid. I cannot save you. I will inform you of final decision, but I suggest you to write the letter of apology to Mr. J. Ueno nevertheless. I trusted you. Now I am sadly disappointed.

   S. Kato

AKIKO

The black woman sits on the couch, watching the white woman next to her. The white woman is nuzzling and calming the two coffee-colored little girls, fixing the bright ribbons in their soft brown ringlets, tucking their striped jerseys back into their denim overalls. The little girls squirm and dance. Pensively, the black woman starts to speak.

"Even when I was very, very small I knew I never wanted to be with a man, you know?"

Slowly, slowly, as she speaks, the camera moves toward her face. Her voice is tentative and thick.

"Never wanted a man, never wanted to get married to a man or have his children. I knew it when I was as little as these babies are here."

The little girls glance up, eyes bright from the tussle, breath rapid with the possibility of more. The white woman smiles at them and shakes her head.

"And there was something else I knew for certain."

The camera holds steady on the black woman's face. She falters, her voice cracks, and she frowns with concentration to control it.

"The one thing I wanted, *ever* wanted, was to have a woman to love and to make a family with. Even I thought that was crazy, let me tell you—impossible, loco . . . but look." The tears well up in her eyes.

"I got it all. Here they are. . . ."

Wonder underscores her words, belies her ferocity. She scowls through filmy tears at the white woman, who reaches over and gently touches her cheek. The two little girls throw their arms around her, kiss her, and she gives in to it all and starts to laugh. The *My American Wife!* theme song swells, a wave of sound that washes over them, confirming their joy with closure and sealing it with a commercial break.

Akiko stared at the television screen as a thick red streak hit a griddle with a splat, followed by a deafening sizzle.

She was kneeling on a cushion, hugging herself, rocking slowly back and forth. She stopped and saw that her hands were shaking, so she put them on the edge of the *kotatsu* to steady them. Then she noticed that she was crying. She was not sure why. Possibly it was fear of John's mood when he came home. It would not be good, she was afraid. From what she knew of his tastes in programming, she sensed that it might be wise to throw away the recipe for Pasta Primavera right away and perhaps serve a Beefy Burrito instead.

But it was not just fear of his anger or even of getting hit. As she watched the sun set on the vast American landscape— "Beefland!" the logo proclaimed—she realized that her tears had nothing whatsoever to do with John. These were tears of admiration for the strong women so determined to have their family against all odds. And tears of pity for herself, for the trepidation she felt in place of desire and for the pale, wan sentiment that she let pass for love.

Akiko buttoned her coat in the *genkan* and let herself out. The hollow metal door echoed behind her. Yes, and there was something else as well. Something that the black woman had said, which resonated in her. Something about impossibility and desire, or lack of it. It was a new thought, slow in coming, but by the time Akiko had walked down twelve flights of stairs to the playground, passing the mothers on her way, it hung in front of her, tentative but with its parts fully formed: She wanted a child; she'd never wanted John; once she became pregnant, she wouldn't need him ever again.

At the neighborhood butcher's shop, she splurged and bought two fat sirloin steaks, some potatoes instead of rice, to bake with butter, some tender tips of asparagus. For dessert she chose a muskmelon, bursting with sweet juice and seeds. Or so she hoped. That was the problem with melons, she thought. You never knew what they were like inside.

MORE FAXES

Dear Takagi,

Well, you are very lucky this time. I just got a call from your mole, Tashiro, at the Network, and the show passed and aired. The network producer wasn't even aware of the storm that was brewing, and he said he found it "humane and moving," however the word on the street is that what really appealed to him was the novelty and shock value of putting lesbians on Saturday morning. Anyway, Kato is still very annoyed with you and he says that if you want your job, you are to write that letter of apology to Ueno and obey whatever conditions he places on program content in the future. Obey being the operant word, here. Got it?

    Cheers,

      Kenji

Dear Mr. Ueno,

Please accept my most humble apologies for making yet another program that violated the mandate of BEEF-EX while receiving, yet again, some of the highest ratings of the season.

Please allow me to continue directing *My American Wife!* Although my programs have been full of mistakes, I really think I am getting the hang of it now. With your patience and your wise guidance, I am confident that I will be able to make programs that will convince every housewife in Japan to buy BEEF-EX for her family's next dinner.

Sincerely yours,

Jane Takagi-Little

Dear Miss Takagi,

Please be advised that Mr. J. Ueno has receive your humble apologies and reluctantly agree to give one more chance to you providing that you make next programs only about normal people and regarding the appropriate topic of meats.

Please tell what is next program idea as soon as possible, since from now on you must tell every details about your program before shooting. You may not make a program before you get approval from him first.

He additionally say that you should feel shame for teaching unwholesome ways to young Japanese people.

Sincerely yours,

M. Nakano

(for Mr. J. Ueno)

cc. Mr. S. Kato

Dear Mr. Ueno:

Thank you so much for this chance to redeem myself. From now on I will only make wholesome programs about beef and normal people. Accordingly, I would like to propose a certain Mrs. Payne from Peerless, Montana, who has written a cookbook called "Best O'Beef" that includes the following:

BEEF FUDGE

2 cups white sugar	1/2 cup ground roast beef
1 cup brown sugar	3 tablespoons butter
1/2 cup white corn syrup	2 oz. unsweetened chocolate
1/2 cup milk	1/2 cup chopped walnuts
1 teaspoon vanilla	

Cook all ingredients together without stirring in a heavy pot to 238° F. Remove from stove and cool to room temperature. Add vanilla and walnuts. Beat until thick. Pour into greased baking dish, chill, and cut as for fudge.

Doesn't this sound delicious?
    Sincerely,
        J. Takagi-Little

AKIKO

Meats are no longer enough, thought Akiko. However unique and well prepared they might be. She'd outdone herself these past few evenings, even taken out some of the Japanese meat cookbooks John had bought her a year earlier, thinking that a more refined approach to meat preparation might be more to his liking. New England Pot Roast smothered with tender baby vegetables. Delicate mignon with a rich sesame-pepper sauce. Steak marinated in sake and lightly broiled, crisp on the edges and pink inside, with a delicate dipping sauce of *yuzu* citrus and ginger. But all for nothing. John simply hadn't noticed the attention she'd been paying to his appetites. It was time, she felt, to try something new.

Ever since the show with the lesbians, he had become withdrawn and silent, or drunk and gregarious, but always a nervous rage simmered right below the surface. His complexion had turned sallow, and he was losing weight. Akiko, on the other hand, had color in her cheeks, and her hipbones were once again integrated into the line of her figure. She noticed these things in the mirror, that she sort of had a figure again, that she'd lost the dark hollows under her eyes. Her mind dodged the thin white scar above her eyebrow. On the whole, looking at her body didn't frighten her as much anymore, now that her bones were more covered up. Still, she thought critically, craning around to inspect her buttocks, she had a ways to go. The sides were not so concave anymore, but they were not round and plump, either. Not enticing.

On the way home from the market, she passed the vending machines near the train tracks where she first bought condoms. She hadn't bought condoms for two years, not since John decided it was time for them to have a baby. The machines looked much the same, except that now, in addition to the condoms, magazines, and batteries, there was a fourth machine, which sold sports drinks. Poccari Sweat. She stopped in front of the magazine machine, then stepped closer and peeked behind the foil. The women looked the same too: high school girls in their sailor middies, airline stewardesses, office ladies neat in polyester blouses and fake pearls. And the nuns. Akiko surveyed the women available, trying to see what was hidden under the foil. She had Bobby Joe plugged into her ears and felt quite bold. He was singing "Backwoods Preacher Man," and she didn't care which of the neighbors came by and saw her standing there, even in broad daylight. She pondered her choices. She was going to take her time.

The nuns were out of the question, although she suspected that in disposition she might in fact resemble them most. The high school girls were too young and silly, and the steward-esses would require a uniform. There were S-M women too, bound and gagged, but their mute pain scared her and she didn't even consider them, barely even saw them, in fact. That left the office ladies. She had sort of been an OL once, and she still had the clothes, although most of them would be too large for her now. She fed six one-hundred-yen coins into the slot and pulled the knob for the *All Nudo OL Special!* The magazine slid from the slot and she retrieved it, tucking it discreetly into her grocery sack, around the scallions.

At home she took the magazine into the bathroom. She drained the old water from the previous week out of the bathtub, washed the tub carefully, then filled it again. It was early in the day for a bath, but it was part of the program that she'd studied in a women's magazine: "12 Steps to a Sexy Feeling." Step One was a hot bath to relax you, but you had to use brand-new fresh water and special-smelling spa salts. She'd acquired an assortment of these last week from the department store. When the tub was full and the water hot, she slipped in. She closed her eyes and tried to empty her mind of all her daily concerns, tried to be fully aware of the warmth of the water against her skin like the caress of a lover, tried to concentrate on her own sexy feeling. It was difficult. She opened her eyes again and decided to take a breather. She put some water on her face, then sat in the deep tub with her arms wrapped around her knees, rocking gently so the warm, scented water lapped her shoulders. The bathroom was pleasant, and the cedar drainboards on the floor gave off a nice smell when they were wet. The sun shone through the lace curtains, which fluttered in the breeze from the open window. The breeze felt good on her face too, fresh, brushing away the warm steam. It was nice to take baths in the afternoon sunlight, Akiko thought. Not so sexy, maybe, but pretty and bright.

She remembered the magazine. She propped it on the edge of the tub and started to flip through, looking at the pictures. The OL were quite young, maybe just out of college. Ten girls were featured, and each one had a little story and several pictures with different poses. The stories were very authentic and told what company the girl worked for, when she had started working, and what her main office duties were. Then it told about her hobbies and what kind of boyfriend she liked and what she liked to do with him on the weekends. The first picture looked like a normal snapshot of the girl at work, sitting at her desk, or taking dictation from her boss, or answering the phone. But as you turned the pages, the poses got more and more risqué. Sometimes the girl was sitting on her desk instead of behind it. Then she was unbuttoning her blouse and taking off her brassiere. Her skirt was pushed up high around her thighs. She looked straight at you, like you were the man she was undressing for. It was disturbing, but at the same time Akiko was intrigued.

The girl was coy, reluctant to show you her breasts at first, and she kept her hands cupped over them, which sort of pushed them up and made them look bigger on top. Akiko stood the magazine on the faucet, against the taps, and tried this. It sort of worked, although her breasts were somewhat smaller than the girl's. Still, it made a nice little swelling.

In the next picture, the girl had dropped her hands. Her nipples were soft and pink and perfectly round. They were cute, like tiny lips, pursed for a kiss. Her eyes were downcast— she was too shy to look directly at you—and her long black hair curtained her blushing cheeks. By the next picture, though, she'd gotten over her embarrassment: she reclined back on the desk, legs spread, papers pushed onto the floor. She was wearing only a garter belt and panties, and one hand was pinching her nipple and making it erect, while the other hand tugged at the front of her panties, bunching the fabric together to make it narrow, so that it sort of fit up in between. She didn't have any hair down there at all. Her head was tilted back and her eyes were closed, but she kept her mouth open a little, biting her bottom lip. In the next picture she was on her knees on the desk, with her bottom looming up in the air, toward the camera. Her breasts hung down in front, and she was twisting her body to look back over her shoulder. She had reached one hand up from below, to cup herself between the legs. Her fingernails were long and manicured and looked dangerous, like they would hurt if she weren't careful. Looking at the fingernails, Akiko suspected this wasn't a real office lady at all. How could she type?

After her bath, Akiko stood with her back to the mirror, wearing a lace garter belt and pearly white nylon stockings that she'd gotten from the lingerie boutique at the Ginza. She pushed her bottom out to make it look bigger. She reached down and touched herself between her legs with her finger, checking the girl in the picture for reference. The girl stared boldly at her. Akiko stared back, moving her finger around a little. She liked looking at the pictures. Even though they weren't so authentic, she found them sexy—but she was not sure whether she wanted to make love to the girl or simply to be her.

JANE

I called Sloan collect from the town jail.

"Well, it's one of those good news/bad news situations. . . . Yeah, well, I'm in Montana. . . . No, that's fine, because you're not invited. I don't think you'd particularly like it here. . . . It's a long story. I'm in jail. I'll tell you about it sometime. . . . No, thanks. Kenji's wiring bail.

"Anyway, that's the good news. The bad news is—well, you remember that time in Fly, Oregon? Yeah, well, I didn't think it could happen, but I'm pregnant. . . . I know. I thought I was sterile too, believe me. . . . I know. . . . I know. . . . I know. . . . Well, I am sorry too, for what that's worth. Far sorrier than you . . .

"Yeah, well, that seems like the only sensible thing to do, right? I mean, I can't really see us raising a kid in a Motel 6. . . . Yeah, well, I thought you'd agree. . . . Also, I guess, I think we should kind of take a break, not see each other. . . . Fine. And the last thing is the cost. I'll send you a bill for your half. . . .

"Okay. Well, bye. . . ."

I had access to a pay phone and time on my hands—jail was the perfect opportunity to take care of some of those nagging things that I'd been putting off, didn't want to deal with, didn't want to think about, even.

There had been this small confusion with a freight train, but I really blamed our predicament on Gulf War fever, which still held the country in its grip and made everyone see ghosts. We had been standing by the railroad tracks, shooting scenery in a remote part of Montana, when the train went by. Spotting us, the engineer radioed the dispatcher and reported our coordinates, describing us, somewhat hysterically, as a band of Mexican terrorists with a rocket launcher—a logical mistake: He'd never seen a Betacam on a tripod. The dispatcher called the sheriff, who brought a posse to arrest us.

"Mexican?" I asked as he confiscated the Betacam. "Mexican *terrorists?*"

"Aw," said the sheriff, "y'know . . . engineer prob'ly just got the news confused with some old TV western."

At the police station, I convinced him the Betacam wasn't loaded with anything more incendiary than Mrs. Payne from Peerless—a normal American carnivore—and her Blazing Steak on a Plank. Well, maybe she wasn't so normal—she did make the Beef Fudge for dessert.

Anyway, by the time I got hold of Kenji, the sheriff had dropped the conspiracy charges. The trespassing was still under negotiation. We were waiting for the bail money to arrive.

The jail was small and clean, just a couple of cells at the back of the renovated police station. I had one of them to myself for two nights, and like an unscheduled stopover at an unfamiliar airport, it gave me time to think—an activity I'd been carefully avoiding.

When I first learned I was pregnant, I just assumed I would abort, either spontaneously or deliberately. Then, after the ultrasound, there were those suspended weeks when I was working with Lara and Dyann and just couldn't think about the pregnancy at all. The fetus was there, growing, but I had been unable to act, to make the call, to terminate. Now I had reached the twelve-week mark and was pushing the deadline for a safe abortion.

If the impregnation had paralyzed my will, it had also quickened my emotions, but I failed to kindle a like response in Sloan's lackadaisical heart. After New Jersey, I had waited for him to call. I phoned him once, maybe twice, but he was always busy on his cellular phone, driving in and out of roam. And eventually I got the message. Sloan was making it abundantly clear that a loopy, random orbit was all he could sustain. It became more and more difficult to tell him about the pregnancy.

Why couldn't I tell him? What was I afraid of? On an obvious level, I didn't want him to think I was one of those women who would get pregnant to entrap a man. But more than that, I knew he would want me to abort, and I just didn't want to hear him say the words "You'll have an abortion, of course . . . ," as though it was a foregone conclusion. So when he did say it, over the phone at the jail, it just confirmed how painfully little our relationship meant to him. But the odd thing was that I realized simultaneously and with shocking clarity that my pregnancy was no longer contingent upon him.

I had wanted a child so badly at one point in my life and that much desire is hard to erase. Maybe it was Dyann and Lara, and all their love and self-sufficient fertility. Or Gracie Beaudroux and her ever-growing brood. Or Miss Helen Dawes and her softball team of tall, strong girls. Even Mrs. Bukowsky, with only one crushed child of her own, and enough love to nurture the hundreds who showed up on her doorstep. All my American Wives and their brimming, child-filled lives had awakened my desire all over again. So by the time the sheriff released me and the boys, I was considering motherhood seriously enough to call it quits after only two shots of Jack Daniel's.

We were sitting at the hotel bar, celebrating our freedom and the dismissal of all the charges against us. The sheriff was a nice man after all and bought us all the first round of drinks. In halting Japanese he made a toast to us, a phrase he had learned from Suzuki in jail, along with the numbers from one to ten and the names of the most interesting parts of the human anatomy. Oh was cradling a tiny kitten, the offspring of the jail cat, who had given birth to a litter on Oh's sweatshirt, then abandoned this one as the runt. He'd adopted it, named it Butch, and fed it with an eyedropper that the sheriff's deputy brought from home. The sheriff told him he could keep it as a souvenir of Montana, and Oh was beaming and cooing like a proud mom. The bartender had gotten some heated milk for him from the kitchen, and now Oh was dipping his little finger in the milk and letting the kitten lick it off.

After watching Suzuki knock back a fourth shot, the sheriff went home for dinner with a warning not to celebrate too strenuously. But Suzuki was determined to make up for two nights on the wagon.

"Jane-chan, *nomé!*" he ordered, drunk as a monkey. "Drink! Drink!" Tennessee whiskey had made his blood boil and stained his face like a new bruise. He lifted his shot glass and drained it, summoned the bartender and ordered another round.

"*Kampai!*" he cried, picking up one of the brimming glasses that were aligned in front of me, untouched. "You are not keeping up!"

"Suzuki-san," I began, "*chotto, damé*—I can't drink. . . ."

"Can't drink!" He exploded with drunken laughter. "Don't make me laugh! Of course you can drink. You are a splendid

227

drinker! For a girl, no less! Most girls haven't got what it takes, but you! You are the finest—"

"Suzuki-san . . . *ninshin da yo*—I'm pregnant."

The news stopped him dead. He stared straight ahead, then slumped against the bar; his head thumped solidly on the counter.

"Suzuki-san?" I placed my hand on the back of his sweaty neck. "*Daijobu desu ka?* Are you okay?"

And then he surprised me. Straightening up again, he swiveled on his stool to face me, draped his arms around my neck, and pressed his shiny forehead against mine.

"Takagi-san," he announced, in slurred Japanese, "you will never have to worry about the child as long as I live. I will marry you tonight if you wish. Whatever you want, you must simply tell me and I will do it for you. If your baby needs a college education, I will work hard to provide one. You are my dear comrade, and I will always support you."

And with that, he slid off the barstool and fell to the floor.

There's a fairy tale about the first Japanese wanna-be astronaut, another drunken monkey, who saw the moon in a deep and quiet pond and bragged to his friend the badger that he could fly all the way there and bring back that moon in a bucket. He drowned in the attempt. I suspect it was the lunacy blooming in my face that galvanized Suzuki. His offers were sincere and I was touched. I got him back onto his barstool, thanked him warmly, and left him there, staring gloomily into the bottom of his glass.

The next morning we went to Cemetery Hill to shoot the panoramics of the town. It was one of those beautiful Montana mornings, when you wake up and walk outside and it hits you: Oh, right, this is why they call it Big Sky country. I mean, the sky is so big and so blue, you can't really think about anything else.

Cemetery Hill wasn't much of a hill at all, but it provided enough of a rise to simulate a vista. A chain gang was working at one end of the cemetery, weeding and tending the graves, though most of the men were just enjoying the weather, smoking and sitting on the headstones. These guys were from the penitentiary, where at one point the sheriff had threatened to send us. I recognized a deputy, who waved to us. After a brief discussion of my editorial needs, I left Suzuki to get the shots of the town. He tends to work better on his own, especially when he is hungover, which is most of the time.

Two white moths were chasing each other, and finally they locked together and tumbled out of the air, landing on the thick green grass of a grave, where they fluttered and mated, then came to rest. The small battered headstone read:

our
Belov'd daughter
Ann Wren
born March 10, 1848
died March 24, 1848

Ann Wren. It was a sweet, plain name. Her parents had given it to her, known her for two weeks, fourteen short days, before she slipped away from them—buried here, belov'd for eternity. I wandered on, moving from stone to stone, reading off the names of the early settlers and the dates of their lives and deaths: Nathan Field, 8 years old; Jasper Beckwith, 3 months; Elsa May Foster, 2 years.

So many children.

There were adults buried here too.

But the tiny, crooked headstones were the ones that drew me.

Then suddenly it came to me, why I was here.

Whispering the beautiful names of these dead pioneer children, I was testing them for sound, invoking their identities, trying them on the nascent son or daughter who had settled inside me. It was unreal. *Name is very first thing. Name is face to all the world.*

But you shopping for one in graveyard?

I could hear Ma's horror and it made me smile. One thing was finally clear—I wanted my baby.

AKIKO

The loose bow at the collar of Akiko's silky white blouse looked like moth wings, glowing in the flickering candlelight. She sat primly at the *kotatsu* next to John, like an OL or a hostess at a bar, adding ice cubes to his glass. As she leaned forward with the whiskey bottle to pour a drink, the loopy wings closed, and as she sat back, they softly opened again.

John was big and bombastic, and his face was maroon. He grabbed the bottle of Suntory Old from her hand and poured a huge swig into her glass.

"Drink," he slurred. "Drink up. It's good to see you having fun. I like having a wife I can drink with."

Around her neck she wore a choker of pearls, and a pearl-studded barrette held up her hair on one side. Tucked about her knees was a straight, rose-colored skirt. Underneath it was the garter belt. Just before dinner she turned off the overhead fluorescent light and lit the two candles, which she placed on the *kotatsu*.

She had intended to tell John about her periods right after dinner, but it was so hard to bring up such topics of conversation. So then she thought perhaps a little whiskey would make it easier, but even after several drinks, she hadn't spoken. The candles had burned down and the wax was hardening onto the tabletop. Still hopeful, she was reluctant to break the mood to clean it up.

John was recounting the successes of the BEEF-EX campaign, all due to his skillful handling of the American sponsors. This was a good sign, thought Akiko. He seemed to have forgotten her lack of enthusiasm for some of the programs.

"They liked the Thayer Show very much," he told her. "So it's very fortunate I made that trip to Memphis to intervene, don't you think? They would never have stood for that black family. And so far I've managed to keep the Lesbian Show from them. The Wyoming Show was a success. . . ." He sighed and drank another shot of whiskey. "All you see is the finished programs," he told her, suddenly morose. "You cannot possibly imagine what I have to go through to keep the sponsors happy."

She leaned forward expectantly, but he fell silent, elbows on the table, head in his hands. Perhaps she should ask him a question, Akiko thought.

"What is wrong with them?" she ventured. "The sponsors are American. Don't the Americans find their programs interesting?"

John snorted. "BEEF-EX is just a bunch of cowboys pretending to be international traders. They don't know the first thing about television. And neither does the New York staff, for that matter."

"Is the staff not competent? Don't they do as you say?"

John laughed out loud. "Do as I say? Hah. Not that stupid woman. She goes out of her way to do the opposite. She makes a point of it." His voice was getting louder, and his face glowed. "She knows nothing of loyalty or obedience. All she thinks of is herself. Lesbians on Saturday morning! It's disgusting. I mean, *families* are watching! No proper Japanese person would enjoy a program like that!"

John slammed his palm on the table to emphasize his dissatisfaction. Akiko knew she should change the subject, but she couldn't help herself. She was too curious. "Is this Takagi-san?"

"Yes. Takagi . . . Last thing I heard, she managed to get herself and her whole crew thrown into jail! I wish they'd kept her there. Thrown away the key." He laughed and seemed very pleased with this, so Akiko laughed too.

"She must be quite a woman! I should think you'd like a woman with so much spunk."

"Spunk, hah! She must be a lesbian too." Then John looked at her, and his eyes narrowed. "Why did you say that, anyway? Are you jealous?"

"Oh, no." Akiko shook her head. "That's not what I meant at all. I only meant—"

"Well, you should be, you know. A proper wife would be very jealous, with all the traveling I do, to Austin, Texas, and places like that." He watched her. "Do you know what they have in Austin, Texas?"

Akiko looked down at her hands, folded in her lap. She had given herself a manicure this afternoon, but one of the nails had already started to chip. She shook her head.

"They have this big club you can go to for lap dancing. Do you know what lap dancing is?" He leered at her and then drained his glass. He stared sullenly at the melting ice at the bottom. "Forget it."

"No, please tell me. . . ."

"Forget it," he said. "You don't care. You don't care about sex. You are a cold, dead fish."

"No I'm not!" Akiko cried out. "Look at me! I'm not like that anymore." She stood up so he could see her skirt and blouse. John watched her, his face expressionless. As an afterthought, she spread her fingers in front of her so he could see her manicured nails. Then he grinned.

"*Kimi wa kawaii, ne,*" he grunted, patting her cushion on the floor with an amused, conciliatory nod. "You are cute. You look very nice."

Akiko knelt slowly back down. He was not acting at all interested. She wondered whether she should try doing something erotic. Maybe she should lift her skirt and show him the garter belt. He poured her a drink and pushed it across the table.

"Here, don't sulk. Drink up. I'm sorry I said that."

She caught hold of his hand and raised it to her mouth. Now what? She kissed his fingertips one by one and glanced up in what she hoped was a coy and provocative manner. He pulled his hand away, but she held fast, then she bit his little finger as hard as she could.

"Ow!" He gasped in pain, then he snatched his hand away from her and belted her across the face, knocking her sprawling.

"You fool," he snarled. "How dare you . . ."

Akiko lay on her side, holding her head, her skirt pulled up to reveal the top of her garter. John stared at her leg, then leaned over and yanked the skirt up farther. He frowned. Akiko watched him through the tangle of her hair. Her nose had started to run from his blow. She sniffled and wiped it as discreetly as she could on the back of her hand, hoping it wasn't blood. He crawled over and straddled her, rolling her onto her stomach and pulling down her panties. She heard him unzipping his fly and held her breath. She waited, her bottom in the air, for what seemed like a very long time, but nothing happened, so she twisted around a bit and peeked. He was kneeling above her, pulling violently at his limp penis. His eyes were closed and his face was deep red and sticky with sweat. He looked like a red-faced *oni*, she thought. Then he opened his eyes. She averted her face as quickly as she could, but it was too late. He'd seen her watching. Abruptly he stopped and put his penis away. He got slowly to his feet. He zipped up his fly and walked toward the *genkan*, then sat down heavily on the little step and put on his shoes.

Akiko rolled over and sat up quickly. Her head was throbbing. She pulled down her skirt and followed John and knelt just behind him. She placed her palm on the center of his broad back. His white shirt was wet with sweat, and his back was hot and humped.

"*Anata . . . ?*" she said. "Dear . . . ?"

His back started to shake. She left her hand sitting there until he turned and put his arms around her waist and buried his face in the front of her blouse.

"*Daijobu . . .*" She patted him gently. "It's all right. . . . It's all my fault. I'm sorry."

She held him, wiped her nose surreptitiously on the top of his head, and let him cry. When he quieted down, she took his shoes off and helped him to his feet. She walked him back into the apartment and undressed him and tucked him into bed.

"Next time," said John as he drifted off to sleep. "I promise you, next time it will stand right up. It will be all right."

It was the bite, she thought, arms folded, watching him snore. She shouldn't have bitten so hard. She didn't mean to. Her jaws just sort of snapped shut.

234

THE LONG MONTH

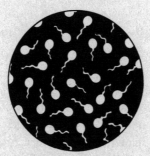

SHŌNAGON

Annoying Things

A woman is angry with her lover about some trifle and refuses to continue lying next to him. After fidgeting about in bed, she decides to get up. The man gently tries to draw her back, but she is still cross. "Very well then," he says, feeling that she has gone too far. "As you please." Full of resentment, he buries himself under his bedclothes and settles down for the night. It is a cold night, and since the woman is wearing only an unlined robe, she soon begins to feel uncomfortable. Everyone else in the house is asleep, and besides, it would be most unseemly for her to get up alone and walk about. As the night wears on, she lies there on her side of the bed, feeling very annoyed that the quarrel did not take place earlier in the evening, when it would have been easy to leave. Then she begins to hear strange sounds in the back of the house and outside. Frightened, she gently moves over in bed towards her lover, tugging at the bedclothes, whereupon he annoys her further by pretending to be asleep. "Why not be stand-offish a little longer?" he asks her finally.

JANE

FAX

TO: J. Takagi-Little
FROM: J. Ueno
DATE: September 1
RE: Wyoming

Dear Takagi-Little:

    It is good that you have corrected your way and are
showing proper respect for beef as sovereign of meats. The
Montana show is most original one and the Beef Fudge was
delicious. Please continue to make such quality programs
that BEEF-EX, the American sponsor of meat can feel pride.

    Sincerely,

       J. Ueno

P.S. Please do not forget that you must sending me ALL
ideas for next show so that I can make the right decision.

Ueno wants beef, and beef he shall have. Went to the library and found more books on the meat industry. The DES stuff was only the tip of the iceberg. Why didn't I pursue this? I call myself a documentarian, but I've learned almost nothing about the industry that's paid for these shows. Paid *me* for these shows.

So here we go. I will probe its stinking heart and rub Ueno's nose in its offal. No more fudge. I'm thinking slaughterhouses for the next show. A meat-packin' mama in Chicago, perhaps? Or a feedlot family?

FAX

TO: Lara and Dyann
FROM: Jane Takagi-Little
DATE: September 2
RE: Wives, Meat, etc.
Dear Lara and Dyann:

I hope this finds you all well. I write it with some trepidation. . . . Did you get the copy of *My American Wife!* that I sent you? I haven't heard back from you and I'm worried that you didn't like the show. I hope this isn't the case, but if it is, I also hope you will let me know.

I am writing to ask for some advice. I am researching my next *My American Wife!* This time I happen to be featuring a wife whose family is involved in the livestock, specifically beef, industry. I started to research the topic and I'm finding it very disturbing.

I remember that during the cooking scene you both

talked a little about being vegetarians by default because
of the practices of factory farming meat. I wasn't able to
use it in the final program, but could you tell me more
about this? I have read quite a bit, but I want to hear what
you have to say.

If this is presumptuous of me and you don't have time,
or you hated the show and don't want to have anything
else to do with me, I understand and apologize. I hope I
will hear back from you.

Sincerely,

Jane Takagi-Little

FAX

TO: "John" Ueno
FROM: Jane Takagi-Little
DATE: 9/3/91
RE: Blatszik & Dunn
Dear Mr. "John" Ueno:

As per your instructions, I am attaching a copy of our
research thus far for the next *My American Wife!* program.
As you will see, we have found two promising candidates,
Mrs. Anna Blatszik, the wife of a meatpacker in Chicago,
and Mrs. "Bunny" Dunn, the wife with a Colorado cattle
ranch. I have asked each of the ladies to tell us her *best
beef* recipe to share with the Japanese audience.

Sincerely,

Jane Takagi-Little

FAX

September 3
Takagi,

You won't return my calls so I have to resort to faxes. I don't know whether you've gone and had the abortion already, but I have to see you regardless.

I reacted very badly to your phone call from the Montana jail. I'm sorry. Collect calls from prisons make me nervous. But you did sort of railroad me, you know. Anyway, can we please talk? I need to know what's going on.

Please, call me.
Sloan

FAX

September 4
Dear Jane,

Thanks for your fax. Don't worry. The show is a hoot and the girls in particular loved it. They think it is hysterical that they are on TV, talking in Japanese. They took it to school for show-and-tell, and now they prance around acting like goddamn movie stars. Actually, they can't decide between being stars or directors. Any suggestions?

When we were trying to get pregnant, I started getting interested in fertility rates and I ended up writing a series of articles (which I will send you) for a local ecology magazine, surveying recent studies of natural and synthetic hormones in the environment and their impact on human reproduction. Do you know that some studies show that sperm counts have dropped globally in the past fifty years by about fifty percent? This coincides with the start of factory farming and the heavy use of estrogens and other hormones in meat production. Granted there were a lot of other chemicals and pharmaceuticals just starting to saturate the environment around that time too, and the research is disputed, but my feeling is how could it not take its toll?

Anyway, the meat thing in particular interested me, so I pursued it and started to dig up all sorts of nasty information about the industry, which I am sending to you. That's when Lara and I became vegetarians. Basically, at first we didn't believe that there was anything inherently wrong with eating meat. We simply decided to try not to eat contaminated foods when we were pregnant, or to feed them to our daughters. But then we started to feel that eating meat was, not wrong exactly, but not the best of all ethical choices, either, you know? So that's where we stand.

Best of luck on your show.

Fond regards,

Dyann

P.S. The girls want me to ask why there are black sections in the tape? Is that where the commercials go?

Beef Junkies
by Dyann Stone

How do you know when your cows are in the mood for love?

This is a serious question for cattle ranchers, who need to know which of their cows is in estrus and ready for artificial insemination. In the good old days, the rancher relied on a "teaser bull." He was a bull of inferior stock, who, like any bull released into a herd of cows, promptly found and mounted those in heat. The difference was that the teaser bull had a paint marker around his neck, which left behind an identifying smear of paint on the cows' rumps.

But that was all he left behind. Naturally you do not want this bull's lesser sperm weakening your gene pool, so it was important to keep him from actually fulfilling his biological imperative. A simple surgical alteration took care of this problem. A slit in the skin of the bull's penis rerouted it out the side, so when the bull became aroused and mounted the cow, his skewed erection circled futilely around his target. Accordingly, these bulls were nicknamed "sidewinders."

The use of sidewinders, however, is old technology. The Upjohn Company now markets a new estrus-synchronizing compound called Lutalyse. Injected into all the cows in a herd, it forces them to come into heat simultaneously, within a matter of hours. Imagine! No more "Not tonight, honey, I've got a headache." This is modern love—efficient, assembly-line artificial insemination and controlled calving. Upjohn's slogan? "You Call the Shots."

Lutalyse is a prostaglandin, a chemical that functions similarly to a hormone, affecting almost everything that a body does, including respiration, digestion, nerve response, and reproduction. Prostaglandins work equally on both cows and women, and are being used in human medicine to stimulate menstruation as well as to abort fetuses in the second trimester of pregnancy.

Lutalyse is only one of many "growth-enhancing"

drugs, hormones, and other pharmaceuticals used in beef production. In America, 95 percent of cattle routinely receive estradiol, testosterone, progesterone, and anabolic steroids, not to mention the huge doses of antibiotics needed to control disease in feedlots, where cattle are crammed into pens, standing knee-deep in urine, feces, and mud, with no place to move.

Trace residues of these drugs end up in the beef we eat, along with concentrated doses of herbicides used in cattle feed, and pesticides and insecticides needed to control the rampant fly populations in feedlots.

These drugs, hormones, chemicals, and poisons are being blamed for a host of modern human health crises, including dropping sperm counts and fertility rates, cancers, and our rising resistance to antibiotics. In addition, the "diseases of affluence"—the heart attacks, strokes, and stomach cancers caused by too much meat in the diet—are killing Americans, Europeans, and increasingly the Japanese. . . .

Journal: September 4

The creature inside craves meat. This is the month of manic growth, they tell me, when the manikin will double in size, from a puny three inches, crown to rump, to a whopping six. I take out my ruler and stare at it in disbelief. This much baby in my belly!

Meanwhile, a massive rift has occurred between the seat of my so-called intelligence and my dumb, stunned body. With my mind, I am studying meat. I am immersed in accounts of pharmaceutical abuse. I recall Purcell Dawes, the DES, and the cute young doctor in Oklahoma with his warnings about antibiotics. I am reading chilling descriptions of the slaughterhouse, the caked filth, blood coursing down the cement kill floor, the death screams of a slaughtered lamb (exactly like the cry of a human baby) going on and on, long after the lamb's throat has been cut. And yet . . .

And yet my body still craves the taste and texture of animal between my teeth. I read, I shudder, I gnaw a spare rib. How is this possible? I've had a long course in psychic numbing, but if this is the outcome of my documentary career, then I'm doubled to a psychotic extreme.

Found a health food store that sells organic beef. I don't want this child born with two penises or half a brain if I can help it.

Sloan's been calling. Now he's faxed, asking to see me. What does he want from me?

FAX

TO: "J." Ueno
FROM: Jane Takagi-Little
DATE: September 4
RE: Sausages and Prairie Oysters

Dear Mr. "J." Ueno,

I am delighted that you approve of our researches for *My American Wife!* thus far. I spoke to Mrs. Anna Blatszik, who told me that she often makes sausages with the "leftovers" from the meatpacking plant and she would like to make these for our program. She said she has a dish that she likes to make when her in-laws come for dinner, called "El Quicko Sausage Surprise." The name sounds fancy, she said, but it's real simple to make. She cooks the wieners in a sauce made from a can of cherry pie filling and a cup of rosé wine (or you can just substitute sugar and orange juice, she assured me, if you don't have rosé wine).

Mrs. "Bunny" Dunn loves variety meats and has suggested her special recipe of Pan-Fried Prairie Oysters. Do you know what a prairie oyster is? It is a bull's testicle, a traditional delicacy in the American West, which American men eat in order to increase their strength and their manhood. I think this would be a very nice custom to introduce to Japanese families. However, if you think it is too crass a meat for the refined Japanese palate, she also has a very nice recipe for Scrambled Brains 'n' Eggs or Simmered Heart.

I will visit Chicago and Colorado and scout both women. I will send you my opinions, but of course, the final decision is yours. You call the shots.

Sincerely,

Jane Takagi-Little

FAX

September 5

Sloan,

I will be in Chicago next Monday for a location scout and I can see you then if you want. However, I will be spending most of the day at Blatszik Meat Fabricators. I haven't yet aborted, although I did deposit your check.

Sincerely,

Takagi

TO: Mr. "J." Ueno
FROM: Jane Takagi-Little
DATE: September 5
RE: Wild West

Dear Mr. Ueno,

The more I find out about "Bunny" Dunn, the more I like her. She is a former rodeo queen and everyone says she is physically quite attractive. She was born and bred in Texas, and perhaps you may recall how charming Texas girls can be. In addition she has a warm, outgoing personality. She and her husband, John, have a feedlot, which is different from a ranch and better for the purposes of our program, I think. A cattle ranch may have several hundred or maybe several thousand animals. But at the Dunns' feedlot there are cattle from ranches all over the country, about 20,000 head in all!

The Dunns feed the cattle special food to fatten them up and give them medicine to make sure they do not get sick. The cattle are kept in one place, so they will be easier for us to film and get all 20,000 into one spectacular shot. Now that's a lot of beef! In addition there is a meat-processing business nearby owned by good friends of the Dunns who have agreed to allow us to film all the different and interesting steps involved in meat production.

Aside from the attractiveness of Mrs. "Bunny" Dunn, there is much to recommend the rest of the family as well. Mr. Dunn is quite a bit older than "Bunny," but he is still vigorous, and the two fell in love at first sight. John Dunn has one grown-up son from a previous marriage who works with his father on the farm. John and "Bunny" have a little daughter as well. John sired the girl at the age of 72 and he says his virility comes from the red meat he's eaten every day since he first grew teeth. "Bunny" swears it's her Prairie Oysters. All in all, I feel that the Dunns are a pretty typical American family who would do much to promote an image of the wholesomeness of BEEF-EX.

    Sincerely,

       J. Takagi-Little

Journal: September 5

Bunny Dunn was indeed a rodeo queen, in the small town of Fossil, Texas, when she was in high school. Then she took a shot at the state title and ended up as a stripper and an exotic dancer, moving from town to town until she wound up in San Antonio. John Dunn is old enough to be her grandpa. He spotted her at the club where she was working, bought a ring at a pawnshop next door, slipped it on her finger during a lap dance, and took her back to his spread in Colorado.

If the feedlot is anything like the ones I've been reading about, there should be plenty of opportunity to shoot some pretty horrifying material. And the slaughterhouse—I have high hopes for that.

What am I hoping to accomplish? Am I trying to sabotage this program?

I need this job. I can't afford to get fired now. On the other hand, I can't continue making the kind of programs Ueno wants, either. What am I supposed to do?

FAX

TO: "J." Ueno
FROM: Jane Takagi-Little
DATE: September 6
RE: Documentary Ethics

Dear Mr. Ueno:

There are a couple of things that have come to light in my researches that I think you should know about. I have inadvertently discovered an unsavory side to the meat industry. I am talking about the use of drugs and hormones in meat production, which are being blamed for rising rates of cancer, sterility, impotence, reproductive disorders, as well as a host of other illnesses and harmful side effects. These drugs are routinely given to the cattle that end up as steak on the plates of the Japanese television viewing audience. I am concerned about the ethics of representing either the Blatsziks or the Dunns in a wholesome manner, knowing what I now know about the health hazards of meat production.

I am sending you a summary of all of my research. Since there is so much technical language, I've asked Kenji to translate it into Japanese. Please advise how to proceed.

Sincerely,

J. Takagi-Little

P.S. On a more personal note, while there is still no proven link to meat, did you know that now the average man produces less morphologically sound sperm than an average hamster?

FAX

September 6

Dear Dyann and Lara:

Thank you for your articles. They were very helpful in planning my next show. To answer your question, yes, the commercials for the program sponsor go into the black spaces in the tape. The copy I sent you, without commercials or titles, is called a "white mother." This time I am enclosing the "on-air" copy with the commercials included. Before you watch it there is something you should know—and I'm afraid it's going to make you angry. The program sponsor for *My American Wife!* is an organization called the Beef Export and Trade Syndicate, or BEEF-EX. I neglected to tell you this before the shoot, probably sensing that you wouldn't go along with it, and after the shoot was over it was too late. I didn't have time to reshoot, and your program was so *good*. I felt it could deliver a truly affirming message about sexuality and race and the many faces of motherhood to Japanese women. I know these aren't adequate excuses, nor do they tell the entire story, but there is nothing I can say that would be sufficient to exonerate myself. All I can do is apologize and ask you to forgive me and promise to make it up to you somehow.

　　Sincerely,
　　　Jane

FAX

TO: J. Takagi-Little
FROM: J. Ueno
DATE: September 7
RE: Beef Safety

Dear Takagi-Little:

Please do not be concerned with these matters that are none of your business and which you know nothing about, and that is the wholesomeness of BEEF-EX. They have one good committee called the Meat Affirmation Task Force who assures me of high quality of all meats. So do not waste your time. This is not hobby. If you cannot be professional television director and make wholesome program of *My American Wife!* I have asked Mr. Kato to send some another director instead.

Sincerely,

J. Ueno

Journal: September 7

Well, that settles it. Ueno will have his meats. I leave for location scout tomorrow. I don't want to see Sloan.

That is such a lie. Of course I do. He is picking me up at the airport.

AKIKO

Dear Miss Takagi-Little,

You do not know me because I am only the wife of Ueno of BEEF-EX so I regret to bothering you at all. But I feel compelled to writing for the reason of your program of the Lesbian's couple with two childrens was very emotional for me. So thank you firstly for change my life. Because of this program, I feel I can trust to you so that I can be so bold.

You see, Ueno and I wanted to have the child at first but because of my bad habits of eating and throw up my food I could not have monthly bleeding for many years. But now I can have it again thanks to eating delicious Hallelujah Lamb's recipe from your program of My American Wife!, so secondly thank you for that also.

But I am most wanting to say that I listen to the black lady say she never want man in her life, and all of a sudden I agree! I am so surprising that I cry! (I do not know if I am Lesbian since I cannot imagine this condition, but I know I never want marriage and with my deep heart I am not "John's" wife.)

I feel such sadness for my lying life. So I now wish to ask you where can I go to live my happy life like her? Please tell me this.

Sincerely yours,
Akiko Ueno

Akiko painstakingly finished copying the final draft of her fax. She had written it several times, consulting the dictionary, and felt that she had managed to express herself rather well. She put down her pen and read it over once again, checking for mistakes. The problem that remained was one of courage and logistics. She didn't dare use the fax machine at home because the New York fax number would be recorded in the machine's memory and John might see it and recognize it.

Akiko had found the fax number by accident. She had brought John's suit to Hashimoto Dry Cleaners the week before, and when she went to retrieve it, old Mrs. Hashimoto pulled a plastic sandwich bag carefully labeled with her name from under the counter. In it, folded in quarters, was what looked to be several pages of a fax. Akiko's heart sank. She was usually so careful about checking pockets. The wives in the line behind her looked up expectantly.

"You'd be surprised at the things I find in husbands' pockets!" The old woman cackled. "You are a lucky wife. Only letters. Sometimes I find other things too. . . ." She looked ominously down the line of wives waiting their turn and they ducked their heads or looked in the opposite direction.

Akiko fumbled with her wallet. She paid the bill in a no-nonsense manner, hung the suit over her arm, and held out her hand for the plastic bag. Mrs. Hashimoto ignored her and, instead, opened the zip-lock with her crippled fingers and peered inside.

"It is written in English, your husband's letter! I wish I could read English. Perhaps it is from an American lover? You must scold your husband severely!"

Mrs. Hashimoto had no teeth and no respect. She held the letter behind the counter, just too far for Akiko to grab and still maintain her politeness. The old woman leered at her from underneath wrinkled, hooded eyelids.

"Perhaps that's why . . . perhaps he is spending all his stamina elsewhere. Perhaps you have some nice stepchildren in America—"

Akiko lunged over the counter.

"And none of your own children here!" the old lady crowed as she relinquished the paper to Akiko, who crushed it and shoved it into her pocket.

"Shut up, you old turtle!" she shouted. The waiting wives gasped behind their fingers.

"I don't even care!" She glared at them.

She backed out the door and a tinny digital voice chip thanked her for her continued patronage.

When she got home she looked at the fax. She recognized the name, Takagi-Little. It must be the same Takagi. The woman who defied John, who went to prison, who made programs that were true and authentic and that Akiko could understand. And with that, she made a decision. She poured herself a shot of scotch and sat down to write the letter that would express the contents of her heart.

p.s. please do not tell my husband I write this to you because he will anger and maybe hit me as he is sometimes wont to do.

The nearest public fax machine was at the stationers. Akiko folded the fax from Takagi-san and put it in her pocket just in case she forgot the phone number when she got there. Then she put her own fax in a plastic folder to protect it.

There were two employees behind the counter at the stationers, a studious-looking girl with glasses and a teenage boy with pimples, wearing a Hello Kitty apron. Akiko chose the boy. It was less likely, she thought, that he could read English. He took the pages from her and looked at them curiously. For a moment Akiko thought of snatching them away from him, but then he handed them back to her, along with a cover sheet to fill out. She carefully wrote Takagi-san's name and number, then checked it against the number on the fax in her pocket. When she finished, the boy took the pages away to the machine in back.

Akiko looked at the fax from Takagi again. The first page was a letter, typed, in English. There were several long words—"unsavory," "sterility," "impotence"—that Akiko didn't understand, but it certainly should have been obvious to anyone that this was not a love letter. She turned the page. What followed was a long list of research, covering three pages, in tightly written Japanese. She'd glanced at it earlier but hadn't paid attention to what it said. Now, as she waited, Akiko read it through without stopping, holding her breath. Then she asked the girl clerk for another cover sheet. She took a pink-and-white pen from a plastic Kitty display on the counter, addressed the cover sheet to Takagi, then wrote:

Dear Miss Takagi.

    I read your Japanese fax to my husband Ueno about some dangerous meats. Can it be true? Is the seed of meat-eating man weak from bad medicines, or perhaps he becomes not able to perform the sex act even? Please tell me answer to this important question, too.

    Sincerely,

    Akiko Ueno

"Customer, are you studying the English language?"

Akiko looked up, confused. The boy with the Hello Kitty apron had returned and was standing in front of her, looking at the letter he had just sent.

"I can read some of this, but you are at a level far more advanced than I. May I ask you for your advice? I am studying English conversation myself, and my teacher says that a pen pal from a foreign country is a good method of practicing idiomatic English. Do you agree? Or do you—"

Akiko snatched her letter from his hand, knocking over the plastic container and scattering the pink-and-white pens across the floor. The other shoppers fell silent, watching.

"He was reading my letter," she explained, clutching it to her chest. "He shouldn't read my letter, don't you think? It is private. . . ."

But wives should not be sending private letters in the first place. She backed toward the automatic doors. The boy in the apron was defensive. He had just been making polite conversation. He noticed her new fax on the counter.

"Customer, you didn't pay for your first fax. And now here is a second. Do you expect me to send this for free as well?"

Akiko stopped, realizing she had no choice. She approached the counter again. She took two thousand-yen notes from her purse and put them on the counter.

"Here. For both," she whispered. "I'm so sorry. . . ."

She leaned down and picked up all the pens from the floor and replaced them clumsily in the Kitty container. The boy came back with her second letter. Clutching it, she backed out of the store, under the inquisitorial gaze of the neighborhood. For the second time that day.

JANE

Sloan lives in the penthouse of one of the high-rise apartment buildings that cluster along Lake Shore Drive as it winds around the southern perimeter of Lake Michigan. From his vantage, the horizon line is negligible, obscured by smog and slatted blinds. Floor-to-ceiling windows frame the gray lake and the steel waves that lap the concrete shore. The carpet is gray and mimics the water.

When he picked me up at the airport, I could tell something was different. With clothes on, I was barely showing, but his eyes dropped surreptitiously to my stomach and he immediately took my bags away from me, with an accusatory grimace when he felt their weight. He didn't kiss me or engage in any other proprietary demonstrations, but something had subtly changed. He had a limousine waiting at the curb and he ushered me into it and gave the driver the Lake Shore Drive address.

"Are you tired? Do you want to rest for a while before dinner?"

"Sloan, I have a meeting with a meatpacker in a couple of hours. It's at least a hundred-and-thirty-mile drive to Normal, and I can't show up there in a white limousine."

"Oh." He thought for a moment. "What kind of car would be appropriate for a visit to a meatpacker?"

"I don't know . . . something rented and innocuous."

He phoned his secretary on his cellular phone, and exactly two and a half hours later we were sitting in front of Blatszik Meat Fabricators in a metallic-gray Ford Taurus, and he had changed from his linen suit into a pair of jeans and a T-shirt and a Bulls cap and could pass for the local driver I should have hired.

A rusting sign at the top of the exterior stairway read:

Blatszik Meat Fabricators, Inc.
Precision Meat Products
Custom Slaughter

"You want that I should come inside with you?" He was playing the driver.

"No, stay here."

He dropped it. "Please. I want to see this."

"Okay, but behave. And don't say anything."

Anna Blatszik met us in the small office that overlooked the packing plant. She was large and apologetic. Her husband was seated behind a metal desk, screaming in Polish into an old black phone. The desk was piled high with bloodstained packing slips and invoices. A shipment of lambs was late in coming, Anna explained, and the workers were just sitting around in the slaughterhouse, waiting. Her husband was upset. Every hour that went by was costing them money. The lambs were apparently stuck in traffic on the outskirts of Gary. Anna regretted that she would not be able to show us the plant in operation, but would we like to see the facilities? She took two bloodstained white coats from a steel locker in the corner of the office and offered them to us.

The air in the abattoir felt like cold metal, solid, like something you could hurt yourself against. Yet it was volatile too, permeating your lungs and sinuses so you could taste it immediately as it stained the back of your throat. It was hard to breathe and not choke on it.

The workers at Blatszik Fabricators were sitting around, talking softly, and some were sharpening their knives, so the metal was in your ears too, a rhythmic *shuunck, shuunck, shuunck* of steel against stone. They glanced up when we walked in, and fell silent except for the sharpening. Some drank coffee, others smoked, each cupped his own private thread of vaporous comfort against the cold.

The lambs were expected momentarily, Anna explained. They had been expected momentarily for the last two hours. Apparently, the workers were expected to stay at their posts. They weren't supposed to be smoking, though, Anna apologized. She obviously saw us as inspectors of some sort, which was kind of true, and she treated us with a hangdog deference.

I had been correct about one thing. Anna Blatszik just wasn't right. I knew it on the phone when I talked to her from New York and I knew it now. She was broadly constructed, as I'd suspected, but she wasn't fat or deformed or even unattractive. Her skin was creamy, her hair thin, and her eyes were rimmed in red, with faded blue centers. At fourteen, she might have been a beauty. But the problem wasn't her physical appearance. I don't know how to describe this sense, but it is unmistakable to a television documentarian. Anna Blatszik was dull. Not spectacularly dull, which at least gives you something to work with. But simply, plainly dull. Screen dead. She was like an old gray dishrag, continually wrung and damp and never hung to dry. She exuded her drabness, trailed it around behind her like a low-hanging cloud.

We followed Anna's broad back across the slippery floor. It had recently been hosed down and everything felt damp; puddles of pink water collected in the shallow cement depressions around the drains. Under her white coat, Anna was wearing a floral-patterned dress, possibly in honor of us, but on her feet she wore heavy rubber galoshes, which were too big and made her shuffle. The walls of the slaughterhouse were splashed with blood and now I could hear the sound of dripping behind the *shuunck, shuunck* of the knives being sharpened, and also the low, spiraling drone of bluebottle flies, and everything was in a state of horrible suspended animation, waiting for the lambs. We left before they arrived and drove the two and a half hours back to Chicago in silence.

Sloan came up behind me as I stood by his window, watching the dull waves lick the shore. He wrapped his arms around me and held a glass of wine to my lips, gently supporting my head against his chest as I drank. We had showered and changed, but the metallic aftertaste of the slaughterhouse had lingered at the back of my tongue and only now was cut by the rich red wine. I was suddenly warmed, but wary as well, distrustful of Sloan's solicitous gesture. It felt soft. It scared me, so I pulled away.

There is nothing soft about Sloan's apartment. It is all polished surfaces, acute angles, hard glass, cold chrome, and leather. Like an abattoir, it could be hosed down without too much difficulty if anything unsightly, like an attachment or a sentiment, happened to splatter the walls. So the sudden accommodation in Sloan's manner seemed at odds with his decor as well as with our history. I stood a few feet away from him and waited, hoping he'd adjust his attitude into something that felt more aggressive and familiar, but he just stood there too, watching me.

"So . . . ," he said.

"So . . . ?"

"So here we are. . . ."

I glared at him. It was like bad movie dialogue. I had never seen him hesitate before. I didn't think it was possible. It made me cranky.

"So what? So I'm here. Do you want to talk? Do you want to fuck?"

"Can you?"

"Huh?"

"I mean, is it safe . . . ?"

"Sloan, it wasn't safe *before*. Now it is perfectly safe, believe me."

"I mean, is it safe for . . . our baby."

It was the first time I'd heard him say the words. "Our baby." I had steeled myself against this notion of "our." That was the agreement I'd made with myself. I could have the baby, provided I root out all desire for "our." This baby would be mine, no strings attached. But when I heard Sloan say "our baby," watched him form the words on his lips and launch them into the world, it was like conjuring. It made me gasp. Buckled my knees and triggered the longing. I didn't know how to respond. Words weren't safe, but sex could be, so I walked over to him and pulled his head down and kissed him, and we sort of goose-stepped into the bedroom and took our clothes off. We lay down side by side and he cautiously inspected my abdomen as though there might be a land mine or something equally perilous and as easily triggered concealed there, and when he'd run his hand across its gentle protuberance, satisfied that it was safe and smooth and solid, he hoisted himself gingerly on top of me and prepared to enter. And without really meaning to, I stopped him.

"Aren't you going to wear a condom?"

"Why? You said it was safe, didn't you? It's not like I can impregnate you again."

He was right, of course, and it took me a minute to pinpoint my objection.

"No. It's not about safety. It's a question of manners. I don't want you leaving any more bits of yourself around inside me. It's too ... personal. We've just never had that kind of relationship."

Sloan rolled back onto his side of the bed and looked at me, shaking his head in exasperation.

"Takagi, you are making me insane. What do you want from me?" And at that, I exploded. I sat up in bed. The narrative seemed simple enough to me. He'd duped me into having unprotected sex with him in Fly, implying at the time that he wanted a deeper commitment, and then when the sex was over, he made it quite clear that it had been an experiment, conducted because I, the sterile laboratory animal, was safe, or so we both thought at the time. And then, after New Jersey, despite my obvious distress and my obvious desire for greater intimacy, he avoided me, continued to reject my repeated attempts at—

"What repeated attempts?"

"I called you . . ."

"Once, maybe twice."

"Well . . ."

"I travel. I always called you back as soon as I got your messages. Anyway, you were the one putting me off. As soon as you started directing those damn programs, that was it. You never had any time, or you'd invite me someplace and then

262

cancel. . . . If there were any repeated attempts, they were mine—"

"Yeah, after you knew I was pregnant and you felt guilty—"

"Guilty! I did not . . . I have *never* felt the slightest bit guilty. When you told me you were pregnant, I was scared, surprised . . . I don't know. I was happy. Stupid, maybe. I don't know what I thought would happen. But then in the next breath you call me from some jail to tell me you intend to abort the baby and never want to see me again."

"*You* told *me* to abort!"

"Never. You said you didn't want the pregnancy, that you were sorry. Of course I assumed you wanted an abortion. I was crushed."

"But you sent the check."

"What was I supposed to do? It's your body. But I called and called and faxed, and finally here you are. With the baby."

"So . . . ?"

"So . . . nothing. So there. Everything worked out after all."

We sat there on the bed and glared at each other. I wasn't so sure. It sounded sweet but just seemed too easy. Still, as I watched his frown yield to amusement and a satisfied smile creep over his face, I thought I might be willing to put some of my reservations on hold and consider his version of things. And this took about a second, or maybe two, and then all I could feel was this inane joy, glutting my heart.

"You want me to get a condom?"

"Forget it."

It was odd sex. Odd for us. Suspended and tentative at first, it slowly gathered into something we could both agree upon, negotiating each thrust with a clear-eyed rush of collective purpose. Unlike our insular and lopsided encounters of the past, it was, instead, equally thrilling. Sex was not about

263

mastery, more about choice, which this time did not disappoint me.

On the way to the airport in the Taurus the next morning, I told Sloan about my ongoing research, and he was suitably impressed.

"So what you're basically saying is that the residues in meat from hormones, steroids, pesticides, bacterial and viral contaminants, will lead to cancers, infertility, brain fevers, and a host of other illnesses, which we will not be able to cure with antibiotics because our tolerances have been jacked up by the residues also found in meat? So we are doomed to die young and not be able to reproduce ourselves in the bargain?"

"Well, more or less. You see my quandary? I peddle the stuff.. .."

"Pretty bleak. However, I just heard a story on the news that forensic medicine is having to reinvent itself because the preservatives in food have changed the rate of a body's decay after death. So there's the upside. You die younger, perhaps, but you get to hang around longer after you're dead."

"Sloan, that is *so* dumb."

"No, Jane. It's *faux* dumb."

Dead right. That's precisely what we are—politically, ethically, aesthetically—in premillennium America.

We pulled up at the terminal and unloaded my suitcase, and I let Sloan do curbside check-in for me, then I let him kiss me, too, and left him standing there, leaning against the Taurus, eyes narrowed with what I took to be concern, watching me disappear off to Denver. I liked it. It felt good.

AKIKO

The line of salted smelts hissed and popped over the gas grill. Akiko flipped them, careful not to burn the little bamboo skewer that pierced the bottoms of their delicately gaping jaws. The *mozuku* was ready, a fresh pond-algae salad garnished with vinegar and a pinch of ginger, and the tofu was chilling in the refrigerator. She would also serve some very young flounder, deep fried until the bones were crisp and fragile. But first she had steamed some fresh soybeans for John to nibble on before dinner, dusting them with coarse salt so that they would sweat in their pods. She knew he enjoyed these with his beer, although it was no longer summer.

John was in the living room, watching television. Akiko entered, carrying a large lacquered tray. He watched as she knelt by the low table and unloaded the dozen or so small dishes. His eyes narrowed. She could feel it. He was thinking. And then:

"What's going on." It was not a question. He knew.

"I'm sorry . . . ?"

"Don't play dumb. This is the fifth night in a row that we've had Japanese food. And no meat. You think I don't notice? What is the meaning of this?"

"Nothing . . . There was a nice sale at the fishmongers of young flounder—"

"*Baka!* Stupid. Don't insult me. Why won't you serve me meat? You know I like meat. I work for meat and it is my duty to eat it. I will not be made into a traitor to my company and to my clients by my wife."

Akiko stared down, watching the bonito flakes twitch slowly, then wilt on top of the chilled tofu.

"I just thought it would be nice for a change," she whispered.

He said nothing, waiting for her real answer. She had no choice but to continue.

"And, well, there was something I heard the other day, about bad meat. . . ."

"Where did you hear this?"

"Uh . . . at the dry cleaners. At Hashimoto Dry Cleaners. It was one of the wives. . . ."

"What did she say?"

Akiko's voice was barely audible, not even a whisper now. "That there are things in meat . . ."

"What? What things? Speak loudly. I can't hear you."

"Hormones and other bad medicines that can make a man . . ."

"Can make a man what?"

"Can make a man . . . incapable."

"Incapable of what?"

"Of performing sex. Or of making a child . . ."

John stared, then leaned back and burst out laughing. "You really are stupid. Believing a bunch of gossiping women."

"So it's not true, then?"

"That meat causes impotence? Absolutely not. Quite the reverse. On one of the upcoming programs of *My American Wife!* you will see a man who fathered a child at the age of seventy-two, and he was able to do it because he eats red meat every day."

Akiko relaxed, laughed with relief. "Then that other part, about the hamsters, couldn't be—"

"*What?*"

As soon as she said it, she knew she had made a terrible mistake.

"Nothing . . . I mean . . ."

John was silent, weighing her words, recollecting. "Where did you find it?" he asked.

"What?"

"The fax. The fax from America. From Takagi . . ."

There was no point in lying. "In your suit pocket. Old Mrs. Hashimoto found it. She teased me in front of all the other neighborhood wives. She said it was a love letter from your lover in America. . . ."

"So you read it?"

"Of course I read it. It is my right. As your wife, I mean."

John sat back and watched her, but she knew she had to outwait him; it was her only hope. She had stumbled onto the sole viable self-defense—her wifely entitlement to the contents of his pockets. It was the only maneuver that would flatter him, and if he bought it, maybe she would not get hit. Finally he spoke.

"Kimiwa baka ne," he said, relaxing. "Of course you are jealous. But you don't need to doubt me." He picked up his chopsticks and skewered a salty smelt. "Mmm," he said, biting it in half. "Delicious. Filled with eggs."

Akiko quietly relaxed and set the tray aside. She had been holding it close by, just in case, to use as a shield for her face. She vowed to keep perfectly silent for the rest of the evening. Everything seemed fine now, but she didn't trust herself not to make another stupid error. She picked up the little fish, piercing its fat, oily belly with the tip of her chopsticks, then ground the bones between her teeth.

JANE

The Colorado scout was a great success. Bunny Dunn was all I'd hoped for. I faxed Ueno from the hotel, but I knew he'd go with her. He has a soft spot in his heart for Texas women.

Bunny and her ancient husband drove me to a beef trade show, where I took care of all my souvenir needs. For the boys in the office I got kitchen magnets from Lambert Pharmaceuticals, shaped like voluptuous humanoid cows in cocktail gowns, with the words "Ready when you are ... big shot!" in dialogue bubbles over their heads. For the research girls, I got pink sun visors that said "Beef Babes Are Best," and also these small square green tins of a lanolin substance called Bag Balm, for applying to cows' chafed udders. It looks just like Vaseline, and ranchers and their wives all swear by it. The illustration on the tin is right out of a 1920s Sears catalog, a hand-drawn sketch depicting an elegant set of swollen teats encircled by an oval cameo frame. The girls loved this.

I found a T-shirt for Kenji with a cartoon of a long line of bulls in front of an unemployment office, with a caption that read "Sidewinders." He admired the shirt and thanked me politely, then followed me into my office and closed the door behind us.

"This came for you while you were gone."

He held out three pages of faxes. This was odd. Usually he just posted them on my board.

"When I noticed who they were from, I thought I ought to keep them ... secure."

The cover sheet read "From: Akiko Ueno." The name meant nothing to me. Then I glanced at the first page.

"Oh, shit."

"Yeah, that's more or less what I thought. I read them through, of course."

So did I. Quickly.

"Oh my God. He *beats* her."

"So she says."

"I *knew* he was evil."

"So you've said."

"Yeah, but I never imagined anything like this. . . ."

"Takagi, I don't know whether you can take this at face value. I mean, this woman sounds slightly deranged to me."

I think I must have gasped. He backed off a bit.

"What I mean is simply that a normal Japanese woman would never write a letter like this."

"Kenji, you are a racist and a pig."

He ignored me completely. "Takagi, you're on parole, remember. And I am supposed to look after you. This is just the type of thing ... I mean, you mustn't ... It's the boss's wife, damn it!"

"You don't get it, do you? This woman is in trouble."

Kenji leaned against the door and folded his arms. "So what are you going to do?"

"I don't know. Tell her to leave that disgusting husband of hers. Do you know I saw him cry over a lap dancer in Texas? God, he's pathetic."

"I'm warning you, Takagi. Leave it alone. You're not Japanese. You're just going to make it worse for everyone."

Ma used to do this to me and Dad all the time, cop this attitude of *you are a crude, uncivilized foreigner and cannot possibly understand our delicate and unique Japanese sensibility*, and there is absolutely no point in arguing. They've been practicing this one for over a millennium. So I told him.

"He tried to rape me in Memphis, Kenji."

This brought him up short, for a moment at least. Then he said, "Jane, you don't understand how these things work."

"Screw you, Kenji."

Kenji shrugged. He looked down at the T-shirt. "What does 'Sidewinders' mean?"

"It's a baseball team."

"Oh? Never heard of it."

"Yeah, well, it was a really popular minor-league team until it got bought out. It's a Western thing. You wear the shirt out West, you'll fit right in."

"Thanks, I wish I could. It would be nice to get out of the office. . . ." He tossed the T-shirt over his shoulder and continued to watch me closely.

"You've gained a little weight," he said.

This is something else they do—make these extremely personal observations, like "You have a pimple on your nose" or "You're really fat, aren't you?" I used to think it was just Ma, but when I went to Japan I realized it's a national trait.

"Good-bye, Kenji," I said firmly.

He shrugged and opened the door to leave, then paused.

"Oh, by the way, that Flowers woman has been calling almost every day, asking for a tape. She's driving us all nuts. Can you do something about this, please?"

"Sure, Kenji, I'll handle it. Good-bye."

I had no time for Suzie Flowers today. I sat down at my desk and wrote a final report to Ueno about the Colorado scout. Then I reread the fax from Akiko and wrote her a response. I got as far as putting the sheets into the fax machine, when I realized that it was too risky to send it to her home number. Her husband might get to it first, assuming it was for him. So I telephoned instead. A woman's voice answered.

"Hai, Ueno degozaimasu . . ."

I addressed her in polite Japanese, which I have never been particularly good at.

"Moshi moshi . . . Hello. I'm sorry to bother you at this hour, but is the wife of Mr. Joichi Ueno present?"

"Yes . . ." I could hear her hesitate. "This is she."

"This is Takagi from New York. . . ."

"Oh yes, of course. Thank you." It was clear from her voice that it was bad timing, but I persevered.

"I have written a response to your questions, which I would like to send, but I'm afraid that, given your circumstances, it might be unwise to fax it to you there . . . ?"

"Oh yes, certainly."

There was a long silence.

"Is there a time when I could send it, sometime when you would be alone to receive it? Perhaps during the day, while your husband is at work . . . ?"

"Oh yes." Her voice brightened. "Yes, that would be fine. Tomorrow at noon would be just fine."

AKIKO

"Who was that?" John asked, as Akiko replaced the receiver.

"No one. Just the census taker. They came by today, but I was out at the market. They said they'd come back again tomorrow."

"How rude, to call people at home so late."

The phone rang again. John frowned and stood up. "I'll answer it," he said. "I'll tell them not to—"

Akiko elbowed him out of the way and wrenched the receiver out of his hand.

"*Moshi moshi . . .*," she said breathlessly. "*Moshi moshi . . .*" Slowly she let the receiver drop from her ear. "It's a fax," she whispered, as she stared, stricken, at the humming machine.

John glanced at her strangely, then looked at the top of the paper as it was slowly fed out. "It's from the New York office, from Takagi."

Akiko backed away toward the bathroom.

"I've been waiting for this," John said, as she closed the door quietly between them and locked it from the inside. She sat on the lid of the toilet and listened. There was no noise at all from the living room. She unlocked the door and listened some more, then walked down the corridor. John was sitting at the table, reading the fax. He looked up at her.

"Are you all right?" he asked.

Mutely, she nodded. He smiled a little, then went back to reading.

September 18

Dear Mr. Ueno,

I am back from Colorado, having set up everything for the Bunny Dunn show. I am confident that she will be our best American Wife yet! And talk about beef! You have never seen so much beef in one place! Acres of it.

As a background to this attractive family and their abundant beef, the Colorado setting offers the type of scenic beauty that conforms perfectly to Japanese people's preconceptions of America's "Big Rugged Nature." Wide-open prairies, snow-capped mountains . . . Additionally, it is a state that is rich in history and human interest. There are many interesting examples of "Wild West" stories, including one that the Dunns' son, Gale, told me. It is about a cannibal named Alferd Packer, who killed five traveling companions and ate their remains during a particularly cold winter in 1874. Gale has agreed to tell this story on-camera. It would be an effective way of evoking the hardships endured by the early American pioneer, but if you think it would create a conflict of interest with BEEF-EX product, we certainly don't have to include it in the program.

Sincerely,

Takagi

"*Baka*," said John, throwing the fax on the table. "Fool."

JANE

Akiko's fax threw me for a loop. Maybe it was because my shows were broadcast in Japan, on the other side of the globe, but up until now I'd never really imagined my audience before. She was an abstract concept: at most, a stereotypical housewife, limited in experience but eager to learn, to be inspired by my programs and my American wives; at the very least, a demographic statistic, a percentage point I'd hungered after, to rub in a pesky executive's face—Akiko's husband's face, actually. Now it hit me: what an arrogant and chauvinistic attitude this was. While I'd been worried about the well-being of the American women I filmed as subjects, suddenly here was the audience, embodied in Akiko, with a name and a vulnerable identity.

These dawning recognitions come at you like shock waves. They pass over you and in their wake nothing is the same.

Like in the cemetery in Montana, when I caught myself selecting names, and I knew in an instant that I would have the baby if the baby would have me. I could have aborted a fetus without an identity, but once that fetus had punched through its own anonymity and made its small self known, abortion was no longer an option.

And like in Chicago with Sloan, when he said "our baby." After that, a warm little fantasy bloomed in a corner of my mind, where Sloan and I lived with "our baby," almost a normal family. I won't go as far as a sloping lawn and a two-car garage, or even a freestanding housing structure—I live in New York, and as far as I'm concerned, those things exist only in an America I construct for television in Japan, not one I can imagine for myself. But I wanted our baby to grow up safe and secure, and Sloan could provide that.

You see, the doctor told me that because of my deformed uterus, the baby faced increased risks of miscarriage or premature birth, and provided it survived my womb, then it would still have to survive my life. I was worried. Sloan could provide security, but the fact was he hadn't volunteered to do so, and I didn't trust that he would. And even if he did, I was afraid of being emotionally dependent on him, terrified of becoming financially so. No, it was up to me to provide for the child, and the only way to do that was to keep my job.

And that was my problem. I didn't know how I could. Maybe my shows weren't much as documentaries, but I had believed in them. And Akiko's fax brought my audience, and my responsibility, into sharp focus. It was clear to me that I couldn't continue to celebrate beef. I had to tell some truths about meats, even if it meant getting fired.

I couldn't stop thinking about Akiko, wondering what she was like. Ueno's wife. No matter how hard I tried, I couldn't suppress the memory of the man, his foul and humid aura, the feeling of his fingers trying to penetrate me. How did she endure it? I waited until ten in the evening, phoned her again to make sure she was alone, then faxed my response. Everything seemed fine. Still, I couldn't shake this sense of oppressive responsibility. No. That's not it, either. Not responsibility. More like guilt. Like I'd already done something wrong.

AKIKO

Dear Akiko Ueno:

Thank you for your fax. I am glad that you have enjoyed my programs and that you feel they have helped you. I want to try and answer your questions as best I can.

First of all, I don't think that eating lamb caused your menstruation to start again. And second, you asked if eating meat can cause sterility or impotence. The answer is probably no.

Having said this, however, there is evidence that hormones in the environment, including those used in meat production, may contribute to the overall decline in fertility rates. And I have come to think that American meat is unhealthy and it's probably a good idea to stop eating it.

Now, you asked where to go to have a happy life like Dyann and Lara. I wish I could give you the answer. But there is one thing I do know for sure. If your husband hits you, you must leave him immediately. This is the first step to a happy life. Can you do this? Do you have anyplace to go?

I want to warn you that I will try to make my next program about bad meats. Please watch it, but please be careful, because I am sure it will make your husband very angry.

Sincerely,

Takagi

P.S. If there is ever anything I can do to help you, please don't hesitate to call me.

John put down the letter. A liver-colored cloud blossomed from his stiff white collar, creeping across his face.

"Where is the fax you sent to her?"

Akiko knelt on the floor in front of him. Her back was straight, but her head was bowed. She shook it from side to side, struck mute, then suddenly deafened as well by a blow John delivered to the side of her head with a heavy English dictionary. It knocked her over and was followed by the low-pitched roar.

He got to his feet and kicked her on his way into the bedroom. He came back with her purse. He opened it and held it upside down, showering the contents onto the floor in front of her: keys, lipsticks, a handkerchief, two sanitary napkins, liner notes for her Bobby Joe Creely CD, shopping lists, her little pillow book diary, recipe cards, and the two faxes, folded into quarters. She watched them fall onto the tatami and made a grab for them, but he kicked her hand away, picked them up, and started to read. Very slowly, Akiko reached out her hand toward her pillow book. She had it in her hand when his foot came down, crushing her wrist. He pocketed the diary along with all the faxes and walked toward the door.

"Have my suit dry-cleaned," he said before he slammed it. "And pack my suitcase. A two-week trip. No, better make it three. I'll stay in town until I leave. I'll be back later to pick it up."

JANE

Sloan sprawled on Grammy's love seat. The light from the pink globe lamp was soft in the dusk and burnished his face, and I lay on the rug at his feet, feeling quite content. My great-grandmother Little had hooked the rug we'd just screwed on, and I never had liked her much. My grandfather Takagi's portrait hung on the wall behind Sloan, and their two heads thus juxtaposed formed a striking contrast. All in all I was enjoying the improbable ebb and flow of my personal history and feeling quite smug about posterity. I'd just gotten the results of the amniocentesis and everything was fine.

Sloan was watching me carefully.

"What?"

"Nothing. You look nice lying there naked on your great-granny's rug. What would she say?"

"Before or after she saw you?"

"How about when she saw you?"

"I know exactly what she said when she saw me. Naked on this very rug, in fact. I was a few weeks old. She said, 'How could that little Jap be a Little baby?'"

"Really?"

"Really. My ma told me. Ma had a pretty hard time of it in Minnesota. Mostly from Great-Granny Little, who hung around forever and finally died when I was eight. Ma never had another kid and I think that's why. My grandparents, on the other hand, were wonderful to her and to me. They were dairy farmers. They went bankrupt. Lost the proverbial farm to agribusiness and turbocows. I was really little. I don't remember much about it."

"Where did your parents meet?"

"You know. The old story. Ma was a prostitute on the streets of Tokyo, Dad was a GI—"

"No shit . . . really?"

"Nope. Dad was a botanist with the army. They sent him to Japan as part of a team of scientists doing research in Hiroshima. They were kind of checking up on their handiwork—you know, looking at people and monstrous plant mutations—to see if we should drop an A-bomb on Korea. Dad died of cancer and I've always wondered whether there's some connection."

"When did he die?"

"When I was in college."

"You still didn't tell me how they met. . . ."

"They met at an *ikebana* exhibition. Flower arranging. It's a classy kind of hobby in Japan, especially back then, and Ma was certified as a teacher, but Dad didn't know any of that. He just liked the flowers."

"And they fell in love and got married. . . ."

"Yup. And Ma's parents disowned her and never spoke to her again. I don't know if it was because Dad was white or because he was a farmer."

"I thought he was a botanist."

"He was. He just never had the political or economic ambition it took to make it in academic sciences. After he was discharged he went back to the farm, and after the bankruptcy he got a job teaching at the high school. I guess it was hard on Ma. She didn't speak much English. None, in fact. And there weren't many people who could appreciate her flower arrangements. People were more into hardy roses."

"Takagi . . ."

"Yes, Sloan . . ."

"Would you do me a favor?"

"Maybe . . ."

"Would you be very careful on the shoot in Colorado?"

"Of course, Sloan. I'm always very careful."

"I mean extra careful. The idea of you working those hours . . . It's stupid. You should be taking it easy. Here. At home. Not wandering around in feedlots, you know? There's too much toxic stuff lying around there."

"Sloan, it's very nice of you to worry, but I'll be fine. Really. You need long-term, repeated exposure to these drugs for them to be harmful, and they're not using the blatantly toxic stuff now, anyway. And the doctor said that I don't have to alter my daily routine. . . ."

"Takagi, your doctor doesn't have the slightest idea of your daily routine. Don't be an idiot. How could any doctor know what a TV production schedule is like? I didn't know until I saw you at it. You guys are insane."

I was touched by all this concern, but a bit annoyed too. I'd been in a very good mood and Sloan was spoiling it. I sat up on the rug. He raised his hand.

"Jane, don't even start. It's not worth it." He slid off the love seat, onto the floor next to me. He placed his hand between my breasts and pushed me to the floor. When he had me on my back, he rested his hand on my belly and stroked it.

"You know I'm right to be worried. It's your life and your uterus. However, I probably know better than most that your uterus is a precarious place to hang around in, so cut me some slack. All I'm asking is do us all a favor—you, me, our baby— and be careful. Please. I'm asking you. Take this seriously."

"I always do."

I mean, what could I say? And by the time he finished his little speech he had pinned me once again to the old hooked rug. And still he persisted.

"You don't."

"I will."

"You'd better."

I loved him. That's what I was thinking. That's all I was thinking. He worked his way down the length of my body, kissing my breasts, which were larger now in a way I thought was very sexy, then running his tongue along between my ribs until he reached my stomach, where he rested for a moment, cheek to rounded belly, before descending further.

"Oh my God," I gasped.

"What?" He looked up, startled, and gripped my arm.

"It moved. I felt it move!" I pushed his head back down. "Do you feel it?"

And there it was again, the first quickening, a mothlike fluttering or the twitching of a fish's tail. I'd almost mistaken it for desire. "Can you feel it?" I asked again.

But Sloan didn't answer. He was lying there with his face pressed into my belly, arms wrapped tightly around my thickening waist, waiting with all his might.

AKIKO

John leaned, or fell, against the metal door as he thrust his hand into his pocket, searching for the aluminum key. What came out in his fist and dribbled through his fingers to the ground was a confusion of change, his subway pass, a woman's handkerchief, and a members card from the bar where he'd been drinking. And the key. The door swung open with a hollow clang. He stumbled over the threshold, kicked the shoes aligned in the *genkan*, tripped over the umbrella rack, and fell through the beaded curtain onto the kitchen floor. He lay there and listened. Nothing. The apartment was dark. He fell asleep.

In the bedroom, under layers of futon, Akiko listened too. Nothing. Maybe he would sleep there all night and wake up in the morning defensive and subdued. Slowly, as the silence lengthened, she dared to hope. She lay absolutely still, but her blood pounded loudly in her ears as she strained to hear and evaluate the potential for violence in her drunken husband. He stirred. She willed herself silent, insensate, inert.

"Barren old witch," he muttered. "Poisoner . . ." Or something like that. On all fours, he crawled into the dark of the bedroom and located the lump that was his wife. He stood up unsteadily, wrenched back the covers, and looked down at her. Her body was curled loosely on its side, her breathing light and even. Eyes shut, hands folded, she looked like she was praying. Her flannel pajamas, dotted with small lavender flowers, obscured her from neck to wrist to ankle. The pajamas infuriated him. He poked her with his toe. No reaction. He swung back a stockinged foot and kicked her as hard as he could in the stomach. She gasped but continued to lie there, as limp as a dead cat. The force of the kick, however, caused him to slip on the tatami and fall with a thump onto his bottom. It took his breath away. Legs splayed, he sat there and surveyed his inert wife.

"I know you are alive. You're playing dead, but I know you are alive." He crawled over and straddled her and rolled her onto her back. He covered her mouth and pinched her nostrils closed as hard as he could and waited for a long, long time. When she still didn't respond, didn't crack an eye or even gasp for breath, he lifted her by the front of her flannel pajamas.

"Open your eyes!" he screamed, inches from her face. "Breathe! Look at me!" And when she didn't, he punched her squarely in the jaw. Her head flew back as his knuckle split her lip, and a thin dribble of blood ran down her jaw. He flipped her over onto her stomach so he wouldn't have to look at it. He pinned her to the floor. "You liar, you liar . . ." As though she were struggling or fighting back, as though to control her, he put his knee into the small of her back and pulled down her elastic-waisted bottoms, exposing her thin, pale buttocks. Still she didn't move.

"So I guess it doesn't matter where I put it, does it?" he muttered, as he unzipped his pants. "In the front or in the back, it's all the same! It doesn't matter where, because you are a sterile, useless woman." He lifted her up by the hips and forced his penis into her anus. "So I'll do it like you're a little boy. Do you like that?" He held her by the neck, ground her hips into the floor.

"You deserve worse than this for lying to your husband," he hissed into her ear. "You think I'm stupid?" He lifted her by the shoulders and pounded her against the floor, over and over. "You think I don't know you'd started again? That I couldn't smell you bleeding?" Then, just as he was about to ejaculate, he pulled out. "You think I don't know when you are in heat . . . ?" he whispered, inserting his penis into her vagina now. "So you want to be a lesbian? You want to have a baby but not a man? Well, here . . ." He pulled out, then thrust himself into her as hard as he could. "Tell *this* to that *bitch* Takagi." He ejaculated, then collapsed on top of her.

Akiko lay perfectly still, eyes glued shut, crushed into the tatami by his smothering weight. Her heartbeat deafened her. Slowly the pain began to punch through, like an erratic pulse at points across her body—a dull throb here, a searing tear there. His breath was hot against her neck, his ribs pressing into her backbone as his sleep deepened. She wanted to touch herself, cry, cry out, but she was afraid to move. Hold still, she thought, a little longer—because the worst thing in the world at this point would be to wake him and then have to make conversation.

He started to snore. Gingerly she shifted her body to one side and little by little managed to inch out from beneath him.

Her legs felt sticky and she smelled blood. She reached her hand down. But it couldn't be. She'd just finished her period two weeks earlier. She got to her feet, collected her pajama bottoms, then limped to the bathroom.

The fluorescent light was like a blow to her face. The blood was bright and smeared along the insides of her legs. She sat down on the toilet and started to pee, when a sudden shock of nauseating pain in her anus made her gasp, and she realized the blood was coming from there. She took a deep breath, then washed herself gingerly, flinching with the pain. Turning off the light in the bathroom, she groped her way into the kitchen. On the way, she found her husband's jacket in a tangle on the floor. She picked it up, straightened it, and extracted his wallet from the breast pocket. She looked inside. Then she went to the telephone.

JANE

"Is this Miss Takagi, please?"

The call had been forwarded to my office. I picked it up, desperately hoping it wasn't Suzie Flowers.

"Yes, speaking . . ."

"Takagi-san . . . ?"

"Hai . . . sumimasen ga, donata-sama?" I'd switched to Japanese, but I had no idea who it was on the other end. The whispery voice sounded as though it were coming from a coffin, way underground.

"Akiko desu. Ueno Akiko desu."

"Ueno-san? Doshitano desuka? Are you all right? What time is it there?"

283

"It's three in the morning. I'm all right."

"Did you get my fax?"

". . . Yes. Yes, I got it."

"I can barely hear you. What's the matter? Is your husband there? Can he hear you?"

"He's asleep. It's okay. He's drunk and sleeping. He won't wake up." She paused and swallowed. "He found it."

"Found it? Found what? Oh no—my fax?"

"Yes. I'd put it between the pages of the English dictionary. He is so vain, you know, about his English? He never looks up any words. I thought it would be safe. But this time there was a word he didn't understand, from your fax to him on bad meats? I think it was 'unsavory.'"

"Akiko-san, I'm so sorry. What happened?"

"He became very angry."

"Did he hit you?"

"Yes. A little. It's all right."

"You must—"

"No. The reason I am calling is not that. The reason I am calling is because he has instructed me to pack a suitcase for him with clothing for a trip. He did not tell me where he is going, but I looked into his wallet and found his ticket. He will be leaving on Friday. He is going to Colorado."

THE GODS-ABSENT MONTH

SHŌNAGON

On the Day After a Fierce Autumn Wind

On the day after a fierce autumn wind everything moves one deeply. The garden is in a pitiful state with all the bamboo and lattice fences knocked over and lying next to each other on the ground. It is bad enough if the branches of one of the great trees have been broken by the wind; but it is a really painful surprise to find that the tree itself has fallen down and is now lying flat over the bush-clover and the valerians.

JANE

Colorado is one of the most beautiful states in the country. I love driving from east to west across the vast Great Plains, through Denver and straight up into the mountains, still so young and assertive with their jaggedy upward thrustings, then over the Continental Divide to hook up with the Colorado River and to follow it past the Glenwood Dam and on into the plateau. The westernmost town of any size is Grand Junction, once a thriving uranium production center in the years following WWII. When the mines closed, the Atomic Energy Commission allowed the radioactive mill tailings to be used in over six thousand housing structures and school foundations. Now Grand Junction is a center for fruit production—a rich riparian zone, the countryside bursts with iridescent peaches, sweet pears, luscious cherries, and glowing apples. The old river valley is cupped on either side by wildly eroded sandstone cliffs, like worn hands with fingers softly folded. Gradually these buttes and outcroppings subside even further, flattening into the gray clay deserts of eastern Utah, where ancient seas hid dinosaur bone and prehistoric fossil.

Before going to an area, I would read all about it, keeping track on a map of scenic spots, places of interest, as well as all military and atomic installations.

In Colorado Springs, the North American Air Defense

Command established the Ent Air Force Base in 1957. In 1966, inside Cheyenne Mountain, they opened a new combat operations center.

Just outside Denver was the Rocky Flats plutonium plant. It was closed in 1989 after two major fires and numerous accidents and leaks led to charges that the plant had seriously contaminated the surrounding countryside, causing a significant rise in cancers among Denver area residents and a veritable plague of mutations, deformations, reproductive disorders, and death among farm animals.

I kept track of these places even before our arrest in Montana. On the way to Fly, Oregon, driving through southwest Washington State, we had unwittingly stumbled across the border of the U.S. Department of Energy's Hanford site. I don't remember what we were after—possibly the perfect sunset, or the inflorescence of a rare northern desert cactus—but when we came to the barbed wire and a sign said "Department of Energy—Keep Out," how was I supposed to know that we'd reached the perimeter of the 570-mile nuclear city that produced the plutonium for "Fat Man," the bomb that leveled Nagasaki? Later, as we were passing through the adjacent town of Sunnyside, I happened to ask our waitress at a diner about the facility, and she raised her eyes and whistled.

"You went in there?" she said. "Ooh, that's a no-no."

Hanford was one of three atomic cities hastily constructed in 1943 to produce plutonium for the Manhattan Project. Over the next twenty-five years, massive clouds of radioactive iodine, ruthenium, caesium, and other materials were routinely released over people, animals, food, and water for hundreds of miles. In the 1950s, it was discovered that the radioactive iodine had contaminated local dairy cattle, their milk, and all the children who drank it. As the incidence of thyroid cancer grew, the farmers in the surrounding areas—"downwinders," they're called—began to wear turtlenecks to hide their scars. It was the fashion, the waitress told me.

When I recounted this story to the boys later on in the bar, Suzuki's narrow eyes widened. He'd had relatives in Nagasaki, all of whom had died.

We were lucky we didn't get busted. These sites are hazardous, and I'm not even talking about the environmental fallout. They are well and jealously guarded by men who make a Rodney Dwayne Peairs, the Louisiana butcher who shot the Japanese exchange student, look reasonable and benign. Paradoxically, they have conserved these desolate parts of the country. Often these landscapes hide underground bunkers, but on the surface they are rich with flora and fauna that have flourished, protected from families with fat-tired recreational vehicles, grazing cattle, and other ruminants.

We drove through Colorado in our fifteen-passenger Ford production van, past towns called Cope, Hygiene, and Last Chance. For this trip, it was the eastern part of the state that I was interested in. Early explorers called it the "great American desert," mile upon softly undulating mile, breathtaking and beautiful. Of course, it looks nothing like it once looked, when the first settlers came. The vistas, unbroken then and alive with grasses, are now cropped and divided into finite parcels whose neat right angles reassure their surveyors and owners while ignoring the subtle contours of the land. The fences stretch forever.

"You see that?" Dave, my local driver, interrupted my plains-induced reverie. He pointed to an immense field we'd been passing for several minutes or maybe hours. It looked like all the others, stubbly hacked wheat stalks in neat rows as far as the eye could see. It made me dizzy, like a bad moiré pattern on a videotape, and the back of my eyeballs ached. I squinted, trying to see what, in particular, he was pointing to.

"What?"

"There. The way wheat's been planted up that hillock, with the rows perpendicular, up and down the side?"

"Oh . . . Yeah?"

"Bad. Very bad."

"Why?"

"Erosion." He shook his head morosely.

Dave was an agricultural student at Colorado State University. His last name was Schultz, and he looked remarkably like a baby version of Sergeant Schultz on *Hogan's Heroes*, with an enormous breadth of chest and calm hands like sun-warmed rocks, made for comforting large terror-stricken animals. Suzuki and Oh liked him because he talked slowly and didn't use a lot of words.

One of the first things I ask a prospective driver is whether or not he likes to talk. Then I ask him what he knows about. Dave said, "Nope" and "Farms." I hired him on the spot.

Dave gave me the facts about farms:

The United States has lost one-third of its topsoil since colonial times—so much damage in such a short history. Six to seven billion tons of eroded soil, about 85 percent, are directly attributable to livestock grazing and unsustainable methods of farming feed crops for cattle. In 1988, more than 1.5 million acres in Colorado alone were damaged by wind erosion during the worst drought and heat wave since the 1950s.

"I remember it. I was on my dad's farm," said Dave. "I was just a kid then."

"Dave . . . 1988? That was just a couple of years ago."

"Yup."

Drought and heat waves happen, Dave explained. Erosion didn't have to. Not like this.

"You know what we have here?" Dave asked, an hour or so later.

"No, what?"

"A Crisis. A National Crisis."

"A national crisis?"

"Yup. Nobody sees it yet, but that's what it is, for sure."

"Dave, what are you talking about?"

He turned his head and stared at me, disbelieving, for a long time, so long that I started to get nervous; the Ford was rocketing down this country road, and Dave, though behind the wheel, wasn't watching at all. Finally he shook his head and turned to face forward again.

"Desertification," he pronounced glumly. He had more than his share of profound German melancholy, which seemed at odds with his sunny blond, pink face. He'd wanted to enter the Beef Science Program at the university and had written a paper on the effects of cattle on soil erosion. The paper was called "The Planet of the Ungulates," and it started out from the point of view of a Martian botanist who is circling the planet Earth in his spaceship, making a report on the creatures he sees below, only he's made a terrible mistake because he thinks that Earth is ruled by these large-bodied hoofed mathematicians who own small multicolored two-footed slaves; the slaves work from morning to night to feed their masters and to fabricate over the land their vast intricate geometries. Of course, the Martian never gets to see the inside of a slaughterhouse. But then again, who does?

Dave's professor failed him on "The Planet of the Ungulates," suggesting that he might be better off in the humanities rather than in agricultural sciences. As a result, he was taking a semester off, which was why he was free in October to work for us. He was thinking of dropping out entirely. Dave was not so popular at school because of his "take on things." This depressed him. So did his landscape.

Cattle are destroying the West, he told me, and whenever we passed a grazing herd, I could hear him groan. According to a 1991 United Nations report, 85 percent of U.S. Western rangeland, nearly 685 million acres, is degraded. There are between two and three million cattle allowed to graze on hundreds of millions of acres of public land in eleven Western states. *Public* land, Dave said, shaking his head.

"I read this thing by a guy in a magazine once," Dave said.

"Oh, well, that sure sounds interesting. . . ." Sarcasm, I figured, would be lost on Dave Schultz.

"Yup," he continued blandly, then gave me a dirty look. "It was an article in *Audubon* magazine. The guy was Philip Fradkin. Anyway, what he said was: 'The impact of countless hooves and mouths over the years has done more to alter the type of vegetation and land forms of the West than all the water projects, strip mines, power plants, freeways and sub-division developments combined.'"

"Wow." I took out my notebook to copy it down. Dave was odd, but I was impressed. "Tell me, Dave, did you happen to . . . I mean, did you memorize that?"

"Yup."

"How come?"

"I dunno. Guess I musta thought it was neat."

We drove in silence for another mile or two.

"Did you know seventy percent of all U.S. grain is used for livestock?" Dave suddenly burst forth again. His big hands clutched the steering wheel and he stared straight ahead, as though struggling to control some powerful emotion.

"And with all the tractors and machinery, it ends up taking the equivalent of one gallon of gas to make one pound of grain-fed U.S. beef?

"And do you know that the average American family of four eats more than two hundred sixty pounds of meat in a year? That's two hundred sixty gallons of fuel, which accounts for two point five tons of carbon dioxide going into the atmosphere and adding to global warming. . . .

"And that's not even taking into account that every Mc-Donald's Quarter Pounder represents fifty-five square feet of South American rain forest, destroyed forever, which of course affects global warming as well. . . ."

"No kidding." I was writing it all down. He looked over and gave me a smug grin.

"Nope. . . . Are you at all interested in methane gas emissions?"

Okay, so he'd lied about not liking to talk. I could forgive him, because Dave was obsessed.

"Ready?" he continued. "Scientists estimate that some sixty million tons of methane gas are emitted as belches and flatulence by the world's one point three billion cattle and other ruminant livestock each year. Methane is one of the four global warming gases, each molecule trapping twenty-five times as much solar heat as a molecule of carbon dioxide." He finished on a triumphant note, then sighed, and his powerful shoulders sank.

"This is great!" I said, scribbling wildly. I was excited. I had the beginnings of a solid Documentary Interlude that I could work into the Bunny Dunn Show. "Go on. . . ."

"I just don't know," he said sadly, as though the sight of my enthusiasm had somehow quenched his. "All these figures, but who cares? So what? It doesn't help one bit. Nobody is going to do anything about it, and then slowly, bit by bit, it will be too late."

"I really wish you hadn't said that." I put my notebook away and stared out the window.

Too late. Until Dave said that, I'd been feeling lucky. After Akiko's call, I had rounded up Suzuki and Oh, called the travel agent, and phoned Bunny and then Dave to tell them we'd be on the next plane to Denver. Next I called my obstetrician—I was due for a second ultrasound, as I was approaching the twenty-week mark, but he said it was fine to postpone for a week, until after the shoot. He asked how I was feeling and I told him just fine, which was true. In fact, I'd never felt better physically; although my belly was rounding out, it still wasn't really visible under my clothes and wasn't getting in my way at all. And emotionally I was oddly calm. And happy. And we had a four-day head start on Ueno. Somehow everything seemed to be falling into place.

AKIKO

Akiko stood in the bathroom with her bottom to the mirror, bent in half, peering over her shoulder. She drew her under-pants slowly down around her knees. Two days later, and her rectum was still bleeding. She looked at it now. Little flakes of black crusted blood stuck to the insides of her buttocks, and as she watched, a trickle of bright-red blood oozed from the center. Like a bleeding eye, she thought. She studied it, twisting her body to get a better view. Then she lunged toward the toilet. Tripped up by her underpants, she fell to her knees and vomited repeatedly.

Life is bloody, she thought, wiping her mouth. I don't mind, because it can't be helped.

She got up and shuffled to the sink. She gargled some water from the tap to rinse out the sour taste, then sat down on the toilet. She stuck a fresh sanitary napkin to her under-pants and waited. The worst was this terror of bowel movements. It hurt so much. She'd stopped eating almost entirely, hoping to avoid them until she healed, but it hadn't worked. She still had to go. She sat, shoulders clenched to her ears, fingers laced in prayer. Her knees trembled in anticipation of the pain. Instead she felt a sudden flooding sensation. She got up from the toilet seat. Her eyes went starry, and the world went black. She stood there for a moment, like a cartoon character who gets socked in the nose and sent reeling round and round while all the pretty little birds twitter, then her knees buckled and the floor disappeared altogether.

JANE

The problem with Bunny Dunn was one of framing. Specifically, it was her hair. Suzuki looked perplexed. I watched on the monitor as he framed in tight on her features, studied his composition, then widened out to encompass the perimeter of her hairdo. But this required such a radical expansion of the frame that now her face seemed dwarflike in the center, a small, bright diamond set in cotton candy. Suzuki sighed in frustration and zoomed back in again.

Balanced on the split-rail fence that surrounded her ranch house, Bunny Dunn was amplitude personified, replete with meats, our ideal American Wife. She had dressed for the interview in purple stretch jeans, hand-tooled alligator cowboy boots, and a purple checked shirt decorated with fringe and mother-of-pearl snaps that fought to stay attached across the expanse of her bosom. The upper snaps had popped open to reveal a massive depth of cleavage. The fringe had beads on the tips, which dangled from the edge of her breastline like raindrops clinging to the eaves of a house. Her perfume bent light like an aura. And then there was her hair, golden, like spun metal forged into a nest by a mythical bird of prey, impossible to capture on television. And this was only the head shot. When Suzuki widened out once again to show me a bust shot . . . Well, Bunny gave new meaning to the phrase. Her structure invited a CAD/CAM analysis of its component parts, and watching the monitor, I could imagine the digitized 3-D frame, slowly rotating. Oh waited on the sidelines, fiddling with the pin mike. He was going to have to go in and attach it inside Bunny's shirt. He was stricken with terror.

Maybe she heard Suzuki snicker or saw Oh shake his head in dismay.

"You think I don't know?" she cried, teetering on the rail. "You think I don't realize I look like a goddamn cartoon character with these inflated boobies and this big old butt? You ain't got no idea what it's like. Why do you think I dress like this?"

She was waiting for an answer. "Bunny, I . . ."

"Well, I'll tell you. 'Cause if I don't, I just look fat. Like a block on stilts. At least if I wear tight things I got some shape. You're probably laughing at my hair too. Don't worry. Everyone does, but do you know how limp and pinheaded I look without it?"

"I'm sorry, Bunny. We didn't mean . . ."

"Forget it," she said, recovering her balance. "I'm used to it. Hell, I used to be an exotic, remember? People were always laughing and staring. And darn it, they oughta stare. These babies are Nature's Bounty. That's what John calls 'em. No artificial growth enhancement here."

She cupped her huge breasts and lifted them toward Suzuki, made a little moue into the camera, and then turned on Oh. "Come here, boy. Don't be scared, they ain't gonna bite you. There's plenty of room to hide that little gadget of yours down here. Just stick it in wherever you want."

That's when we all began to like her. Bunny drove a custom-painted purple Sedan de Ville. It was a comfortable car for her husband, John, to ride in and easy to get in and out of as well. John was less active in running the feedlot these days, but he still liked to keep an eye on what his son was up to, so Bunny would drive him on his rounds every day, a long, sleek purple ship cutting through a sea of milling cattle. We set the camera up on one of the feed towers, and it made a great wide shot for the title sequence. At their various stops Bunny would help John out of the car and into his wheelchair. He spent most of his time in his chair, propelled by Bunny.

"I like it down here," he cackled, gazing up adoringly at the shelf of breast that shielded his balding head. "Lots of shade."

Bunny slapped his pate. He pinched her bottom. They had a playful and loving relationship that caused his son, Gale, to shiver with rage. Gale was a pale, flaccid man with a chin that simply receded into the swollen flesh of his neck. A thyroid condition, perhaps. His handshake reminded me of Ueno's. Cold. Damp. Suspicious.

And then there was Rose. Strange Rose. "She's shy," explained Bunny as the little girl clawed her mother's thigh and buried her face between her legs. She was still just a baby at five, but her eyes were haunted, and there was something about her, not timidity, not just the eyes, that was deeply disturbing. She looked ordinary enough, a plump, pretty child with light-brown ringlets, dressed in puffy smock dresses. Her daddy doted on her, but it was Gale whom she adored. From time to time a flicker of doubt crossed Bunny's face when she looked at her daughter. There was a secret. I didn't know what it was, but Gale knew, and he leered at me when he caught me staring at his half-sister.

The Dunn & Son feedlot was a twenty-thousand-head operation located about fifteen miles down the road from Bunny and John's house, in a shallow bowl of land just shy of the foothills. The Rockies rose up in the distance to the west, but the east was horizontal, an endless expanse of griddle-flat cropland.

From a distance, the feedlot itself looked like an island, an enormous patchwork comprising neatly squared and concentrated beef-to-be. Angus, Brangus, Hereford, Charolais, Limousin, and Simmental, these were breeds, not animals, penned with precision and an eye to slaughter that was antithetical to the randomness of living things. The only aspect of their animal nature that could not be contained by the gridwork was the stench, an aggregate of all the belches and flatulence, the ammonia, methane, and hydrogen sulfide gases exuded with the fecal matter and urine of twenty thousand large-bodied animals. It rose and spread like anarchy on the autumn wind. The closer we came, the stronger it got.

The wooden ranch gate that marked the drive into the feedlot proclaimed:

Dunn & Son, Custom Cattle Feeders
John and Gale Dunn, proprietors
"Dunn to Perfection"

Gale was waiting for us in the small feedlot office. He was nervous and had taken special care with his appearance. His baby-blue plaid shirt was buttoned tight around the neck, making his reddened wattles bunch up at the collar. He wore a string tie fastened with a big hunk of turquoise. The polyester fabric of his shirt stuck to his sweaty skin, despite the stale, humid air-conditioning in the office. He fidgeted, removing his cowboy hat to run his fingers through his straw-colored hair. He had the jittery blue eyes of a newly farrowed sow, rimmed in pink, with pale, bristle-like lashes. Periodically he puffed out his chest to levitate his gut, a maneuver that gave him enough room to tuck his shirt into the belt below it.

He was to take us on a tour of the feedlot. We would film the operations, and later Bunny, John, and Rose would join us to shoot some family scenes. I was hoping to get most of the feedlot footage on Day One. On Day Two we were scheduled to go to the slaughterhouse. On the morning of Day Three we would shoot Bunny and John's house and their interior decor, and by the afternoon of Day Three, when Ueno was due to arrive, we would be on to the cooking scenes and the family dining. I thought that the sight of Bunny in an apron, searing bulls' testicles, would soften Ueno, and he could supervise that scene to his heart's content. He had approved the show, after all. I just wanted a free hand with the meat production.

Suzuki got set up and Oh pinned the wireless mike on Gale, although I didn't anticipate getting much usable sound. So far, Gale had been surly and uncooperative, and it seemed he had agreed to this tour only at his father's insistence. Still, you can't shoot cows without a cowboy, and I needed Gale because his father was too decrepit.

"Ready?" I tried to give him a reassuring smile, but Gale was growing more distraught by the minute.

"Cheer up. You don't have to say anything, just show us around. Or ignore us. Pretend we're not even there."

But he surprised me. We filmed him leaving the office, then walking along one of the dirt access roads that cut alongside the pens. Suzuki went handheld, tracking backward with Gale, filming him as he walked. I stayed next to Suzuki, with my hand looped through his belt, steadying him and trying to keep him from tripping in a rut. Oh was attached to us by the camera cable, doing his best to record ambiance, mix, and keep up with us. Dave orbited the periphery with the tripod on his shoulder, staying out of the frame. We made a curious constellation, with Gale as our stiff, silent nucleus. Then all of a sudden, with no warning, he looked straight into the camera and started to speak.

"Well, howdy," he said with a nervous smile. "Uh, I guess I'll just introduce myself first. I'm Gale Dunn, and this here's my spread. I'm the one in charge here."

He had actually scripted his lines and now was going to perform them. Warming to his role, he puffed out his chest and lowered his voice, sounding bass and manly.

"Uh, some guys run their operations from the office, but I'm a hands-on kind of guy, if you know what I mean."

He shifted his pale gaze from the lens and looked over at me. "I said 'guy' twice. Is that okay?"

"Uh . . . yeah, fine." I was astonished. "You're doing just great. Please go on. . . ."

With a renewed sense of confidence, he looked back at the camera and raised his arms in an awkward sweeping gesture that encompassed the acres of pens surrounding us.

"Like I was sayin', I'm in charge of all this here, ever since Dad got remarried to that . . . married Bunny. That's his new wife's name, but she ain't my real mother. My real mother died. Ever since Dad got remarried he ain't too effective 'round here anymore, so I oversee the operations of the entire lot and personally supervise mixin' the feeds and the medicines."

This seemed like a good opportunity to focus the conversation.

"What kind of medication do you give them?"

"When they come in for processin', we give 'em a prophylactic dose of Aureomycin and then implant 'em with Synovex as a growth supplement."

"Are you using DES?"

"No; it's illegal."

"Did you?"

"Oh yeah. Who didn't? It's still the best and cheapest growth enhancer around—"

"Still?"

"No. That ain't what I meant. I meant if it was still around. Which it ain't." He stopped walking and glared at me, his voice rising in pitch and volume. "Wait a minute. What's goin' on here? I thought you were workin' for BEEF-EX. What are you givin' me the third degree here for?"

"Sorry. Just curious. What's Synovex?"

"It's a growth hormone. Perfectly legal. You give the heifers Synovex-H, and the steers get Synovex-S."

"What's in it, do you know?"

He looked at me with scorn. "Estradiol, testosterone, and progesterone. All natural."

My questions seemed to have quenched his enthusiasm for television and he walked along for a while, huffy, ignoring the camera entirely. I didn't know what had gotten into me; I was normally not so blunt and graceless with my interview questions, but the guy just bugged me. Still, now I'd blown it and needed to lure him back.

It was high noon and the desert sun bore down so hard it dimmed vision and made solid objects wriggle. This kind of heat was odd for October. The dirt was parched and the hot wind buffeted your face with a stench you could taste—the sick-sweet smell of manure, cut with searing fumes of ammonia that rose from the urine-drenched ground by the feed bunkers. Black flies buzzed furiously around us, but Suzuki had given up trying to shoo them away from the lens, concentrating instead on clearing his eyes of the sweat that cut rivulets through the dust on his forehead. Dust was everywhere. It got in your eyes, in your throat. The wind lifted up the dust, twirling it into tight little twisters that danced in and out of the pens. The only sounds were the wind, and the flies buzzing, and the eerie wheeze and rattle of twenty thousand cattle coughing. We stopped by the side of a pen. Gale turned to face us, resting the backs of his elbows casually on the top of the gate and hitching his boot heel around the rung at the bottom. He looked at me. His body language was all about openness, a casual cowboy-nailed-to-the-cross sort of posture, but his eyes were wary. The penned cattle in the background turned to watch. It made a lovely picture. Dave sidled up to me while Suzuki reframed.

"Ask him about feed," he whispered in my ear.

I looked over at Suzuki, who turned on the camera and gave me a nod and a thumbs-up.

"So, Gale, what kind of feed do you use?"

Gale grinned. "Well now, I was hopin' you'd ask about that. You East Coast environmental types are always going on about recycling . . . well, that's just what we're doing here with our exotic feed program and we're real proud of it. We got recycled cardboard and newspaper. We got by-products from potato chips, breweries, liquor distilleries, sawdust, wood chips. We even got by-products from the slaughterhouse— recycling cattle right back into cattle. Instant protein. Pretty good, huh?"

"That's cannibalism!"

He looked at me with utter contempt. "They ain't humans," he said.

"Wasn't there a problem with that in England a couple of years back? It caused something—some disease that ate the cows' brains and made them crazy. . . ."

"Nineteen eighty-seven," Dave hissed behind me. "It was in nineteen eighty-seven."

"Wouldn't know," said Gale, spitting. "This is America. Never been a problem here. . . ."

"I think it's illegal," Dave said. He couldn't keep quiet.

"Nah, it's all done local." I didn't quite see how this

addressed our concerns, but Gale continued without missing a beat.

"It's a changing field—there's scientific developments in feed technology happening all over America, all the time. Some guy down at Kansas State I read about has come up with plastic hay. It's these plastic pellets you can feed the cattle instead of regular hay. Hay's a bitch, but this plastic stuff—it's clean, it's easy to deliver through an automated feed system. Works just as good for roughage and you only need a tenth of a pound compared to four pounds of hay. That's a forty-to-one ratio. They say it's a savings of about eleven cents a day per head. And the best thing is they can get back about twenty pounds of it—right out of the cow's rumen at the slaughterhouse. Make new pellets. Talk about recycling!"

"You feed animals *plastic?*"

"And if you like that, well, get this one. Cement. That's right. Cement dust. High in calcium, and the cows in the tests put on weight thirty percent faster than normal feed, and the meat was more tender and juicy."

"Who is doing these tests?"

"United States Department of Agriculture. I got one more for you, but you ain't gonna like it."

Behind him, dominating the center of the pen, was a towering bulldozed mound, which rose above the sea of cattle. The mound was alive with flies. He pointed to it with his thumb.

"See that?"

"What?"

"Shit." He grinned as Suzuki racked focus.

"No way . . ."

"No shit—I mean, I ain't kidding. Out one end and in the other. Now, talk about fast turnaround."

"That's disgusting."

"Nope. It's recycling, only it's recycling animal by-products.

305

You gotta understand the way feedlots work. The formulated feed we use is real expensive, and the cattle shit out about two-thirds before they even digest it. Now, there's no reason this manure can't be recycled into perfectly good feed. There's this one pig farmer in Kansas who ran his pregnant sows underneath his finishing pens? You know what he saved in feed costs? About ten thousand dollars a year." His words resonated with awe and he withdrew for a minute into a private reverie, then he shook his head and continued.

"And another thing you East Coast environmentalists are always griping about is organic-waste pollution. Well, you should be real happy, 'cause this pretty much takes care of the problem, don't it. Feed the animals shit, and it gets rid of the waste at the same time. That's two birds with one stone."

The cattle that formed a backdrop did not look happy at all. Suzuki, picking up on the content of the interview, zoomed in on a cow who was raising her tail to defecate. I was proud of him. His English comprehension had improved immensely over the months of shooting. He adjusted his position and grabbed a close-up of a steer, feeding mournfully at the trough.

Just at that moment we heard a car horn in the distance and turned, to see the purple Cadillac barreling toward us, followed by a massive wake of dust. It stopped about ten feet away, but the dust cloud kept on coming. Suzuki cursed and coughed as he shielded the Betacam with his torso, but an odd noise from Gale made him reframe and turn on the camera.

"Ro-o-osie!" Gale squealed.

The purple car was hidden, but out from the center of the billowing cloud came Rose, running. Gale leaned down to greet her and she threw herself into her half-brother's arms. He swung her up high, tossing her into the air over his head. Her dress ballooned around her little kicking legs as she came to land solidly on his hip.

"How's my favorite little helper today?" he crooned. "Come

to help Uncle Gale mix up a nice dinner for all the cows?"
Rose nodded happily, but when she saw us she withdrew,
burrowing her face into the side of Gale's soft neck and
peeking at us out of the corner of her eye. Suzuki trained the
camera on her as Bunny emerged from the direction of the car,
pushing John in his wheelchair over the rough dirt road.

"What's that lyin' son-of-a-bitch son of mine been tellin'
y'all?" John hollered. "Come on down here, Rosie. Come sit on
yer daddy's lap and we'll go for a ride."

Rose shook her head and clung tighter.

"Leave her alone, John," said Bunny, pressing his shoulder.
"She wants to help her Uncle Gale."

"Well, she's a smart one. He needs help . . . ," John
grumbled.

I liked the idea too. It would make a nice scene—big
brother teaching little sister how to feed the beef—so we
filmed the family walking to the feedmill, and inside we
prepped the scene. Gale would mix feed and medication. Rose
would help. Bunny and John would look on approvingly as the
knowledge and traditions of the American West were passed
on to the next generation. Everyone was in place. Rosie was
helping Gale get ready, dragging a half-empty paper sack that
was almost as big as she was across the floor. Suzuki was
resetting the white balance on the camera to accommodate the
hospital-bright fluorescents, and while I waited for him I took
a look around.

A larger hopper dominated the room, used for funneling
the mixed feed into the auger system. There was a refrigerator
in one corner and an industrial sink in the other. Next to me
was a long stainless-steel counter, which I leaned on. Stacked
against the wall were more paper sacks, like large flour bags,
containing what I suddenly recognized as various brands of
powdered drugs. A thick coat of dust covered every surface.
At first I didn't think anything of it. Dust was everywhere,

indoors and out. But then I noticed I had dust on my hands from the stainless-steel counter, and up close it seemed to consist of a mix of ground-up grains and powder.

Something caught in my chest, a quick little fear, and it traveled straight down to my gut. I went to the sink to wash my hands. Next to the sink was a large metal garbage can filled with small empty bottles. I picked one out and examined the red and white label. Lutalyse, the hormone used to synchronize the estrus of a herd for easier artificial insemination. I didn't understand. Gale was not breeding cattle. Why would he be using Lutalyse in a feedlot? In the garbage can I found the insert that came with the bottle.

WARNING: Not for human use.

Women of childbearing age, asthmatics, and persons with bronchial and other respiratory problems should exercise extreme caution when handling this product. In the early stages, women may be unaware of their pregnancies. Dinoprost tromethamine is readily absorbed through the skin and can cause abortion and/or bronchospasms. Direct contact with the skin should, therefore, be avoided. Accidental spillage on the skin should be washed off **immediately** with soap and water.

Use of this product in excess of the approved dose may result in drug residues.

I was still holding the bottle. I dropped it back into the garbage and turned on the tap. My hands were shaking and the bar of soap kept slipping from my grip and landing on the bottom of the sink with a drumlike thud. There was a brush next to the faucet and I scrubbed my hands with it as hard as I could. I couldn't stop scrubbing. Or shaking.

"Are you all right?" Dave asked, suddenly next to me.

I pointed to the garbage pail. "I touched it."

Dave picked out the bottle and looked at the label. "Lutalyse," he said. "Fairly common. It shouldn't be a problem—"

"I'm pregnant."

Dave stared at me. "You shouldn't be here at all."

Just then Suzuki gave the thumbs-up. I turned to Gale and tried to control my voice.

"Why are you using Lutalyse? Are you breeding cattle?"

John and Bunny looked confused. Gale snickered with pride. "Now, ain't that something? You see what I mean? That's just another example of modern science comin' up with a way to kill two birds with one stone. We ain't breedin' here, but we use that same Lutalyse to abort our heifers when they get accidental bred, you know? Before gettin' here. Actually, we give 'em all a shot when they come in for processin', just in case. They abort so nice and smooth they don't go off their feed for a second, don't even miss a mouthful."

"But why?"

"Jeez," he said, shaking his head. "You can't have pregnant heifers in a feedlot. All they do is eat, eat, eat, and never gain. Our job here is gainin'."

John snorted. Suzuki panned over to him, adjusted the frame, and continued to roll.

"Crazy, that's what it is," John growled. "Used to be you waited till an animal was sick or needed it before you pumped 'em full of drugs. It's all a scam, son. You're just throwin' your money at these big pharmacooticals. . . . My money, I should say. Them scientists of yers, they git their paychecks from the pharmacooticals, and they're all in cahoots with the gov'ment."

"Can't do it any other way, Dad," Gale whined. "I've explained all this to you. Times have changed."

He turned to address us. The pitch of his voice was rising again, the more excited he got.

"Profit's so small these days you gotta deal in volume, and

without the drugs we'd be finished. The math just don't work out. I'm bringing more head to slaughter than he ever did. If it weren't for the modernizing I accomplished around here—"

"Yeah, yeah, I heard all that before," John interrupted loudly. "Maybe it's so, Gale, but that don't make it right. Getting so you gotta be a goddamned chemist to fatten up a cow."

He spun his wheelchair around and headed toward the door. "Come on, Bunny. Bring your daughter. This ain't no place for a child to be playin'."

Bunny looked at us and shrugged.

"Rosie, baby, come on," she called. "Uncle Gale's got work to do."

"Uncle Gale?" Rose whispered, tugging at Gale's elbow as he watched Bunny help his father negotiate the threshold. "Uncle Gale . . . ?"

Gale ignored her, but she persisted.

"Uncle Gale . . . ?"

Finally he noticed, crouched down, and put his arm around her. "What is it, darlin'?"

She whispered something in his ear. He grinned and stood and went to the dusty refrigerator. As he opened it I got a glimpse of the shelves inside, lined with row after row of little rubber-topped bottles. Gale reached into the freezer section above and pulled out a bright-blue popsicle on a little plastic stick from a tray of molds. He saw me watching.

"You want one?" he asked. I shook my head. "You mix 'em up with Kool-Aid. Rosie loves 'em. Can't have a visit with Uncle Gale without an ice pop, hey?"

Rosie took the popsicle in her dust-covered hands and stuck it in her mouth. The heat started melting it almost immediately and the sticky blue liquid ran down between her fingers. Contentedly she licked it off and sucked at the pop.

"Come *on*, Rosie," called Bunny from outside. Rosie reached her arms up to Gale. He bent down and she planted a sugary kiss on his cheek, then scampered out the door. When he stood up again I saw that her kiss had left behind a wet mark on his skin, like a brand, in the encrusted dust.

"He's an old fart," said Gale, more to himself than to us. He stood in the doorway watching Rose run after her father. "Can't see an inch beyond the tip of his pecker." He noticed Suzuki was still filming and put up his hand to block the lens. "Don't you use that last thing I said," he growled at me. "Don't need you stirring up more trouble round here."

I told Suzuki to cut and thanked Gale for his time and for the tour. He grunted, then went back to work, turning his attention to one of the large drug sacks. All I wanted was to get out of that room. I washed my hands again quickly, but by then Suzuki had spotted a cutaway shot—a shaft of sunlight filtering through a high window, illuminating the dust particles that were sent swirling in the air as Gale dragged the sack toward the hopper. I fled through the door before he had time to rip it open, then waited outside in the blistering heat until finally the crew emerged. Suzuki apologized: Gale had started to mix up some feed, he explained, and he had gone ahead and shot the scene without me. He watched me with a worried expression.

"Takagi, are you all right?"

"I'm fine. I'm sorry. You're right, I should have thought of it. Of course we need that footage. I should have stayed. . . ."

"No, that's not what I mean. Are you all right physically?"

"I'm fine, Suzuki, thanks. Really. I'm sorry. It's just . . ."

"You should go home and take care of yourself and the baby."

"I know. But really, I'm fine now. Let's just get this over with."

My throat ached and I felt tears pressing up into my eyes. I was losing it, losing focus, control, forgetting what I needed for the show. The shots of Gale mixing the feed were essential—without them I'd never be able to edit together his interview on the subject. And we needed footage of the entire feedlot too, to show the extent of the Dunn operation. But the heat was sucking the air from my lungs, and for the first time, I was scared.

I wanted to get out of there, to go back to the motel and get perfectly clean and then curl up in cool sheets and hug my belly for the next few months, until it was huge and viable.

Instead I led the crew in the direction of a cluster of long, low buildings that Gale had identified as the processing area, telling myself all the while to stop being self-indulgent.

The Dunns had a custom lot, where ranchers brought their cattle for finishing. Nearby we heard the clatter and clang of hooves striking steel and the *whump* of a hydraulic squeeze chute. This was followed by a bellowing cry of pain. Oh shuddered. The cattle wound in a long curving line toward the chute; confined between high narrow walls, they waited their turn to get processed. A young cowboy was operating the squeeze, and two others were branding and administering injections. Every time an animal was released, the row of waiting cattle reluctantly advanced by one and the animal at the head was forced, struggling, into the chute, where a metal collar trapped its neck and the hydraulic sides of the pen compressed to restrain its body.

"Sonofa*bitch*," said the young cowboy, planting his heel down hard on the bony rump of a recalcitrant steer.

The terrified animal evacuated copiously and the smell of searing hair and flesh from the brand added to the stench.

"What's that?" I asked an older cowboy. He was wielding an enormous hypodermic needle, which he plunged into the steer's neck. The thick hide twitched. The cowboy ignored me and withdrew the needle.

Suzuki swung himself up onto the top of the chute to get an angle on the incoming cattle and the action inside the squeeze. Dave stood next to him, supporting him with one hand and holding the camera with the other. The cowboys watched skeptically, but the sight of Dave seemed to reassure them. I waited for Suzuki to get settled, retrieve the camera from Dave, and turn it back on.

"Lutalyse?" I asked again. "Is that what you're injecting?"

The older cowboy snorted with derision. "This here's a steer, miss. Don't give Lutalyse to no steer."

"Then what is it?"

"Dunno."

"You don't know what you're giving them?"

"Nope."

The young cowboy grinned and winked at me. "Boss's special formula."

The older cowboy frowned at him. "Listen. We just shoot 'em up. Don't ask no questions." He sounded too curt and he realized this.

"It's medicine to keep 'em disease free," he added. "Good clean meat for you city folks. That's all I know."

"Yup, these cows here's goin' straight to Japan," said the young cowboy conversationally. "I heard they even eat the assholes and everything. Is that where y'all are from?"

The older cowboy spit. "Donny, you just shut yer mouth and don't go sayin' shit you don't know nothin' about."

"Well, that's what Roy down at the packin' plant told me. Straight to Japan, Taiwan, and Korea. You ask me, it's a darn shame, wasting all that good American meat on a bunch of gooks. No offense," he added, looking over at me.

"None taken."

It was a great sound bite. Having had his say, Donny settled back into a silent sulk. We watched them process a couple more animals, then headed back to the van down one of the long access roads that cut between the acres of pens. Cows huddled, tails swatting, hides quivering with flies. You forget how big cows are, slow and warm and solid. Sometimes they looked up as we passed, watching us with mournful, seeping eyes. Suddenly Suzuki stopped dead in his tracks and handed me the Betacam. He clambered up the side of a pen and held out his hand. Passing him the camera, I climbed up next to him. On the far side of the pen was a cluster of heifers, feeding at the bunker. Suzuki ignored them and trained the camera on the ground just below us. In the dust lay a slimy, half-dried puddle containing a misshapen tangle of glistening calf-like parts—some hooves, a couple of bent and spindly shins. It was an aborted fetus, almost fully grown, with matted fur, a delicate skull, and grotesquely bulging eyes. Suzuki rotated the lens into a telephoto setting, but even without it, through the swarm of flies, I could see that the eyes of the calf were alive with newly hatched maggots.

We drove to the motel. Inside the van we were all silent. I thought the boys were asleep, but when I looked back they were wide awake, each slumped on a long bench seat by himself, staring out the window at the flat horizon. Dave kept glancing over at me and nervously adjusting the temperature controls. He didn't speak, either. It was cool in the van, but I was sticky with perspiration and dust. I kept imagining what the dust must contain, the microscopic particulates of toxic powder, dissolving in my sweat, now leaching back through my pores, and the thought made my skin prickle and flush and sweat some more.

At the motel, we unloaded quickly. I was desperate for a

shower, for sleep, for even just a short nap. We were due back at the ranch at five to shoot Bunny serving cocktails, still there was time. But as I shouldered my knapsack and headed toward my room, Suzuki stopped me.

"*Takagi-chan, chotto* . . ."

"Suzuki . . . what?" I turned, about to snap, but then I saw his face. And Oh's, behind him.

"*Gomen, ne* . . . ," he said. "Sorry. I know you are tired. But there is something I think you must see."

"Can't it wait? Until tonight after we finish?"

Suzuki and Oh exchanged a quick look.

"No," Suzuki said.

"I will cue up the tape," said Oh. "If you would like to take a shower."

The hot water revived me, washed off the dirt, which ran in soapy rivulets down my legs, spiraling into the drain between my bare feet. But as I watched, it occurred to me that the heat of the water, by opening my pores, might increase the osmosis of any poison that remained on my skin. Panicked, I twisted the shower knobs and gasped as the water turned icy. I stood there shivering. For the first time, I think I was aware of the danger I'd walked into, the effect it might have on the baby. I needed to make a choice. I could continue with the shoot or abandon it right here, turn it over to Suzuki to finish, or call Kenji down from New York to take over. I rubbed my stomach, stupidly, as if that would help, and cried a little, then got out of the shower and dried myself off. My teeth would not stop chattering.

We gathered in Oh's room. He had cued the last half of the interview with Gale. It looked great: awkward and grandiose, Gale leaned against the rail of the cattle pen, gesturing expansively around him. I started to feel a little better.

"How did you know to ask him about feed?" I asked Dave. "It seems to be his little hobby."

Dave grinned. "When we were in the office I saw that he had all these copies of *Feed Sense* and *Feed Stuffs* and *Food Chemical News* all neatly cataloged on the shelf, and when I pulled one out I saw he'd tagged articles like he was seriously studying them. It seemed like a good bet he'd have something interesting to say."

The interview was over and Gale was leaning with his back to the pen and behind him the cautious cattle were drawing closer in a line, doleful and curious, when suddenly a swish pan triggered by a squeal of joy caught little Rose running from the middle of the dust cloud. She leapt into Gale's arms and he swung her up and tossed her high, and the camera followed her arc so that for a moment it looked as though she would just keep on flying up into the bright blue sky. But then she came down and landed on Gale's broad hip and behind them the cattle scattered.

Suzuki had lingered for a moment on this shot of the two of them, then slowly framed in on Rose. She buried her face in the softness of Gale's neck, but met the encroaching gaze of the camera and stared back into its depth. Suzuki kept zooming in, so close you could see the crosshatched texture of Gale's sunburned skin. Rose just stared, unblinking. It wasn't a look of particular intelligence, but once more, something struck me about the girl.

"She's odd, so weird-looking . . . ," I said, and realized I was whispering.

Again, we had all fallen silent, drawn by the camera as it slowly passed across the little girl's face and down her body. Gale had wrapped his thick arm around her. His forearm supported her back and his hand held her in place, tight around her stomach, partially hidden in the folds of her dress. The camera paused there, studying this image, taking it in with a long, steady gaze, when suddenly it tipped, as though an unexpected shift in gravity had rocked the world.

"Oh God," said Dave in a low voice. I looked at him. He was staring at the screen, so I looked back too, but it was the same frame as before—the man's callused hand clasping the little girl's body.

"What . . . ?" I asked. "What is it?"

"She's . . . precocious," Dave said, and it sounded like a dirty secret, a cruel joke that I still didn't get. Rose was hardly precocious. Slow, perhaps even dumb . . .

"No, not her personality," said Dave, shaking his head impatiently. "Her development. Here." He clasped his hands to his chest.

"*Oppai ga aruyo,*" said Suzuki, pointing at the monitor. "Look. Right there. See? I noticed it when I was shooting. I wanted to show you. She has breasts."

His finger tapped the screen where he had zoomed in further to Rose's chest. There, resting on the callused edge of her half-brother's hand, was a pronounced swelling, which had looked like bunched fabric at first but now, up close, had the weight and heft of a woman's breast. Underneath the white smock dress, pulled tight by Gale's hand, you could see the shape of the enlarged areola and the outline of her nipple.

"It's premature thelarche," said Dave. "I read about cases in Puerto Rico. Precocious puberty. These little girls with estrogen poisoning. They thought it was some kind of growth stimulants in meat or milk or poultry. I think they suspected DES. You asked Gale about it, so I guess you know about DES?"

I nodded.

"Yeah," he continued. "Well, it's still easy to get down there. Some of the girls were just babies, like a year old, with almost fully developed breasts. Some of them were even boys."

"What happened?"

"Nothing much. There was this one doctor who tried to get the FDA to do tests, which ended up half-assed and inconclusive. But the media attention was enough to scare off the farmers from using the drugs, and after a while the symptoms just slowly regressed when the kids stopped eating the contaminated foods. But not before a lot of them developed cysts in their ovaries . . . and of course there's the danger of cancer too."

"Do you think it's in the meat, then?" I asked, still looking at Rose.

"It's gotta be that feedroom, something she picks up there . . ."

"The popsicles . . ."

"Or just the dust from her fingers. What I'm wondering is, do you think Bunny knows?"

I thought about it. "She must. Look at the way she dresses her, in those loose clothes. . . ."

"The brother knows too," said Suzuki. "Look."

We all stared at the screen. Suzuki was holding the tight shot of Gale's hand, and after a moment, the large thumb started to move, slowly, surreptitiously, up and down, underneath his sister's breast.

"God," said Dave. "He's fondling her."

Suzuki coughed. Oh turned away from the screen and started to re-coil the camera cables one by one, even though they didn't need it. His cables were never knotted or kinked. He always kept them perfectly wrapped and secured them with little-girls' hair elastics, the kind with pastel plastic balls on the ends. I looked back at the television. Suzuki widened out to a two-shot and something occurred to me.

"You know, I don't think Gale knows what causes it. In fact, I think he's got a dose himself. Look at him. I thought it was just a barrel chest, but now I'm not so sure. And his voice, it sounds like it's changing. He had to strain today to keep it low, but as soon as he got upset it went up about an octave and started to crack."

The tape ran out and cut to static. We sat there for a moment, watching, then Oh got up and ejected the tape and slipped it into its plastic case, and like the moving parts of a heavy machine, we gathered up the camera equipment and filed out to the sweltering van. A TV shoot is like a tank, I sometimes felt, rolling over anything that lies in the path of its inexorable forward momentum.

"What are you going to do?" Dave asked as we drove down the frontage road, away from the motel.

I looked out the window. We were passing a large construction site, where bulldozers had dug a gaping crater in the ground. The site was empty now; the workday was over. A red, white, and blue sign, standing next to the mobile office trailer, read "Future Home of Wal-Mart." Beyond the pit, the fields stretched away into the distance.

"I'm going to talk to her," I said.

Bunny and Rose came to greet us at the door in matching white cotton dresses with cinched waists and wide ruffles around the neckline. Bunny's was quite low-cut, to offer up her cleavage, but Rose's was cut high and prim. They led us out to the patio, where John sat by a low bar, scaled to the height of his wheelchair. He waved a bottle of Jack Daniel's over his head when he saw us.

"Just in time, just in time," he hollered. "I'm servin' bourbon and bourbon. Take your pick."

Behind me I could hear Suzuki gulp. I declined for all of us, and then relented: we'd shoot the cocktail scene quickly, I promised, then the boys could have a drink. They needed it. Suzuki and Oh sprang to a grim sort of attention, and within minutes they had the camera cabled up, balances set, and were tracking backward in front of Bunny as she proudly carried a large silver platter of piping-hot Pigs-in-a-Blanket from the kitchen. She set them on the coffee table next to John. Rose climbed up on her daddy's lap and fed him a plump wiener, skewered on the tip of a toothpick and wrapped in a crusty twirl of golden dough.

"She's gonna be a regular little heartbreaker," John cackled as she waggled another sausage coyly in front of him. "Just like her mama."

He fed her a sip of bourbon from his glass, watered down now with melted ice, and she screwed up her face and shook her curls, then begged for more. Hand on the zoom, Suzuki hunkered down to get a close-up of the two, as John traded her a sip for a sausage.

We filmed a quick setup of the three of them—All-American ranch family spends a happy time together at the end of a long, hard day—then I called it a wrap and John made drinks for the boys. When Bunny went back to the kitchen to fetch some hot hors d'oeuvres, I followed her.

"I have to tell you something."

I know what denial looks like, and what it feels like too. It's a mercurial flicker of recognition in the eye, quickly blanketed with a vagueness that infuses the body like sluggish blood. It is opaque. Murky. Like wading through a swampy dream that drags at your limbs, and no matter how hard you try, you can't move forward. I know this feeling because I make television and try to walk through it on a daily basis. It feeds on convention, cowers behind etiquette, and the only way to deal with it is with a blunt frontal attack.

"Bunny, I think Rose is sick."

Her look was quick and sharp before she turned her back to me. She slipped her hand into a black-and-white oven mitt shaped like a cow's head and bent down to open the oven.

"I think she's received some sort of hormone poisoning, probably from the drugs around the feedlot, and that's why she's got breasts. There's a name for it. It's called premature thelarche."

Bunny extracted a hot baking tray of Pigs-in-a-Blanket, set them carefully on top of the stove, then turned to face me.

"She takes after me, you know, in the breast department," she said. She looked ruefully down at her own chest and sort of pushed at it with the nose of the cow mitt. Her tanned skin was the texture of an old mushroom, dotted with beads of sweat that clung in the cleavage. It was hot by the oven and I was sweating too. "John says I should be proud . . . ," she added.

"He knows?"

"Well, sort of." She took off the mitt and started scraping the pastries away from the tin with a metal spatula. "About her breasts, anyway . . . But he's so old, you know? Like, maybe there's not much difference between five and fifteen from where he stands. . . ."

"What is it, Bunny? Is there something else . . . other than the breasts?"

She piled the pastries onto a platter. "The doctor's a good friend of John's, you know? But he's an old guy too. Said he'd never seen anything like it. But even he doesn't know about . . ." She stopped again and looked out onto the patio. Little Rose was turning pirouettes and squealing with delight as she danced in a circle from her daddy to Suzuki to Oh and finally to Dave, popping the sausage pastries into their mouths, one by one. John was clapping, egging her on. The boys sat with hunched shoulders and frozen smiles while Rose spun round and round.

"It's none of your business, you know," Bunny informed me, handing me the platter.

"I know," I said. I took the platter and turned toward the porch, then stopped. "Well, actually, no, Bunny. That's not true. It is and it isn't."

321

She gave me a long, cool stare.

"I had a kind of estrogen poisoning too. Different—I got it from my mother—but, well, it screwed me up inside. I had a growth, like a cancer, on my cervix. And my uterus is deformed. These things are dangerous, Bunny."

I waited, watching her, but her gaze drifted, looked right past me onto the porch, just staring like she hadn't heard a word I said, so I gave up. Balancing the tray of Pigs-in-a-Blanket, I got as far as opening the sliding patio door when her voice behind me, so low I could barely hear it, made me stop.

"Come back tonight," she said. "After eleven. After they're asleep."

I turned back, but she was already busy at work, head bent, wrapping little canned cocktail wieners in triangles of Poppin' Fresh dough. I wasn't sure I'd heard her right. But then she looked up, looked me straight in the eye.

"Bring the cameraman."

The house was quiet when I pulled up the van and parked. Bunny met us at the door; she had recovered her composure and was as garrulous as ever.

"I gave John a sleeping pill," she offered as we walked down the hallway. "And also a half to Rose. We can tear the house down and they won't wake up." We entered a bedroom.

Rose lay under a white four-poster canopy, awash in crisp floral bedding. She was wearing an oversize T-shirt with a "Babes for Beef!" slogan, from the local Cowbelles Auxiliary, emblazoned across the front. Bunny sat down on the side of the bed and patted the place next to her.

"I'm okay now," she offered as I sat down. "Now that I've decided to do this."

"Bunny, I don't want to force you. . . ."

"Forget it. I gotta do something. You guys are journalists. Maybe you can figure out a way to help."

"I'm going to need you to sign releases, you know. . . ."

"Yeah, that's fine."

"And I'll need to interview you about Rose's condition, like when it started and what the doctor said. . . ."

"I can do that. But let's just get this part over with first, okay?"

She reached over to her daughter and smoothed a wisp of hair from her forehead, then lifted the T-shirt to reveal her belly and the two concentric arcs of her lower rib cage.

Rose's skin was still a baby's, milky white and downy, and underneath this translucent sheath, her rib cage rose and fell with her shallow breathing. The bones were blue and achingly fragile. I thought of the tiny curl of a child inside me, and my heart leapt. I wanted to put my head against this small belly, blow warmth across it, inhale her sweet baby-sour smell. Then Bunny pulled the T-shirt up farther. Naked, Rose was not plump at all. The plumpness was an illusion created by two shockingly full and beautiful breasts, each tipped with a perfect pink nipple. Suzuki, behind me, shuddered. The girl was five years old. She lay on her back with her arms spread and bent upward at the elbows. Her soft little fingers were tangled in the hair on her pillow. The breasts were firm, but they had separated the way breasts do and slid to either side of her thin rib cage, into her armpits. Disturbed, perhaps, by our presence in the room, she arched her back and turned her head toward the light that was shining from the hallway door. Her mouth opened and closed like a little fish's. She rubbed the hair out of her face with the back of her hand, then her mouth found her thumb and closed around it, and she started sucking.

She was wearing little white cotton underpants, hiked up high over her belly. Bunny stood over her and raised her small hips and drew the underpants down around her thighs. The baby skin continued, smooth and uninterrupted, down over the swell of her belly to her pubic bone, where suddenly, like grotesque graffiti, her skin was defaced by a wiry tangle of hair.

"She's had some bleeding too," Bunny said sadly.

I turned on the sun gun and gently panned the beam across the child as Suzuki hoisted the camera and focused. My hand was shaking and I couldn't make it stop.

"Just . . ." Bunny tapped Suzuki lightly on the arm. "Please, not her face . . ."

And then she dropped her hand to her lap and looked down at her daughter. Her spine, formerly so straight and tall, strong from counterbalancing the weight of her chest, collapsed into itself, and in that instant Bunny looked old and fat.

"Oh, what the hell. It's not like it's her fault. And with a body like that, who's gonna be looking at her face, right?"

Gently she stroked the tendrils from her daughter's forehead. Her tone, part defeat and part bravado, was filled with the echoes of strip joints and neon, of tinsel and tassels and the hooting of men. All the pain of her own freaky career seemed to hang in the gaps between her words and then spread like an oily wake, wide, in the silence behind them. Suzuki heard the pain and slowly panned the camera to her face.

"Bunny?" My voice sounded harsh even though I was whispering. "I'd like to do the interview now. Tell us about Rose."

That night I dreamed it was time to give birth. It was odd, because my stomach was still taut and concave around the hipbones, and Ma laughed and pointed to my chest and said it couldn't be time since I still didn't have any *oppai* to feed my baby with, and she handed me some small white pills to make them grow bigger. But I knew she was wrong, because this is America and she just didn't know, so I went out behind the milking barn where I used to play on my grampa's farm before he went bankrupt and sold it, and I pulled up my dress and waited. As I stood there with my legs spread, it started to emerge, limb by limb, released, unfolding, until gravity took the mass of it and it fell to the ground with a *thump*, gangly and stillborn, from my stomach. It was wet, a misshapen tangle, but I could see a delicate hoof, a twisted tail, the oversize skull, still fetal blue, with a dead milky eye staring up at me, alive with maggots.

I woke and had to pee, but it was a strange motel and I couldn't remember where the bathroom was, which sometimes happens on the road in the dark. And I forgot the dream until I had groped my way to the toilet and was sitting there with my elbows on my knees, staring into the blackness, and maybe it was the release of my bladder that brought the birth dream back, but suddenly I remembered it and started to cry. And when I was finished I turned on the light and checked the toilet bowl carefully, but there wasn't anything there except water and pee.

I went back to bed, shivering, so cold. I wanted to call Sloan, but then I'd have to tell him about the feedroom and the Lutalyse, and it made me sick with shame to think about. So I decided, just tomorrow, just the slaughterhouse, and that's all. It will be easy after that, no danger, and after this show I will quit, and even though we've never talked about it, I'll make Sloan support me while I grow fat and happy; maybe we'll move in together somewhere, not Chicago, maybe New York, maybe the country somewhere, where I can grow organic vegetables and learn to pickle things . . . and I drifted back off to sleep.

*

Mornings had once been filled with a secret joy, but not any longer. Now they were cold and overcast, no place to linger.

The weather had changed overnight, suddenly bleak and autumnal. The wind whipped up the tumbleweed and sent it skittering across the road in front of Gale's oncoming Dodge. He had come to meet us at the motel to take us to the slaughterhouse. I opted to ride with him in his pickup, while the van with the boys followed behind us. I told Dave what I was planning and asked him to stay close. Now, as we hurtled down a rutted back road, I could see the van in the rearview mirror, swallowed up in the dust.

I turned to face Gale across the wide bench seat in the cab of the pickup.

"Bunny showed me Rose's breasts last night. You know about that, right?"

I watched his head slowly swivel on his mottled, turtlelike neck. He stared at me, then swiveled back. Maybe he thought that if he didn't respond I would just disappear.

"Well," I continued, "then you may already know that she's also got pubic hair and she's starting to menstruate. The problem is that this condition almost always coexists with ovarian cysts and often leads to cervical or uterine cancer, which can kill her. I told Bunny. I'm pretty sure it's estrogen poisoning from the feedlot. There were cases like this in Puerto Rico, where they kept using DES—"

"You still goin' on about that?" He was trying to sound light. "What is it with you and this DES business, anyway?"

"Gale, I think you've got it too. I heard about a case of hormone poisoning in the South where grown men started developing symptoms. . . ."

He drove with both hands, and his knuckles whitened. I thought the steering wheel would snap, but I kept on going.

"Enlarged breasts and elevated vocal—"

He reached across the wide front seat and grabbed my hair and yanked my head to within inches of his face.

"You shut your mouth!" he screamed, spraying me with rage and spittle. "You go spreadin' these filthy lies around here and I'll kill you, you fuckin' bitch, I swear I will."

His eyes were cold and insanely blue. The truck was veering wildly from side to side.

"I saw you, Gale!" I screamed right back at him. "We have it on tape. You were feeling up her breast, you pervert. I saw it."

"Shut up!" Gripping my hair hard in his fist, he shook my head like a dirty onion. Finally he let go, but his voice continued, tightening with rage, spiraling up and up into a high-pitched squeal.

"I never touched her, I swear it! I love that little girl. I wouldn't ever do that, not ever. And about the other, well, you think you're so fuckin' smart, if you got somethin' to accuse me of doing illegal around here, you just go right ahead and try. You and that whore my daddy's married to. This here's ranch country, girl, and we do *what* we want, *when* we want, without no government's say-so. You got that? Your East Coast politicians can't say boo out here. We take care of our own. We got our own kinda justice, frontier justice, and don't you forget it. . . ."

"Are you threatening me?"

His small eyes were fixed on the road ahead and he spoke through gritted teeth. "I'm just tellin' it like it is. So don't say I didn't give you no warning."

"Right. Got it," I answered. "Likewise."

He didn't answer, but his knuckles stayed white and ready, and my heart stayed pounding in my ears.

We drove the rest of the way in silence. When we got to the slaughterhouse, I climbed down from the Dodge and my knees buckled. Dave saw and came over.

"You all right?" He put his strong, calm hand on my elbow to steady me.

"Yeah. He didn't take it very well."

"I figured."

"Come on. Let's go do this and get out of here." I shouldered the heavy knapsack full of batteries and spare tapes. The boys were ready.

We were surrounded by enormous trucks rattling in, backing up, raising dust. It was hard to talk over the noise of the engines and the crack of gunshots, which were not gunshots at all but whips striking hide, and the bellows of pain that followed the whipcracks, and the hooves thundering down metal off-ramps, and the clatter of cattle against the sides of the corral.

The slaughterhouse was a long, low-lying rectangular structure made of cement and cinder block, embellished here and there with curlicues of razor wire and stuck on top with tall smokestacks, like candles, belching a rank steam into the steely gray sky. Sticking out from the side was a pipe like a sewer duct, spewing a viscous, thickened gruel of blood and offal into the tank of a waiting truck. The effluent red sea.

The boys were all business today, silent, bent to the task. Suzuki's sensory receptors were twitching, and though he was ten feet away and had his back to the duct at that moment, he knew that I wanted the shot and spun around and nailed it. When he lowered the camera we went inside.

The boss was a man named Wilson, a buddy of Gale's. He met us in the office, a wood-paneled panopticon decorated with a large poster of a young blonde Amazon in jungle bikini, who overlooked the meat-cutting operations below. The only plant life in the room was a ratty aspidistra in a green wire plant stand. Wilson stood beside it, sized us up, and shook his head.

"I don't care who yer workin' for, I don't like this one bit.

Never woulda agreed if it wasn't for Gale's daddy twistin' my arm an' sayin' as it would be a favor to his wife. Said y'all want to take some pictures to take back home with you to Japan, but I'm damned if I know why. Kill floor's no place for sightseein'."

"Well, I'll tell you now, Wilson," I shot back. "Folks in Japan are real innerested in seeing all them new and advanced technologies for killin' comin' from the United States of Ameriker. . . ."

Dave trundled by me with the tripod and whacked me in the shin with the pan arm.

"Sorry," he said, but I got the message and shut up.

"We'll be real quick," he said. "Be outta here in no time."

Wilson still seemed reluctant, but then Gale spoke up from the back of the office, where he'd been talking on the telephone.

"What's the problem, Wilson? Get 'em suited up and out there. We gotta educate these city folks, show 'em how we murder our animals round here, ain't that right, Miz Takagi? How we stick it to 'em. That's what you want, ain't it? That's what you been askin' for. . . ."

Wilson's eyes narrowed, then he shrugged and walked over to a row of metal lockers. He took out four yellow hard hats, a bundle of bloodstained white lab coats, safety goggles, and four pairs of knee-high rubber galoshes.

"Well, yer gonna need to put these on, now. . . . An' I got earplugs if you want 'em."

He looked at Suzuki. "And you girls with long hair gotta wear a hair net too. We run a sanitary operation here."

Suzuki looked at the limp net cast in his direction, looked at me, then grimly started tucking his ponytail into it. Dave had been to a slaughterhouse before and had told Oh to bring the rain cover for the camera and garbage bags for other pieces of equipment that shouldn't get wet. We were ready. Wilson made a phone call, summoning a young employee named Joey, who was still talking on his cell phone as he walked through the door. Wilson directed him to show us around, and he stayed behind with Gale. As we walked down the staircase and away from the office, I looked back up at the wide glass observation window and saw the two of them, their heads perfectly aligned under the jungle girl's large proffered breasts. They were watching me, and when I turned around they both burst out laughing.

Stepping into the slaughterhouse was like walking through an invisible wall into hell. Sight, sound, smell—every sense I thought I owned, that was mine, the slaughterhouse stripped from me, overpowered and assaulted. Steam hissed, metal screeched against metal, clanging and clamoring, splitting the ear, relentless. Chains, pulleys, iron hooks, whipped around us with unbelievable speed, and as far as the eye could see, conveyors snaked into the distance, heaped with skinned heads and steaming hearts. Overhead a continuous rail system laced the ceiling, from which swung mammoth sides of beef, dripping, and heavy with speed as they rattled toward us.

Blood was everywhere: bright red, brick red, shades of brown and black, flowing, splattering, encrusting the walls, the men. The floors were graded toward central drains for easy cleaning, yet the place was caked with a deep, rotting filth. And thick with flies.

As we walked through the processing area, we passed cows being sorted by parts—brains, tongues, livers, intestines, kidneys—all scooped or severed, then tossed into separate steel carts. I looked into a cart filled with hundreds of large livers, spotted with blood and oozing a viscous yellow liquid. Dave tapped me on the shoulder and pointed to the secretions.

"Hormones!" he hollered over the din.

I grabbed Suzuki and trained the sun gun on the glistening, seeping meat.

It was very, very cold. An acrid, humid stench sucked us forward toward the heart of the place, located behind steel vault doors, which opened slowly and let us onto the kill floor, a huge atrium that was known as the "hot floor," Joey informed me, screaming into my ear, *"because blood is hot when it pours from a living body!"*

Suzuki had been shooting all along, but when we walked through the steel doors, his focus became even keener. He had the camera on his shoulder, pressed against the side of his head for stability, but the hard hat and the safety goggles kept knocking against it, getting in his way, so he whipped them off and tossed them to Dave. Joey started to object, but I tugged on his sleeve and gave him a supplicating smile. "Pleeeeese?" I mimed, pressing my palms together, and he shrugged and grinned and turned his back on us.

There was no place to stand, so we kept moving, and it was like some sort of obscene square dance, with us doing the do-si-do around massive swinging animals that had been hoisted into the air by a hind leg, suspended between the incremental stages of life and death and final dismemberment. Trying not to get clobbered, we sashayed in and out between the bodies along a slippery grate, beneath which the blood flowed like a dark red river. The workers stood on raised platforms, all in identical blood-drenched coats, yellow hard hats, goggles that obscured their faces, and earplugs that shut out sound. They used power tools to perform various operations on the hanging carcasses—lopping off hooves, decapitating, eviscerating—and the whine of the saw severed the air, its blade slicing bone, searing bone, scorching hide and hair. Skinning a giant carcass is like peeling the pajamas off a dozing twelve-foot child. Evisceration is done with a quick slice up the belly, releasing the entrails, which pour out in a cloud of steam.

We found the knocking pen. Suzuki and I climbed up next

to the operator. Down below, a cow was herded into the pen by a worker wielding an electric prod. The cow balked, minced, then slammed her bulk against the sides of the pen. She had just watched the cow before her being killed, and the cow before that, and she was terrified. Her eyes rolled back into her head and a frothy white foam poured from her mouth as the steel door slammed down on her hindquarters, forcing her all the way in. The worker next to us leaned over and, using a compression stunner, fired a five-inch retractable bolt into her brain. He pressed a button and the metal side of the pen rose up, to reveal the stunned cow, collapsed and twitching on the floor. But the stun was incomplete. He shrugged. He climbed down and wrapped a chain around her hind leg. It was attached to a winch that hoisted her up into the air, where she hung upside down, slowly spinning, head straining, legs kicking wildly in their search for solid ground. The worker approached and took a knife from his belt.

Suzuki had climbed down. With the camera braced on his thigh, he crouched in front of the dangling cow, getting a low-angle shot and waiting for the kill. The worker motioned for him to step back. Suzuki nodded but didn't move. The cow was breathing hard, raspy breaths through the foam and the spittle, and from time to time she let out a strangled cry. Oh stood just behind Suzuki, trembling and bloodless, holding the boom. His headphones looked like goofy plastic ears, feeding the amplified cries of the animal directly into his brain. His face was all screwed up, leaking tears, like a little kid trying hard not to cry out loud. I climbed down next to him and tapped his arm, pointing to the exit and to the camera mike, which we could use if he wanted to leave, but he shook his head. He would stay.

The worker put his hand on the cow's arched neck to steady her, and I stood behind Oh and turned on the sun gun and aimed the beam at her pulsing throat. The worker was talking to her all the while, saying, "There now, girl, calm down, it's gonna be all over soon," and then he did the most amazing thing. He bent down and looked straight into her bugging eye and stroked her forelock, and it seemed to calm her. And when he straightened up again, he used the upward movement of his body to sink the knife deep into her throat, slicing crosswise, then plunging it straight into her heart. This is why it is important that the cow be stunned but not dead when her throat is cut—the blood gushes out in rhythmic spurts, expelled by the still-pumping heart muscle.

Suzuki had no idea. He did not anticipate the force of this expulsion or the distance the blood would travel, so when the bright-red torrent spewed toward him, he leapt back to protect the camera, knocking into Oh, who knocked into me and sent me sprawling into the path of a thousand pounds of oncoming carcass. I must have caught the meat just as it swung around a corner at the peak of its centrifugal arc. It slammed me, lifting me right off my feet, and that's as much as I remember, because on the way back down I hit the base of my skull against the edge of the knocking pen, which, appropriately, knocked me right out.

THE FROST MONTH

SHŌNAGON

When a Woman Lives Alone

When a woman lives alone, her house should be extremely dilapidated, the mud wall should be falling to pieces, and if there is a pond, it should be overgrown with water-plants. It is not essential that the garden be covered with sage-brush; but weeds should be growing through the sand in patches, for this gives the place a poignantly desolate look.

I greatly dislike a woman's house when it is clear that she has scurried about with a knowing look on her face, arranging everything just as it should be, and when the gate is kept tightly shut.

AKIKO

When she woke, she was lying in a hospital bed with a needle in her arm and a plastic label attached to her wrist. She lay there for a long time. There were beds on either side of her, and she could hear subdued movement and voices, but a curtain had been drawn around her bed. She coughed a little, then hummed to see if her voice was working, but she didn't dare speak out loud. Someone would come, she was sure of it. Eventually, if she waited, someone would come and tell her what was wrong with her. Because something must be terribly wrong for one to be in a hospital all of a sudden and not even remember how one got here.

It was bright inside the curtains, and the light hurt her eyes. It was fluorescent, not real light from the sun, nor was it fresh air that made the curtains shimmy and sway, but rather a backdraft from urgent bodies moving quickly back and forth outside. This light and movement made Akiko nervous, and so did the sounds around her, especially the torque and squeak of rubber soles on hard acrylic tile. She closed her eyes. It was good to shutter it out, stay dark and still behind her eyelids. The darkness she made helped to muffle the noises in the room, and now maybe she could think. So she tried to remember how she'd gotten here, what had happened, but the only thing that came to mind (and she could see it projected like a burst of light against the velvety dark backdrop of her lids) was a crying eye, with tears of blood seeping from its center.

"Still asleep, are we?"

Akiko's eyes popped open in surprise at the exact moment the nurse wrenched back the curtain.

"Did you have a nice nap, then?"

How to answer? Was it just that she'd been napping? She had been especially tired recently, but she'd never heard of being brought to the hospital in order to take a nap.

"Have I been napping?"

"You've been in and out for about eighteen hours now. 'Sleeping it off' is what we call it. You got here yesterday afternoon, and now it's this morning."

The nurse was changing the bottle attached to the opposite end of the tube that terminated in Akiko's arm.

"What happened to me?"

"Well . . . I should wait until Doctor gets here to tell you, but . . ."

She stopped and looked around, then leaned over and lowered her voice.

"You lost some blood, but don't worry. You're okay."

"Blood?"

"At first Doctor thought you were having a miscarriage, but then he realized it was coming from your bum." The nurse stuck a thermometer under Akiko's tongue and wrapped a blood pressure sleeve around her thin upper arm.

"Your husband found you unconscious on the bathroom floor. He was quite shaken. He must be a very kind husband indeed, to become so upset."

The nurse pumped up the sleeve and placed the cool disk of a stethoscope on the inside of Akiko's wrist.

"Is he . . . ?" Akiko's words were distorted by the slender glass tube in her mouth, and her voice shook.

The nurse looked up from her watch, frowned, and readjusted the thermometer.

"Don't talk. He left yesterday afternoon. But only when it was clear you weren't in any danger." She listened carefully to Akiko's pulse. She looked into Akiko's face. "He must be a very kind husband . . . mustn't he?"

The thermometer was in Akiko's mouth, so she didn't really have to answer. The pressure from the inflated sleeve squeezed her arm, tightening, stopping all the blood. She closed her eyes.

"Maybe not, then," said the nurse. "Maybe not so kind at all." With a hiss, she released the pressure. The sleeve deflated and the blood began to circulate again, making Akiko's arm tingle. The nurse tore off the Velcro and rolled up the sleeve, then plucked the thermometer out of her mouth and squinted at it. She made some entries on the chart, then peered over the edge of it. "He left you a note. I've got it here somewhere. . . ."

She put down the chart and fished around in her pocket for a bit, then pulled out a folded piece of paper. "Don't you want it?"

One arm had the needle in it. The other was still tingling and refused to move at all.

"Well, I'll just leave it here for you, then. You can read it when you feel up to it."

The nurse put the note on the bedside table, then placed her hand on Akiko's side. She pressed. "Does that hurt?" she asked. Akiko winced. "Mmm. Doctor said he suspected a fracture. He'll probably want an X-ray. . . . What happened to you, anyway? How'd you do this?"

She was nosy, Akiko thought. The nurse was about her own age, short and a bit stocky. Her uniform trousers were stretched tight around the tops of her thighs. She had a round, pleasant face, and her badge said her name was Tomoko, written with the Chinese characters for "friend." It would be so easy just to say, "My husband kicked me," thought Akiko. Or "My husband punched me in the face," or "My husband . . . ," but somehow she couldn't make the words come. She just looked at Nurse Tomoko and shook her head helplessly from side to side. It wasn't so easy to say at all.

Nurse Tomoko shrugged and patted her arm, then peered at Akiko's face, where the lip was healing but was still a bit swollen. She touched it, ran her finger gently over the bump, and shook her head. "Must have hurt, huh?" she said. Then she took a step back. Her quick nurse's eyes skimmed over the surfaces of things—the nightstand beside the bed, the sheet covering the bed, covering Akiko—checking to make sure she hadn't left anything lying about.

"Well, I'll be back later to check on you, and Doctor will stop by too. Is there anyone . . . I could call someone for you. . . ."

"No, thank you," Akiko said. "No one."

Nurse Tomoko gave another quick shrug and a smile. "Well, I'll be back. You can think about if there's anything you want." Then she left, snapping the curtain shut behind her.

The note read:

My dearest wife: I hope you are feeling better by the time you read this. What a shock it was to find you unconscious and bleeding on the bathroom floor. My first terrible fear was that you'd had a miscarriage. That you had somehow become pregnant and hadn't told me. But then the doctor told me it was not a miscarriage, and I was so relieved. But how heartless this sounds. Of course I was not relieved. I have caused you so much pain and I am sorry. I humbly beg your pardon and I hope you will forgive me and we can work things out between us.

The doctor said you would be fine, so I have gone to

Colorado for my business trip. I had no other choice. I wish I could be there beside you, but I will telephone my mother and ask her to look in on you and help you with whatever you need. (Of course I trust you will understand that what happens between a husband and wife is private and should not be discussed, even with one's closest relatives or in-laws.)

I am sitting in the waiting room, writing this. There is another young husband waiting here, anxiously pacing up and down. His wife is having a baby. My heart is heavy with grief and envy. Please forgive me, dear wife. Promise me that the next time, that other anxious young husband will be me. That is my fervent wish. There is nothing else I can say.

Your husband, J. Ueno

Nurse Tomoko found the note crumpled in the wastebasket under the bed. She looked up at the sleeping woman and smiled with grim satisfaction. She knew what the letter said. She had carried it around in her pocket, after all, and had read it earlier that day. Quietly and efficiently she replaced the IV bag on the hanging end of the unit; she must have brushed ever so lightly against Akiko's arm, but it was enough to make Akiko gasp in her sleep, roll her head to one side, and utter a groan that wrung Nurse Tomoko's heart. She studied the woman's battered face: the lip was split and had started to heal; the fading bleed of yellow, green, and blue skin that ringed both eyes told of older battles, as did the thin white scar above her brow. Nurse Tomoko had undressed Akiko when she was admitted. She knew there were other bruises, had stood next to the doctor as he examined the dull green-ocher rings forming around the points of impact on Akiko's slight body. Akiko groaned again, as though suffering under this scrutiny. Tomoko sighed and placed her cool palm on

343

Akiko's brow. The weight of the hand seemed to calm her; her bruised features relaxed again as she drifted back into a deep, blank sleep.

JANE

When I came to the first time, all I could comprehend was the lurching of the van and the sound of the rocks spit up by the tires hitting the underside of the chassis. The second time, it was Suzuki's big moon face, and he smiled and it was warm, so I fell back asleep. The third time, I stayed conscious. The boys had laid me out on the narrow seat of the van and Dave was tearing along the county roads and Suzuki was cradling my head in his lap and Oh had wedged himself between the seats, holding me as still as possible. My face was feeling odd and sticky, so I scratched it, and that's when I saw that my hand was caked with blood and the other one too, and not just my hand but my whole arm, in fact my entire body had been drenched in blood, and so I started to scream. And Suzuki held me down and explained that it wasn't mine, that I'd fallen on the slaughterhouse floor, into the lake of blood, and by this time I was crying, and every time I wiped my eyes the tears were bloody too. My clothes were drenched and sticky and my jeans had grown stiff, and this scared me even more, because it was hard to move my legs.

And then we were at the emergency room. Dave carried me in his arms, and when the first nurse saw me her eyes widened and she said, "Oh God!" until Dave explained about the blood. Then the doctor examined my head while the nurses undressed me, and as they were pulling off my bloody jeans I had a sudden moment of searing clarity. "My baby!" I cried out, and they all just sort of stopped what they were doing and stared at me, and then I passed out again.

And then I was lying in a hospital bed in a clean gown, and the blood was gone and no one was there, but the late-afternoon sun was shining through the window and I could hear the activity of the ward beyond the door. And then I realized I wasn't alone after all, that Bunny Dunn was standing by the window, her cotton candy hair glowing like a halo, backlit by the sun. She turned just then, saw that I was awake, and smiled.

"Mornin'," she said.

"Is it morning?"

"Nope. It's afternoon." Bunny came over and stood next to my bed.

"How long have I been asleep?"

"Couple of hours."

"Am I okay?"

"Yup. Nothing to worry about. Just a small fracture and a concussion, but the doctor wants to keep an eye on you for a couple of days."

Suddenly my head started to throb, as though catching up with this information. "How did you . . . ?"

"Dave called me. He thought . . . Well, the boys didn't know . . ." She stopped, unsure of what to say next, how much to tell me, how much I remembered, and the throbbing expanded to fill her silence and turned into dread. Icy, it coursed down through my gut and into my groin.

"They thought maybe you'd feel better if there was a woman here with you," Bunny concluded.

"It's the baby . . . ?" I looked at her, and she met my gaze and held it, firmly.

"Yes."

"It's gone?"

"Yes."

I turned my head away. I couldn't look at her. As I stared up at the ceiling, the tears collected behind my eyes, and suddenly I couldn't breathe for the pressure of them.

"Jane, the doctor said something real important."

I could barely hear her. Inside my head, the pressure had plugged my ears.

"Are you listening? Jane, you gotta listen."

I shook my head. "Please." I ground my teeth around the words. "Go away."

But Bunny persisted. "No, you gotta hear this first. You're blamin' yourself, but it's not your fault."

"Don't be ridiculous," I spit. "Of course it is."

"No. There wasn't nothing you could do. The doc said the fetus had . . . well, it had stopped growing. The miscarriage woulda happened sooner or later. Do you understand? It wasn't just the accident. The pregnancy couldn't have come to term."

"What do you mean, it stopped growing?"

"Well . . . it was dead."

"Dead?"

The tears just started then, trickling down the sides of my face, and I started to cough up these great hacking sobs from the depth of my empty belly. Bunny leaned over the bed and took my fractured head and cradled it against her chest, and I let her. Let her comfort me like I've never been comforted before, certainly not on the bony breast of my cool, dispassionate Ma. I cried on and on, fed by the reservoir of all my dread made real. My thwarted progeny. My poor hope. I had robbed it of viability by my lack of conviction. Of course it was my fault. It was all my fault.

"I wanted the baby . . . ," I gasped.

"Of course you did," Bunny murmured into the top of my head. "Everybody wants their baby. . . ."

"No. You don't get it." I pulled away from her, bitter,

despairing, determined to make her understand. "It's my fault that the baby's dead. I didn't have to do this shoot. I could've stopped. But I didn't. I went to the feed shed and touched the medicines. I knew better. . . ."

Bunny was confused but resolute. "But none of that's what caused the miscarriage."

"Of course it is, don't you see?" I cried. "Maybe not one thing, but a combination—"

"Jane, it ain't got nothing to do with the feed shed or medicines, either. It was already dead, Jane. Doc said it probably died several days ago, maybe even a week."

"A week?" I choked. It was horrible, made me shudder, then I started to laugh. I'd been carrying my dead baby around inside me for a week, and I never knew. Bunny released me, stepped back, stared.

"You see?" I think I was screaming the words. "So much for my maternal instincts! Never even knew my baby was dead, and it was right here inside me! Great mother, huh?" I started to weep again. "You see, it *is* my fault. I didn't care enough, right from the start. I even thought about having an abortion. If I had just stopped working, stopped everything else . . . I should have thought just of the baby, but I didn't. I let things slide . . . and now . . ."

Bunny wrapped me in her arms again. "It ain't your fault," she whispered, cradling me, "but I know what you're sayin'. It's hard to make things stop once they've gotten goin'." Her voice was far away. "Things you'd never even believe could ever happen just start seemin' as normal as pie. Well, maybe not normal, but still you accept it. Like Rosie . . . You just get used to it. Until something happens, that is, that wakes you up and makes you see different. That's what happened when you all showed up. I saw her with your eyes, and everything looked different. Wrong."

She relaxed her hold and laid my head back on the pillow.

Looking down at my face, she stroked my forehead the way I'd seen her stroke Rose's. "I ain't never been brave," she said, then she laughed. "Here I am, talking about myself when I'm supposed to be comforting you. But I wanted to tell you this because it's something I just figured out. After you left the house last night I was thinkin' back, and I realized that I ain't never really ever made a single decision in my life, you know. Just kinda drifted from one thing to the next, following the direction these darn things pointed me in, you know?" She cupped her breasts in her hands and looked down at them ruefully. "The pageants, the strip clubs, John . . . On the whole, I've been darn lucky. But last night? Well, it was like I finally made a choice, talkin' for the camera, and it felt good. Like I was takin' a stand."

She reached out and took my hand and held it. "So I guess what I'm sayin' is that some things are your fault and some things ain't, and the ones that ain't, well, you oughtn't waste your time tryin' to blame yourself for those. But the other ones, the ones you can control? Those ones are different. You gotta do something about those. . . . I'm gonna get to the bottom of this thing with Rosie. Thanks to you."

She smiled, grimly, and I tried to smile back but I couldn't, so I squeezed her hand instead. Good for her. But it didn't change the way I felt about me.

On her way out the door, she stopped and turned around.

"One other thing . . . ?" she said.

"Yes?"

"Gale wanted . . . well, he said he was sorry about what happened."

"But that I'm a bitch and I got what was coming to me, right?"

Bunny looked away. "Yeah, well . . ." She paused, then walked back toward the bed and leaned over close. "Last night he came out to the house to talk to me. About Rosie. First

348

time he's said a civil word to me, far as I can recall. He told me what you said to him, but that he's never, you know, done that to Rosie. Not in a dirty way."

"Yeah?"

"Yeah. I guess I believe him. He was real upset about it, and Rose thinks the world of him, after all."

"That's good, Bunny."

"Yeah."

"He's a prick, Bunny."

"Yeah."

Soon after she left, Suzuki poked his head in, followed by Oh and Dave. They'd been waiting outside in the lobby. Suzuki and Oh were oddly formal. They knew about the miscarriage, but of course they were too polite to mention it. I was glad. I didn't want to talk about it. Dave sensed this, and while he gave me a searching look, he too refrained from saying anything. It was awkward. They stayed only a short while, and then they left to pick up Ueno at the airport.

I must have drifted back to sleep then, because when I woke it was dark in my room, except for a rectangle of fluorescent light that shone through a small window cut into the door. During the day, the corridor beyond had been full of noise and activity, but now the entire ward was still, blanketed by a kind of tentative night that waited for a sudden scream, a hemorrhage, a death, to shatter its rest. Pain returned, like a pulse or a heartbeat. Sometimes it feels as if the mind has fingers, and in this lull of sound and light and motion, I let mine probe—gently, tentatively—at the pain's source. Trying to locate the exact moment—*When did it happen, when did I let it die?*—I forced myself to sink through the chronology of the past few days, peeling back layers of event, certain that the instant would reveal itself, undeniably. How could I not know? But no matter how hard I tried, I could not remember. I could not break through the jumble of chaotic fragments: the bleeding cattle and the bloody meat, the farmer's rage, the mother's stupor, and the child's disfigured and unnatural grace. Trapped by these images, I caught myself trying to edit them, to put them in an order that made sense, and all the while, I was waiting, listening to the hush outside my room and the noises of the ward, straining toward a sense of imminent disaster.

So when it came, I was surprised only at the shape the realization took, not at its coming.

I had forgotten the tapes.

I had been planning to send all the footage we'd shot back to New York before Ueno arrived, so he couldn't get his hands on it. Now he would demand to see everything, and once he'd seen Rosie's deformed body and Bunny's tragic interview, he would confiscate the tapes or, worse, destroy them. I felt for my watch on the table beside me. It was three in the morning. I called the motel and left an urgent message for Suzuki, but I realized it was too late. Ueno would not have wasted any time. He had already seen the tapes. There was nothing I could do. I started to cry. All this for nothing.

Eventually I slept again, and I dreamed about the slaughtered cow, hanging upside down, her life ebbing out of her as she rotated slowly. In my dream I saw her legs move in tandem, like she was running, and I realized she was dreaming of an endless green pasture at the edge of death, where she could gallop away and graze forever.

In the morning, I called Suzuki again, but the crew had left the motel. I called Sloan. He wasn't home, so I left him a message to call the hospital. Then the doctor came. He was young, looked middle-aged. He stood away from my bed and squinted at the chart, keeping it at arm's length too.

"How's the head feeling this morning? Any pain?"

I was confused. I couldn't answer. I had forgotten all about my head.

"No," I finally said. "My head is fine. Where is my baby? Can I see it?"

The doctor took another step backward. "No. The fetus was removed yesterday."

"I know that. I want to see it. Where did you put it?"

"I'm afraid that's not possible. All the products of conception are immediately incinerated."

"Oh."

"Now, don't you worry about that," he said, switching demeanor and trying out an avuncular tone. "You're an attractive young woman, and there's plenty of time to try again. Just think how much fun that will be!"

I didn't understand what he was saying. And then I did.

"Oh. You mean sex."

He consulted the chart again. "Yes, well, I've ordered a D and C for you this morning to make sure everything's all spick-and-span inside and nothing got left behind—"

"You mean, like an arm or something?"

This time he ignored me completely. He made a note on the chart and approached the foot of the bed to hang it back up. When he was close, I tried again.

"Doctor, listen. I need to know. Why did the baby die? What caused the miscarriage?"

The doctor sighed. It was obvious that he didn't want to go into it. He looked hard at me, then seemed to decide I wasn't the type to give up easily so he might as well get it over with.

"In the case of a missed abortion—that's what it's called

when a nonviable fetus is expelled—it's almost impossible to determine the cause of fetal death. Possibly your uterus was too small and failed to enlarge rapidly enough. Possibly the placenta failed—maybe it was too low in the uterus or didn't get sufficient blood. The miscarriage would have happened anyway—sooner or later nature takes its course. The accident might have helped it along a little."

"Oh. Thank you."

"You're welcome. They'll be by to take you in for the D and C in about an hour." He turned to go.

"Doctor . . ."

He paused, patiently.

"I have a misshapen uterus, probably due to DES exposure in the womb. I've also had a neoplasia removed from my cervix. Could this have been the cause?"

He raised his eyebrows and nodded, vaguely intrigued. "Could be, yes." He turned again and headed toward the door. When he reached it, one last thing occurred to me.

"Doctor . . ."

He turned around again. "Yes?" He sighed.

"Was it a boy or a girl?"

He sighed again. "It *would* have been," he emphasized, "a boy."

When the phone rang, I grabbed it, but it wasn't Sloan or Suzuki. It was Kenji. He'd just arrived at the ranch, called in by Ueno to take over the shoot.

"I'm sorry, Takagi. I didn't have any choice."

"I know. Listen, Kenji, just do me one favor."

"What?"

"Find the tapes that I shot and save them for me. They won't be any use to you. You'll have to more or less start over again from scratch. Just don't erase them. Don't throw them out. I'll tell you all about it later, but I need this footage we shot of Rosie. I promised Bunny."

"I can't. I'm sorry. It's too late."

"What do you mean?"

"Didn't you know? The last batch of tapes you shot got destroyed in the accident yesterday. Oh had forgotten to take them out of the knapsack you were wearing, and they got crushed. Ueno was furious, threatened to fire Oh, but then Suzuki said he'd quit too. It was ugly for a while there, but things have calmed down now and Ueno thinks we can use most of what's left. You can have copies of those, but there's not much of Rose. . . ."

"Oh."

"Sorry about that."

"Yeah, well . . ."

"Takagi? Another thing . . ."

"Yeah?"

"This is a lousy time to have to tell you, but Ueno is insisting . . . he doesn't want you working on the show anymore."

"I figured. That's fine. Good luck with it. Give Bunny my love."

"No, Takagi. Not just this show. The series. *My American Wife!* What I mean is, you're fired."

"Oh."

The phone rang again as soon as I'd hung up. It was Sloan.

"Jane, are you all right? Why are you in the hospital? What's going on?" He was scared. So was I.

"I'm okay. We were filming at a meat-processing plant. I, uh, got knocked out by a side of beef. Pretty funny, huh?"

I paused, but he wasn't laughing. "It's just a minor concussion, Sloan. I'll be fine."

He was silent. Waiting. I paused again, to take a breath, to swallow my heart. "Sloan? I had a miscarriage. The baby's dead."

Still there was nothing but silence on the other end of the line. Then I heard breathing, a cough, maybe, a sigh, or a sob, and then nothing again.

"Sloan? Are you still there? Say something . . . please."

"What is there to say, Jane?" His voice was cold, a million miles away.

"It isn't what you think. The doctor said the fetus had stopped growing. It wasn't the accident. . . ."

"I asked you to be careful. I begged you. You promised. . . ."

"It was already dead, Sloan. It died sometime last week, possibly even when I was still in New York. You see? The point is, it would have aborted sooner or later. . . ."

But as I was saying this, I realized it was sounding all wrong. Utterly beside the point. The words trickled off and disappeared into the black, empty space between us.

Sloan broke the silence with a bitter snort of laughter. "Sooner or later? Oh, good. That's a big relief," he said.

It felt like all the air in the room had been sucked out. There was no answer, nothing else to say. I started to cry, but no tears would come, either. I was all dried up.

"Sloan, I . . . I don't know what to say. . . ." It was the truth.

"Yeah. Me too." And that was it. He hung up.

Because of my concussion, the D and C was done with local anesthesia. I lay there, feet in stirrups, tears trickling down into my ears again, thinking this should have been a delivery table instead. After it was over, the doctor said both my head and my womb looked fine, ordered me a supply of maxipads, and told me I would be able to leave the next day. I booked a ticket to New York. Dave came to pick me up at the hospital the following morning and drove me to the airport. The crew was with the Dunns, filming happy family scenes to replace the ones I'd shot.

"You wouldn't believe it," said Dave, glancing over to where I sat, frozen in the passenger seat.

"Ueno is coming up with all these ideas, and Kenji is just going along with them. He made Bunny dress up in her Miss Teen Rodeo banner and tiara, and sit on John's lap with a plate of prairie oysters. Then he did a scene of Gale and Rose riding off together on horseback into the sunset. It was really creepy."

I was holding a clear plastic bag on my lap, which I'd been given at the hospital when I checked out. It contained the bloodstained clothes I had worn at the slaughterhouse.

"Suzuki and Oh are just like automatons. They do what Ueno says, but it's like there's no life to it, you know? Everyone misses you."

The bag was depressing. I wanted to throw it away, but then I thought I might look suspicious stuffing a large bag of bloody clothes in the trash can at the airport, and also I wanted to go through the pockets first. I leaned over to the seat behind us, opened my suitcase, and tossed the plastic bag inside.

"While you've got your suitcase open, you might want to pack this too. Suzuki and Oh asked me to give it to you."

Dave reached under his seat, pulled out a box, and handed it to me. I opened it. In it were twelve Betacam tapes, neatly packed. I looked up at Dave, and he was grinning.

"I guess Kenji told you the tapes were destroyed? Well, it wasn't exactly true. Oh smashed a couple of blank ones to show Ueno, but the ones you guys shot of Rose and Bunny that night, he had stashed at the motel the whole time. Then he and Suzuki stayed up all night and copied the rest of them for you too, including the interview at the feedlot with Gale and all the slaughterhouse stuff, so you have a complete set. Everything we shot. I took Ueno out for some lap dancing."

At that moment I forgot all about everything except how much I loved my crew, and I told Dave to go back to them with that message.

"Listen, Jane," he said at the curbside after he'd checked my bags. "I really enjoyed working with you, and if there's ever anything I can do, you know, even working in New York . . . well, just let me know."

"Thanks, Dave. But I doubt it. I don't have a job myself."

"Yeah, well, just keep me in mind." He hesitated, then wrapped his immense arms around me and gave me a hug that could have brought down a steer. "You remember what I said?" he asked. He was talking into the top of my head, but I could hear his words rumbling in his massive chest. "About nothing helping and no one caring and it being too late?"

I nodded, and he squeezed me harder.

"Well, I don't believe that anymore." He released me abruptly and looked embarrassed. "I'm really looking forward to seeing what comes out of those tapes."

I bought a *People* magazine at the airport and read it very carefully on the plane, cover to cover, every word of it; I cannot recall a single story I read during the five-hour flight, but I cannot remember having a single thought of my own, either, and that was the point.

The air in New York stinks some days, like a viscous sludge in a turbid swamp. I took a taxi from La Guardia into the city, creeping fitfully, in jarring starts and stops, through the congested streets until finally we reached my block. The apartment was stuffy when I opened the door. I dragged my suitcase in and closed the door behind me. I unlocked the suitcase and overturned it, dumping its contents in the middle of the kitchen floor. The first thing I put away was the box of tapes, carefully, on a shelf at the back of my closet—it was too soon to think about them. Then I extracted the plastic bag of blood-drenched clothing. I opened it, and the searing stench of the slaughterhouse hit me like a blow to the face. I pulled out the jeans, and as I unfolded the stiff, leathery creases, it occurred to me: How much of this blood is slaughtered cow and how much is my baby? And then the sadness was back again. I pressed my face into the rigid fabric and wept, which got me all covered in blood again, and then I didn't know what to do with the clothes, and in the end I just walked out onto the street and threw them in the garbage, figuring, It's New York; there's something bloody in everybody's dumpster.

AKIKO

"Imagine," said Mrs. Ueno. "Calling me from an airplane!" Akiko's mother-in-law clasped her hands in front of her chest. "An airplane in the sky! It was flying. He said it was somewhere over the Pacific Ocean!"

Akiko lay perfectly still and stared up at the ceiling. She was pretending to be in a coma. When her mother-in-law first came, she had greeted her and tried to be polite, but it soon occurred to her that this wasn't necessary. In fact, it was not a good idea. A good idea was to try to discourage her and make her leave as quickly as possible.

". . . I couldn't imagine how you could make a telephone call from a moving airplane. At our house we have wires connected to our telephone, and the voices go through the wires. So at dinner I asked my husband, Joichi's father, and he said it was done with radio waves. He is smart. He knows these things. Joichi takes after him. It is such a comfort for a woman to have a smart husband, don't you think?"

It was strange to hear her say "Joichi."

"I told my neighbor, Mrs. Saito, about Joichi's telephone call, and she said, 'You are lucky to have a son who is getting on so well in the world!' Of course I denied it vehemently, but between you and me, Akiko-chan, I do think she is right. I am lucky. And so are you. . . ."

She reached out and tentatively patted Akiko's hand. Akiko lay there and tried to feel lucky. There must be a trick to it, she decided. A knack to luck.

"'It is expensive to telephone from an airplane,' Mrs. Saito told me. 'Very expensive indeed.' So you see, Akiko, he must care about you very much."

"Fractured," the doctor said. "Most definitely fractured. I want you to have an X-ray tomorrow, so we can see how bad it is. Nurse, can you take care of this?"

Nurse Tomoko nodded and smiled reassuringly at Akiko, who nodded too and braced herself.

"Do you remember how this happened?" the doctor asked.

"I fell," whispered Akiko. She was nervous, but this time she was prepared. "When I fainted I must have fallen onto the edge of the bathroom counter. I hit my face too." She pointed to her lip.

The doctor leaned in to look at it more closely. Then he stood up and shook his head.

"Mrs. Ueno, I'm sorry to have to say this, but that cut on your lip is at least several days old. And the black eyes, the bruises on your abdomen, they are not fresh, either. I hate to doubt your word, but . . ."

Behind him, Nurse Tomoko cleared her throat. "Doctor . . . ?" she said. He paused for a moment, then continued.

"Well, you've had a long day. Why don't you just get another good night's sleep and then think about it some more tomorrow. Maybe it will come back to you." He smiled and placed his hand on her forehead. His hand was dry and cool and heavy. It triggered memory, comforted her and made her feel like a child. "You've had a bad time, that's for sure. But don't worry. Nurse will take care of you here. Nurse, could you come with me. . . ."

"Good night," whispered Nurse Tomoko as she slipped through the curtain. "Sleep tight."

As the curtain swung shut behind her and her gum-soled footsteps faded away, Akiko relaxed. The hospital was exhausting, but it was night again, so she could sleep without interruption—she had been sleeping a lot, even during the day, dropping off without warning into a profound oblivion, from which she woke needing to sleep again. Now, feeling the luxury of her privacy, curling deep into its folds, she ran her fingers over her fractured rib and thought about her bleeding anus and the X-ray the following day. Nurse Tomoko and the doctor frightened her with their questions, their almost clairvoyant intimations. They made Akiko feel like a child caught lying, yet at the same time they inspired in her a child's total confidence in their custody. She felt secure. Protected.

It was dim in the ward now, and hushed. Akiko lay there, listening to the muffled creaks and humming, the snores and shuffling, when all of a sudden an overwhelming sensation of well-being flooded through her, rising from the pit of her stomach and radiating out to the tips of her fingers and toes. Amazing, she thought. You wake up one morning in a hospital, battered and bruised, and you should feel scared. But I don't. At all. I feel wonderful.

It was the first time she'd felt wonderful in a long time. It seemed as if a fresh breeze had blown in from somewhere out-of-doors and was making the curtains around the bed billow and glow. The air in the room eddied about her head and Akiko watched its particulates glitter in the moonlight like a bloom of phosphorescence on the incoming tide. Something was happening, she realized, though she didn't know quite what. But she could feel it and knew it was a miracle of sorts, watery, lunar, and profound. She looked down the length of her body, skeletal beneath the thin hospital sheet, and that's when she saw. Not saw, as with her eyes, but conceived, in her mind,

a whip-tailed armada!
zona pellucida, penetrated, now
a small round egg made lively, and
propelled downstream on ciliary currents through the darkness.

Meanwhile, inside, changes,

cleavages and shiftings,
thickenings,
zygote into morula into hollowed blastula, still suspended,
free-floating, until . . .
now . . .
it brushes up against the soft and spongy wall. Parasitic,
it sticks tight, begins to burrow.

Akiko lay there, enthralled. It was a bloody business, full of

ruptures,
engorgement,
hemorrhage,
secretion,

until finally the pugnacious morsel of life bores into the wall's
warm embrace.

Holding her breath, Akiko watched it happen. And when her child-to-be was safely embedded, she let out her breath with a long sigh and fell sound asleep.

In the morning, Nurse Tomoko came to take her for the X-ray.

"I can't," Akiko said apologetically.

Nurse Tomoko looked surprised. "But yesterday it was fine. . . ."

Akiko looked at her, and for the first time, she smiled. "I know. Yesterday I didn't know. But last night, you see . . ."

Nurse Tomoko waited.

Akiko wasn't sure, but she decided to continue. "I don't know if you can say this or not, seeing as he is my husband, but, well, about a week ago . . . he sort of . . . he raped me. He did it in the back and the front. . . ."

Nurse Tomoko took Akiko's hand and squeezed it hard. "That's terrible. . . . I thought something like that might have—"

But Akiko interrupted her. "It's not important. What I wanted to say was it fertilized the egg, you see, and last night I conceived . . . so I can't have the X-ray."

"You what?"

"A baby. I'm pregnant."

"How . . . how do you know this?"

"I watched the whole thing."

Nurse Tomoko frowned. She laid her hand on Akiko's forehead, checking for a fever. She looked deep into Akiko's eyes. Akiko looked up at her, met her gaze, and laughed.

"You think I'm a crazy woman," she declared, suddenly bold. "A fool. That's it, isn't it?"

Nurse Tomoko nodded. "Yes," she agreed. "You sound crazy. What exactly did you see?"

"It was so beautiful." Akiko sighed. "Like one of those science documentaries on television. I could see it up close in my mind, from the fertilization right through the implantation, the little blastocyst burrowing deep into my uterine tissue. Well, it's going to take a while longer to really settle in there, but to all intents and purposes, I'm pregnant. . . ."

"How do you know about all this?" asked Nurse Tomoko, amazed. "These words: blastocyst, implantation . . ."

Akiko lowered her eyes. "I used to write articles for maternity magazines," she said modestly. "It was my specialty."

Nurse Tomoko leaned her hip against the bed and folded her arms. "I don't know what to say," she said finally. "I'll have to tell Doctor, of course, but if you do think you are pregnant, then you certainly shouldn't have the X-rays. We could order a pregnancy test. . . ."

Akiko shook her head. "Too early. The HCG won't show up for another couple of days."

This time Nurse Tomoko laughed. "Fine," she said. "You're the expert."

"You can't just go back there," Tomoko said, sitting dolefully on the edge of the bed.

A week had passed. The doctor had told Akiko that if she refused the X-ray, she would have to stay longer in the hospital for observation, but Akiko suspected that Tomoko had talked him into it. Tomoko was worried about her state of mind and Akiko appreciated her concern, but she also knew that her state of mind had never been better. She was impatient to leave. She didn't want to hurt Tomoko's feelings, though. They had become friends.

"I have to," said Akiko. "I can't stay here. I've been here too long already."

"Don't you have any relatives you could stay with?"

"No, not really. I'll be all right."

"How long will he be gone?"

"At least another week."

"Look," said Tomoko, blushing. "I could take you back to your place and help you pack, and then you could come stay with me. For a while. Until you work things out . . ."

Akiko didn't know what to do. She'd never had a friend before and didn't know if it would be rude to say no.

"Thank you, Tomoko. But I really must go home. . . ."

Tomoko scowled. "You're not going to stay with him when he comes back, are you? You're not going to stick around so he can beat you up again . . . ?"

"I don't know. . . ."

"Akiko, please," said Tomoko, grabbing her arm and shaking it. "You must leave him immediately. Can you do this? Do you have someplace to go?"

The first step to a happy life . . . , Akiko thought to herself, and she smiled at her new friend. "Yes," she answered. "I have someplace to go."

JANE

Ma could tell right away, just by looking. "You throw away your baby," she said with disgust.

We were standing in the kitchen and I'd just barely taken off my coat and the accusation caught me off guard, so cruel and sudden. I'd spent a week in New York by myself, unable to edit, unable to do anything but cry, and I couldn't bear it, so I'd come running home to Ma for comfort. Stupid. I stood in the middle of the kitchen, holding on to my coat, with the damn tears dripping down my face. Ma looked terrified. Now that I think about it, she probably hadn't seen me cry since I was seven or eight and much smaller than her, a size that could still be comforted. Not that she ever did much of that. But in a small child, sorrow is manageable. Now she shuffled suspiciously over to me, looked up into my face, then took me by the wrist and led me to a chair. I held tight to the coat, but she pried it from my fingers and hung it carefully on a hook by the door. Then she turned and came back and stood next to me.

"Why you throw away baby if you gonna be so sad?" she asked, but her tone was softer and she placed her hand on the top of my head, not stroking, not patting or pulling me to her, but just resting it there firmly as though to keep my head from rolling away.

"I didn't mean to . . . ," I said in that normal voice I can use even when I'm weeping and my heart is breaking. "I didn't mean to throw it away. It was a miscarriage. I lost the baby. It was a boy. I really wanted him, Ma."

And then she did the last thing I expected, even from Ma. She laughed. She laughed and then patted my head briskly and withdrew her hand. The shock stopped my tears, and I stared at her. She went over to the stove and poured hot water into the teapot and brought it to the table. She sat down and poured us each a cup of green tea.

"Drink this. You feel better."

"Ma, why did you *laugh?*" I could hear the childish whine and accusation pinch my voice. "You think it's funny?"

"No," she said, wrapping her hands around the teacup to warm them. "No funny. I lose four babies before you. You only one tough enough baby to last. But I keep trying, you know? Until success."

"Ma, that's terrible. I never knew that."

"Why say? Not your business. Now it your business, so I say."

"When did you lose them? How many months?"

Ma shrugged. "One, two, three . . . I forget. All different."

I took a deep breath. I had to ask again.

"And are you sure Doc Ingvortsen didn't give you some pills to make your pregnancy last? With me, I mean?"

"Why you keep talking about some pill? I can't remember. Sure, I try everything. Some vitamin, some Doctor Ing-san medicine. It don't matter. Only one thing matter." Ma's face suddenly closed, and her expression turned furtive.

"What's that?" I've been trained to know a secret when I see one.

She looked at me long and hard, then sighed and gave in. "After losing number four baby, I try new method. . . ."

"Yes?" I prodded. "What was that?"

"You know Japanese *go-en*?" she asked.

"You mean the five-yen coin? With the hole in it?"

"Yes. You know what other meaning for *go-en*?"

"What, like a connection? Like when you have a good connection or relationship with someone?"

Ma nodded grimly. "I think I need *go-en* with my number five baby, so I put it in my mouth when I sex with your father. But I not have real *go-en* from Japan, so I use American nickel instead. I think, This is America, so close enough." She shrugged.

"You mean you had sex with Dad with a nickel in your mouth?!" I burst out laughing. "Ma, that's crazy."

She looked at me, distant and haughty, then suddenly she

smiled. "Dad think so too. He wonder, 'Why you don't like kiss me anymore, Michi?'"

"Ma, how long did this go on?"

"Long time. Every time. And every time it not work. But I never give up, you know? I think, This is my good idea. And then one night was . . . special night. And then you came!"

As an editor, I knew she had jumped ahead in her story and was forcing the conclusion. The note she ended on rang false. She was leaving something out. "Ma, what do you mean? What was special? What happened?"

She paused and took a long sip of tea. And then another. Then she poured another cup.

"Not your business," she concluded, and looked at me out of the corner of her eye. But I was not going to give up on this one. I don't know what I expected. Some clue to my own reproductive difficulties, perhaps. Or maybe it was just a prurient interest in my own conception.

"Forget it, Ma. It is totally my business. I need to know about this. You have to tell me."

She sighed again. "Dad, he come home with bottle of France wine and say he going to make me romantic again. Make me want to kissing again. And he give me France wine, much too much. And then we get ready to bed, so I look all over house for nickel to put in my mouth, and finally I find one and go up to bedroom and lie down. And then we sex, and just at that time, he kiss me so hard I swallow my nickel just like that! And that was night you are made."

I shook my head in disbelief. "I can't believe this, Ma."

"It is truth. I swallow nickel and you come. And stay with me for whole time. We have go-en, you see? Next time, you try with your husband. It work, you see."

"Ma, you know I'm not married. And I'm sorry. I just don't believe in these ancient Oriental superstitions."

Ma stiffened. "What ancient?" she replied.

"You know what it means—like 'old-fashioned.'"

"I know *meaning* of 'ancient,'" she said, affronted. "Nickel in mouth is not *ancient* custom."

"I thought you . . ."

"No," Ma answered. "I am modern woman. I just make it up."

I don't know why I got so annoyed. Maybe because she was so stubborn, so adamant, so sure she was right. Or maybe because she was so credulous, which is why she would have taken the DES in the first place. Or maybe it was her carelessness I blamed her for. Or maybe mine.

"Ma, I have something to tell you. You say the medicine that Dr. Ingvortsen gave you didn't matter, but that's not true. It did matter. It made me sick, when I was still inside you. That's why it's been so hard for me to get pregnant. That's why I miscarried this baby."

Ma just stared at me.

"The pills damaged my uterus and my cervix—inside me, all the parts you need to make a baby, Ma. They never developed properly. Do you remember the tumor I had operated on in Japan? That was part of it. I had *cancer*."

Ma shook her head. "Why Doc Ing-san give me bad medicine?"

"He didn't know. Nobody knew then."

She pursed her lips and shook her head. "No," she concluded. "It is not possible."

I lost it. "How can you sit there and be so sure?" I shouted. "You think you're so smart, that you know everything. But you don't. You just did whatever people told you to—Dad, Doc Ingvortsen, Grammy and Grampa. . . . The drug was a hormone. It fucked me up so I'll probably never have a baby. And I could get cancer again. When I'm in my forties, the risk increases again. I could still *die* of this, Ma."

Ma sat very still. "It is my fault?" she asked quietly. She

looked so little all of a sudden, and crestfallen, but her spine was still ramrod straight and her hands were folded tightly in her lap. I couldn't look at her.

"Jane-chan, I feel sorrow for you. But why you blame me? Only I try everything possible to make healthy baby—maybe take some pills, maybe swallow nickel. I try everything. Did you?"

I couldn't answer.

"I am sorry for taking bad medicine that hurt you, Jane. I did not know it. But you are wrong for blaming me." She reached over and held my wrist. "I never blaming you. I not blaming you for being too big baby that break me to pieces inside when you come out. Doc say I almost die. And bleeding and bleeding, so he take out my inside woman parts. No more chance for babies. All gone. But it's okay, I think. Because I am so lucky to get my big, tough American baby like you." She smiled at me and patted my hand proudly.

I put my head down on the linoleum tabletop and cried. Ma didn't say anything, just kept patting my hand.

I stayed in Quam for two weeks. Ma and I didn't talk too much about the sad stuff anymore, but we were gentle with each other and she made all my favorite Japanese foods, the ones she used to make when I was little and sick—savory egg custards, rice gruels, pickled plums. We ate quietly and talked about the past a lot, because the future had been taken away. But I couldn't forget it. My breasts were swollen and painful and leaking a little, and I was still bleeding heavily. I drove to the county clinic where I'd first gone to get the pregnancy test, and remembering made me cry again, and I sat in the car in the parking lot until I was finished.

The doctor examined me and said the bleeding was normal, and he gave me a prescription that he said should ease the swelling in my breasts. I had it filled at the pharmacy and on the way home I stopped at the Quam Public Library.

The interior hadn't changed since I was a child: the same heavy wooden furniture, the same smell of sunlight striking dust. I had spent many hours here, studying mankind in Frye's *Geography*, designing my progeny and daydreaming about a future, far away from Quam. And here I was, back again, bitter and aborted. The irony was not lost on me. I went to the reference section and found *The Complete Home Reference Compendium of Pharmaceuticals* and hauled the enormous book into an empty corner. My prescription was for a medication called Tace, a hard, two-tone green 25-milligram capsule, made by the Merrell Dow Company. I found it under "Estrogens." It was related to the generic drug diethylstilbestrol. Among the indications, the reasons to prescribe the drug, was "post partum breast engorgement." That was mine. The list of indications took up about one-quarter of a page. The remaining page and three-quarters consisted of warnings, precautions, adverse reactions, and contraindications, the very good reasons never to prescribe this drug. Among these was "known or suspected estrogen-dependent neoplasia." That was mine too.

Dust motes shimmered in the afternoon sun, gave body to the angled shafts of light. I sat there for a long time, watching the air drift until the sun sank below the horizon of the leaded window and the librarian told me the library was closed. Then I drove home. I emptied the vial of Tace into the toilet and started packing. It was the beginning of a new month, time to return to New York.

I told Ma at dinner, and she nodded approvingly. "No good you just stay home with mama like little baby," she said. "You fall off horse, you get back on top and riding again."

"Sure, Ma . . ."

"No 'sure Ma' to me! This is true thing I say to you. You go back to baby's father, you get on top and try again. Maybe get married this time."

"Ma, I don't think I want to. . . ."

"This is trouble with you. You *think* you want, you *don't think* you want—always back and forth. Me, when I want, it is with whole heart. I look at wanted thing with eyes straight on. But you! Neither here or there. Your looking always crooked, from side of eye. It has no power to hold. So wanted thing, it slip away from you."

She was right, of course. I've always blamed my tendency to vacillate on my mixed ethnicity. Halved, I am neither here nor there, and my understanding of the relativity inherent in the world is built into my genes. Nothing is absolute, and certainly not desire. But knowing this was not enough anymore. It was time to suspend knowing and decide, What do I want? What do I want, absolutely, with my whole heart?

When I left the house, Ma and I hugged, and when we separated, she held on to my wrist again and slipped something into my hand. It was a shiny nickel. I burst out laughing. Ma looked offended, then she shrugged.

"Maybe it work. Maybe nothing, only Oriental superstition, but American doctor Ing-san not so smart, either, after all. So you never know."

She was dead right about that too.

AKIKO

The door swung open and clanged against the cinder-block wall. Akiko listened. The apartment sounded hollow and still.

She took a step into the *genkan*. Inside, it felt damp, and chilly too, the way concrete apartments get when the heat's been off for a while and no one's been living in them. Akiko felt like a small mouse, perched at the threshold, peering and sniffing at the unfamiliar air. She took off her shoes and stepped up, listened again, then switched on the overhead fluorescents, waking the room with the flicker and hum.

"*Tadaima . . .*," she called softly. She was just testing, but there was no response. That was how it should be. Still, she needed to be absolutely sure. Clutching her bag, she tiptoed from room to room, checking in the closets, in the bathroom, behind doors. No one. No sign of him. She relaxed. She went into the kitchen and put her bag down on the table, then put on some water to boil.

The phone rang while she was pouring the tea. She took her cup and stood in the living room doorway, listening. The answering machine clicked on and played her own recorded greeting. When she heard John's voice on the other end, she walked across the living room and picked up the receiver.

"*Hai*," she said.

"*Ah, iru ka.* You're there," said John. "I heard the machine pick up and thought you hadn't returned yet."

"I just got back."

"How are you feeling? Have you recovered? You must be feeling better if they let you out."

"Yes." She took a slow sip of hot tea. It scalded her tongue.

"Still angry, huh?"

She didn't answer.

"Well, I don't blame you. You have a right to be."

"No, I'm not angry."

"Good. I'm glad to hear it." He paused. "Did you get my note?"

"Yes, I got it."

"I meant everything I said in it. I'm very sorry I hurt you. I give you my word it will never happen again. But now there's no more secrets between us. Now we can start over. Start fresh. I'm sure we'll be successful this time. We'll be more scientific about it, and make a chart and time things precisely. . . . I am quite confident."

"Yes, so am I."

"Good, I'm glad. I'm glad you are committed to trying again. Now, I'm in New York and I will have to stay here for another couple of weeks—we have decided to do the edit here. I'm sorry, but it can't be helped. But I'll be back on November twenty-first. Can you manage without me for that long?"

"Oh yes. I'll be fine."

"What will you do with yourself? Will you find enough things to keep you busy?"

"Yes. I will clean the house and get it ready for your return."

"Fine. That's just fine."

When she hung up, she pulled out the phone directory and looked up Travel Agents.

"May I help you?" the agent asked.

"I'd like to buy an airplane ticket, please," she said. "To New York."

"Certainly, and the date of travel?"

"November twentieth."

"And the return?"

"Oh. I don't know. It doesn't really matter."

The first thing she did was to throw out all her maternity magazines. Then she cleaned the house from top to bottom, beat the futon, washed the tatami, and arranged all the cookbooks on the shelves. On her hands and knees, she scrubbed the surfaces of the bathroom until every trace of her misery was washed away. She even dusted the shelves and the tops of all the bottles of John's mouthwashes in the medicine cabinet. Then she practiced packing all her clothes and her CDs and her Shōnagon and her pillow book (she'd found it hidden in John's golf bag), until she could fit everything she owned into two suitcases. What wouldn't fit she threw away.

In the evening, she prepared simple meals for herself, consisting of small, calcium-rich fishes, steamed vegetables, and a pickled plum to help her digest.

At night she lay in bed and watched her baby grow. At seven days, it was a single-layered ball of cells that folded over and over again to form layers of cells, the outermost of which, at thirteen days, began to bulge; it was the primitive streak, a marker for the main axis of the body, tracing the path for an eventual spine. The organizing design principle of human symmetry was now in place.

At eighteen days, the embryo entered the neurula stage, initiating the development of the nervous system. By the end of the month, it had grown from a single microscopic cell of perfect simplicity to an exquisitely intricate organization, the size of a grain of tapioca. Now millions of differentiated cells performed diverse functions: nervous, digestive, muscular, vascular, and skeletal. . . . There were rudimentary indications of eyes, whispers of ears, and even the whiff of a nose.

At twenty-two days, she watched as a nonfunctional set of kidneys appeared, looking like those of a primordial eel. (Later, she knew, these would be displaced by another pair, like the ones found in fishes and frogs, until finally the human kind developed.) The embryo now grew four pairs of gill arches and even a temporary tail; like the tadpole it resembled, it would lose both. The foundation for integrated human complexity was laid. Her baby-to-be was full of promise, from the tip of its tail straight through to the beginnings of its chambered yet primitive heart.

Akiko didn't turn on the television, not even once.

Two days before she left, she invited Tomoko for dinner. It was her friend's night off, and Akiko had prepared a wonderful meal: glassine mung bean noodles served cold, with crumbled bean curd and julienned vegetables in a tart, savory sauce; sliced lotus root, lightly fried with chili peppers in peanut oil, then steeped in soy sauce and *mirin* wine, and finished with a dash of Szechwan pepper; a sweet sesame *goma aie*, made with steamed chrysanthemum leaves, mildly bitter to offset the sweet; and a piece of cod, marinated for three days in sake and mild white miso, and then broiled until the skin was crisp but the insides were still succulent.

It was a party of sorts, Akiko mused. A party to celebrate their new friendship. But it was also a farewell party. And a birthday party too. Akiko took out a package she'd bought at the pharmacy and showed it to Tomoko. It contained a home pregnancy test kit.

"I want to prove it to you. So you don't think I'm crazy."

She went to the bathroom and urinated, then Tomoko came in and helped her with the test. It was positive. Akiko smiled.

"See? I told you."

"I believed you."

"It's going to be a girl."

"How do you . . . ? Forget it. I believe you."

Akiko cleaned up the packaging and threw it away, then wiped the sink. They stood side by side, leaning up against the bathroom counter and talking to each other in the mirror.

"That's why I'm going to America," said Akiko. "It doesn't matter so much for a son, but since she's a girl, I want her to be an American citizen. So she can grow up to become an American Wife." She had told Tomoko all about the program.

Tomoko frowned. "She doesn't have to be a wife at all, you know. . . . She could be a nurse, or . . ."

374

Akiko reached over and took her friend's hand and turned to face her. "I know. I'm just kidding. Sort of." Then she took her other hand.

Tomoko looked away, but Akiko leaned over and kissed her cheek. Then she kissed her lips, once, very lightly. Tomoko's lips were shockingly soft. It was hardly a kiss at all. Akiko pulled away and regarded her.

"Are you a lesbian?" she asked.

"I don't know," answered Tomoko. "I've never thought about it."

"I have," said Akiko. "I've thought about it. But I don't know, either." She squeezed Tomoko's hands again and then let go. "I don't know if I'm really going to stay in America. Maybe I'll come back after she's born. Anyway, you can be her aunt."

"I'd like that," said Tomoko, following her out of the bathroom.

The day before her departure, Akiko went to her bank branch office and withdrew exactly two-thirds of the money in the joint account she had with her husband. She converted a little over five thousand dollars into U.S. currency, which she thought would do for the time being. Then she went home and reserved a taxi for the following morning.

The following day, she took the taxi all the way into the city, to the Hakone City Terminal. It cost hundreds of dollars, but she didn't want to take any risks, lifting her heavy suitcases on and off the trains and subways. At the terminal, the driver helped her to the baggage check-in line. Then, with just a small knapsack and her CD Walkman, she boarded the limousine bus for Narita Airport. She found a seat at the back of the bus and checked the outside pocket of her knapsack for her airline ticket and her passport. Tucked inside the passport was a fax, carefully folded. She unfolded it now and glanced at the last line for reassurance. "P.S. If there is ever anything I can do to help . . ." She folded up the paper and put it safely away. She would telephone Takagi-san from inside the airplane, once it was too late to turn back.

Too late. Akiko's heart constricted with quick fear, and her palms broke sweat. What would Takagi say? Takagi was a woman who went to jail. She was tough. She could take on men like John and argue with them. Other than that, Akiko knew little about her. What if Takagi refused to help, or called John, or sent her away? She hadn't quite thought this through, but it was too late. She sat back and plugged the Walkman into her ears. Clearly there were times when it was better not to think.

Bobby Joe Creely was singing as the bus spiraled up the ramp onto the web of cloverleaf overpasses that laced the heart of Tokyo. Just outside the bus window, over the edge of the embankment, the office buildings hugged the freeway like the tall walls of a narrow gorge. They were so close she felt she could reach out and run her fingers across their facades. As the bus passed slowly by, she could see right into the row upon row of identical windows, into the sickly fluorescent-lit cubicles, crammed with desks spilling paperwork, where office workers, dressed in dark-colored office smocks, hunched over the desks or shuffled from one desk to another.

The beginning of a mournful tune, plucked from Bobby Joe's low, slow guitar, made Akiko shiver. It was her new favorite song, and she had studied all the words, looking each one up in the dictionary. Bobby Joe started to sing.

> On the midnight train,
> The lonesome train . . .

The bus shuddered, as if to the music, straining against the tight curve of the on-ramp. It wasn't a midnight train, Akiko thought, but it was just as good. Better, even. Because it took you to the airport.

> You can't feel no pain,
> You can't heal no pain . . .

That used to be true. It wasn't anymore.

> You been hurt so bad
> You been cryin', you been sad

That part would never change. You can't change what has already happened, she thought. But the future . . . Up and up the bus spiraled, until the ramps of the viaduct fed onto the expressway that led out of the city.

> So you pack your bags
> Without a word of good-bye,
> And you don't care if he never even knows
> The reason why . . .

Akiko smiled. Finally she'd done something—something worthy of the women in Bobby Joe's songs. And it pleased her to think that John would never know the reason why, that right now they were headed in opposite directions, and that in a couple of hours they would be passing each other in midair, somewhere, she figured, several thousand feet over the frozen tundra of Alaska.

THE END OF THE YEAR

SHŌNAGON

Things That Are Near Though Distant

Paradise.

The course of a boat.

Relations between a man and a woman.

JANE

> I remember that month of January in Tokyo, or rather I
> remember the images that I filmed of the month of
> January in Tokyo. They have substituted themselves for
> my memory. They are my memory. I wonder how people
> remember things who don't film, don't photograph, don't
> tape. How has mankind managed to remember?
>
> —Chris Marker, from *Sans Soleil*

First I quote Chris Marker, who is a filmmaker of note and
also a fan of Shōnagon. I think about him a lot when I'm
editing. Then I tell you that suspended by her leg, the dead
cow spins, drained but still dripping from the mouthlike
wound that bisects her throat. Then, as though in response
to some unearthly cue, the wound gives a muscular throb,
and a bright-red geyser springs upward from the floor. The
wound opens, wraps its lips around the thick red stream,
greedily sucks in the blood. When it's finished and the blood's
all gone, the mouth closes and the lips seal—satisfied, seamless. The cow is thrashing, frightened, but whole again. Alive
and kicking.

I do it again. And again. Twisting the dial, shuttling
the tape backward and forward, running my finger across
the cusp of life and death, over and over, like there's a trick
here, something that if I practice I might get good at. Suck-

ing life back into a body. Sometimes when I think about it I cry.

Last night, the police came. The neighbors upstairs complained about the screaming.

"Lady said it sounded like there was animals being slaughtered down here or something," the cop reported.

"Yes," I agreed. "She's right." I showed the scene to the cop and his partner, two big, beefy Polish guys from Long Island; like most cops on the Lower East Side, they commute from the suburbs to police the inner city.

"How can you watch that stuff?" the cop said, screwing up his baby face.

"I don't know." I shrug. "How can you eat it?" I rewound the tape, sucking the screams back into the cow's throat, along with the blood.

"Hey, that's kinda neat," said the cop's partner. "Like you're God or something." He shook his head, suddenly somber. "I'll tell you, I sure wish I could do that sometimes."

"Yeah," I agreed again. "So do I."

I came back from Quam resolute. I would edit my video. The act would redeem my insufficiency, my lapses, my sorrow. But the sorrow is too severe, and the guilt too intransigent.

It costs six hundred dollars a week to rent the crappy editing decks and the monitors. I've had all the Beta masters dubbed down to VHS work tapes and striped with time code. Projecting ahead and calculating the costs of a final on-line edit, I realize I'll be broke by the end of the month. Assuming I can edit something together at all. So far, all I've been able to do is run the footage back and forth, replaying the images until they substitute themselves for memory, until nothing exists except what remains on the screen.

At night, though, the displaced fragments float to the

384

surface. I shuttle back, dream the baby is alive, I feel him kicking. The body remembers.

It is cold in the apartment. I finger Mom's nickel, call Sloan. There's no answer, just his machine. I try his cellular; nothing. I hang up, don't leave a message.

I watch Rose sleep, the camera (my eye) tracing her baby-soft skin like a surrogate digit. Belly, ribs . . . Bunny lifts her shirt.

I call Bunny, speak to John.

"Bunny's taken the girl down to Texas for a spell," he tells me. "To visit her folks. Said they both needed a change of air." He paused and cleared his throat. "Awful sorry 'bout what happened," he concludes.

Okay, I'll buy that. Here's what I conclude: John is an awful sorry but essentially decent man who participates in inhumane and mechanical mass slaughter and the corruption of his own daughter. His son, Gale, is a dangerous fool, yet some of what he says about recycling livestock feed makes good ecological sense, however unappetizing it may sound. Of course, some of what he says makes no sense at all. And some of what he practices, like implanting hormones and feeding offal back to cows, could be downright deadly. Nothing is simple. There are many answers, none of them right, but some of them most definitely wrong.

I phone Sloan again, leave a message this time. Still no answer.

I watch Bunny's hand as she strokes Rosie's curls. The bedroom is dark and close, feels clandestine; like a flashlight, the wavering ray of the sun gun finds Bunny's face, illuminates it. I ask her questions: *When did you notice? Why didn't you do anything?* Watch her slippery eyes slide away, so practiced in evasion. But then she gives herself a little shake and raises her head. She looks into the camera, focuses. Like a beam, she meets my gaze; she tells me everything. *Secrets are like ghosts,* she says. *It's like livin' with ghosts. . . .*

Words that haunt, slice open my own abscesses of shame and dread.

Names leak into the air, hang around like a refrain. My litany: *Suzie Flowers. Helen Dawes. Lara, Dyann.*

It's cold in the apartment, but I shiver and sweat. I'm losing it. Haven't bathed or changed my clothes in a week.

Ghosts require ceremony. Like the babies, carefully named, then buried up on Cemetery Hill.

Name is very first thing. Name is face to all the world.

"Product of conception" was my baby's name, before he was tossed into an incinerator.

My son. He had a face, a penis, he sucked his thumb. . . . If he'd had another week or two, he could have opened his eyelids inside my inhospitable womb.

If he'd had another week or two, he might have survived outside it.

The phone rings. I lunge for it, knock it over. Scrabble on the floor to pick it up again. Sitting on the floor, legs splayed, I hear, *"Takagi-san? Akiko desu. Ueno Akiko desu."*

A woman's voice, muffled, disembodied. "Who . . . ?"

"I am Akiko . . . Ueno," she said, clearer now, in English.

"Akiko?"

"I am sorry to bothering you. . . ."

"What is it? Is something wrong?"

"No. Not wrong, but . . ."

"I can barely hear you. Where are you?"

"I am sorry to bothering you, Takagi-san," she said, raising her voice. "But in your fax . . . you said, Please do not hesitate . . . if I need help . . . ? I am calling to you from inside of the airplane."

"Airplane? What airplane? Where are you?"

There was a pause. "I think . . . it is over Alaska."

She was on my doorstep about eight hours later, then in my living room, standing there awkwardly because I'd moved out all the furniture to make room for the editing equipment. I dragged in a kitchen chair and she sat down next to the monitor, which displayed the image of Bunny, perched on her fence. It was a funny juxtaposition.

Akiko was exactly what I'd imagined Ueno's wife to be. Petite and shaking.

"I've left him," she had told me in the cab from the airport. Now I gave her tea, asked her why.

"He hit me," she said simply. "Many times. And kicked me too. But I got used to that." She spoke in quiet, polite Japanese and kept her eyes fixed on her hands, which were folded in her lap. "Then he did something that was wrong. He shouldn't have treated his wife like that." She looked up at me. "*Totemo yurusenai*. I can't forgive him."

I nodded. I had no idea what she was talking about. "Does he know where you are?"

"No. I ran away. He has been in New York, you know. He said something about the editing of the program?"

I grimaced. "Yeah, he took the show away from me."

"I'm sorry. I thought if I could warn you in time . . ."

"You did," I told her. "There was an accident."

She looked concerned. It was sweet of her. "Were you hurt?" she asked.

"Yes." I shrugged. "But I'm getting better." I smiled at her. "And thank you. At least we tried."

She smiled shyly back, then looked at her watch.

"He should be getting home to our apartment soon." There

was nothing shy about her smile now. "I wonder what he's thinking."

"Did you leave a note?"

"No. Nothing." She paused, then said in halting English, "I pack my bags without a word of good-bye."

She looked up at me and asked if she'd said it right. I told her she had. "It's from a song," she explained.

I dragged out an extra futon, gave her towels, and she took a quick shower. Then we went out to dinner.

"I'm not eating meat these days," I told her. "If that's okay with you?"

Akiko nodded. "John made me cook every recipe in your programs," she said.

"No, really? Even the Coca-Cola Roast?"

"That was one of the best ones," she said. "Anyway, I never liked meat so much to begin with."

We ate at a Chinese restaurant just off Mott Street, where the chef fashions mock beef out of wheat gluten, drenched in a black bean sauce. It is indistinguishable from the animal itself.

"What are your plans?" I asked her as we were finishing dinner.

"I want to make a trip," she said. "I want to go to Louisiana. I have wanted to visit there ever since I saw the program about the family who adopted the Korean children. It was one of my favorites. I gave it very high marks."

"Thank you." I was flattered. "If you'd like, I can call them for you. Maybe you could even stay with them."

"Yes, I'd like that." She paused, then tried another line in English. "I want to ride lonesome midnight train, please."

"Okay," I said. "The train is much more interesting. I'll help you buy your ticket."

"Thank you."

"And after that?"

"*So desu ne*," Akiko said, smiling her shy smile. "I'm going to have a baby."

It felt like a punch in the stomach.

"I just lost one," I said. I couldn't help it. The words just happened.

Akiko flinched. "The accident?" she asked. I nodded. "I didn't know. I'm so sorry," she whispered. I shook my head, managed to hold back the tears.

"Don't be," I told her. "I'm getting used to it. I'm happy for you. Is it John's?"

Akiko nodded. "Of course," she said. "He raped me. Just before he left for Colorado."

Over the next three days, she told me the whole sordid story of her marriage and her struggle with fertility. And I told her mine. We spent the days walking, from Battery Park all the way up to Harlem and back, crisscrossing the island. I was worried that the exercise would be too strenuous for her—she looked so fragile—but she assured me that she could see her baby very clearly and knew just what it was doing, what it needed. I assumed this was some Japanese idiom at first, then realized that she meant it quite literally.

"She has limb buds," she said, closing her eyes.

We had ducked inside Macy's to warm up for a moment, and Akiko sat down to rest on a bench just inside the door.

"Her spinal cord is just beginning to form. It shimmers through her skin." She opened her eyes and smiled. "Her heart is beating. She looks like a sea horse."

Her gaze drifted past me, to the busy shoppers milling through the scarves and belts and accessories.

"Since we're here," she said apologetically, "do you think

we could go inside for just a little while? I like department stores. I like to look around."

She asked about Colorado, so I showed her some of the footage on the editing deck. She was interested and listened carefully.

"So that's the deal," I told her. "It's good footage, but I can't seem to edit it. It's too complex, you know? I can't find the story." I ejected the tape and powered down the decks. "Maybe I should just leave it for a while. Come back to it in a couple of months. . . ."

"You are not at all what I expected," she mused, watching me intently. She sounded almost disappointed.

"You mean the way I look?" I asked, surprised that she'd expected anything at all.

"Well, yes, that too. You are surprisingly tall." She looked down at her hands. "I am afraid this may sound rude," she said, "but I expected someone more . . . *shikkari shiteru*. Tougher. More resolute." She looked up hopefully. "Do you remember the song sung by Mr. Bobby Joe Creely? You used it in the program about the Beaudroux family. It's called 'Poke Salad Annie'?"

"Yeah, I know it. . . ."

"'A woman who is carrying the straight razor' . . . that's what I expected you to be."

She was good for me. When I saw her off at Penn Station, she gave me a timid hug and promised to return in a couple of weeks. I was sorry to see her go. But as I rode the subway back downtown, I felt a bubble of anticipation tickle my gut. It took me a moment to figure it out, but then I knew. I was ready to edit.

GRACE

The little cabin was clean and cozy. They had washed the curtains and put a bouquet of fresh-cut winter-flowering jasmine in a vase on the dresser. The scent was heady. Grace stretched the sheet taut and made a neat hospital corner, then tossed the comforter in the air, letting it billow over the bed.

"Mom!" Joy glared at her. The eyebrow ring made her broad, tranquil face look fierce.

"What?"

"You're kicking up all the dust. I just swept." She chased the fleeing dustballs with her broom. Grace watched her. Joy was her least tranquil child. Maybe that's why she needed the ring, to disrupt the placid facade.

"Sorry." Grace paused. "Joy, it just occurred to me. Did you get your eyebrow pierced so you could look fierce?"

Joy rolled her eyes and leaned on the broom. "Mom, lay off the ring, will you?"

"Joy, really!" Grace sat down on the edge of the bed. "You did it over a year ago and I've never said a word. It's your face; you can do what you want with it. But I'm curious."

"I got it pierced to bug you."

"Really?"

"Yeah, but it didn't work, did it? Anyway, I like it. It looks good. Exotic."

Grace cocked her head and examined her daughter more closely. "Exotic. Exotic is good?"

Joy looked up from the floor, where she was crouched over the dustpan. "Yeah, exotic is good. And extreme too. That's real good."

"Your dad and I aren't exotic, I guess."

"No, Mom." Joy was laughing now.

"Who's exotic?"

"Jane Takagi is exotic. Did you see her tattoo?"

"She said hi, did I tell you? I told her about the Juilliard audition, and she said you should call her when you get to New York. She sounded real impressed."

Grace paused. Joy had ducked her head again, furiously digging the straws of the broom between the floorboards to dislodge every last bit of dirt. Was she annoyed? embarrassed? pleased? Grace couldn't read her. When Jane called, Grace had asked her to look after Joy for the week she would be in New York, but this would certainly rouse Joy's fury if she knew. She did not like being looked after. But it was a perfect trade. Jane would keep an eye on Joy, and Grace would take care of Akiko.

"When's she getting here?" Joy asked.

"Akiko? She's coming in on the train. We'll go pick her up in New Orleans. You wanna come?"

"I dunno. Maybe."

Joy stood up and dumped the dust from the pan into the garbage bag. "I'm gonna be real busy in New York, Mom. Should I really call her?"

"Well, actually, she wanted to ask you for a favor."

"She did? What?"

"She's thinking about adoption and wants to talk to you about it. She asked me, but I told her she should really talk to you. You're the expert. I mean, you know more than just about anyone else, from every angle. . . ."

Joy looked genuinely pleased. "Yeah, sure. I'll call her. I'll talk to her." She brushed her thick black bangs from her forehead. "So she wants to adopt, huh? Cool."

JANE

Editing my meat video was hard. It was not a TV show, which was what I'd become accustomed to. It was a real documentary, the first I'd ever tried to make, about an incredibly disturbing subject. There were no recipes, no sociological surveys, no bright attempts at entertainment. So how to tell the story?

Information about toxicity in food is widely available, but people don't want to hear it. Once in a while a story is spectacular enough to break through and attract media attention, but the swell quickly subsides into the general glut of bad news over which we, as citizens, have so little control.

Coming at us like this—in waves, massed and unbreachable—knowledge becomes symbolic of our disempowerment—becomes bad knowledge—so we deny it, riding its crest until it subsides from consciousness. I have heard myself protesting, "*I didn't know!*" but this is not true. Of course I knew about toxicity in meat, the unwholesomeness of large-scale factory farming, the deforestation of the rain forests to make grazing land for hamburgers. Not a lot, perhaps, but I knew a little. I knew enough. But I needed a job. So when *My American Wife!* was offered to me, I chose to ignore what I knew. "Ignorance." In this root sense, ignorance is an act of will, a choice that one makes over and over again, especially when information overwhelms and knowledge has become synonymous with impotence.

I would like to think of my "ignorance" less as a personal failing and more as a massive cultural trend, an example of doubling, of psychic numbing, that characterizes the end of the millennium. If we can't act on knowledge, then we can't survive without ignorance. So we cultivate the ignorance, go to great lengths to celebrate it, even. The *faux*-dumb aesthetic that dominates TV and Hollywood *must* be about this. Fed on a media diet of really bad news, we live in a perpetual state of repressed panic. We are paralyzed by bad knowledge, from which the only escape is playing dumb. Ignorance becomes empowering because it enables people to live. Stupidity becomes proactive, a political statement. Our collective norm.

Maybe this exempts me as an individual, but it sure makes me entirely culpable as a global media maker.

So editing my meat video was hard. It was not a TV show: just the feedlot with its twenty thousand head of cattle, and Gale talking about food and drug technologies; the drugs in the feedmill, and Rosie and her bright-blue popsicle; the cowboys with their hypodermic needles and the aborted calf fetus; the slaughterhouse, and the vat of hormone-contaminated livers, oozing viscous yellow; and Bunny, talking about Rose, who was sleeping. I still couldn't imagine what I would do with the tape, once I'd finished editing it. I mean, who would want to see it?

Well, Bunny, for one. I wrapped up a copy of the tape and sent it to her. And Dyann and Lara. I sent them one too. And Sloan.

AKIKO

The train crossed Lake Pontchartrain on a low, narrow bridge. The tracks were so close to the blue water, and the water was so vast on either side, stretching as far as she could see, that Akiko felt like she was riding on a magic train, skipping across the surface of the ocean.

Leaving Louisiana, the train headed back up north, into *Mississippi, Alabama, Georgia, the Carolinas.* As she stared out the window, she whispered the names of the Deep South to herself, matching their syllables to the rhythms of the train. No wonder people sang songs about these places: deep-blue swamplands cloaked in tattered mists; enormous fields of tobacco and cotton and wheat, forming horizons, bigger and more American than anything Akiko had ever seen before.

The approach into the small towns was heralded by the quick accumulation of wooden shanties lining the tracks, where men and women sat outside on crooked porches and children played in the street. Mangy dogs ran loose, and sometimes she caught sight of a chicken in a yard, pecking in the gravel by the skeletal wreck of a car. The cars parked along the streets were old and rusty too, as were many of those she saw actually driving down the dirt roads. Akiko had never seen a rusty car, and she realized with a shock that the people who lived here were poor. She'd never thought of Americans as poor. Maybe in the past, or in the movies, but not now. Not these days. Not in real life.

Many of the towns were too small to have stations anymore, but the train still stopped in the larger ones. Most of the passengers who got on and off were black. Families hauling huge bags and suitcases with broken latches and lots of children. There were some single men and women, traveling home, or away from a home, perhaps. Akiko tried to imagine it. Like herself, they were on the road, taking the train to find their happy life.

It was time now, eight weeks, and her breasts were tingling. Time to settle down. Oddly, she'd suffered not a moment of nausea during the early weeks, but instead felt a more or less continuous flush of well-being, which had ebbed and flowed from the moment of conception. Alison Beaudroux told Akiko that she'd had a terrible time with morning sickness. Her son was eight months old now, a plump, blond, bouncing ball of a baby, tossed from lap to lap around the dinner table by his adoring aunts and uncles. A rough 'n' tumble family. They were authentic, exactly what Akiko had seen on TV, what she'd traveled thousands of miles to see for herself, in person.

She'd never had meals like that before, platters passed around the table, heaped with steaming mashed potatoes, chicory and kale, and Vern's prize-winning kudzu-fried chicken. But the biggest surprise had been a turkey! Golden, glazed and resplendent, carried triumphantly to the table by the eldest boys and placed in front of Vern, who presided over it. Wielding his carving knife like a sword, he addressed the bird, but before he did so, he saluted Grace across the length of the table, where she sat, regal, her contentment running deep and feeding them, all fifteen members of the Beaudroux family and Akiko too, like a taproot. There was singing afterward. It was Akiko's first Thanksgiving.

When Grace learned that Akiko was pregnant, she offered the cottage and pressed her to stay, to have the baby there. It was tempting, but Akiko declined.

"If you ever change your mind," Grace said, "you are welcome to come and live here for a while."

Akiko was stunned at this generosity, this amplitude of feeling and the openness of Grace and Vern's life. She promised to return and accept the offer sometime. It was nice to have options, Akiko thought, as she watched the varied scenery go by. She'd never had any before. Now she had two.

The train families had settled noisily into their seats. The children were frothing with activity, climbing over the seat backs, falling in the aisles. The parents, laughing and screaming at the kids, unpacked their toys and coloring books, blankets and pillows, card games, tape decks, and bags and boxes of delicious-smelling picnic food. They knew this train, Akiko thought. Treated it like home. They reminded her of country people in Hokkaido when she was a child, off to the seaside or to a hot-springs resort, with their *ekiben* lunch boxes and bottles of hot tea and sake, bought from the train girls who came right to your seat with carts that they wheeled up and down the narrow aisles. There were no train girls dressed in neat cotton uniforms and pillbox caps who came to your seat on Amtrak. On the trip south, Akiko had waited for several hours for one to appear, growing hungrier as the miles slipped by. In Japan, the *ekiben* lunch boxes featured regional specialties of the areas through which the train traveled, and Akiko had been looking forward to her first taste of Southern cuisine. But she soon discovered that the Amtrak train served only microwaved hot dogs or cold ham and cheese sandwiches, and you had to go to the lounge car to buy them.

The Amtrak coach attendant on the southbound train had been kind enough to explain this system to her. The attendant on this train going back north was equally kind, a wiry black man, wearing an apron over his navy-blue vest. Three hours out of New Orleans, and he knew every person's name, even Akiko's, which he'd pronounced "A-KEE-kow." His name, he told her, was Maurice. Now he was carrying a broom and a large garbage bag, and as he sauntered down the aisle, collecting the trash, he stopped to talk to the passengers seated on either side.

"Well, now, Miss A-KEE-kow," he drawled, perching on the armrest and leaning on the seat back in front of her. "I can tell you're not from around these parts. Where y'all coming from, anyways?"

"I coming from Japan," Akiko said.

"Whoooey! Y'all hear that?" He stood up and addressed the passengers seated around her. "This young lady here's come all the way from Japan!" He turned back to Akiko. "You ain't come all that way on this here train now?" Everyone laughed, and Akiko shook her head.

"That's *still* a real long trip, I'd say," Maurice continued, raising his voice for the benefit of the people seated in the far rows. "So the rest of you, I don't want to hear any of you complaining 'bout how long this train's taking and how many hours you been riding now, 'cause I'm just gonna send Miss A-KEE-kow over to give you a talking-to, y'all hear me now?" The people laughed and craned their necks to take a look at Akiko. They smiled at her, and she blushed and smiled back.

"You know what train you're ridin' on?" he asked her.

She shook her head. "I'm sorry?"

"You know what this here train is that you're ridin' on?"

"It is train to New York, I think?"

"Well, that it is, but it's more than that. This here's the Chicken Bone Special, Miss A-KEE-kow, and you know why that is?"

Akiko shook her head. The passengers up and down the coach car were hooting and calling out things to Maurice, egging him on.

"It's called the Chicken Bone, Miss A-KEE-kow, because all these poor black folks here, they too poor to pay out good money for them frozen cardboard sandwiches that Amtrak serves up in what they call the *Lounge Car*, so these poor colored folk, they gotta make do with lugging along some home-cooked fried chicken instead, ain't that right now?" The passengers cheered. "Which one of you's got a piece of home-cooked fried chicken to share with Miss A-KEE-kow who's come all the way here from Japan? Give her a taste of some Southern hospitality now. . . ."

And as soon as he said this, suddenly Akiko was surrounded by people offering her drumsticks and paper plates of potato salad and chips and pickles and drinks of soda, and Maurice, giving in to the demand of the crowd, had retreated to the head of the coach car, where, with an ear-splitting screech and clatter, he activated the train's public address system. Clapping his hands and slapping his knees, he started the passengers chanting a background chorus, *chicken bone chicken bone chicken bone chicken bone* . . . and then he joined in:

Let me tell you a story 'bout
train one-nine—
She's a mighty old train
But she's runnin' just fine,
An' the folks who ride her,
They have a good time,
on the Chicken Bone, Chicken Bone, Chicken Bone Special!

Akiko clapped her hands in time and looked around her at the long coach filled with singing people. This would never happen on the train in Hokkaido! For the second time since she left Japan, she shivered with excitement. She'd felt it at the dinner table at Thanksgiving, and now, again, even stronger— as if somehow she'd been absorbed into a massive body that had taken over the functions of her own, and now it was infusing her small heart with the superabundance of its feeling, teaching her taut belly to swell, stretching her rib cage, and pumping spurts of happy life into her fetus.

This is America! she thought. She clapped her hands and then hugged herself with delight.

JANE

"Lara, pick up the other phone!"

Muffled, on the other end, I heard Lara call out, "Just a minute . . . ," and then her voice came through the receiver. "Hello?"

"I've got Jane Takagi on the line," Dyann told her. "She wants to know if we're still mad at her."

"Oh," said Lara.

This did not sound good. I had sent them the fax and the tape of their episode with the BEEF-EX commercials, but they'd never acknowledged either. Nor had I gotten any response to the Bunny and Rose tape. I don't know why acquittal meant so much to me—from these ghosts, in particular.

"Well, are we?" Dyann said.

"I don't know. What do you think?"

"I dunno. I mean, it was a pretty lousy thing to do, tricking us into being *spokeswives* for the meat industry. . . ."

It *was* lousy, but I'd admitted that already and apologized.

"Yeah, but look how subversive we got to be." I thought I could detect a trace of amusement in Lara's voice.

"I suppose . . . but she could've told us, you know," Dyann countered sternly. "Beforehand."

It's true. I agree. There's no excuse.

"Yeah. But she did apologize."

What else could I do? I was wrong.

"Yes, but was she *really sincere?*" Dyann's voice was warming up.

"Hard to say," said Lara.

"Yeah, it's that inscrutable Asian thing. . . ." They were both laughing now.

"Excuse me," I broke in. "When you guys get finished here, just let me know. . . ." They only laughed harder. "I almost got fired trying to air your show," I continued, somewhat indignantly. "I got in deep shit with the ad agency. 'You can't put vegetarian lesbians in our Saturday-morning family meat slot!' That's what they told me. It was hell."

"Sorry, Jane. But you deserved it."

"I know. I know. I'm sorry. How many times do I have to say it?"

"Basically, forever, I'd say. What do you think, Lara?"

"Yeah, forever should do it."

"Fine." I was relieved but edgy still, so I went straight to the point. "Did you see the other tape?"

The pitch of the conversation shifted, and silence filled the wires.

"The tape was remarkable," said Lara, finally.

"Very fucked up," said Dyann. "Very, very disturbing. It's what convinced us you were really serious about being sorry."

I sighed, partly with relief, I think. And contrition, and a lot of sadness, which just wouldn't go away.

"What are you going to do with it?" asked Dyann. "It's going to be hard to get it shown, don't you think? I mean, it's pretty intense for TV. . . ."

"I don't know yet," I said. "I haven't thought that far ahead. I'm still waiting to hear back from the woman, the mother. From Bunny."

"Oh, *good* for you. You sent it to her *beforehand.*"

"Dyann, lay off," Lara chided.

"It's all right," I said.

"It must have been hard to make," said Lara.

"It cost me everything," I answered, without thinking. Then I realized I didn't want to go into it. "It's a long story. I'll tell you the whole thing sometime. Listen, there's something else. Remember I told you in my fax that the reason I wanted to broadcast your show was that I thought it was important, that it would make a difference in Japan?"

"Yeah . . ." Dyann sounded apprehensive.

"Well, apparently it did." I didn't know exactly where I was going from here. It wasn't a situation like the Beaudroux family. Welcoming strangers into their home was a way of life, and an extra body was negligible. This was different. "Uh, I have something else I want to send you," I concluded gracelessly.

"I don't like the sound of this," said Dyann. Her tone was ominous.

"She's a young woman. Japanese. A fan . . ." There was very little response from the other end. "She's a friend . . . of a friend . . . sort of. She saw your show and then appeared on my doorstep, looking for you guys. She's run away from her husband, who beat her up pretty badly, and raped her too. But the point is, she wants to meet you. You guys meant a lot to her. Gave her the courage to leave a really bad situation. She wants to come to Northampton. . . ."

"Fine," said Lara.

"Lara!" said Dyann.

"What?" said Lara. "We have a guest room. She can stay with us."

"Oh, all right," Dyann groaned. "How long is she coming for?"

"Well, that's the thing." Now I was in real trouble. "You see, she's pregnant. . . ."

LARA & DYANN

When she hung up the phone, Dyann tracked Lara down and cornered her by the extension in the kitchen.

"Do you really think that was wise?" she asked.

Lara leaned against the kitchen counter, cocked her head, and considered the question.

"Yes," she concluded.

"Okay." Dyann shrugged and sat down at the table. "You know, when Takagi calls, we should learn to be really on guard with her. She gets us into these damn situations."

"Yes, she does," Lara agreed.

"Weird, huh? How someone just drops into your life like that. I mean, there we were, minding our own business. . . . What did we do to deserve her?"

Lara shook her head and smiled. "I don't know. But nothing really bad's come of it so far, right?"

She crossed the room to the kitchen table and stood behind Dyann, putting her hands on her lover's shoulders.

"I think Akiko's story is touching," she said, pulling Dyann gently to her stomach. "You should write about her. I mean, this woman has guts. Escaping from a husband who beat her, coming all the way here to America, to Northampton, Massachusetts, to have her baby, all because of us. No, because of you! What was it she wrote? 'I feel such sadness for my lying life. So I now wish to ask you where can I go to live my happy life like her?' That's you, darling, your happy life she's talking about. Makes me proud. . . ."

Dyann caught Lara's hand and kissed her palm. "Okay. You win. It *is* my happy life, truly it is."

JANE

"Domo arigatoo gozaimashita," said Suzuki, bowing slightly. Oh did the same.

They were sitting on the floor of my apartment. We had just had dinner, then watched the tape. The boys were silent, and then when it was over, Oh shuddered and Suzuki turned to me.

"Thank you very much. I feel like I've filmed something very important. I am proud."

"What are you going to do with it?" asked Oh.

"I don't know. . . ."

"You'll never get it on TV, not in Japan, anyway. It's much too . . . real."

"Yeah," I said. "It's no different here."

"It's too bad. People ought to see this."

"Yeah."

We went down to Houston Street, to the Parkside Bar, an anachronistic tribute to a stretch of green long since tarred over. I told the boys I'd buy them drinks because I owed them for lying about the master tapes and saving them and risking getting fired. But they objected, saying they owed me for making a documentary they could feel proud of—and for *really* getting fired in doing so. And because I was dead broke, I gave in.

"I'm warning you guys," I told them. "I'm not pregnant anymore. I'm serious about drinking tonight. . . ."

We ordered a round of double shots of Jack and pints of Brooklyn Lager.

"*Jane-chan wa mada wakai...*," Suzuki said, toasting me decisively. "You're still young. You can get pregnant again."

Oh raised his glass, supporting this notion.

"I'm not so sure about that. I can't do it on my own, you know." Suzuki gave me a puzzled look. I laughed. "What, you thought it just happened? Like immaculate conception? I broke up with the guy I was seeing, the baby's father."

Suzuki puffed out his chest and leaned in close. "*Ja, boku wa?*" he said in a manly tone of voice. "Can I help?"

"*Boku mo!*" said Oh, shoving Suzuki off his barstool and out of the way. "Me too!" he said eagerly. "You don't need the Commissioner. We can do the job."

"*Baka!*" I laughed and threw a handful of soggy pretzels at them. Then I realized what Oh had said.

"You knew about the Commissioner?"

"Do you really think we are stupid?" Suzuki asked. "How could we not notice an identical very tall man showing up week after week, in Nebraska, Texas, Oregon...? Please, give us some credit."

"How come you never said anything?"

Suzuki looked at me, affronted. "You didn't want us to know. We were being polite."

"Oh," I said.

"What happened, anyway?" Suzuki asked. "How come you broke up?"

"I think it was the miscarriage," I said, tipping my head back and polishing off the shot. "But I don't know for sure, because he's dropped out of sight. I have no idea where he is. Won't return my calls. Nothing." I held the glass in the air.

"Oh."

The bartender filled our shot glasses, and the three of us drank them off, then had another. When we left the bar, we were leaning on each other for support. We went up to Saint Mark's Place for a bowl of *ramen* noodles, and then they walked me home. It was a weekend night and the streets were restless. People were on the prowl, humming with an edgy, inconsolable desire.

"It's none of my business," Suzuki said as we crossed Avenue A, "but the Sloan Rankin Band was playing at the Mercury Lounge last weekend."

I stopped short. "How did you know that?"

"I read it in the *Village Voi*—"

"No. The Commissioner. How did you know he was Sloan Rankin?"

"Oh, really, Takagi," he said, disgusted. "You have got to give us more credit. Sloan Rankin is a very popular indies star in Japan. He's in the Suntory Dry Beer commercial. Playing his sax."

The next day I called the Mercury Lounge. After a bit of a fight, the bartender put me through to the owner, who did the bookings. Rankin, he told me, was on tour with his band.

"They don't usually tour like this, at this time of year," he said.

"Do you know where they were headed?"

"Yeah, that was weird too. They were doing a Southern circuit. Smaller gigs. I was surprised."

"Do you know where I can find them this weekend? Like tomorrow?"

"Yeah. I think he said they were heading down to Memphis."

AKIKO

The first evening she was alone in her new apartment, she walked from room to room, perching for a moment on a windowsill, leaning against a bare wall, or crouching in a corner to gain a new perspective. Not that it was a big place. There was a kitchen with space enough for a table, a tiny bedroom, and a living room with a big, deep window seat that looked out onto the tree-lined street called Pleasant. Akiko liked that. In her old neighborhood in Japan, the streets were generally called by numbers.

Dyann and Lara had been wonderful. Lara had helped her find the apartment, and Dyann had introduced her to a woman doctor, who would help her have the baby. They had lent her pots and pans and a chair, and then taken her shopping for the futon mattress on a frame that folded into a couch, which was clever and very American. As she tiptoed from room to room, Akiko decided that, all in all, this certainly felt like the beginning of a happy life.

The window seat was her favorite spot. She'd bought a thick pillow to sit on and another one to lean against, intending to spend the next seven months perched right there, curled and ripening. It was a place where one could watch the first snow dust the skeletal branches of the maple out front, then deepen as the winter grew deep. Then, when the weather warmed, the snow would grow heavy and slide from the neighbor's slate roof and splatter wetly to the ground, where it would melt, baring patches of dark, raw earth. Quickened by the fury of early spring, red spikes would spear the earth from underneath (as dark and sharp as anger or as loss), and one could watch that too, until finally the days grew long and mild and the tiny leaves unfurled into a dense green canopy. Just when the breezes blew warm through the window, it would be time to hoist oneself to one's feet and trundle off to the bedroom to pack a bag, to go to the hospital, to have a baby.

She tested the window seat now, jumping up from time to time to fetch something that would make it even better: a blanket, a cup of tea, Shōnagon, and her own pillow book too, and finally a pen and some writing paper that she'd bought at the stationery store earlier that day. She leaned back and looked out the window into the darkness, then picked up her pen.

"Dear John," she wrote. "I am writing to tell you that I am fine. I have left you and I am never coming back." She took a sip of her tea. She had changed her mind about telling him. She had to write, otherwise it would never end.

> So you pack your bags
> Without a word of good-bye,
> And you don't care if he never even knows
> The reason why . . .

Not that John would ever write a song about her, but it was an example of how not saying something made it hang around in the air, like a refrain that just keeps coming back at you, again and again. Akiko had plenty of very good reasons for leaving, and she wanted him to know each one. Only then could she be done with him, once and for all.

JANE

On Beale Street, a greasy rain smeared the neon as it fell, then scooped up its light in asphalt puddles. Beale Street. The name is full of blues and magic, conjuring up a time and place, gritty with lost authenticity, that embarrasses the sham of here and now. Now Disney is the model for magic, and conjuring has turned America's more colorful streetfronts, like Beale and Bourbon and Broadway, into self-referential shadows of their former, bad-ass selves. On warm sunny days, sporting emblazoned T-shirts, the tourists are sheepish as they graze Beale Street in search of the real thing, but in the night, *this* night, the few seekers who were out and bent against the rain bled seamlessly into the sax-filled air.

It was Sloan's sax. I could hear the thread of it blocks away, so I slowed, then stood there on the corner, wavering. The notes fractured the night, absolute in their dissonance, irreconcilable. I thought about turning around, returning to the ducky comfort of the Peabody, but instead I walked on, stomping through puddles like a Japanese monster, to give me courage. At the doorway I fingered Ma's nickel, pushed in.

Sloan commanded the stage and the place was rapt. He was deep into the middle of a long, slow riff. Rope thin, his rangy body curled around his instrument, then magnificently unfurled as he rode its crescendo. No one could let loose like Rankin. I stood at the back, watching him through a thick blue haze, across a pebbly expanse of backs and heads that I knew I would have to cross to get to him, and it suddenly was very clear to me: I wanted that proximity again. I wanted that muscled mouth against my mouth, and the sure pads of those fingertips stroking my bones. So when the last set was over and Sloan wiped the sweat off his forehead and turned his back to the crowd, I stomped over all of them to get to him first. But when I got close, I stopped.

There were girls. Already there. Shadowy girls, tall like me, better dressed, like the ones we met in SoHo boutiques or the garden cafés in L.A., whose talent was simply to belong, no matter where they found themselves. One, in particular, belonged to Sloan. Gamine, tainted with the pallor of youth, she made an art out of gawky. I stood there and watched as she suffered a kiss to her cheek, then languidly she turned and draped her slim arms around his neck, pushed back his sweaty cowlick, and blew on his forehead. He closed his eyes, tilted his head, moved it slowly from side to side to direct her breath across it.

So maybe I didn't believe it. Maybe I didn't believe that she was real, or that he was, or maybe it was Ma's nickel, but when he opened his eyes again, I was standing behind her, more or less over her shoulder, directly in his line of vision. I didn't have a plan or anything. I mean, there I was, sodden, gaunt, deflated. No competition. If I'd been talking to the girl, that's what I'd have said, and given her arm a reassuring pat or two. All I really wanted to do was watch them. And understand. And then get the fuck out. But as soon as he saw me, he released her, walked right through her.

I put out my hand. The waif was watching us with bruised eyes. "Sloan Rankin?" I said in a voice meant to carry. "Pleased to meet you. Jane Little, Tennessee Commissioner of Jazz. It's a pleasure to welcome you and your band of outstanding musicians—"

He grabbed my outstretched hand by the wrist, twisted it up behind my back, turning me, then moving his body in behind mine. "Walk," he ordered roughly in my ear. I struggled, but he lifted my pinned arm up between my shoulder blades, and it hurt. He marched me across the emptying room, through the door, and out into the rain. Then he released me against the side of the building. "What the fuck are you doing here?" he asked.

I stood there, rubbing my elbow. I didn't really have an answer prepared. I shrugged. "Here on a job. Heard you were in town."

"Bullshit."

"Yeah."

We stood there, facing each other. It was raining harder now, and the big, fat drops were running down my face, and his too, as he loomed over me.

"Just say it." His voice was tight and his teeth were clenched and I could see the muscle in his jaw working.

"What?" I lifted my shoulders, cocked my elbows, raised my palms to the weeping sky. "What do you want me to say?" Trying hard for insouciance.

"You're sorry. Just say you're sorry."

"Sloan, it's too late for apologies—"

"Fuck you!" He slammed his fist into the brick wall next to my head. "Fuck apologies. I don't want apologies. I just want to hear it. I want to hear *once* that you are sorry, like you really mean it. No fucking excuses. No explanations. Just once, that you are as sorry as I am . . ." He was crying, I think. I was too. I sank back against the wet brick and covered my face with my hands, then slid down the wall, like a body shot through the heart.

"I'm sorry," I sobbed. "You don't know how sorry—"

And then suddenly he was all around me, gathering me up and crushing me against the wet brick, kissing the rain. And I realized I'd never been gathered up before, never been so broken apart or so recovered, and it was shocking, but before I could think about it, we were walking really fast through streets that flowed like a river, to arrive, dripping, at the stolid Peabody. Up the brass elevator, across the densely carpeted hall, to the door where I fumbled for the key (remembering the last time I stood at a door at the Peabody, fumbling for a key), but before I could think about it, the door swung open and Sloan backed me through, across the room, and onto the big, redeeming bed.

It wasn't easy. It wasn't like we made love and it was this enormous flood that washed away all our sins and insufficiencies, although from time to time that was how it felt. Rather, we had to negotiate a way through layers of nakedness and conjunction, stopping and starting, asking questions, filling in gaps and testing the waters. But we did it. Dove, then rose again to reach a plateau where we could rest, breathing deep and easy. Until another accusation surfaced. A doubt insisted on address. And so we would start again, and so we continued, off and on, all night, until morning.

I made him get up. It was Sunday, and I made him get out of bed and shower and get dressed, and it was a good thing that he always wore a suit and tie onstage, because by eight o'clock he looked presentable. We grabbed coffees, stumbled into my rented car and I drove across the border into Mississippi, and an hour later, at a little before nine, we were parked in the dirt lot of the Harmony Baptist Church, watching Mr. Purcell and Miss Helen and the kids unload from their car and greet their neighbors. When Miss Helen looked up and caught my eye and recognized me, I saw her confusion, so I walked over to her and stretched out my hand.

She held it, and shook it, but said nothing.

"I came back to say I'm sorry."

It took her a while, but finally she spoke.

"You said you'd come back," she said, nodding, "and you did." She patted my hand.

"I don't know how to explain what happened," I told her. "I didn't agree—"

She pulled me toward church, tucking my hand under her

arm. "You come back to the house afterwards." She caught sight of Sloan. "Is that your friend? Bring him too." She stopped, and we waited for Sloan to catch up, and I introduced them.

"You didn't tell me we were going to church," Sloan whispered as Miss Helen turned to greet a friend on the front steps.

"Yeah, well, I didn't know. . . ."

"Takagi, I don't do church. . . ."

"Neither do I. Usually."

We climbed the steps. At the top the buxom usher in the white nurse's uniform greeted us and we followed her through the doors and into Harmony.

"I get it," Sloan continued, whispering as we walked down the aisle. "This is a trick, and when we get to the altar there'll be a guy with a shotgun. . . ."

I glared at him. "Don't flatter yourself." Miss Helen was still holding my arm, and pointing out people I'd met on the previous visit, who waved and called out to us.

"Takagi, we'll get married, that's fine. A nice civil ceremony . . . but just not in a church, please!"

And just at that moment, the Yamaha organ launched a triumphant chord, and the Harmony Five burst into a rousing rendition of "It Remains to Be Seen What He Can Do for Me."

"Relax, Sloan," I said, patting his hand as we took our seats next to Miss Helen. "Just sit back and enjoy the music."

EPILOGUE: JANUARY

SHŌNAGON

It Is Getting So Dark

It is getting so dark that I can scarcely go on writing; and my brush is all worn out. Yet I should like to add a few things before I end.

I wrote these notes at home, when I had a good deal of time to myself and thought no one would notice what I was doing. Everything that I have seen and felt is included. Since much of it might appear malicious and even harmful to other people, I was careful to keep my book hidden. But now it has become public, which is the last thing I expected. . . .

Whatever people may think of my book, I still regret that it ever came to light.

JANE

Hah!

As a fellow documentarian, I can say this with authority: Shōnagon's covering her ass. It's false modesty, so don't believe a word of it. But I'm getting ahead of myself.

The rest of my story is a matter of history. Sloan and I parted in Memphis knowing that we would try once again to forge our respective uncertainties into something that resembled a family and a future. We talked a little about adopting kids. I called Grace Beaudroux, and she promised to take the family to hear him play in New Orleans at the end of his tour, then I flew back to New York to find a job.

When I walked into the apartment that night, I knew something had happened. It was just after eleven, and the phone was ringing, and somebody had shoved dozens of little pieces of paper underneath my door. I waded through them to answer the phone, but when I got there, I noticed the message light flashing on the answering machine and, looking closer, saw that I had twenty-seven messages, and the twenty-eighth was being recorded as I stood there listening.

"This is Ivan Singer calling from the CBS news desk again. *Please* give us a call. . . ."

I waited until the machine had reset, then rewound it and hit Play. One after the other, every major television news program and talk show in the country had left an urgent message requesting that I get in touch immediately. There were messages in Japanese as well, from the networks there, and also from several European stations. "Mrs. Dunn gave us your number," each first-time caller prefaced his request, and then: "We want to talk with you about the footage."

Finally, there was a message from Bunny.

"Howdy there, Jane. I'm real sorry about all this. I've been trying to call you all morning, but I can't get through 'cause your line is always busy, so you probably already know what's happening. But I just wanted to tell you that the documentary tape you made was put together real good, and thanks for blocking out me and Rosie's faces like that. Guess it sort of bothered me after all, even though I said it was okay. . . . Anyway, I gave a few people your number. Hope it's okay with you."

I disengaged my call-waiting feature and phoned her immediately. I got her answering machine.

"Bunny, pick up, it's me, Jane. Bunny, are you there? It's Jane. Jane Takagi-Little. Bunny . . . ?"

"Hey there, Jane."

"Figured you were screening your calls. . . ."

"You said it! Ain't this something!"

"Bunny, what the hell is going on?"

"Yeah, well . . ." Bunny sighed. "It was the documentary tape that you sent? Of Gale and the slaughterhouse and me and Rosie?"

"I figured. What happened?"

"Well, what happened was, a couple of weeks after y'all left, I took Rosie to Texas, to a big hospital there, and sure enough, it was just like you said, some kinda hormone poisoning, and they speculated it was from the feedlot. I couldn't bring her back here, so I left her with her grandma in Texas for a spell and came back to make things right with John. I told him, not everything, but a little about what was wrong, and he didn't believe me, you know? I mean, it all sounds pretty crazy, right? So just then, your tape came in the mail, and I watched it. . . . I showed it to him—" And right there, Bunny giggled and couldn't go on.

"Bunny, what happened?"

"He went ballistic!" she shrieked. "I shouldn't laugh. But I was so relieved, you know? Like finally he understood. He made me drive him down to the feedlot and get Gale, and then he showed him the tape too. And I'll never forget Gale's face, all twisted up and pink when them pictures of Rosie's chest and down below came on. . . . I mean, that boy was sorry! He was sobbing, 'I never knew, Daddy, you gotta believe me I never knew. . . .'"

"He did know. I told him."

"That's what I said. So John made him get on the phone and call the guy at the local USDA office? And he made Gale 'fess up to everything, the whole thing."

"Whole thing?"

"Yeah, well, it seems like he's been using that DES stuff and injecting the cattle with it. Getting it from somewhere, I don't know. Him and a lot of other guys around here . . ."

"But I still don't understand. How'd this get to the press, then? And how'd they find out about the footage?"

"Well, after Gale finished telling about the DES and the cattle, John got on the line and he told 'em about Rosie. And then we get this call from the USDA in Washington, D.C., and then another from the FDA, all wanting to know exactly what he was talkin' about. I guess this kinda thing happened before. Anyway, somebody in one of them offices musta leaked it to the press, because before you know it, it's all over the place and we're gettin' calls right and left from the TV stations and everybody, and there's John, sittin' in his wheelchair on the porch with a shotgun in his lap, holding them reporters off. No pictures, we told 'em. Of course, Rosie ain't even here, but nobody knows that, you see. But then me and John talked it over and figured, hell, we'll just turn 'em all over to you. Seeing as you blocked out our faces and everything. John liked that. Figured you're to be trusted. You'll know what's best to do with 'em. And as far as Gale and the feedlot is concerned, John is fed up with all of it and figures Gale's just gittin' his just deserts."

"So what is it you and John want me to do, Bunny?" I asked helplessly.

"Spread the word," said Bunny. "Give 'em your document-ary. Nah, you ain't got no money. Sell it to them. Whatever you want. The main thing is, people gotta know."

And that was that. A feeding frenzy ensued during the next couple of weeks. I sold pieces of the footage to all the major U.S. networks and to foreign TV as well, in Europe and Asia, including the network in Japan that carried *My American Wife!* Aside from the footage sales, public television in the U.S., England, and Japan bought the edited documentary in its entirety. But people wanted my story too, how I uncovered the illegal hormone ring. I was so swamped I couldn't handle it all, so I called Dave Schultz in from Colorado and we rented a little office, where he slept on a couch. With his grasp of the facts and figures, it took him no time at all to get up to speed, fielding the questions from the press.

Kenji called to tell me that he and Ueno were in deep shit. Apparently, the Bunny Dunn episode of *My American Wife!* (directed by "John" Ueno) was a virtual celebration of the wholesomeness of beef, and the program aired the same day that the DES story broke. As the Dunn feedlot figured promi-nently in both, it didn't take long for the press to catch on. Now, in addition to the beef scandal, they found themselves at the heart of a media controversy over reliability in television and the power of corporate sponsorship to determine content and truth.

And there was yet another angle. Gale's interview about cattle feed, especially the practice of feeding cow parts back to cattle, stirred up a wave of media concern about bovine spongiform encephalopathy and its human equivalent, Creutzfeldt–Jakob disease. It had first made the news back in 1987, when the disease was identified in England and given the media-sexy name "mad cow." Yet despite awareness of the dangers, the practice of feeding offal to ruminants continued in America. The Japanese didn't like this.

Ueno was demoted, sent out to one of the regional offices in the provinces to make local TV commercials for hot-springs resorts and conference centers. This made me very happy, but I felt truly sorry for Kenji: *My American Wife!* was being canceled, and the New York office was closing.

"Well, at least you'll be able to go back to Tokyo, right?" I asked.

Kenji sounded glum. "I'll never direct, you know. Not after this."

"I'm sorry. . . . But you know, Kenji, it's not what I thought it would be. It's no fun directing for TV. Too many compromises."

"Yes, well, I don't mind compromises. *Shikataganai* . . ." He sighed deeply. "Oh, I almost forgot. I sent that damn tape to Suzie Flowers. I'm sorry, Jane, I had to. She was driving us all insane. But it didn't help, and she's *still* calling every other day. She wants to speak to you. You simply have to make her stop."

My heart sank but I finally did it. I called her.

"Jane!"

"Suzie, I'm so sorry—"

"I got the tape! Of the show!"

"I know. I'm so sorry—"

"It was wonderful!"

"What?"

"It was so beautiful, and so . . . I don't know . . . so *authentic*, you know?"

"Authentic?"

"Uh huh. Especially that part after the Survey, where you guys put in that *boinnggg!* I mean, that's *exactly* what it felt like to me at that time. Like I'd been hit on the head with one of those rubber mallets or something."

"Really?"

"Uh huh, so I sent the show to Fred, you know? And you'll never believe . . . He actually watched it, and then he brought it back to me, in person! Like, I opened the door and there he was, just standing there holding the tape in one hand and roses in the other! *Roses!* I couldn't believe it. And then he asked me for a second chance, and it was just like the show, the way you guys ended it, with a big kiss and everything! I just had to tell you . . . !"

And suddenly—*boinnggg!*—there it was. Suzie hit me on the head, and the puzzling and multifaceted shape of my year became clear to me. Like Mrs. Bukowsky had said to the Mayor, "You never know who it's going to be, or what they'll bring, but whatever it is, it's always exactly what is needed."

I had started my year as a documentarian. I wanted to tell the truth, to effect change, to make a difference. And up to a point, I had succeeded: I got a small but critical piece of information about the corruption of meats in America out to the world, and possibly even saved a little girl's life in the process. And maybe that is the most important part of the story, but the truth is so much more complex.

I am haunted by all the things—big things and little things, Splendid Things and Squalid Things—that threaten to slip through the cracks, untold, out of history.

Like all the parts of the Gulf War we didn't see on TV,

424

parts that were never reported. That war was certainly a Thing That Gained by Being Painted.

And like Suzie's tale, a small but Outstandingly Splendid Thing. I mean, I take a Japanese television crew out to Iowa to film a documentary about this American wife, we make a total fiction of the facts of her life, and now, a year later, she tells me that those facts have turned right around and aligned themselves with our fiction. So go figure.

I hung up the phone after my conversation with Suzie and stood at my window, looking out through the iron security bars onto the street. Fresh snow was falling, covering up the dirty slush and the urine-stained embankments of hard-packed snow that lined the sidewalks. The forecast was for a record-breaking blizzard, another "Storm of the Century." The city looked sparkling clean and white.

There's no denying, I thought. In the Year of Meat, truth wasn't stranger than fiction; it *was* fiction. Ma says I'm neither here nor there, and if that's the case, so be it. Half documentarian, half fabulist . . . Maybe sometimes you have to make things up, to tell truths that alter outcomes.

As a DES daughter, I need hope for my outcome. I don't know if I'll ever be able to bear children of my own, but still, I'm one of the lucky ones—the peak-risk age group for developing fatal adenocarcinoma is fourteen to twenty-three, and I made it. I not only survived but did so in blissful ignorance. But there is a strong chance of a second "age-incidence peak," starting in my forties, and I might not be so lucky the next time around.

I don't think I can change my future simply by writing a happy ending. That's too easy and not so interesting. I will certainly do my best to imagine one, but in reality I will just have to wait and see. For now, though, it is January again. Like Shōnagon, I have "set about filling my notebooks with odd facts, stories from the past . . . ," or at least this past year, and "everything that I have seen and felt is included." However, unlike Shōnagon, living in the Heian days, for whom modesty, however false, was still a prerequisite, I live at the cusp of the new millennium. Whatever people may think of my book, I will make it public, bring it to light unflinchingly. That is the modern thing to do.

So here it is. My Year of Meat. Not so easy. But done.

BIBLIOGRAPHY

AUTHOR'S NOTE: Although this book is a novel, and therefore purely a work of my imagination, as a lapsed documentarian I feel compelled to include a bibliography of the sources I have relied on to provoke these fictions.

—J. T.-L.

Choy, Christine, and Spiro Lampros, directors. "The Shot Heard Round the World" (a documentary film about the trial following the shooting death of Yoshihiro Hattori). Distributed by NAATA, 346 9th Street, San Francisco, CA 94103, and Filmmakers' Library, 124 East 40th Street, New York, N.Y. 10016.

Coe, Sue. *Dead Meat.* New York/London: Four Walls Eight Windows, 1996.

Fenichell, Stephen, and Lawrence S. Charfoos. *Daughters at Risk: A Personal D.E.S. History.* New York: Doubleday, 1981.

Marcus, Alan I. *Cancer from Beef: DES, Federal Food Regulation, and Consumer Confidence.* Baltimore and London: The Johns Hopkins University Press, 1994.

Mason, Jim, and Peter Singer. *Animal Factories: What Agribusiness Is Doing to the Family Farm, the Environment and Your Health.* New York: Harmony Books, 1990.

Orenberg, Cynthia Laitman. *DES: The Complete Story.* New York: St. Martin's Press, 1981.

Rifkin, Jeremy. *Beyond Beef: The Rise and Fall of the Cattle Culture.* New York: Dutton, 1992.

Schell, Orville. *Modern Meat: Antibiotics, Hormones, and the Pharmaceutical Farm.* New York: Random House, 1984.

Shurtleff, William, and Akiko Aoyagi. *The Book of Kudzu: A Culinary & Healing Guide.* Brookline, Mass.: Autumn Press, 1977.

Ziegler, P. Thos. *The Meat We Eat.* Danville, Ill.: The Interstate Printers and Publishers, 1948.

For more information about DES, please contact:
DES Action U.S.A.,
1615 Broadway, #510, Oakland, CA 94612
Tel: 1-800-DES-9288 or 510-465-4011
E-mail: desact@well.com
http://www.desaction.org

DES Cancer Network,
514 10th Street, N.W., Washington, D.C. 20004
Tel: 1-800-DES-NET4 or 202-628-6330
E-mail: DESNETWRK@aol.com

For more information about the use of pharmaceuticals in meat production, please contact:
Beyond Beef,
1130 17th Street, N.W., Suite 300, Washington, D.C.
Tel: 202-775-1132
Fax: 202-775-0074

NOTES

1. Ivan Morris, in his translation of *The Pillow Book*, eschews literal translations of the pre-Heian names of months: "Charming though many of these names are, I have avoided them in my translation for fear that they might produce a false exoticism of the 'Honourable Lady Plum Blossom' variety." As a coordinator for television, I know that false exoticism is my trade. It's what sells meat.

2. "A genus of deciduous shrubs, native in Asia and belonging to the Saxifrage Family. They are attractive in early summer with their wealth of flowers, mostly white but some tinged pinkish." *The Wise Garden Encyclopedia* (New York: William H. Wise & Co., 1970), p. 383.

3. The following definitions are taken from Webster's *New World Dictionary*:

> **CAPITAL n**. [ME. & OFr. < L. capitalis, of the head < caput, the HEAD: see CHIEF] wealth (money or property) owned or used in business by a person, corporation, etc. **1**. an accumulated STOCK of such wealth or its value **2**. wealth, in whatever form, used or capable of being used to produce more wealth **3**. capitalists collectively: distinguished from labor **make capital of** to make the most of; exploit

STOCK n. [ME. *stocke* < OE. *stocc*, akin to G. *stock*, Du. *stok*. a stick < IE. base **steu-*, to push, hit, chop] **1.** *a)* the first of a line of descent; original progenitor, as of a human line, or type, as of a group of animals or plants *b)* any of the major subdivisions of the human race **2.** short for LIVESTOCK; farm animals collectively **3.** the CAPITAL invested in a company or corporation by the owners through the purchase of shares, usually entitling them to interest, dividends, voting rights, etc.

CATTLE n. [ME. & Anglo-Fr. *catel* (O Fr. *chatel*) < ML. *captale*, property, stock < L. *capitalis*, principal, chief < *caput*, the head: orig. sense in var. CHATTEL: CF. CAPITAL] **1.** farm animals collectively; LIVESTOCK **2.** domesticated bovine animals collectively; cows, bulls, steers, or oxen. **3.** people in the mass: contemptuous term

4. Ivan Morris, in his footnote to this passage, says, "Normally the soup and vegetables were eaten together with the rice; to finish each of the dishes separately and with such speed was unspeakably ill-mannered." *The Pillow Book*, p. 373.

ACKNOWLEDGMENTS

My deepest gratitude, as follows:

To Marina Zurkow, for her risks and her rigor; to Cliff Colnot, for real help at the right times; and to my parents for urging me to do what I love . . .

To Arthur Levine, Judy Klassen, and Ann Yamamoto, for their generous and careful reading; to Molly Friedrich, for her breathtaking speed; to my friend and editor, Carole DeSanti, without whom this book simply would not be . . .

And for their wisdom, to the whole wide world of wives.

RUTH L. OZEKI

All Over Creation

PICADOR   £15.99

Lloyd had raised these heavens for me – they were luminous decals that came in a kit. The Friendly Stars That Glow. The day he applied them, he stood in the middle of the mattress, my tall rickety father, as I jumped up and down. He was trying to consult his map of the nighttime sky . . . He told me to hold still, so I lay down on my back to watch as he stood on his tiptoes and stretched across the heavens with Polaris balanced on his fingertip.

The Fuller family are cultivators of Fullers' Seeds in Power County, Idaho. With a lifetime of patient nurturing of potatoes and seeds behind them, Lloyd Fuller and his Japanese wife, Momoko, have begun to feel the ravages of time. Their only daughter, Yumi, left home twenty-five years ago, and now they must attempt to consider the future of their precious yet fragile livelihood.

Meanwhile, a troupe of young revolutionaries are scouring the land in their faithful Winnebego, their eccentric, volatile lives focused on restoring farming practice to its basic beginnings and curbing genetic modification once and for all. As these extraordinary and loveable people come crashing into Fullers' Seeds so too does Yumi return to the fold, and the lives of Lloyd and Momoko are certain never to be the same again . . .

SID SMITH

A House by the River

PICADOR   £15.99

There was a startling volume, nibbled by beetles, about missionaries who stained themselves with tea to map forbidden provinces – counting their paces with a rosary, measuring altitude with the boiling point of their kettle, their compass in a false-bottomed bag – until they were heroically lost and bamboo grew through their bones. Often they were murdered.

A House by the River is a story of love and adventure in the highlands of China. John and Grace Gerrard grew up among the wild streets of Hong Kong and Canton. And this understanding of China proves crucial when they travel among the peoples and landscapes of the interior. But, struggling to reconcile her mixed heritage, Grace provokes a murderous conspiracy. Meanwhile, John has been claimed by China's ancient gods. Now, as they journey to the headwaters of a torrential river, only their knowledge of East and West can save them.